# EVERMORE

### *heart* of the *raven*

## CHRISTINE



## ROBERTS

# CONTENTS

## EVERMORE: SOUL OF THE LION SNEAK PEEK

Published by Christine Roberts in the United States of America

First Printing, 2022

ISBN= 978-1-7366543-8-5

*For Kris. For challenging me, inspiring me and, in more situations than I'd like to admit, forcing me to always be better. For being a damn fine beta reader, a hell of a bridesmaid and the friend of a lifetime. Here's to you and the crazy auto fill on my email that accidentally sent you a novel in progress all those years ago. And, of course, for being kind enough to read it.*

# ACKNOWLEDGMENTS

My thanks and appreciation to all of the people who helped me make this work possible:

— My amazing beta readers who poured through not one, but two novels about this amazing couple and their epic road trip.

— The fans and support network who encourage me daily on social media.

— Morgan, Karen and Heather of Paper Raven Books for your support and expertise throughout this process. I didn't die.

— My husband and children for providing the innumerable interruptions needed to force me to leave my home, head to a quiet spot at the local library and just write this darn book.

— To the Autauga/Prattville Public Library and all the librarians who keep my favorite writing spot ready and waiting when I need it.

— B.R. Curry for always providing just the right amount of carbs and cocktails to inspire me and keep me on track.

— To Mayhem Cover Creations for designing my dream cover.

— To my editor, Nancy Prenzno, for being brutal. I love you! You make me a better writer.

— To my muse, Brock O'Hurn. I'll probably never get a chance to meet you in person, but you were the man who inspired my hero, Connor Rose. So, thanks for the hours I got to spend looking at your pretty face online.

## ABOUT EVERMORE

Advertising executive Raven Elaine Flynn needs a job. Instead of landing at one of Atlanta's premiere ad agencies, the universe tosses her into the *Journey's End,* a jungle themed local pub. This pub has more than decent cocktails and daily specials. It also has Connor Rose, a long-haired, tattooed Tarzan look-alike, for a proprietor. A job rejection leads to whiskey, too much whiskey, and lands Raven in Connor's hands and his bed. There they find instant attraction that moves quickly into more. Hoping to leave all her regrets behind, Raven takes a bold step towards moving from merely earning a living, to living her life.

As the miles pass during a road trip with Connor in an RV dubbed the *Minnow Bucket*, Raven finds herself sharing the pain of her past and discovering a way to move into a future with promise — but will the future include Connor? He can help her relax and enjoy a summer vacation, but can he teach her to really spread her wings and fly into the future — as she was meant to do?

But Connor is guarding dark secrets of his own. The demons of his past fight for control over his heart leaving little room for love unless he can learn to let them go. Lost one and battle wounds leave deeper scars than the ones seen on his skin. Could Raven be the answer to filling all the dark places of his soul? Or will she be left to live the life she wants without the man she wants to live it with?

This is an HEA with no cliffhangers. A stand-alone novel with ties to the previously published HEATHEN BROTH-ERHOOD series launched in 2021. Be sure to look for a companion novel, *Evermore - Soul of the Lion*, which will be released in the summer of 2022 to complete Raven and Connor's story.

This novel contains mature content and is not intended for persons under 18.

Trigger warnings for *Evermore - Heart of the Raven* include references to parental neglect, romantic cheating, Post Trau-matic Stress Disorder and violent acts of war.

# AUTHOR'S NOTES

Music has a unique and profound way of giving a voice to the intangible aspects of the human experience where mere words fall short. The deepest emotions: sorrow, loss, and love can all be experienced through a few notes of a song. Tune and lyric evoke powerful feelings, spark memories and leave a permanent bookmark in our hearts that signify pivotal moments in our lives. I chose to give Raven the gift of music and provide her with the innate sense to allow it to speak for her when words failed. It connects her to events, people and to her inner self because I think that's what music does for us — at least, what it does for me.

Throughout both novels penned for Connor and Raven, you will see several works of great music referenced. I encourage you to pause in your reading and listen to the piece. Allow the sounds to collide with the words to give you an additional dimension that reveals more of the story, more of the characters to you as you let yourself become a part of the lives of Connor and Raven.

Here are the pieces in order as they appear in the stories:

1. *Bach's Cello Suite No.1 in G Major*
2. *Dvorak's Cello Concerto No. 2*
3. *"Blackbird" by the Beatles*
4. *"Desperado" by the Eagles*
5. *"Moonshadow" by Cat Stevens*
6. *Bach's Cello Suite III in C Major*

# CHAPTER ONE

### Wednesday, June 2

THE MAN SITTING across from me smiles politely. I offer a polite smile back. He holds my future in his hands, after all. The least I can do is offer him a pleasant smile. He shuffles some papers and then clears his throat — for the fourth time. Lord, but that's an annoying habit. It's nearly as annoying as that pencil tapping thing he's been doing since I got here. Honestly, how can he not know how irritating that is?

"We appreciate you coming in today, Miss Flynn," *Bounce. Tap. Tap. Tap.* "But I'm afraid you're not quite what we're looking for here at Pinnacle." *Bounce. Tap. Tap. Tap.*

For a single second — which, honestly, feels like an hour or two — I sit there motionless. It's like I've left my body and floated up to the top of the ceiling, looking down at what is happening as if it isn't happening to me, but to someone else. Did he just tell me I *didn't* get this job? *Bounce. Tap. Tap. Tap.*

"I ... I don't understand," I hear myself murmur out loud. "I meet all of the qualifications you require. I'm a very dedicated, hard-working, loyal employee."

"Perhaps, Miss Flynn, but we are looking for the entire package here at Pinnacle." *Bounce. Tap. Tap. Tap.*

"Maybe we could work out a trial period? Let me prove myself." From my disembodied spirit's place among the dusty fluorescent light fixtures above the scene, I hear myself practically begging. How humiliating. But I need this job.

The man across the table holds up a hand to silence me. I stare back at him. He's so young-looking. He doesn't even look thirty. His five o'clock shadow looks like he's been working on it since last Thursday. And he has a baby face. Smooth skin, still battling the last years of pubescent acne. His hair curls around his ears. He must be growing it out because it looks to be in that awkward, too short to be long and too long to be short phase of the process. I'm pretty sure he gets highlights, too. His eyes are bright and he just sits and stares at me with this fabricated smile as if I've stepped in a pile of dog crap, and he's trying to tell me in a nice way that I totally stink.

"Miss Flynn, I just don't think you'd be a good fit here." *Bounce. Tap. Tap. Tap.* "I'm sorry. I am glad to have met you. Perhaps another time, in other circumstances."

"What other circumstances?" My mouth responds automatically.

He sighs and then starts tapping the rubber eraser of his pencil on the table again. I watch nearly transfixed as the soft pink end bounces several times before he picks it up and lets it tap its quick staccato again. *Bounce. Tap. Tap. Tap.* So! Damn! Annoying!

"This is a creative firm. We're looking for people with outside interests they can bring to the table. You have virtually no social media activity, no hobbies or interests outside of work, you don't travel or take vacations. Forgive me for saying so, but you're only a couple of years away from a workaholic's burnout. And that's just not something we really want here. You understand, of course."

He spits out those last words as if he's confirming a fact, not asking a question. I do not understand. I definitely do not understand.

"Does this have anything to do with Morgan Wright?" I hiss out. Good for me, standing up for myself. Wait, I'm actually standing up. Why am I standing up?

"Who?" Mr. Pencil Tapper asks, his head cocked to the side.

"Morgan Wright, my old boss?" My index finger jabs the top of the desk, pressing so hard, that the first joint bends back awkwardly and the whole tip turns white.

"Um ... actually no. Should it?" His brows furrow together in consternation.

"Never mind," I huff. I tug my black leather bag over my shoulder. "Thank you for your time, Mr. ..."

Holy crap! I completely blank on this guy's name. Mr. What? I glance down at his desk and wouldn't you know it, no nameplate. Lord, what's with these Gen Z-ers anyway?

"Cyrus. Just Cyrus."

"Of course, thank you for your time, Cyrus."

I make a hasty retreat to my car through the modern building into the sticky summer air. Tucked in behind the wheel, I press my forehead against the scorching leather and let out a long shuddering breath. I cannot believe I didn't get this job because I don't vacation or have an Instagram account.

Seriously? I have a life outside of work. I have friends. Mrs. Fernelli from apartment 6B. She knocks on my door nearly every Saturday. Of course, it's usually because she's missing her newspaper, and she thinks I've stolen it.

And I have a Facebook account. At least, I think I do. I follow all sorts of interesting people who encourage and inspire hard work, creativity and a growth mindset. But my posts aren't anything like the ones my so-called friends make. No selfies of me skydiving, no video of a marriage proposal or check-ins at the newest clubs in town. #loser

I have a life. I mean I ... that is, I ... well, crap. Who am I kidding? Mr. Pencil Tapper is right. I don't have any meaningful pursuits or hobbies outside of my job. And now, I don't even have a job.

Maybe that's why I've felt so lost since leaving Pittman & Wright. It was such a great advertising agency, and I loved my job there. I'd given them every minute of the past four years of my life. They were going to miss me in the coming months. Especially if they were serious about Tucker Cole taking over my accounts. That guy is a total idiot. He'll be in above his head. No one did as much work as I did. Although I didn't mind the work. But having my boss hit on me and being the topic of watercooler gossip that I was sleeping my way to the top were is just a bridge too far for me. I cannot go down that road again.

I press the ignition button on my hybrid and maneuver the car into the slow-moving traffic of downtown Atlanta. The towers along Peachtree Street loom over me like the trees in an ancient rain forest, blocking the sun and casting cold shadows on the teeming life that struggles for its existence below. The small and helpless animals slinking through the shadows. Insects. Like me.

Pittman & Wright transferred me here from Chicago just a year and a half ago. My performance reviews were perfect. I like the city. I definitely love the weather. I want to stay. I am quickly becoming desperate to find something — anything to keep my Roswell, Georgia address. I'm a two-time Clio award winner for crying out loud — doesn't that count for anything? Apparently, it doesn't because I'm being rejected by twenty-somethings who get highlights? Oh, how the mighty have fallen — well, at least how the mildly mediocre have fallen.

Six interviews. Six interviews in the past two weeks and not a single offer. At least Cyrus told me right away. Two firms still haven't responded. Maybe they'll call. Oh, please, let them call!

I pause for a red light two blocks from my mid-rise just outside of Roswell. Pulsing lights from a neon sign suddenly catch my attention: *Journey's End*. I must have driven past this little hole-in-the-wall bar two hundred times since I moved here. How have I missed it? It looks cozy and quaint. Peering into the window, it seems like the kind of place where locals become regulars and visitors make memories. A fun place. In other words, the last place you'd ever find me. Well, no more. I decide to take a chance and find a parking place in one of only three reserved slots for the bar. The tears I'm swallowing are bitter. I rationalize I could really use a drink to wash them down.

Typically, I'm not a drinker. Like, ever. I got totally plastered one night right out of high school on peppermint schnapps. And after the two-day hangover that had me literally hanging over a toilet a whole day, I vowed never to drink again. And I've held mostly true to my own promise. I occasionally enjoy a glass of wine at office dinner meetings or the company Christmas party. And I did have half of a glass of cheap champagne at my sister's wedding last year, so I'm not a total teetotaler. But as a general rule, I'm a ginger ale kind of a girl.

Today, however, I definitely want a big-girl drink. It isn't like I need the job I interviewed for today in order to survive. I am responsible with my money and try to live within my means. I save as much as I can. I could easily go for five months, six if I cut back on luxuries like gourmet lattes and haircuts, before I have to take some job out of desperation. It is the reason Mr. Pencil Tapper didn't hire me that keeps needling its way under my skin.

Since when does a company tell a qualified candidate with a proven track record for performance that she's not "what they're looking for"? I am so angry. I'm also disappointed and frustrated. For the first time in my life, I want to swallow it all down and cover it with the bitter bubbles of a beer.

I make my way to an empty stool at a long dark wooden bar, shellacked and shiny, and look around. *Journey's End* is equal parts bar and restaurant. It's clear this place is for meeting friends, having a few drinks and occasionally enjoying a bit of fried pub fare.

The whole place is almost completely decked out in dark carved wood. The walls are painted a deep green with some sort of faux finish that gives them the look of rich, shiny leather. The booths and chairs are covered with a glossy cordovan brown material that blends with the earthy colors and jungle-like motif that moves throughout the entire space. It's definitely a man's place.

The focal point of the decor is the four oversized animal heads mounted above the bar — a zebra, rhino, cheetah ... and a male lion. They've got to be fakes. But they are pretty darn good ones. They look terrifyingly real to me. The lion's teeth are massive, his face looks menacing and powerful. The cheetah is chilling, too, with his curled lip and long ivory teeth, bared like razors ready to rip the flesh from your bones. My body gives an involuntary shudder.

Above the bar is a hand-painted sign on a piece of distressed wood: *"It's good to have an end to journey toward, but it is the journey that matters in the end." — Earnest Hemingway.*

The quote certainly explains the decor and name on the neon sign outside. I inhale and savor the fragrance of grilled meat, French fries and lemony furniture polish. I have no doubt it takes gallons of it to keep this place clean. Overall, the bar looks fairly new. Perhaps that's why I haven't noticed it before today. Not because I'm oblivious.

As a rule, I avoid fried foods. But my mouth instantly waters from the smells coming from the kitchen, and I'm tempted to skip the beer and drown my sorrows in a bacon cheeseburger instead. Hell, with the way today has turned out, maybe both. It sure beats the ramen dinner I had planned for tonight.

My gaze travels back to the lion looming above me. I know his eyes are just glass orbs, but it feels like they're looking at me — almost into me. As if, in some strange way, the lion has chosen me to be his next meal. The world is set to devour me — the weakest of the pack.

"What can I get you?" A bartender glances down at me. The rumble of his voice startles me out of my daydream. My eyes suddenly feel huge. Well, they'd have to be to fit the whole of him within my vision.

The man in front of me is by far and away the largest human I've ever seen. And not in a way that would make him seem overweight. He's simply ... huge. He's tall and muscled. His chest and shoulders are broad and the cotton T-shirt covering them is straining to contain the flesh underneath. Clearly, he knows his way around a gym.

His long light brown hair is tied into a neat ponytail at the base of his neck. If it were loosed, it would probably flow past his shoulders. And this guy's scruffy beard is no amateur five o'clock shadow. It's a bit darker than the hair on his head and looks a bit ragged in that super sexy sort of way.

Swirls of black ink peek out beneath his sleeves and above the collar of his black T-shirt that bears the bar's logo in a neat font across the right breast. My eyes are roving to take him all in. My TikTok addicted sister would brand this man as a walking thirst trap. And I would have to agree with her. He's definitely making me thirsty.

His face, etched with tiny lines around his eyes and mouth, proves he's no pretty boy Gen Z. This is a full-grown man. My lady parts instantly react. And my stomach begins a ballet pirouetting back and forth with flutters that float from my belly and then drift lower. My Inner Sex Goddess just licked her lips. What on earth? A man has never affected me this way before.

"The view's included, but you have to buy a drink," he says boldly. Whoa! He's got this sexy bedroom voice that slides over me like a cashmere caress. I want to bury myself in its rich tones. It sounds like the deep notes of a cello and it thrums through my ears and nestles straight into my heart.

Holy crap! I'm staring. My eyes snap to his, and I'm instantly lost. His eyes are the most dazzling cobalt blue I've ever seen, and the contrast of his tanned skin against them makes him look like some sort of a mythical warlock.

His fingers drum on the sleek shiny bar top while I lick my lips and try to act as if I am totally contemplating my beverage options and not staring at this gorgeous hunk of a man who is staring back at me. I doubt I'm very convincing.

"Um, a beer, I guess." My voice sounds foreign to me — scratchy and oddly strained. Thirsty. Well, of course, it is. Just look at what's standing in front of me.

"Sure thing, what kind?" He rumbles back. His gravelly voice stirs a darkness that vibrates through every bone inside me.

"Excuse me?" I squeak.

"What kind of beer do you want? We have lots on tap, and if you don't like any of those, we have bottles."

I twist my head to consider the row of colorful plastic taps that provide an impressive assortment of draft options. I have absolutely no idea what to order. I shrug and try not to gawk at him again. Of course, trying to avoid his presence is impossible, and before I realize it, I'm staring again.

I blink to bring the rows of glass liquor bottles behind him into focus. They're backlit with some sort of iridescent greenish glow that makes them look almost as if they're alien favorites from the starship *Enterprise*. I can almost picture Guinan pouring one of them for a Klingon warrior.

"Your day that bad, huh?" He asks. I can feel my shoulders drop. Tough day? Tough week, tough month, tough year.

"Yeah, you could say that. I was really hoping to land this great job, and I honestly thought I had, but they turned me down."

"That sucks. Maybe a beer isn't what you need. Maybe you need something stronger. You like whiskey?" Who knew thunder could rumble into words like that.

I've never had a whiskey in my entire life. I know that makes me sound like a complete loser: thirty-two years old and never enjoyed a whiskey. But I usually play it safe and stick to my seven-dollar glass of wine, trying to avoid drinks that require a payment plan option when ordering.

"I don't know, maybe." I shrug, still not sure whose weak voice is coming out of my throat.

The bartender gives me a little half-smile and sort of laughs at me. I honestly don't know whether he is amused by me or feels sorry for me. Quite frankly, I don't even know why I care which it is, but I do.

"How about you try one of my favorites? It's a small batch brand out of Colorado. They age it fourteen years in rum casks. Smooth as a baby's ass. No bite or burn at all on the way down. I think you'll like it.'"

I nod. All of that sounds fine. Especially the way he says it. My Inner Sex Goddess could listen to him talk about smooth asses and burning body parts until the cows come home.

"OK, how much?"

"It's on me," he insists. He reaches for a small bottle

behind him with a baby-blue label that has the word *Brecken-ridge* scrawled across it in black letters. He pours an inch of the dark leather-colored liquid into a short glass and slides it across the bar to me.

I lift it to my nose and inhale. It smells sweet. I can detect hints of cinnamon and other spices and what smells like cocoa or maybe caramel. I swear I could dab this stuff on my wrists as perfume, it smells so tantalizing. Of course, I'd probably attract every AA dropout from here to New York City. But honestly, that would probably be an improvement over the guys who have shown interest in me lately. Just more evidence of my complete lack of a life. #single.

I throw the contents to the back of my throat and work to swallow it in large gulps, praying my esophagus neither catches fire nor dissolves under the slow-burning heat of the alcohol.

Choking and gasping, I reach clumsily for the glass of water the bartender is sliding toward me and guzzle it down within seconds to hopefully extinguish any flames. Doesn't burn going down, my left ass cheek!

I watch the image of him wobble and roll around through my watery eyes. He's laughing at me. And not a light little chuckle, either. No, he's enjoying a full-on belly laugh over me. Jerk.

"You're not supposed to shoot it, honey. It's a sipping whiskey. That's why I didn't pour it into a shot glass."

Well, that would have been good to know before I nearly died on 1.5 ounces of Colorado's finest.

"Thanks for the lesson," I manage to rasp and pick up my purse to leave. A flush of embarrassment washes over me. Or maybe it's the lingering flames from the firewater Tarzan here tried to kill me with.

"Oh, no you don't," he asserts and grabs my glass. He refills it and drops in a huge sphere of ice. The splash sends ribbons of amber liquid trailing down in long, thick fingers against the sides of the glass. "You need a do-over there, Tenderfoot. And don't worry. It's still on me."

I cast him a warning glance, but resettle myself onto the stool and try again. I take a tiny sip. My throat closes up in anticipation of the burning sensation, but it doesn't come. Instead, my mouth and tongue explode in a cacophony of flavors that slide and smash into one another in the most unexpected ways.

The sugar sweetness of honeyed caramel and the perfume of the rum and spices all marry together with the hints of flavors I detected earlier. This time, there's no burn as the whiskey eases down my throat and gently heats a line from my mouth to my stomach. The warmth spreads back up into my cheeks and down into my arms. It feels like a magic spell twinkling through my entire body. A warlock's magic potion of sorts.

"Wow," I confess, fully experiencing the drink as it was intended. And more than a little grateful he challenged me to try it for a second time. "That's terrific."

"Glad you like it," he winks and gives me a sly smile.

I scan the room to discover hardly anyone else inside. A real shame, if you ask me. This is a cool place and it's got a mellow vibe. A balding man with a protruding belly hunches over a beer at the opposite end of the long bar where I'm sitting. Sadly, he looks nearly too drunk to hold his barstool down for much longer. In a corner booth, an elderly gray-haired couple shares what looks to be a basket of fish and chips. And in the center of the small dining room is a group of six young professionals in their power suits, obviously discussing their next big business deal or where to club on Friday night.

"Not very busy today, are you?" I comment. I'm not sure why I always feel as if there needs to be conversation in the air. But my whole life, it seems, silence has always made me feel uncomfortable. Silent people think. And it's been my fear that all they're thinking about is me. And not in a good way.

"Well, it is two o'clock on a Wednesday, so ..." Tarzan, the bartender, informs me.

"True," I add, realizing with more than the slight embarrassment that he's right. Oddly, I don't worry about feeling embarrassed like I normally do. This place seems homey to me somehow — like I belong here among the people and the silence and stories that have been written within these walls. Or maybe I'm just feeling the effects of the whiskey. It's a bar for goodness' sake. It's just the whiskey.

"We tend to get busy after five and on the weekends." He lets his head drop to an odd angle and studies my face for a split second before asking, "Have you eaten today? You want a menu?"

I shake my head. "No, I'm good. I had a granola bar and two bottles of water earlier today."

He blanches as if I'd told him I eat puppies for breakfast.

"Birdseed and water isn't a meal, honey. Let me grab you a menu."

He slides a laminated list of offerings in front of me and I have to admit, the smells emanating from the kitchen combined with the irresistible photographs of their food make my stomach rumble. I read over the menu, finding my eyes struggling to focus properly. Hmm ... must be the dim lighting in here.

"What sorts of salads do you have?" I ask. My voice finally sounds more like my own.

My burly tattooed bartender rubs a long-stemmed wine glass to a gleaming shine before reaching up and sliding it into an overhead rack. His bicep flexes and the thick veins that map over his hands and arms make me want to order him, lightly tossed, with dressing on the side. Inner Sex Goddess mentally places her own order.

"No salads, honey. How about a cheeseburger? If you're a vegan or something, we can do mushroom or black bean."

My mouth waters at the mere mention of a cheeseburger. Well, and the view of him. I hum almost audibly and then nod slightly. I really am hungry. For the cheeseburger, that is.

"OK, cheeseburger, I guess." I stammer. "But can I get it with cheddar instead of American? Oh, and I'd like steak sauce instead of mustard. And no lettuce, unless it's not iceberg. If it's iceberg, then none. But if you have something else, go ahead and put the lettuce on. Oh, and no mayo."

I watch his eyebrows lift nearly disappearing under his hairline as I order. I give him an apologetic one-shouldered shrug and offer a "please" in the kindest voice I can muster.

A few short minutes later, my very sexy bartender slides a perfectly plated dish across to me. It looks exactly like the photograph on the menu, complete with cheddar and steak sauce and — crisp butter lettuce. I couldn't be more delighted.

Usually, I'm disappointed because the food never looks as appetizing in real life as it does on TV, or on the menu. But this is perfect. A tower of fluffy, fresh white bun; meat grilled to perfection; gooey, melted cheese; bright green lettuce; a fresh, ruby-red tomato; spicy onion and a Kosher pickle stand erect on my plate surrounded by a sea of thick-cut fries sparkling with a light dusting of salt. The smell is divine. The taste is even better. My Inner Foodie just wrapped her napkin around her neck.

I'm pleased to discover, as I bite into my burger, that thick slabs of applewood smoked bacon are layered between the meat patty and the cheese. It is, by far, the best burger I've ever eaten. Probably one of the best things I've ever eaten, to be honest.

I nibble on the fries, which come with some sort of mayonnaise-based sauce I'm initially skeptical of. I'm not a mayo girl. But being brave, and practically shamed into trying it by the hunky bartender, I'm surprised to find it's delicious.

"I make that myself," he boasts proudly.

"It's good. What's in it?" I ask, instantly regretting the question. I'd rather not know in case it has some strange ingredient that totally ruins it for me.

"Mayo, ketchup, fresh black pepper, hot sauce and Worcestershire."

"Really? It's so good."

I sip on another whiskey, which I insist on paying for, and clear my plate. A baseball game comes on one of the large screen TVs over the bar and the place starts to fill up. I order another whiskey, justifying that it's a dessert of sorts. I mean, it's not really that much alcohol after all. It's practically only a single swallow in each glass. It would take like six or seven of these to equal the volume that's in a beer bottle or four or five to equal one glass of wine. I mean, it's not like I'm going to get drunk or anything.

---

# CHAPTER TWO

---

**Thursday, June 3**

I AM GOING TO DIE. I swallow dry stale air and feel my head pulse with just that slight motion. Nope, not going to — I'm already dead. I've died and sadly, I've been sentenced to an eternity of licking used kitty litter boxes because that's what my mouth tastes like right now. Gross.

I clutch my throbbing head and try to sit up. Waves of nausea slosh over me, and I'm forced to breathe through my mouth to keep my body in check. I press my fingers into my eye sockets, hoping the pressure will keep them embedded in my skull where they belong. Because, honestly, they feel like they're going to pop out of my head.

An intense bright light surrounds me. Even though my eyes are closed, I know it's there, and it makes me afraid to open them. When I finally find the courage, the blinding rays stab into my brain and I quickly clamp my lids closed again. That was such a bad idea.

I hear a light tapping and then work to refocus my vision and adapt to the blinding morning sun. Geez, it's so bright this morning. Is the sun always this bright? Maybe it's the light of heaven and I really am dead after all.

"Good morning, Little Bird," I hear a deep, sexy voice say. It's definitely a voice I've heard before. Like last night. At the bar. Crap on a cracker! Tarzan!

My eyes flip open like spastic window shades on a roller, and I blink to get a look at where I am. I'm tucked into the soft white sheets of a king-sized bed that isn't mine. The bed is in a room that isn't mine or even one I'm familiar with. Oh God, Oh God, Oh God! What have I done?

The burly bartender who forced his evil firewater and half-masticated cow into my body last night has the nerve to smirk at me.

"Well, you don't look as bad as I expected. How do you feel?" He inquires, thankfully, keeping his volume low.

I flop back against the pillows and let my eyes fall shut.

"I'm dying." Hearing the croaking sound of my voice, I'm immediately concerned and work to sit up again, gripping my throat.

"You're not dying, honey. You're just hungover. I guess whiskey isn't your thing, huh?"

"How many did I have?" My voice sounds scratchy, and it's almost painful to speak.

"Last I counted, four, possibly five." He lifts one hand and splays out all five of his enormous fingers to be sure I understand how many he means.

"Aren't you supposed to cut me off at some point when I've been overserved?" I accuse. This really is all his fault. I wanted one beer. He talked me into five whiskeys. How did that happen? One look at the black tee stretched tight over a muscled chest and well-worn, low-slung jeans and I know exactly how.

"Yep," he agrees. "But you seemed fine. Until you weren't. I wasn't going to let you drive home, but you were chatty and coherent the whole time. Well, until you went to the bath-room and passed out."

"I passed out in the ladies' room?" My voice screeches. Crap! I clutch my head. Another terrible idea.

"Yeah, one of the waitstaff found you. She wanted to call an ambulance, but I told her you were a friend of mine, and brought you here."

"Where is here?" I ask, glancing down to be sure I'm covered by the sheets only to realize that I'm dressed in an oversized T-shirt that doesn't belong to me. It has the logo of one of my all-time favorite bands on it, *Climax*. It's old and soft from washings. And it smells clean and like some sort of man spice I can't quite put my finger on. It takes a moment for my brain haze to lift and realize I'm in his T-shirt. His T-shirt and nothing else!

"Where are my clothes?"

"Relax, Little Bird. You're at my place in the city," he explains. "And you threw up on your clothes, so I washed them and put you in my T-shirt."

I can feel my cheeks reddening with the flame of mortifi-cation. This is not happening. I blew chunks all over the hottest man I've ever met? Now, I really wish I could die and spare myself this humiliation.

"Calm down, I didn't try to fuck you or anything. You're perfectly safe. I just didn't want you waking up with a char-coal tube down your throat while EMTs tried to pump your stomach. I figured you'd wretch it up on your own, and you did. But I wasn't putting you in bed covered in vomit, either."

I'm not listening to a word he says. My brain cannot process language at the speed it's assaulting my ears. I'm still focused on him washing my clothes.

"You washed my clothes? Like in a washing machine?"

"Um, yes?" He looks a bit worried. He should be.

"Listen here, Tarzan, that was a three-hundred-dollar suit. Silk. It's dry clean only. Didn't you read the label?"

"Shit," he leaps up from the foot of the bed where he'd rested one hip to sit slightly and dashes from the room. I untangle myself from the sheets and try to steady myself on my feet. Well, *I'm* perfectly steady. It's the room that seems to keep tipping from side to side. I reach out and try to balance myself by leaning on a side table next to the bed.

"Oh, shit. I'm so sorry." The King of the Jungle holds up my skirt and blouse, which now look as if they could fit a child's doll. I roll my eyes, nearly causing my body to fall over onto the bed.

"Great. Now, what am I supposed to wear?"

"I'm sure we can find something for you in here." He turns and pushes open two bi-fold closet doors along one wall of the cream-colored room he's put me in. Inside is a closet full of a woman's clothing. Oh. Hell. No.

"You want me to wear your girlfriend's clothes?" I practically shout and instantly regret the volume. A battalion of tiny elves hammer on my brain with pickaxes.

"Relax. They're not my girlfriend's," he growls.

"You're married?" Again, the elves remind me to keep my voice down. I squeeze my temples. Message received, boys.

Tarzan gives me a look that makes all of the air in the room stop instantly. Our breath, the whisper of the air conditioning and the whir of the ceiling fan — they all seem to pause for a heartbeat. For a single second, time stops, and I have no idea why my question forced such a reaction from him.

"No, Lainey Bird, not married. My niece stays with me sometimes. This is her room. She's got a shopping addiction and keeps some stuff here. You two look to be about the same size."

He tosses a pair of jeans and a vintage T-shirt to me from one of the shelves in the closet.

"My name is Elaine," I say more quietly. The elves seem pleased. "Elaine Flynn."

"I saw on your license," he says. "It also says you live in Chicago."

"I know. I've been meaning to get it changed, but I keep forgetting." That is actually a lie. I haven't forgotten. I've just been working such long hours every day. I never made time to go to the DMV to get it changed. The lines are always so long, and it would have wasted valuable time I could have used to get ahead on important projects at work.

"I'm Connor Rose. But I kind of like Tarzan better."

"Thank you for taking care of me, Conner Rose," I mutter shyly, "but I'd really like to just take my doll clothes and go home now. Give me a few minutes. I'll change and call an Uber. I'll make sure your niece gets her clothes back."

"Look, why don't you get a shower. We can grab some food, and I'll take you back to the bar to get your car. You'll feel better with something in your stomach."

I can still hear the elves hammering although they seem like they're using dull rubber mallets now. Honestly, if I tried to drive right this minute, it would be a disaster. Then again, I could walk home from the bar. My apartment is only a couple of blocks away. But the the thought of getting cleaned up does sound heavenly, especially after my hellish night.

"Thanks," I mumble. I don't want to admit to him that he's right.

"The bathroom is through there," he points to a partially closed door to my left. "Ginger uses all sorts of different soaps and shampoos. I think she has one for every part of her body. Help yourself. You'll find clean towels in the basket under the sink and extra toothbrushes in plastic wrap in the cabinet above the sink."

The bathroom, like the bedroom, is a mixture of textures more than colors. It's like a variation on the theme of cream. The fixtures and finishes look expensive and the spaces are large. An apartment like this in Atlanta costs a fortune. Maybe bartending could be a potential career option if this whole job search thing in the advertising world doesn't produce fruit soon.

The hot water feels amazing. When I finally force myself to leave its steamy embrace, I find my bra and panties clean and folded on the bed. A glass of water and a couple of Tylenol are on the nightstand beside them. I'm grateful for both.

I slide on the jeans and the T-shirt. I really love the way the jeans fit me. I haven't worn jeans in years. I don't even know if I still have any in my closet. My typical outfit of choice is a suit or a dress. When I'm at home, it's yoga pants, sweats or pajamas.

I twist to look at my ass in the jeans. Dang, the cut of these things does wonders for my backside. Even my legs look longer. I turn and face myself in the mirror. My long brown hair hangs in damp waves down my back. I can't believe how long it's gotten. When was the last time I got a haircut, anyway? My eyes have always been my favorite feature — they're almost a bit too large for my face, almond-shaped and a dark brown. So dark brown, depending on what I'm wearing, they can appear almost black. Today, though, they're streaked with red. They're not amazing. I sigh and twist my hair up into a messy bun with a ponytail holder I found in the girl's bathroom.

I couldn't remove all my makeup from last night and dark gray smears of eyeliner and mascara linger under my eyes. I rub at them with my fingertips, but it's no use. I pinch my cheeks to try to put some color back into them. They look bony and a little hollow. I remember a bathroom scale beside the shower and jump on it. Holy crap! I've lost fifteen pounds? I've always yo-yoed with my weight, but whoa!

Maybe Tarzan is right. Oh, he said his name is, what...? Maybe Connor Rose is right. Apparently, I can't live on birdseed and water.

The house is a maze of hallways and staircases. I get lost a couple of times and accidentally stumble into some sort of library or office filled with books, another bathroom and finally what appears to be a music room. There's a grand piano, several guitars on stands, a giant hand-carved harp and ... a cello. My heart instantly stops beating.

I pad slowly over to it on bare feet as if I'm approaching a creature in the wild. I just want to touch it. I won't play it, I promise myself. Just one touch.

Brushing my fingertips over the strings, I feel the delicate etched grooves along their length and the sharp bite as I press against them. I carefully slide my hands over the satiny finish of the neck and body. My touch is more like that of a lustful lover admiring the curves of his beautiful woman. Cellos are built like women, curvy and delicate. Held and caressed by a master, they can be made to sing and moan in haunting harmonies that can force the hair on your neck to rise in a standing ovation.

My fingers instinctively begin to twitch in midair, tapping out the easy dance of the warm-ups I played for more years than I didn't. I can almost feel the notes hum from the strings. Bouncing and rising and then falling in scale after scale. But I won't play it. I only touch, hearing the music in my mind.

"Do you play?" Connor's voice rumbles from the doorway. I'm lost in my daydream and his low growl makes me jump.

"I used to, a little," I stammer. It's a gross understatement of the truth, but that doesn't matter to him. My heart has resumed beating again and now it's racing. I'm not sure if it's the cello or the man or both. Maybe it's the hangover.

"Play something for me," he says, motioning to the instrument.

"No, it's been too long." I turn away from it, feeling like my child has been plucked from my arms, and start to walk toward Connor and the doorway to leave. But he's already moving closer to me. The press of his personal space against mine compels me back toward the cello like two like-ended magnets. I'm forced to stand beside the instrument in order to maintain an appropriate distance from him.

"Please." He asks so softly in his low, velvety tone. My head and my heart bob a yes before my brain can wake from its fog to think.

Like an old familiar love come home to me, the instrument is heavy against my spread legs, finding a natural fit in the sacred space there. I position my fingers, curl my hand to form the first note and drag the bow across the strings. My eyes drift closed as the note embraces me into a familiar hug. To my surprise, the cello is barely out of tune. I wonder why it is here and who plays it. Perhaps Connor?

I force out hums in the first few familiar notes. My body slowly begins to move back and forth, rhythmically, gracefully, as I bring the wooden beast to life. In an instant, the melody has captured me completely. By the time I reach the climax of the piece, I am transported. Once again, I feel my soul floating above me as it did in Mr. Pencil Tapper's office, but this time I'm not watching. This time, I am dancing, twirling, spinning and whirling as the notes lift me and carry me away with them.

My mind empties and the world around me dissolves into sound, vibration and tone. The earth no longer spins out of control, but turns as predictably on its axis as the movement of the strings under my fingers and the bow gliding across them.

My love is speaking to me now, telling a story of hope and love and of all things that are earth and life and music. And I am lost. Bouncing, tossing and lifting, dropping and rising again, the notes seesaw and float from the strings, propelling the piece ever forward in staggers and steps. I coax the tones from the instrument with my entire body now.

The music swells and crests and I feel myself sway and then hold as I pull my bow across the strings for the last time. The beautiful haunting blend of the final chord echoes through the room.

I sit as the last of the sounds ripple away like the rings on a pond, until they all dissolve around me and my spirit falls back into my body. I feel the warm wood against my legs again and finally, I let my eyes drift open to see Connor studying me, his voice mute, his lips parted in what I can only assume is surprise.

What looks like a tiny crystal of a tear twinkles in one corner of his eye, but it is gone before I can brush one from the corner of my own.

"Wow, Lainey Bird," he struggles to speak. "That was gorgeous. What was that?"

"*Bach's Cello Suite No.1 in G Major.* Just the prelude though. I doubt I could remember the whole thing."

I clear my throat and manage to get back on my feet, rest the body of my beautiful old friend back into the stand and lay the bow at the base. I let out a long breath. Suddenly, I don't feel the elves hammering anymore. My head is clearer and my heart is lighter than they have been in a very long time. Oh, sweet love, I've missed you.

"That was the most beautiful thing I've ever heard. Where on earth did you learn to play like that?"

I give him a half-smile, thinking back to the first time I

ever held a cello. How my awkward fingers worked to hold the bow. For weeks, I could only force screeching noises from it when I attacked the strings. I think of the hardened callouses that formed on my fingertips and on the insides of my knees because I refused to practice in pants one summer.

"Mrs. Dean taught me at PS 163 — middle school," I explain, smiling as I think of the patient woman who led me to my first, and probably, the greatest love of my life. My fingers still drum along my thigh, finishing the piece as I stand and talk.

"Are you OK?" Connors asks.

I blink and realize I have tears streaming from one eye. I nod furiously and sniff and swallow away the rest of the emotion.

"It's just been a really long time since I've played." I say the words as if that is all the explanation I need to give as to why playing a three-minute prelude has made me so emotional. Apparently, it is because Connor doesn't ask me anything else about it. And I'm thankful he doesn't press.

"Let's get you some food, Lainey Bird," he says and offers me his hand.

I don't know this man. I don't know where I am or what his real intentions are. Visions of all those serial murder shows I binge on Netflix flash through my mind. And yet, something about him makes me feel safe. Something that tells me on a deeper level, he understands me.

"My name," I correct him, straightening slightly, "is Elaine."

"I know," he says, grinning at me. "But Lainey fits you better."

I slide my feet into a pair of flip-flops that Connor's niece ordered and then didn't like. They're a bit too big, but relatively comfortable, and I love the colorful beads that cover the straps.

"I was supposed to return these for her and never got around to it. I guess it's a good thing I didn't," Connor says, looking a little embarrassed. "I'm sorry about your suit. I'll replace it."

I shake my head. "I appreciate the thought," I admit. And this isn't a lie. It is nice of him to take care of me. I'm a complete stranger to him as well, after all. I wonder if he binge-watches serial murder shows, too.

We walk outside and my eyes are immediately stung with the bright sunshine. Connor hands me my purse and I rummage through it half-blind until I can find my sunglasses. I slide them over my face, and instantly feel the tiny hammering elves ease their pounding.

When I can refocus, I am face-to-face with a cherry red two-seat roadster. The top is pulled back to enjoy one of the rare days of Georgia summer that isn't hot enough to melt plastic. A silver pony on the front of the grill rises up on his back legs. I instantly recognize the Ferrari symbol, but this car looks like a vintage model. Its smooth round edges have a total James Bond vibe. It is nothing like the sleek spaceship angles of the newer body styles.

"Wow! She's pretty," I say as he cracks open the passenger door and I sink down onto the supple tan leather seat. The dash is basic, showing only the essential dials for speed, gas and oil levels and a rudimentary tachometer.

"Thanks. It's a 1960 Ferrari LWB California Spyder," Connor says with pride, as if he's introducing the President of the United States.

"Really?" I say, gushing. This has got to be a seriously rare car.

"Well, sort of. I rescued the body from an old junkyard and had a crew resto-mod it for me. We got as many original parts as we could, but there's still too much new stuff in here for it to be considered the real McCoy."

"This is seriously the coolest car I've ever seen." I'm completely fawning over this guy's car. But honestly, it's as hot and gorgeous as its owner.

"Thanks. I don't usually take her out, but it is so nice today, I'd thought I'd let her stretch her legs a little. We've got about twenty or thirty minutes depending on traffic to get to the bar."

"Wait," I pause, giving him my best impression of a flirtatious smile. "But only after breakfast, right?"

The corners of his mouth quirk up slightly, and I can tell he's pleased I'm asking to spend more time with him, although for the life of me I can't understand why I want to. Maybe I just want to sit in this beautiful car for a while. Or maybe it's the beautiful driver I want to sit beside.

He winds the car through a green canopy of trees that rise and fall like the waves of an ocean. We finally come to a stop outside a cute little cafe in a small Atlanta suburb I'm not familiar with. It's called the *Day Old Bagel*, and I really hope they also have egg white omelets. I'm suddenly starving, and granola isn't going to cut it today.

A line of people wait for tables and sip Bloody Marys and mimosas. It's a Thursday morning, for crying out loud. Don't these people need to be at work?

When the hostess spots us, she gives a big smile. "Hello, Mr. Rose," she says, gazing up at Connor. "Table for two?"

Connor nods and I notice we're getting some pretty envious glances from the mimosa-sipping crowd around us. I can't blame them.

"Would you like to be seated inside or on the patio?"

"Patio, please," he says. We're immediately escorted to a quiet table outside. At a small pocket park across the street, a couple of guys throw a frisbee and some ladies power walk along the trail. The laughter of a child, squealing as his mom pushes him in a swing, comes floating faintly over a light summer breeze.

Our server comes over immediately carrying two cups of coffee, a tiny steel pitcher of cream and a glass holder of sugar packets.

"Good morning, sir. It's good to see you again. Would you and your guest like a few minutes to look over the menu?"

"Yeah, thanks Micah," he says, and we're left to peruse the sheet of paper placed in front of us.

The menu is printed on brown parchment in a pretty font that looks like someone's handwriting. The options seem much more upscale than just your basic scrambled eggs and bacon. I see lobster eggs Benedict and a crab cake sandwich with an over-easy egg, arugula and a side of fresh berries. Everything looks seasonal. I glance down toward the bottom of the menu and see a list of local growers who are providing the ingredients for today's menu offerings.

"This place is great. You must come here a lot?" I offer, perusing my options. Everything sounds so good.

He nods and adds cream and sugar to his coffee. "I pop in from time to time," he says and leans back in his chair taking a long, slow sip.

The server reappears, and I order the tomato pie with a side of sage sausage and fresh berries along with orange juice.

Connor simply smiles and waves dismissively. "You already know what I want, Micah."

Pops in from time to time, huh? He has a usual order. This must be his regular go-to breakfast place where he brings all the women who spend the night with him, lose their clothing and ride in his fancy red sports car. His little extra for the ladies during their drive of shame the morning after. When a man looks like he does, that's probably a weekly occurrence at least.

While we wait for our food, Connor surveys me up and

down with a frank curiosity. He's not even trying to be discreet about it. He just sits and stares. His face has an expression like he's trying to make up his mind about me, and is debating an inward pro/con list. This judgment is why silence is scary.

"What?" I finally say, taking a sip of my coffee. It's strong, but not bitter at all. Probably the best cup of coffee I've had in a long time. And that's saying something. The gourmet blends I buy on Amazon are like thirty bucks a pound. Well, used to buy when I had a job.

"You've really never been on vacation?" He begins as if we've been in the middle of this conversation for several hours.

"What? How would you know that?" Talk about rude and presumptuous.

"You're a real chatty Cathy after about your third whiskey," he says with a slightly amused expression.

"What ... what did I say?" OK, so maybe not so presumptuous. Maybe just an eavesdropper. My fingers slowly begin picking away at the edge of my napkin. It takes several long minutes before I realize I'm fingering the notes of *Dvorak's Cello Concerto No. 2.*

Connor swats at a lone red wasp that has flown in to investigate our beverages. "You said the man who interviewed you wouldn't give you the job because you didn't go on vacation."

"I said that after the third whiskey?"

Connor nods.

"Well, then let it be known throughout the land, I am officially a two-whiskey girl." Connor chuckles a little, but doesn't comment.

I jut out my lower lip and blow upward, forcing my bangs to fly up off my forehead in a wave. I know he's waiting for some kind of explanation, but I honestly don't know what to say. I settle for brazen honesty and hope for the best.

"The guy who interviewed me said while I was qualified ... he just couldn't help but think that work was my whole life. I guess he was afraid if he hired me, I'd be on my way to Workaholics Anonymous.

"Is it true?" Connor asks, sipping his coffee. I love how the oversized mug seems so small in his hands. My eyes trace the veins that map over them and up his forearms disappearing under the sleeves of the graphic tee he is wearing today. It's red and has a logo I don't recognize on it. It looks like it could be a beer logo. From a vendor maybe? I stare at it, but honestly, I'm imagining what his chest must look like underneath it. No doubt Tarzan here hits the gym with a regularity that shows.

"What?" I ask, not quite registering his question.

"Would you be on your way to Workaholics Anonymous?"

The server delivers our food, and I'm grateful for the pause in conversation. On the one hand, I could lie. I have never been a good liar, but I could tell him I've traveled the world, lived my best life and have loads of friends who occupy every second of my free time. Or I could tell him the unvarnished truth — I am a lonely, nearly middle-aged woman who works so much I can't even keep houseplants alive. I am married to my job and sacrifice living for earning one. That the seemingly innocent rejection of a pencil-tapping, throat-clearing man just out of his teenage years has finally forced me to admit my life is depressingly empty and really, really boring.

After taking the first bite of the pie, I decide on option two — but without the colorful metaphors.

"Maybe," I finally answer and then quickly turn cowardly before disclosing more.

"Where did you go on your last vacation?" he asks, spreading preserves on his toast.

"San Diego," I pipe up, feeling a bit prouder. I have been somewhere.

"Oh? When was that?" He licks off a dollop of jam and holy cow! Inner Sex Goddess can't help herself and imagines all sorts of tricks that tongue could do.

I clear my throat and feel my cheeks pink a bit. I hope he'll think it's the heat of the sun and not my embarrassment that is causing it. Where the heck did all that come from?

"Seven years ago," I confess.

"Seven? And you haven't been on vacation since then?"

"OK, I admit. It wasn't technically a vacation. It was my grandmother's funeral. My family lives there. So, no. I guess the last time I went on vacation for fun was the summer before my freshman year of high school when my parents took my sister and me to Disneyland in Anaheim for the day."

"Whoa! I hate to say it, Little Bird, but Mr. Pencil Tapper may be right. You gotta live a little."

"Mr. Pencil Tapper? Is that what I called him?" I can't help laughing out loud at myself a little.

Connor nods. "What about your boyfriend? Doesn't he take you places?"

Subtle, Connor. Real subtle. I shake my head. "I had a fling with a coworker years ago, but it ended badly, and I don't waste my time anymore." Connor arches his right eyebrow and, if I'm not mistaken, a pleased little smirk begins to curl at one corner of his mouth.

"Girlfriends? You know like a girls' night out kind of thing. You do that?"

I shake my head again.

"Bowling league?"

Another shake.

"Canasta? Knitting circle? Book club?"

"Nope. My life is as pathetic as it sounds. I work. But I'm very good at my work. And the field I'm in is very demanding."

"What is it you do?"

"Advertising and marketing." My answer earns a low, quiet hum from Connor as he spreads more blueberry jam onto his toast.

We finish the meal and he doesn't ask any more questions, for which I am extremely thankful. I still catch him staring at me from time to time, though. Each time, he has that contemplative look on his face as if he's trying to make up his mind about me. I have no idea what he's trying to decide, but it's incredibly unsettling. I wonder if this is what is meant by "undressing you with his eyes"? Wait, is this flirting? No. I dismiss the idea immediately. I feel exposed, not desired. The look isn't lustful. At least not like the lust I've seen in a man's eyes before. The memory of the last time I saw that makes me shudder and feel slightly nauseated. I push the thoughts aside.

We leave the restaurant after Connor drops a stack of bills on the table even before Micah brings our check. Then we climb back into his vintage sports car and cruise through traffic to the *Journey's End* bar and soon the sanctity of my apartment.

I click the remote to unlock the door of my hybrid and turn to face Connor, who leans against the fender of his car, arms crossed over his chest. His biceps are flexed, threatening to rip his tee at the seams. Sweet baby Jesus in the manger, this man is so incredibly hot! He's Kevin Creekman and Brock O'Hurn knit together by Aphrodite herself and cast down from Mt. Olympus to live among us mere mortals. And he bought me breakfast. And drove me around in his fancy sports car. And lent me clothes. Oh ... the clothes.

"I'll get these things laundered and returned to you as soon as I can," I say swallowing. Uncomfortable silences wreck me again. Like in the cafe earlier this morning, while he sat and stared and all I could do was wonder how he was judging me. People are always judging me. Always finding all the ways I fall short. There are so many.

"Tomorrow," he says firmly. "Noon."

"Oh, OK. I can do that." I stammer out. "Should I meet you here at the bar? Are you working tomorrow?"

He nods his head, and I don't know whether he's agreeing I should meet him here or that he's working tomorrow. He uncrosses his arms slowly and then suddenly walks to me in three long steps. His legs are so long. He's at least a head and shoulders taller than I am. But against, my five-foot-three-inch frame, most men are taller than me.

There's no warning before he does it. No preamble. No nonverbal cues of what is about to happen. He just reaches out, cups my face in his oversized paws, leans down and kisses me. His lips are intent, hot and aggressive. He dominates my mouth, forcing himself inside to lick and taste me like a starving man lapping at his last meal. And, oh heavens, can this man kiss!

I resist, of course, pressing my hands on his shoulders, but moving Connor is like trying to move a mountain. I feel his muscles flex under my touch and when my hand finally relaxes and snakes around to the back of his neck, he hums contentedly into my mouth, sending happy little vibrations throughout my entire body. With that sound, I allow myself to surrender to him. He's forceful, but tender. His lips are soft and so hot. He tastes of coffee and spicy man that can be described in no other way than ... just Connor. Our tongues tangle and my mind empties, allowing him to stoke long-forgotten flames of passion deep within me. Inner Sex Goddess is on her hands and knees bowing in worship to the

Ruler of the Realm of Kissing. He is its master. I am happily his slave.

I don't know how long he stands there in front of the bar kissing me. A minute? Three? But it feels as if it's my whole life. As if we'd always stood there kissing and we always would be standing there kissing far into the future. Forever, just locked together like this — our lips and our breath coupling and entwining in a sensual dance.

When he finally breaks our kiss, I'm left with my tongue out. It falls against my lower lip and I lick it to soak up the last tastes of him before he steps back and turns to the door of the bar.

"Noon. Tomorrow, Lainey Bird. Be here."

He disappears into the darkened pub, and I stand there simply murmuring to myself, "My name is Elaine."

At least, I think it is.

# CHAPTER THREE



AT SIX O'CLOCK THE following morning, I jump on my stationary bike for my daily virtual spin class. I wash my laundry, mail out six more resumes and cover letters, apply online for three more positions, make a grocery list, change the sheets on my bed and try not to think about Connor.

I spend all morning debating whether or not to accept his invitation. Was it even an invitation? It had sounded more like a command. But a command for what? Did he want to see me again? Or did he just want me to return his niece's clothing? Ugh, I wish I were better at deciphering this whole flirting thing.

I glance down at the jeans and T-shirt neatly folded on the kitchen table. I made a note of the brand of the jeans, but couldn't find them online anywhere. I have to admit I'm tempted to keep them. They're buttery soft. The seams don't pinch, and they fit like they were made for my curves — or my lack thereof. When I look at myself in the mirror, I usually feel like I have the figure of a twelve-year-old boy. But in these babies, I feel like a sex goddess. Curvy, sultry and alluring. The kind of woman who gets kissed in broad daylight in front of bars on the streets of Atlanta. The kind of woman that could totally give in and be taken under by this wave of attraction I have for Connor Rose.

I'm almost worried that if I do go meet him, he'll feel like he's conquered me somehow, and I don't want to be a woman who can be conquered with a growl and a kiss. Do I? If I don't go, then ... oh, what the heck am I saying? I'm totally going to go. If there's even the slimmest possibility that he'll kiss me like he did yesterday, I'd travel to the far corners of the globe to meet him.

I glance at the clock. It's already after ten. I take a shower and then get dressed, donning the jeans again. If he wants them back, he'll have to take them off of me. Now, there's a thought that has my Inner Sex Goddess brushing off seven years of dust from her book of "how-tos."

A sign on the bar's front door says it's closed and reserved for a private party, and it will open at three. But inside, the place looks dark. I give a sharp knock and see Connor's broad frame begin to emerge from the shadows.

I'm ten minutes late. On purpose. I can't have him thinking I'm too eager. Although I was dressed and ready at eleven. Man, I really suck at this.

He greets me with a warm smile, and my heart instantly begins to flutter. I study his mouth and the curve of his lips, remembering the way they felt on mine. He's got a three-day stubble around his jawline that's super sexy and his hair isn't tied back today. It's soft and slightly wavy and falls just past his shoulders in long dark blond locks just like I knew it would.

"Hey Lainey Bird, I thought maybe you wouldn't come." He gives me that happy little smirk of his. It's his smile that's melting me into a puddle right now, not the oppressive

Georgia summer heat. I need to keep my guard up with Connor. He's complete kryptonite.

I smile and walk through the door that he's opened widely in invitation for me to come in further. Inside, I am immediately assaulted with the pungent smell of baking yeast dough, fresh garlic and melting cheese. My stomach growls and my Inner Foodie salivates. I've eaten two meals with Connor Rose and both have been stellar.

We walk through to a large corner booth toward the back of the restaurant and I see another large man emerge from the kitchen wearing a chef's toque and a long white apron. He's covered in flour and has a red sauce smear on his cheek. He smiles and I feel my eyes grow wide. I know this man. Hell, everyone on the planet knows this man. Posters of him and his rock band papered my high school bedroom.

"Ox Carr?" I gush, feeling my Inner Fangirl start to reach for her pom-poms. "You're Ox Carr!" I stare, mouth agape, at the lead rocker of the world-famous band, *Climax*. Fangirl is now in full-on cheer mode as I feel my heartbeat ratchet up a notch and a pulsing heat sink into my cheeks and neck.

"Bryan Carmichael," he corrects and extends his hand. "But you can call me Ox."

"Ox, I'd like you to meet my Lainey Bird," Connor says behind me. I can tell by the smile on his face that his inner Tarzan is totally laughing at Fangirl. Thankfully, she is unfazed. How on earth am I standing in the same room with Ox Carr?

Ox is built exactly as his name would imply. He's tall, pushing six-foot-six if I had to guess. He's at least a few inches taller than Connor. And he's broad and thick. Colorful ink swirls over his arms and neck. Blond hair, now streaked with a bit of gray, falls in waves around his face and down past his shoulders. He has deep creases around his green eyes that fold into happy crinkles when he smiles. He's older than he was back when *Climax* was in its heyday, but every bit as hot. Sexy has no expiration date on this man.

"Nice to meet you. Connor didn't tell me he'd invited a friend." Ox replies to me as if I'm not completely drooling over him. Which, of course, I am.

Fangirl deflates. "Oh?" I look back to Connor. Shit. He did just want me to give back the clothes. "I'm sorry if I'm imposing, I ..."

"I don't tell you every detail of my life, Ox," Connor cuts in. "Now, how much longer on those pies. I'm starving." Connor slides behind the bar, filling four glasses with ice and what looks like some sort of soda. Connor's huge hands easily grip all four glasses and he carries them to the back booth.

Ox glances down at his watch. "Seven minutes and twenty-three seconds," he announces.

"Ox here makes the best deep-dish pizza you've ever had. You eat pizza, don't you, Lainey Bird?" Connor gives me a wink.

"Connor," I lower my voice to a conspiratorial whisper and hustle closer to the bar where he stands. "If you just wanted the clothes back, you should have told me. I can see you're busy. I can drop these and ..."

"Don't you remember? I invited you yesterday, Lainey. You don't want to stay and have lunch with me and a has-been rocker?"

I cock my head to the side and give him a skeptical look.

"My pizza's great. You're staying." Ox says and turns to go back behind the swinging stainless steel door to, what I assume, is the kitchen. "And I'm not a has-been, asshole," he adds in a sing-song voice from behind the door.

As his voice fades, a woman pushes through the front door. She's stunning with long black hair that flows down her back in loose curls. Her eyes are the same fierce blue as Connor's. She's almost as tall as he is, too, with strong arms and a lean torso. She's wearing black leather pants and a flowing tank in some sort of silver-gray that makes her look almost magical.

"Hey, sorry I'm late," she says. Her voice sounds like a melody. She kisses Connor on the cheek and hollers to Ox in the kitchen. "I'm here, babe."

"Be right out ... five minutes and sixteen seconds," he calls back.

"He's got it timed to the second," Connor explains, stepping to the side to reveal me to the new dining companion.

"Oh, hello," she says, looking a bit startled to see me.

"Tori, this is Lainey. Lainey Bird, this is Tori, Ox's wife."

Tori extends a hand and I greet her. She smiles warmly and gives Connor a sideways glance I can't interpret.

"My name is Elaine, actually," I stammer to this gorgeous woman. She looks me up and down and her gaze falls on my jeans.

"Nice jeans," she says. "And don't mind Connor. He and Ox give nicknames to everyone. I'm Victoria. And my husband's name is actually Bryan. Although I can't remember the last time anyone ever called him that." She waves her hands, dismissing her brain's obvious desire to remember.

"What's your nickname then?" I look up at Connor who is still giving this woman an odd look.

"I like Tarzan," he smirks.

"Tarzan?" Tori says laughing. "He used to be known as Heathen once upon a time, which I think fit him pretty well while it lasted."

"Heathen?" I ask, raising my brows at him in question.

"Enough show and tell. Ox, seriously man. Just bring it already."

"It's done. It needs to rest a minute though," Ox calls out from the kitchen. He enters moments later carrying a steaming pie that looks to be nearly two feet across. It's shaped like a dormant volcano filled with cheese, sausage, peppers, mushrooms and bits of bacon. The smell is unbelievable. My mouth immediately waters. Inner Foodie polishes up her fork and knife. This is going to be so good.

Ox drops it in the center of the table and Conner pulls over a stack of plates. A huge knife shaped in a semicircle rocks across the pizza, neatly dividing it into eight giant slices.

Tori slides into the booth and pats the bench beside her for me to sit next to her. I slide in and watch long strands of mozzarella cheese stretch up as Ox serves each person a fat slice of deep dish.

"I've been thinking since it is such a nice day, maybe we should take the bikes out after lunch. Can you spare the day, Tarzan?" Tori asks, taking a sip of her soda and giving Connor an inquisitive smirk over her glass.

Connor returns her gaze with what I'd call an icy glare. But his voice remains calm and kind. "Possibly. I'll see if Lincoln can cover for me. Where did you want to go?"

"The ride along the river is always fun," Ox chimes in. "What do you say, Lainey, wanna go with us?"

I chew what can only be described as pure heaven melted onto the most delicious crust known to man. It's crisp and buttery, oozing with a garlicky sauce. Stuffed with sausage and spicy pepperoni, I feel it slide down my chin and I don't even care. Connor wasn't kidding. Ox knows how to cook a deep dish. I lived in Chicago for years and never had anything this good. My Inner Foodie fights the urge to moan out loud.

"Um ... ride?" I ask, cooling the heat of red pepper flakes in my mouth with my soda. Something tells me they're not talking about bicycles.

"Yeah, you've been on the back of a bike before, right?" Ox interjects, chewing. "Or are you a virgin?"

I flush slightly at his use of the term. "Um, if you mean a motorcycle, then no. I've never been on one before."

Ox shoots Connor a look. He only nods back and then pulls out his phone and taps a quick text. Within seconds, it buzzes with a reply. He stuffs it back into his pocket and gives me a glance that hints I'm very much going to regret coming here today.

"Well then, today's your lucky day, Lainey Bird."

Connor's "bike," as he calls it, looks more like a piece of art than a machine. He tells me it's an Indian. It's solid black with bright flames of chrome that spiral and weave through the exposed motor. The tank has a subdued Indian head, the manufacturer's logo, I learn, embossed with iridescent pearl black paint. The long leather seat can easily fit two people. It looks sleek, fast and like I should make sure my health insurance policy is all paid up before I get on it with him. But there's no time for second-guessing. The peer pressure weighs down on me like the heat of the summer sun, forcing me to muster every ounce of courage I can. I throw my leg over the bike, feeling my inner thigh muscles stretch. I'm not an overly religious woman, but I pray as if my life depends on it. Because at this moment, I honestly feel like it does.

"OK," Connor begins, stuffing my head into a helmet that feels much too tight. "Keep your arms around me and hold on tight. Try not to fight the movement or tilt of the bike. Go with it. I promise I won't let you fall off, and I won't dump us onto the pavement."

I nod and swallow hard. Good to know that dumping onto the pavement is a thing. I hadn't imagined that particular disaster yet. My stomach twists in knots around the pizza I just ate. It's a warm June day and sweat starts beading on my lip and in my hair under the helmet, which is also black to match the bike.

"We're not going far," he promises.

Tori and Ox look like they were built to be on the massive bike they just mounted. Tori tucks herself behind Ox like a pro. He has a Harley with long handlebars that would stretch any mortal man out like a medieval torture device. But for his oversized frame, they seem just right. Tori snaps on her helmet and I can somehow hear her voice in a tiny speaker over my ear inside my own helmet.

"Don't worry, Lainey. Riding a bike is just like having sex. You hold onto the man and let him do all the work."

Laughter now floods my ears as the two men enjoy Tori's joke. But it manages to break the tension, and I do feel slightly more at ease.

Connor revs up the engine and the entire machine between my legs rumbles to life. The vibrations hum through my body, shaking my bones and tickling my nerves. Connor's legs push us off the stand and we're balanced perfectly. Although, I admit, I feel as if I'm going to fall off at any moment. It's like trying to stay on a tightrope. Suddenly being dumped onto the pavement seems like a very real possibility.

I slowly snake my arms around Connor's body, holding tentatively onto the tight muscles around his rib cage. He pulls my wrists up so that my arms are on his chest and not where I grabbed for him. He presses his hand over mine as if to indicate I should keep my hands over his pecs while he drives. My Inner Sex Goddess happily complies. His body is like iron under my grip. I dig in and hold on for dear life.

"Ready?" he asks into the microphone. I don't trust my voice to respond. It will sound high-pitched, nervous and scared. I don't want to sound scared, even though right now, I'm totally terrified. I pat my hand against his chest in an effort to confirm I'm as ready as I'll ever be.

With a twist of his wrist and the tap of a foot, we lurch forward.

I can feel every muscle in Connor's body. Pressed against my chest, his back muscles flex under his shirt. Neck twisting, he checks the traffic. His hips twitch against my inner thighs and knees when he adjusts positions or changes gears. His abs tighten in the turns and corners. His heartbeat quickens. The soft thump of it ebbs and flows in hot waves under my fingertips. Holy macaroni balls! This is the most erotic experience of my life. It should probably upset me to think that riding on the back of a motorcycle through downtown traffic fully clothed in broad daylight is the most erotic thing I've ever done. But it doesn't.

Mr. Pencil Tapper would be giving me his full-on "I told you so" look of pity again, I'm sure. But I don't care about that either. This is sexy as hell. #bikerchick

I love how Connor's body responds to curves, stops and turns. I love the way he feels so close to me. The heat is trapped between us, his heart pulsating wildly.

We finally escape the city and turn down a nearly empty road away from town. Connor sits up a bit and begins to relax. I mimic his actions, letting my spine settle. I slide one hand to his hip to straighten, but I feel his giant claw of a hand move to cover mine and place it back on his chest. Then, he holds it tightly against him as we ride. The gesture is small and innocent. But I know he wants to feel my touch there. I close my eyes, relishing the sensation of his body and mine on this machine. And the thought he wants me touching him like this — so intimately — gives me a rush that nearly makes me dizzy.

The sky is perfectly clear and blue without a single white

puff of a cloud to mar its flawless beauty. The sun is hot, but the wind that we push through cools me so much, I actually feel goose bumps rise up over my bare arms. Well, it could be the breeze. It could also be because Connor is now slowly stroking my wrist and forearm laid over his chest with the pad of his thumb. The feeling is extraordinary. It's somehow familiar and automatic, even though it's also completely new and totally unexpected. I breathe in and let the glory and the wind and the sun and vast blue sky take me in. I let Connor take me in, too.

Connor's definition of "not far" really needs some serious revision. We ride for nearly an hour before coming to a stop. The insides of my legs scream in pain. When we first started, I kept them clenched around Connor's hips like a vise grip — my body's way of silently praying that we didn't end up a mushy spot on the Georgia 400. After we left the city, however, I simply stretched and held them until they began aching. My back and neck, too, have grown stiff from being still for so long. Connor kills the engine and I happily dismount.

We stop alongside what looks to be some sort of a ranch or farm. A split rail fence runs along the roadside. Often, fence posts are just existing pines that grew up into the property line. A metal gate breaks the endless line of fencing. Ox and Connor push the bikes out of sight of the road and under the shade of a large oak tree.

I pull my helmet off and immediately try to smooth and fluff my helmet hair. Tori twists off her helmet and gives her head a quick shake, sending every hair into its place among the effortless curls that drip and coil down her back. I so want to hate her. But it's impossible. I attempt to shake out my own tangles and hand my helmet to Connor who secures it to the bike.

"I need to stretch my legs. Let's walk." Conner, again, asks through command. But I nod, eager to try to use different muscles in my legs and arms and give my inner thighs and back a break.

Tori and Ox pull a blanket out of some saddlebags attached to the side of his bike and disappear, giggling behind a tight knot of trees.

Connor and I walk down a gentle slope of grass and clover toward a tiny trickle of water. Before we've taken a dozen steps, the trickle becomes a small creek. And with another fifty paces or so, the creek widens into a shallow river. Connor toes out of his boots, peels off his socks and rolls up the cuffs of his jeans.

"Damn, it's hot today," he says, wading out into the fast-moving water. "You coming, or what?"

I repeat his actions and wade in beside him. The soft mud of the river squishes between my toes. The water is cold and rushes by me so fast that I almost lose my footing. But the movement of it against my ankles somehow manages to cool my entire body.

Connor bends over and splashes his face with a handful of water. Then, he reaches behind him and pulls his shirt off over his head. He tosses it beside his boots on the sloping bank. He pulls his hair into a loose bun and secures it with a tie, turning so the full vision of his naked torso is revealed.

My mouth falls open. His entire back and shoulders are a tapestry of some of the most beautiful tattoos I've ever seen. A lion's face and mane spread across his shoulder blades. The animal is done entirely of black lines and gray shadows and he looks as if he could open his mouth and roar at any minute. He wears a crown on his head made of the American flag and other small pictures: a rifle, a bullet of some sort and tiny boots. Beneath his chin, the hair of his mane morphs into the eyes of a predatory bird. An owl or an eagle perhaps? The image is a tangle of smaller pictures fitting and melting together to create a tapestry of ink on his skin. And the most stunning feature is the electric blue eyes of the lion. Lost in a sea of flesh and black, they completely hypnotize me. I gasp at the sight of the extraordinary beauty.

Connor turns and looks behind him before his eyes meet mine.

"Is all that noise for my tats?" He's wearing his little smirk. I've seen it before. The first time was when he watched me throw back the sipping whiskey in a single shot. Then again when I said I'd never been on a motorcycle and Ox called me a virgin for it.

"I'm sorry to, but wow!"

I'm dumbstruck by its beauty. The artistry and skill it must have taken to create a piece like this. It moves me in a way I can't explain. Sorrowful and yet hopeful at the same time. Connor's lion looks angry and vengeful, but also peaceful and protective. It's so much more than a tattoo. It's a work of art.

"So, is that a good wow or a bad wow?" he asks, turning to me and raking his wet hands over his hair to dampen it down.

"A good wow, definitely. I don't mean to stare. I'm sorry. I've just never actually seen anything like that before. It's stunning."

He gives me the playful smirk again. "You've never seen a tattoo?"

"I mean, you know, those silly frat boy things they get on their ankles and forearms, but nothing like this."

I am drawn to the lion. Inexplicably pulled to him. I wade out deeper, feeling the rushing water soak my jeans to the middle of my calves. I reach a hand up toward his shoulder, and then pause, leaving it inches away from touching his body. A half hour ago, I held tightly to every inch of him, but now touching his skin feels like an act that's too intimate.

He turns around revealing the lion to me again. Twisting

his head to look at me, he says invitingly, "You can touch it if you want to. It doesn't bite."

I grin. I must look like I am afraid the life-like animal will open his mouth and devour me in his jaws. Because he totally looks like he could. And I feel like I could let him. I could let the lion consume me entirely. Get lost in the piercing blue of his eyes and the silken waves of his mane.

My fingers reach for Connor and I touch his skin. It's damp from the river water and sweat and it's hot. So hot. I trace the edge of the lion's regal crown, now discovering other tiny images tangled into the larger design: soldier's stripes, like from a uniform, a star, a tube of lipstick ... I could stare at the artwork for hours, but I blink and take my hand away.

Connor shifts his feet and faces me, stepping closer. He leans forward and this time, I'm ready for what he's about to do. I steel my body for the force of his kiss, but the impact doesn't come. Instead, his lips brush mine softly. He kisses my bottom lip and then the top and then presses against my mouth, opening me to be tasted, licked, savored. And just like that, I'm slowly being devoured by the lion.

After a single, long kiss, he lets his hand drift to hold mine. Our fingers gently tangle together as he tugs me up on shore to a cool patch of clover in the shade.

We sit and then let our bodies stretch out to lie alongside one another. He's cradling the back of his head in cupped hands, eyes closed. I watch as his chest and abs rise and fall softly with his steady breath.

Silence closes in around me and I feel the need to fill it, to fill his head with words and sounds so he's not thinking of me — judging all the ways I'll never measure up.

"Where do you think Ox and Tori are?" I ask innocently. I sit up and cross my legs and pluck at a white tuft of dandelion by my knee.

"Probably having sex somewhere over there." Connor

doesn't open his eyes or move his body other than to tip his chin up to indicate somewhere on the other side of the creek in the dark shadows of a cluster of trees.

"Seriously?"

"Yeah, those two never got out of the honeymoon stage. They fuck like rabbits."

I blush slightly at his candid language, and try to push the vision of the two of them from my mind.

"My mother used to tell me dandelions are good luck," Connor motions at the one in my hand and several of them scattered throughout the field. "After the yellow flowers turn into white balls of fluff, you can blow on them and make a wish. Mom used to say you're setting your wishes free when you do that. Go ahead, Lainey Bird, make a wish."

All of my wishes got squashed years ago, not that I want to discuss that with him. "I guess I'm not one for making wishes," I offer lamely.

"You should," he says. "They just might come true." He plucks a nearby dandelion and puckers his mouth, sending white fuzzy seeds into the breeze. I smile at his obvious optimism.

His eyes lock with mine in a long embrace of silence. I wonder what a man like Connor Rose could possibly wish for. Sweat erupts across my forehead and my face grows pink.

"It's getting late. We should probably get back, don't you think?" I force out. I instantly regret the words. The last thing I want to do is leave.

Conner keeps one eye the squinted to block the sun and looks at me. "You're not having a good time?"

"I feel like I'm living a dream," I admit. "Meeting one of my rock star heroes and finding out his wife is this wonderful, beautiful creature, and then my first motorcycle ride and being in this beautiful place. With you. You're kidding, right?"

"Then why do you want to leave?"

I shrug my shoulders because I'm not really sure.

"You don't like the quiet, do you?" he suddenly asks.

"What makes you think that?" I feel exposed that he can see through the thin veneer of my facade. Like he's unearthed some hidden part of me.

"You chattered on and on like a little bird all night. Even drunk. If we stopped talking about one subject, you started in on something else."

It's a terrible habit, my incessant chattering. Still, no one has ever called me out on this before. Not even my family. I'm not sure how to respond. "I guess you're right. I don't like the quiet."

"It's loud here," he says twisting his head to look up into the trees again and closing his one open eye.

"Loud? Maybe for you. You could hear a fly burp," I say. This draws a laugh from Connor. It's such a good sound. I want to hear it again and again.

"Lie down, Lainey Bird, next to me." I do as he commands.

"Close your eyes." Again, I comply, not really sure what it is about the way he orders me around that makes me want to do everything he says. I slowly let my lids fall closed, and I feel his fingers reach out and touch mine again. He curls them around my hand and we lie there in the grass under the hot Georgia summer sun.

"Now, just listen, Lainey. You can hear the wind in the trees, the birds, the river, even your own heart. But you have to stop talking to hear all the noises around you. You don't have to fill the space. It's already full."

I take a deep breath and try to calm my nervousness. Why does the quiet bother me so much? "You're thinking I'm a nut, aren't you? Because I always need to talk?"

"Shh," he whispers.

"I always think people are judging me in the quiet. I

always like to know what people are thinking, and when they're talking, I think I'm distracting them from thinking about me."

I feel the coolness of a shadow cover my body and think a cloud has managed to appear and block the sun. But when I open my eyes, Connor's body is looming over me.

"I am thinking about you," he says softly. "I'm thinking about how badly I want to kiss you again."

"Why?"

"Your mouth, it's ... irresistible. It reminds me of a ripe plum. Such a pretty color, so soft and sweet."

His hand cups the back of my head and he presses his mouth against mine. He kisses me, softly at first, and then harder. He gently releases his weight and then devours and nips. And while we lie there, I hear the sound of our mouths, wet and hot, sucking and licking. The click of teeth. The chirp of birds chattering among the branches of the trees. The leaves applaud the soft summer breeze as it drifts lazily through the branches. I can hear the water tumbling in fast giggles over the stones in the creek bed. I can hear Connor's breath and my heart. A symphony of music and noises. Connor is right. It is loud.

From somewhere beyond the trees, I hear a woman scream softly, followed by a man roaring. My body goes rigid and Connor stops kissing me, leaving his lips just a centimeter from mine.

"Sounds like Ox and Tori are finally finished." And we both break out into a giggly laugh.

We take our time putting on our shoes and walking back to the bikes. Connor's shirt covers his lion tattoo again, but knowing it's there feels like knowing a secret about him that is hidden from the rest of the world. And I feel special, somehow, for knowing a secret about him. The thought flashes through my mind, and I grin as it settles and takes a firm hold. I want to know all of his secrets.

"Hey, anyone else hungry?" Ox asks. He and Tori slip out from a knot of trees carrying the blanket. His shirt wrinkled and her cheeks and neck pink with a flush. "How about we stop at that cool fish place up the road for some dinner?"

"What do you say, Lainey? You game?" Tori asks me. She has a leaf in her hair. Ox plucks it away and then leans down to kiss her cheek. The hand that carelessly tossed the leaf to the ground reaches around and tweaks her backside. They're so cute with one another. I can't help but wonder if she was a fan first or his wife first. Every single one of my friends in high school would have given anything to have been loved by Ox Carr. And this woman has him forever. He loves her. And she loves him. It's so perfect. And enviable.

We ride to the restaurant, which is nothing more than a small cabin alongside the Chattahoochee River. It's cozy and filled to overflowing on a Friday night. Ox steps up to the hostess stand and smiles. "How long is the wait?"

The hostess, a small slip of a girl, barely twenty, doesn't bother to look up at him and mouths almost robotically, "About twenty to thirty minutes. Seating around the bar is first come, first served. Domestics are $5 until six if you care to wait at the bar. Name?"

"Ox Carmichael," he answers.

At this, the woman glances up, taking a serious inventory of the man standing in front of her. A look of shock and utter disbelief crosses her face. It washes away almost instantly as Ox gives her a sly smile and waggles his eyebrows.

"Ohmigod! Mr. Carmichael. Um ... give me a couple of minutes, sir. How many in your party?"

"Just four, darlin'. I sure do appreciate it." And just like that, we are getting a table, and our hostess is getting hot and bothered. I can't blame her. If Ox Carr had walked into a place where I worked when I was her age and waggled those brows, calling me darlin' ... I would have fainted on the spot.

She smiles, blushes and rushes away to clear a table recently vacated by four women who look as if they've been drinking since lunch.

"You guys never wait for tables, do you?" I mutter quietly to Connor.

"Not usually," Connor replies, his mouth close to my ear. I can feel the heat of his breath and it sends a happy shiver into my belly where the butterflies are taking wing inside again.

The hostess seats us right away and I drop my purse before heading to the bathroom where I see her motioning to another young woman, tapping an order onto a keypad by the bar.

"You guys must be big fans, too?" I say a bit offhandedly. If they are *Climax* fans, then we're practically family. Although, they look a bit young to be true disciples of the band, but honestly, their music is timeless and really transcends generational limitations.

"Fans?" She asks. "Of ..."

"*Climax*? The band? I saw the way you looked at Ox when he came in, and ..."

"Oh, he's in a band? Cool. No, Mr. Carmichael owns this place."

My eyebrows shoot up in surprise, although I shouldn't be. So that's why they never wait for tables. They're not frequent customers, they're owners.

Returning to the table, I see a hard cider at my place. "It's a girly beer. Not too strong," Conner says. "Do you mind?"

"No. It's fine. Thanks."

I see that Ox and Connor are both drinking some sort of non-alcoholic beer and Tori has ordered something pink in a champagne glass with a cherry bobbing at the bottom of it.

The cider is sweet, and I'm thirstier than I realize. The bubbles feel good sliding down my throat.

"Just don't swallow it all in one shot," Ox says with a playful jab. I glare over at Connor who nearly chokes on his drink.

"Damn, Ox. Really?" he scolds.

Ox laughs out loud. Hearing him laugh reminds me of how Santa Claus would sound if I ever actually met him. It's a jolly rumble that rolls out and then catches on itself into a happy bounce that fills the hearts of all who hear it. It's infectious. Fangirl swoons again.

"You'll have to excuse him, Lainey. He was raised by wolves," Tori says, joining the laughter and diffusing Connor's frustration.

"Which one?" I ask, giving her a wink. At that, the entire table, including Connor, erupts into laughter. Connor instantly relaxes and whatever irritation he seemed to have had with Ox is forgotten. It seems we couldn't stop laughing. Through two rounds of ice water, four baskets of fish and chips and two shared molten lava cakes with ice cream. By the time we return to the bikes, the sky is rapidly fading from a light blue to a deep purple and my sides burn from the reverie of the night.

I hold onto Connor even more closely than before, the night air chilling my skin as we wind our way back to the *Journey's End*. Ox and Tori both hug me, Ox clapping my back in a hard slap.

"It was so nice to meet you, Lainey," Tori says politely. "I do hope we see you again sometime."

I took my time driving to the bar from my apartment earlier that afternoon. I wanted to be late on purpose and now I regret not getting ten more minutes with these lovely people who so quickly and unexpectedly have become my friends. Ox and Tori take off on their bike leaving Connor and me alone in front of the bar.

"Thanks for such a great day. I wish you'd have let me pay for my dinner tonight, though," I say, rubbing my shoulders. The air has turned thick with the coming of the evening. But I'm not shivering from the cool air. I'm shivering with the joy of reliving the day in my mind as I share my gratitude with Connor.

"Nah, it's no big deal." Connor moves closer and I can feel the heat of his body next to mine. His hands drift up my arms to my shoulders and he leans forward and drops a single, soft kiss on my cheek.

"I want you to meet me at this address tomorrow at three. Can you come?"

I feel him slip a small card into my hand. I look at it and see it's a card for the *Journey's End,* but on the back, he's written an address and two sets of numbers.

"It's a house near where we were riding today. That's the address," he says, running his finger along the top line. "This is the gate code. And this is my cell if you need me."

I instantly go into my bobblehead doll routine, nodding that I'll be there even though I haven't checked my calendar or my emails to see if I have any interviews. It's not likely I will on a weekend, but I'd have to cancel if I did. Two days ago, I'd have driven cross-country for an interview on a Sunday, but now I suddenly find myself hoping no one wants me. Well, no one but Connor Rose, that is.

"See you tomorrow, Lainey Bird," Connor says and disappears into the enveloping sounds of laughter, drinking and celebration inside the *Journey's End.*

# CHAPTER FOUR

### Saturday, June 5

I FIND myself traveling along the same road Connor, Tori, Ox and I rode along yesterday. Even though it's much hotter and insanely humid today, I roll the windows down so the breeze can brush against my skin again. Being on the back of the bike with Connor was like nothing I've ever felt before. It's a feeling I've been trying to identify since I got back home last night. But I can't.

I pause when my GPS announces I've arrived. I recognize the metal gate where Connor and Ox parked the bikes yesterday. I hadn't noticed the keypad then, however. I type in the number Connor wrote on the business card and hear a loud buzzing noise as the gate slides open to let me pass. I follow along the gravel drive through a cluster of trees for nearly half a mile before I see the house.

It's perched on the edge of the riverbank tucked under towering oaks and age-old pines. It's definitely modern construction, but has this old-world feel to it, as if it was built to look old. There's a circular drive with a three-tiered fountain in the center. A plaster lion is perched at the top. Two more copper statues of the king of beasts flank a massive wooden door. I ring the bell and a short balding man answers. He says nothing, just simply raises his eyebrows.

"I'm looking for Connor," I say quietly. "He's expecting me, although I think I may be a bit early." I glance at my watch and see it's ten minutes until three. "I'm Elaine. I mean, that is, Lainey."

He smiles, hearing me say Lainey, and pulls the door open wider, sweeping his hand back to invite me inside. But he still says nothing. After closing the door, he walks through a massive foyer that reveals a second story above. A rounding staircase offers visitors both the opportunity to go up one side and down the other. I follow the mute little man until we get through a spacious living area dotted with heavy deep couches and accented by a large stone fireplace. A bank of glass doors leads out onto a deck that overlooks the river. The view is spectacular.

I walk outside to see Connor barking out instructions to an army of people moving furniture, setting up tables and arranging some sort of a stage.

"Wow. What's all this then?" I ask as I step outside. Connor turns and his face instantly lights up seeing me. Holy crap! When was the last time anyone looked at me like that? My heart flutters and my Inner Sex Goddess starts to toss her mane of glossy hair over her shoulders like a woman in a shampoo commercial. Lord, he makes me feel sexy.

"Hey there, Lainey Bird." He greets me with a big hug and a deep penetrating kiss that has my Inner Sex Goddess now choosing between a black lace teddy and a white silk negligee. I met this man two days ago. Two days. Why does it seem OK for him to be touching me, kissing me and holding me? Inner Sex Goddess ignores the question. Quite frankly, she doesn't care. And I decide that if she doesn't care, then I don't either. I let my arms wrap around him and embrace the lion for a few more kisses.

"I'm glad you found me. I'm having a party."

"What's the occasion?"

"It's my birthday," he reveals, almost bashfully.

"Your birthday? I didn't bring you a gift. And a party? Am I dressed all right?"

He glances over me. I've ditched the jeans for the day and opted instead for a pair of khaki-colored linen capri pants, a cropped navy tee that shows just a tiny sliver of my stomach and a pair of strappy sandals. I've braided my hair and topped my coiffure with a light straw fedora.

"You look great. And you are my gift, Lainey Bird." He drops another kiss on my cheek. "Ox will be here in a few minutes to oversee the setup for the band. Can you show him down when he gets here? I really want to take a shower."

"Sure. Is there anything else I can do, old man?" I give him a wink.

Connor looks over me with a salacious glare that immediately sets Inner Sex Goddess completely on fire. "I'm thirty-five today, not old yet. And let's jump off the bridge of 'what you can do for me' later, OK?"

He disappears into the house and I wander to the back deck and find another staircase that leads to the lower level where all the action is. Caterers fill massive smoke pits with huge cuts of pork, sausage and whole chickens. Bartenders scurry about carrying bottles of wine, beer and assorted liquors. Construction workers build a stage complete with professional-looking concert lights and a soundboard that looks like it could launch a space shuttle.

"Hey, it's the Lainey Bird," I hear a voice growl behind me. Ox shuffles forward wearing a ripped T-shirt, long cargo shorts and tattered flip-flops. Tori floats behind him wearing a floral printed dress that comes to her knees, a large sunhat and oversized dark sunglasses. She looks amazing.

"Lainey," she sings out and wraps me in a hug. It somehow feels forced today when it was more friendly last night. "I'm glad you're here. Where's Connor?"

"He said he wanted to take a shower, and I should show you to the stage. Not that you need me to. You can't miss it."

Ox gives me his warm Santa Claus laugh. "Letting you play hostess, is he?"

I shrug and take Tori's outstretched hand in mine as she drags me over to the bar. I hear the Santa laugh trail off as Ox makes his way toward the general direction of the stage.

"We need to test your frozen margaritas," she tells the bartender. "It's my brother's party, and everything has to be just right."

My heart skips a beat. Her brother? Connor is her brother?

"I'm glad we can have a few minutes to chat, just you and me," she says, handing me a frosty glass with a little yellow umbrella sticking out of it.

"You want to ask me what my intentions are with Connor?" I joke. But her expression is anything but joking. My blood freezes colder than the drink in my hands.

"Yes, actually, I do." She lowers her sunglasses off of her face and I see the ice in her eyes.

I choke on the swallow of sweet and tart frostiness and stare at her with wide eyes. She's glaring back at me and, I don't know why, but I suddenly feel as though I'm guilty of some sort of a trespass.

"The jeans you had on yesterday ... those are mine." Her voice is as chilly as her stare.

I flush, feeling embarrassed. "Oh, I'm so sorry. I didn't know. Connor told me they belonged to his niece. I ... I was just borrowing them."

"Oh, they're Ginger's. But they're my design. I mean they're my fashion creation. They haven't gone to market yet, so it was surprising to see them on you yesterday. They looked good on you, though." She pulls a long draw from her drink before setting it down and leaning back, her arm draped across the back of the chair.

"Thank you. Again, I'm so sorry. I should have just washed them and returned them. I ..."

Tori holds up her hands. "You're misunderstanding me, Lainey. I don't care if you wear the jeans. Keep them. They're yours. I care that you're fucking my brother."

My mouth drops open and my face burns scarlet. "Oh, my God! No. We're not. That is, we didn't sleep together." My brow crinkles in a tight V over my forehead, pinching so hard I nearly give myself an instant headache. Did Connor tell her we slept together? Crap! An embarrassed flush spreads across my cheeks, heating my entire body. We could have, I suppose. I wouldn't have remembered. I was too blitzed. But he did tell me he didn't try to sleep with me. What the ...?

"So ... how do you explain the jeans then?" She picks up her cocktail and takes another long draw.

It's none of her business, but I suddenly feel the need to explain myself to this woman. To earn back the sweet feeling of acceptance and friendship we shared yesterday. Or at least I thought we shared. I can't have her judging me. My heart squeezes tight as I choke out my words.

"I got drunk at the bar where he works. I kinda passed out, and he took me to his house. He washed my suit, because I got sick apparently, and it was ruined, shrunk, so he offered me clothes from Ginger, that's her name, right? He offered me clothes from her closet. We didn't sleep together. We're not ... I mean ..."

"And he invited you to lunch yesterday?" She asks, narrowing her eyes.

"Not exactly. He just barked 'Noon. Tomorrow,' at me when he dropped me at my car. I thought he was asking for the clothes back. That's why I wore the jeans. I kinda wanted to be a bit ... I don't know, defiant? I thought maybe we were flirting. But I swear that's all it was, flirting. And you don't have to worry, because I'm really bad at it anyway."

Tori smiles broadly as I talk and nods. "I see. Well, this is interesting. And I think you should know that Connor doesn't work as a bartender at the *Journey's End*, sweetie, he owns it. He and Ox own six different restaurants around the area."

"Like the *Day Old Bagel*?" I ask, thinking back to the morning after I woke up in his bed.

"Yeah, it's one of their newer ventures. Connor inherited a large sum of money a few years back, and he and Ox have been investing it and managing it. My brother is a very wealthy man, Lainey. This is one of the many houses he owns. And he's a bit blind when it comes to games women play. I need to be assured that no one is ever going to take advantage of that."

"I understand, and I respect and appreciate how much you clearly must love him. He's lucky to have you. But I can assure you, I'm not playing any kind of a game, Tori."

"Christ, Tori. What the hell are you doing?" I hear Connor's voice like a low rumble coming closer behind me.

"Connor, I asked, you didn't answer me, so I'm asking her. I told you I would. Someone has to look out for you." Tori pops to her feet and instantly crosses her arms over her chest in a defensive posture.

"You two were discussing me?" I pipe in, also rising to my feet, but no one even listens to me. Connor looks murderous, and Tori looks ready to take him down. It's like I'm standing in the middle of a World Wrestling Federation match for the national title.

The stare-off between them mounts. My Inner Miss Insecurity wants to suck her thumb and slink back into a corner. They're judging me. Tori is, at least. They're discussing me behind my back. She thinks I'm using him. She thinks I'm not good enough. I'm not. I'm nowhere near good enough to attract the attention of a man like Connor, or be accepted by people like Ox Carr and his beautiful fashion-designer wife. I suddenly feel too hot. I can't breathe. And I want to just ... just get out of here.

"You know what? I'm going to go. You two obviously have a lot to talk about, and it's clear that I don't belong here." I drop my glass onto a stone patio table next to the chair where I was sitting and dart toward the stairs that will take me up to the ground floor level and back out the way I came in. If I knew of a faster route of escape, I would have taken it.

I can hear Connor's and Tori's voices in angry tones with one another although I can't make out what they're saying. I wipe tears from my eyes and pump my legs up the stairs and through the house to the massive wooden front door. I'm only a few feet from my car when I see Connor running from alongside the house toward me. Clearly, he knows where all the shortcuts are in this place.

"Lainey Bird. Wait. Please. Don't go." His voice is strained.

"What sort of game are you playing with me?"

"I'm not playing a game." His fingers reach for me. I want to swipe them away, but I can't. My hands are shaking at my sides, so hurt and angry. His thumb wipes away a tear and I flush with color. I'm such a baby crying like this. Why? Because Tori doesn't like me? No. Because they were judging me. Showing me again how much I fall short.

"Oh no? You kidnap me when I'm drunk and passed out — a situation which I totally blame you for, by the way. Then, you whisk me away in your fancy vintage sex machine to breakfast and kiss me as if your life depends on it before demanding I come to you at noon the next day. I must have seriously lost my mind, because I actually show up, and you seduce me with your rock-star brother-in-law and your amazing sister and that ride to the river. Why didn't you tell me she was your sister? Why didn't you tell me you weren't the bartender at the *Journey's End*, you are the owner? That you own the *Day Old Bagel* and the cute catfish place where we ate last night? That river where you kissed me, that was your land too, wasn't it? Jesus, I knew you probably had money. I could tell by the sheets I slept on. But I don't want your money or your sympathy or anything else. Hell, I don't know what I'm doing here. This is nuts! I'm going back to my boring life. At least I knew what was coming."

"Lainey, please. Don't go." His fingers clutch mine, and I feel the heat and need penetrating into my skin. "It's my birthday, and all I really want is for you to be here. Ox and the band are going to play. Please, just stay."

A car full of people pulls into the drive and voices call out to Connor.

"Hey man, Happy Birthday," they intone in a cheerful chorus.

"Thanks, Dax, Marcus. Hey Mags. Glad y'all could come." Connor plasters a mask of delight on his face, but it falls away when he turns back to look at me.

"Please. I'm sorry, Lainey. Just give me one dance and eat a piece of cake. Then you can go. Deal?"

I heave a heavy sigh. Inside, I am at war with myself. Inner Sex Goddess pants at his pitiful eyes, clearly sorry and truly wanting me to stay. Fangirl salivates at the thought of hearing *Climax* perform in a private concert. Inner Foodie can't wait to taste the culinary delights I can smell cooking in woodsmoke. Miss Insecure seems to be the only one with an intelligent, rational-thinking brain.

And she tells me to get in my car and forget this weekend ever happened.

"Connor, hey man. You've got guests. They're all wanting a drink with the birthday boy," we hear Ox calling from behind Connor. He's walking toward him with two beers in his hand and a smile stretched over his lips. He thrusts one bottle to Connor and they clink their drinks together.

"I'll be there in a minute. I'm talking to Lainey right now." His voice is more of a bark than words. He is clearly annoyed at being interrupted.

"Well, I tell you what. You go greet your guests, and I'll talk to Lainey. How about that?" Ox gives him a wink.

"I don't think that's a good idea, man." Connor's annoyance level just went up about fifty notches. I feel the air between them prickle with testosterone.

"It's a great idea. Trust me. Now, off you go." Ox turns Connor around and gives him a swift kick in his backside in the direction of the front door. I actually hear Connor growl at him as he takes a swig of his beer, rakes his hands through his hair and stalks off in the direction of the foyer. He is going the long way back to the party. Probably to cool off before greeting the people who've arrived. They must be coming in by boat along the river, too, because I only see a few cars park while we are standing out front. But I can hear the laughter of a lot more people coming from the back deck.

"Lainey, I want to apologize for my wife. She was way out of line earlier. It's not an excuse, but Connor got really hurt by a woman several years back. He was a total mess. He's just started getting himself back together and she feels like she needs to protect him."

"She's not his mother, Ox. And I haven't done anything wrong." I protest. I actually cross my arms over my chest. Love for a sibling is fine. But it doesn't excuse overstepping. Ox was right about that.

"Tori and Connor's parents died when Connor was just thirteen years old. Tori and I are a lot older than him. We took him in. Ginger was already almost eight, I think. Those two practically grew up together. And, yeah, Tori isn't his mom, but we raised him. So she does tend to go full-on Momma-Bear on people she feels threaten her young cub." He gives me a shrug and a half smile. "We're working on it."

I didn't know that about Connor. No wonder he seems so close to his family. "I promise she won't say another inappropriate word."

"Ox, I appreciate what you've said. Thank you for telling me. But I barely know Connor and I'm not sure I really want to get into all this with him right now."

"He likes you," Ox says flatly, the half-smile disappearing from his face. "The night you passed out at the bar, he told me everything. He said he liked you from the minute you sat down. And he was as thankful as he could be that Marie's kid got lice, and she had to go pick him up early from school. That's why he was behind the bar that day. Fate totally brought you two together. And some poor kid had to get head lice to do it. The least you can do is stay a couple of hours at his party. I think it would really mean a lot to him."

"He said he liked me?" Fangirl and Sex Goddess hold hands and dance in a circle together.

"Yeah, he did. He said, and I'm quoting here, 'Ox, I met the most beautiful woman tonight.' Then he went on and on and on about your job interview and the whiskey and how funny you are. You make him laugh. I haven't heard Connor laugh in a really long time, hon. A really damn long time."

Ox takes another sip of his beer and my heart flutters a little at his words. Connor isn't the talkative type. I acted like a total idiot the first night we met and he thought I was, what? I was endearing? He likes me and he wants me to be here. And he was plenty pissed at his sister for giving me a hard time. I use these thoughts to soothe Miss Insecure, who's packed away her thumb-sucking blanket for the moment.

"Tori called and gave him the third degree after you went home last night. He wouldn't tell her shit. When she found out later that I knew about you, she got a bit nuts. But this ain't about Tori. It's about you and Connor. My wife, I can handle. So ... you gonna stay, or what?"

"OK. I'll stay." I concede with a long puff of breath I let out in a rush.

"Awesome. Now, I'm going to buy you a drink." He drapes his arm around me and we walk into the party together. Fangirl just high-fived my Inner Sex Goddess.

"It's an open bar, Ox." I truly feel better after our talk. Ox's tone of voice and his words of encouragement have me wanting to learn more about Connor Rose.

"Exactly."

*Climax* has still got it. Granted, most of the band members are in their mid-fifties now, but age doesn't matter. Their voices, their instrumentals and the eerie harmonies they were known for still ring out like they always have. There's a lot less running and sliding across the stage on their knees, of course, but the sound ... the sound is all there. My Inner Fangirl just lit her lighter and holds it high for the world to see. I am captivated. #climaxrocks

Music has always had that effect on me. It transports me. It frees me. This weekend, I realize how much I've missed it. How much I really do need it in my life. It was so much more than a paycheck for me. It was a passion. I knew it then. But

I let the people around me influence me. Swaying to a ballad, I can't help but wonder if it's too late to go back to it. I wonder if my cello would treat me like a jilted lover — angry and resentful, or if it would embrace me as the prodigal child come home.

"I bet this is your favorite song of theirs, isn't it?" Connor's mouth is against my ear so I can hear him over the din of the music. I shake my head.

"*Youngest Lover* is," I confess, talking directly into his ear so he can hear me.

Connor's eyebrows lift and his eyes widen in something more akin to delight than surprise. "You know what that song's about, don't you?" I can't hear him, but his lips are easy enough to read.

I do. It's not a ballad, but it has less of the rock vibe *Climax* usually uses to push the beat of their music. An older man makes love to a young girl, legal of course, but very young. He takes her virginity with compassion and teaches her to love him and love sex. The song is sensual, very descriptive and quite erotic. I always wanted it to be like that with me someday. It wasn't, of course.

"Wow! You keep surprising me, Lainey Bird," Connor says into my ear. "Dance with me."

He commands me again. Just like his lunch invitation, he's not requesting but directing. Before I can answer, he has me in his arms and spins me around to the band's cover of a popular new love song. They're giving it their trademark sound, and it's so much better than the original recording.

I like Connor's arms around me. He's strong and hard, but there's a softness inside of him that I can tell he keeps safely hidden behind all the strength. Ox said he'd been hurt badly by a woman a long time ago. It must have been pretty bad to have forced him to keep such a protective fortress around himself now.

Me? I talk incessantly. When I run out of small talk, I tend to overshare. I'm always embarrassed by it, though. Like Mr. Pencil Tapper said, my life is way too boring. But right now, I'm not talking. I'm listening to the music, the laughter of the party and dancing with the most surprising man I've ever met. *Yeah, you keep surprising me, too, Tarzan.*

A half a pound of smoked pork, two ears of sweet corn on the cob — absolutely dripping in butter — three of Tori's frozen cocktails, four dances and two pieces of cake later, the party finally starts to break up a little after 1 a.m. *Climax* finished their second set more than two hours ago. The crew busily dismantles the stage while guests linger a little while at the bar. A little after two o'clock, Connor leads the last of his friends out to their rideshares and finds me coming out of a dark hallway from where I luckily managed to find a much-needed powder room.

"You throw a hell of a party," I say sincerely.

"It was a great night." Connor stalks toward me. Right now, he's the lion.

"Well, anytime you have good food, an open bar and *Climax* playing live — you've got all the makings for a wonderful night."

"It was wonderful because you were here." His eyes soften a bit when he says that. I blink and the softness seems to fade somewhat. Too many margaritas, I suppose.

"Stay with me tonight," he says. Once again, I know he's asking me even though his words and his tone would indicate it's more of a command. I don't know him well. But I don't think he's the kind of person who would command me to do anything. And my Inner Sex Goddess never complains that he "asks" me the way he does. She's already calculating how many kisses it will take to let him have sex with me, but I'm less certain. I think it's much too soon to sleep with Tarzan.

"Connor, I don't know. I'm not sure I want to ..."

"No sex," he says suddenly. I know by the way he says it, he means it. "Just sleep beside me in my bed. I swear I won't try anything."

My brow creases with skepticism. "You want me to stay, but you don't want sex?"

He nods and I'm not sure why, but I completely believe him. He has this look on his face that reminds me of a little boy who is scared of the dark. I can't quite explain it, but I think Connor needs me to stay with him tonight even more than he wants me to be here.

"I don't have any of my things, and it's too late for me to go home and ..."

"You can sleep in my T-shirt again, and I've got plenty of extra toothbrushes. Please."

This is the third time he's said please and I swear, I'll never get tired of hearing this man, who looks like a brute and has a ravenous, blue-eyed lion tattooed on his back, utter the word "please".

I give him a smile, and, much to my Inner Sex Goddess' delight, I agree to stay. The part of me who prays is on her knees asking the Ruler of the Universe that this not be the biggest mistake I ever make. All those serial killer shows, you know.

We go back outside to find Tori and Ox seated around a firepit. Ox has an acoustic guitar on his lap, picking out a song and singing to his wife. My heart clutches with a little pang of jealousy over what they have. They're soul mates, true loves. And you know just by looking at the way they steal glances and the fact he still smacks her on the ass when she walks by, they'll be together forever.

"Hey, Lainey, Connor tells me you're a musician. Cellist, right?" Ox confirms. He kicks a chair toward me with his foot. I suppose it's his way of inviting me to join them.

I nod. "A long time ago."

"She played for me a couple of days ago, and it was beautiful," Connor offers.

"Play anything else besides the cello?" Ox is plucking out the melody of one of *Climax*'s most popular love songs.

"I dabbled with the violin, but it affected my cello playing, so I had to put it down. I do know five or six chords on the guitar." I nod to his instrument, a bit shocked at how brazen I am to volunteer this information. I know he's going to ask me to play, and for the first time in a very long while, I'm not hiding from the opportunity. I actually want it. The Maestro inside me is already thumbing through my limited repertoire.

Ox hands me his guitar and slides out of his chair to retrieve another.

I feel the wood, already warm from his grip, melt into my palms. I pick a few strings. The sound is amazing. Without thinking, I began to pluck out the first few notes of an old Beatles' tune called *Blackbird*. It was a pretty difficult song for a beginner, but it was the first one I learned. My father has always loved this song. I must have played it for him a thousand times. No matter how long it's been since I've played it, my fingers always remember how to pluck out this song.

By the time I've gotten halfway through the long introduction, I'm improvising and Ox is playing an accompaniment part. At the start of the first verse, Connor, Ox and I all start singing. We all naturally seem to know how to split the parts. Connor takes the lead. He has a gorgeous tenor voice that makes my skin tingle. I sing harmony and Ox chimes in with a bass line that gives the whole piece a strange harmony that is hauntingly beautiful.

The notes wrap around me, and for three minutes I am gone. I am here fully, but I'm also inside myself and a thousand miles away at the same time. It's the power music has always had on me. It will always have on me.

When we finish, I open my eyes. I didn't realize I'd closed

them. I usually do when I play. It helps me concentrate. I look up beaming. Ox, Tori and Connor are staring. Ox's mouth is actually hanging open.

"Blow me blind, woman," he says, breaking the spell of silence. I'm thankful he did. The single heartbeat of quiet was almost too much. Judgement threatening to fill the vacuum of sound. "You're incredible."

I shake my head and try to hand the guitar back to him. "I'm terribly rusty."

"Shit, if that's rusty, you could have been a professional."

"I was. Sort of." I hear myself say it, and I instantly regret it. I was always proud of my achievement, but with the way my short career ended, I don't like to bring it up. Everyone always wants to know why I don't play anymore. And that story is one I don't care to share.

Connor glances at me with another one of those amused grins of his. I'm really beginning to like them. It gives him this sexy boyish look that resonates down into the bottom of my belly.

"Of course you did. Cello, guitar or were you in a rock group we don't know about?"

I laugh at that. "I played the cello for the New York Phil-harmonic for about three years."

"Holy shit!" Ox says. "Where did you learn to play?"

"She told me middle school, but I don't believe that," Connor chuckles out.

"I did. My family moved from San Diego to Chicago the summer of my seventh-grade year. Moving into a new school was pretty tough. My music teacher, Mrs. Dean, said that joining the orchestra could help me meet new friends. She handed me a cello, and I guess the rest is history."

"Yeah, but you're not that old. You must have been playing with them when you were pretty young."

"I started right after I left Juilliard." And there goes

another piece of this story I never like to share. What is wrong with me? Note to self: no more margaritas.

"You studied at Juilliard?" Connor raises an eyebrow and lifts his glass, which I notice is filled only with water, toward me in salute.

"A couple of years. It's really not that big of a deal. Thousands of people go to Juilliard, you know." Thousands of the most awful, mean-spirited people I'd ever met.

"Well, I'm impressed." Tori chimes in. She's been quiet for a while and the way she slurs her words tells me why.

"All right, one more. Then, I've got to take my girl home," Ox says, setting down a bottle of water on the ground and adjusting his guitar on his lap. I notice his is a twelve-string. It's a such beautiful instrument, all polished red and burled wood. And even though his stage persona is a total bad-boy rocker, Ox really understands and knows music.

"You guys should know this one, you did an amazing cover of it once in your early days," I say to Ox and start picking out the introduction to the Eagle's *Desperado*. I have no idea why my Inner Maestro chose this song, but it's a favorite. I never completely mastered it, but I don't think this crowd will fault me for a couple of mistakes if I flub a chord or two.

Ox smiles and Conner starts to laugh. "I'll be damned," he says as we begin our unique three-part harmony. "She's playing our song, Ox."

When the song is done, Ox shakes his head and mutters "Holy shit!" in approval. "We've got to do this again, Lainey, when it's not so late, and my beautiful bride hasn't had seven margaritas."

I set my guitar down in the chair and the four of us start to move to the stairs that lead up to the ground floor and the driveway where Ox and Tori have parked their car. We walk together, pausing in the foyer to say goodnight.

For a little while tonight, I felt like I belonged here and

these people were my family. We shared music, and that is a bond that connects me instantly to people. People who don't feel the need to compete with me or challenge me or try to discourage me. Just people, like me, who feel the music flow through their souls the way blood flows through their veins.

"We have a driver tonight, Lainey. We can take you home if you want," Tori offers. She's resting her head on Ox's shoulder with a sleepy little pout. His arm is around her and he kisses the top of her head. I'm not sure what he said to her, but she's been great all night. Well, at least she's been quiet all night.

"Lainey's sleeping over tonight, but thanks," Connor pipes in.

"Cool. We're actually just going to our cabin up the road. I enjoyed this tonight," Ox says. "Happy birthday, old man." He claps Connor on the back in a big bear hug that sends their long hair flying up around them.

"Happy birthday," Tori says and kisses Connor's cheek before giving me a side-eye. My Inner Sex Goddess sticks a tongue out at her.

"So, brunch tomorrow then, Connor?" she poses the invitation exclusively to him, casting a cold gaze my way. Yeah, nothing obvious about the fact this woman doesn't like me. "Ginger's going to be there."

"We've got some things to do. Maybe next time," Connor speaks with a tone that makes it clear he wants to be left alone with me. No interruptions. And it makes me feel ... fuzzy under my skin. Because, I want that with him, too. His arm moves possessively around my waist and the tips of his fingers begin to stroke up and down my spine from my bra strap to the waistband of my pants. Holy cheese and crackers! Chills ripple through my entire body. His touch is like electricity.

Tori opens her mouth to speak, but Ox claps a hand over

it and smiles, speaking over whatever it is she was about to say.

"Well, you two have a good night. See you later, Con. Let's go, wife," Ox asserts, pulling Tori away amid one of his deep Santa laughs that steals my heart every time.

Connor's river house is large and has too many rooms to count. First, can I just say ... I'm spending the night with a man who owns a second home! This whole weekend feels surreal. I actually did get lost about an hour ago just looking for a powder room, though. But every time I discover a new space, it is well furnished and nicely decorated. Despite their sizes, the rooms don't feel cavernous or lonely. Cozy pockets that invite sitting and reading and just being are everywhere. It feels like a home, more than just a house.

His bedroom is massive. There's a sofa and chair in one corner and of course, a huge king-sized bed in the center. Two small nightstands sit on either side with cool wall-mounted sconces over each. A large screen TV opposite the bed makes it look like he watches as he goes to sleep. I used to love falling asleep to the TV when I was in college. My roommate, Martha, and I would put on something soothing like a documentary on the History Channel or a nature show and drift off to the low, monotone of the migratory patterns of the monarch butterfly or something.

With a glance at the bed, I know immediately which side is his. It's piled high with a stack of books. Who would have thought Tarzan was such a voracious reader? While he digs out a T-shirt for me to wear, I meander closer and glance at the titles.

*Tax Code Changes That Affect Your Small Business; Simply Organic: Cooking with Seasonal, Local Ingredients; The Boyfriend's Guide to Oral Sex: How to Make Your Woman Beg; Seven Ways to Market Your Small Business; 11 Days to Leaner Abs.* I'm intrigued to find Mary Shelley's *Frankenstein* as well as a copy of C.S. Lewis' *The Lion, the Witch and the Wardrobe.*

The last sits on top, and it's a beautiful book. Bound with a soft tan leather cover and engraved markings on the spine in gold and silver. The edges of the pages are tipped in gold, but there are worn spots where it becomes obvious that, despite its pristine condition, it has been well read over the years. When I open the book, I discover that the pages are a thin onion skin with beautiful hand-drawn pictures tucked inside. The sketches are mostly in pen and ink or in pencil, and it's clear they've been drawn and added in, since they're not bound into the book like the rest of the pages. The paper is a much heavier linen weight, too. The fine quality allows the charcoals and inks to be absorbed between the fine linen strands.

They're quite possibly the most stunning drawings I've ever seen. I pull out a couple, one incomplete sketch of each of the four Pevensie children and ... the book is suddenly lifted from my fingers and replaced onto its stack.

"I'm so sorry," I say, immediately releasing the book and stepping back. "That was rude of me to pry." Miss Insecure, born in middle school, now insists on yammering on to fill in the silence so he'll forget what a horrible mistake I just made and stop thinking bad things about me.

"Stop chatting, Lainey Bird," Connor says, leaning down to kiss me softly. "I don't care if you look through it. I just want to let you go change and ... and I am dying to kiss you. I've wanted to kiss you all night."

I smile, thankful he wasn't upset about my rifling through his things.

"Bathroom is through there. I set out some clean towels and a new toothbrush."

"Thank you," I murmur and make a run for the bathroom with his T-shirt clutched between my fingers.

The shirt he gives me is from a rock concert from so long ago that most of the screen print on the front has dissolved in the hundreds of washes it has endured. I can barely make out the name of the band. But it's so soft and smells like Connor. I'm thankful, too, it comes down long enough to cover my behind since I have nothing on under it except my powder blue panties.

When I, along with a very minty mouth, emerge from the bathroom, I can see Connor already changed into a pair of long cotton basketball shorts and a loose tee. He looks comfy and so super sexy. My Inner Sex Goddess applies her lip gloss.

We awkwardly switch places in front of the bathroom door, so he can take his turn, and I snuggle down into the sheets. They are, quite frankly, the softest sheets I've ever felt. They're not cotton or satin or even silk. But they're so soft my body just slides down into them. He has a lightweight down comforter thrown over the bed that provides the perfect weight without making me feel like I might suffocate. My body is so tired. I unclasp my watch and place it on the nightstand and see it's well after three o'clock. I have never stayed up this late in my entire life!

When Connor comes to bed, I catch a glimpse of his face before he turns off the lamp. He looks exhausted, too. He settles himself on his back and then whispers into the darkness that surrounds us.

"You're too far away. Come closer."

Barking orders at me again. I want to roll my eyes, but I'm too tired. And, to be honest, I want to comply. I want to be closer.

I scoot toward the middle of the bed and feel his arm

extend out, reaching to cup my head and draw it onto his shoulder. His shoulder and chest are absolutely the perfect height and firmness to be the best pillow ever. I could sleep curled next to him like this all night. And I kinda hope I do.

"I really feel bad I didn't get you a birthday present," I admit, filling the quiet around us with words again. I feel nervous. He said he didn't want sex, but I still feel a bit ... anxious. Cue catfight between Inner Sex Goddess and Miss Insecurity.

"This is my gift, Lainey Bird. You can't know what it means for me just to hold you. Now, no more chatting. I'm beat."

"You look tired."

"Yeah, well I ended up working at the bar last night after you went home until we closed around 3 a.m. And the caterer and party people were here at the house at six this morning to get started setting up."

His fingers curl around my body and begin lightly stroking my back. He's tugged the shirt up so that I can feel his touch directly on my skin. A slit of flesh just above the waistband of my panties. But he does nothing to make it seem like he wants to get under the blue cotton. The slow, soft stroking somehow has the same effect on me as talking to fill the quiet spaces. It's soothing and makes me feel as if there is nothing to worry about. I'm safe — my body and my heart.

"Connor?" I ask, not thinking he'll still be awake. We've been lying still and quiet for what feels like an hour, although it's probably only been a few minutes.

"Hmm?"

"Why do you call me Lainey Bird?"

He turns his head and kisses the top of my hair. His sweet amused smile presses against my scalp.

"You'll think I'm crazy, but there's something about you, Lainey. When I look into your eyes, I think I can see so much there that no one knows. Like you've flown with the clouds on your cheeks and no one knows about it. Plus, you chatter like a little bird in a tree to fill in the quiet. Does it really bother you that I call you that?"

"No, it's just ..." I pause, not sure I want to reveal anything more about myself.

"What? Tell me. I'd like to know." His commanding tone is gone. Perhaps from his fatigue or perhaps because lying like this together in the dark, we can't see one another's expressions. We can just hear. Whatever it is, I'm compelled to disclose my first tiny secret to him. I can't help but wonder if it is the first of many.

"It's just, my name isn't Elaine. Well, it is. Elaine is my middle name. My parents were these weird hippies. So, my sister and I both got these odd first names. But my grandmother insisted we have 'normal' middle names in case we ever wanted to be like everyone else."

"Tell me your name, Lainey Bird," he whispers, smoothing my temples with his soft kisses.

"Raven."

# CHAPTER FIVE

### Sunday, June 6

I WAKE to the sounds of birds singing. Dozens of them. Their songs are happy, short and filled with messages mere humans can never fully comprehend. I secretly wonder if all their chattering isn't talking about us. Sizing up us non-flying bipeds. Delivering their verdict on how well we take care of the world they live in. Well, Miss Insecurity wonders, anyway.

During the night, I've inched away from Connor and am on the edge of the bed now. I stretch and pull my arms over my head, letting my back twist and arch to relieve the stiffness of sleeping so hard and so well all night. I have seriously got to get a set of these sheets.

"Stop writhing around in my bed like that, or I won't be able to keep my 'no sex' promise to you, Lainey Bird."

I turn and see Connor half-sitting up in the bed. He's typing on his phone, no doubt handling matters at one of his restaurants. How many did Tori say he owned again? I can't remember. Even with just one, he's a very busy man. He's got to be.

"Sorry, I can't help it. I want to stay in this bed forever. It's so comfy and warm."

Connor tosses the phone onto the nightstand and rolls over onto his side so that he's facing me. He props his head upon his hand and gives me that little trademark smile he makes when he's amused by me. When he does it, his eyes twinkle. Or maybe his eyes twinkle and that's why he smiles. I can't tell. I just know that when he does it, it sends a rush of happy warmth that slides over my skin and seeps into my bones. And the aftereffects linger with me for a while even after the smile fades.

"Sounds like a plan to me." A solitary finger reaches out to brush a strand of hair from my face and then curves around to my jaw. When it gets to my chin, he removes it.

"I can't. I've got too much to do." My body flexes so I can sit up, but Connor rolls over on top of me, pinning me down with his body over mine. His entire hard length is hovering inches above me. His breath, warm and inviting, brushes across my face. He's so close, I can see tiny flecks of black inside the blue irises that give them such a deep hue. My breath hitches and I realize I've stopped breathing. I catch it again when he speaks. His voice barely hovers above a whisper.

"It's Sunday. There's nothing that has to be done on Sundays."

"I need to look for a job today. I could get some interviews lined up for early next week."

Connor leans down in a push-up and kisses me. It's soft at first, but quickly transforms into something deeper, hungrier and so filled with lust it leaks from his mouth and drips into mine. I swallow it down inside me. I can feel an erection pressed against my belly and I know he wants me. I reach to touch him. My fingers skate over his hip and then up to his waist, when he suddenly breaks our kiss and rolls off of me back to his side of the bed.

He's lying on his back staring at the ceiling. His breathing is a bit ragged.

"Sorry about the boner. It's pretty impossible not to get turned on with a beautiful half-naked woman in my bed who lets me kiss her like that."

I laugh and roll onto my side now so I can see him. His eyes are closed and I can tell he's working to restore his breathing and wrangle in his lust — for now.

"No worries, Tarzan. But I seriously need to get up. What time is it?"

"Almost eleven."

"What?" I audibly gasp. The last time I slept past seven was the morning after I'd passed out at the *Journey's End*. I've never slept past nine. Ever. "It's so late."

I throw the covers off of my body and nearly jump from the bed. Walking around Connor's side of it to get to the bathroom door, I feel him reach out and grab my wrist. He's sitting on the edge of the bed. He pulls me to him. Mr. Swellington hasn't left the building just yet, I note as I'm brought down onto his lap with a hard thump.

"We need to have a talk. Get a shower. Meet me downstairs, and we'll have some coffee."

"A talk?"

"Yes, but not here. I can't think with you in my bedroom, wearing my T-shirt and that whole tousled sexy look. And I need to think."

Inner Sex Goddess just did a roundoff back handspring with a half twist. Who knew I had a "tousled sexy look"?

"OK." I get up and can't help but glance downward to take a peek at the thick stick I've been sitting on. He tries to tuck it away with a surreptitious flick of his wrist but, seriously, the man is huge. He'd need a full-on demolition crew to pack away that stack of concrete he's got in his shorts.

"Sorry about him," he says, giving me a shrug.

"No, you're not," I say, grinning. I return his gesture with a wink and a coy little smile, which is the best version of flirting I can muster before I've had coffee.

"I'd lock that door if I were you," he says, teasing. But I do click the lock into place before I strip and step into the warm shower.

I have to admit, I've never had a sleepover with a man before. It was nice to enjoy all of the sweet parts of sharing a bed without the stress of sex. My poor Inner Sex Goddess has gone quite a while without it. Seven years to be exact. Strangely, I haven't missed it much. Sex for me has always proven to be stressful and messy and leaves me with everything hurting so badly I want to stay in bed for a week. Especially my heart. And my heart always took way longer than my body to heal. I like being able to enjoy getting to know Connor without that kind of pressure. And the fact that he is turned on by me isn't a downside. It makes me feel pretty ... sexy even. So Inner Sex Goddess is happy. But I also feel respected. So Miss Insecurity is also happy. And both of them have to be happy or whatever this is will be over before it starts.

I wash my hair and my body with Connor's assortment of soaps and shampoos and towel off before sliding on the clothes I wore yesterday.

Whatever this is. What is this? Ox said Connor liked me, and I'll admit, I like him, too. We've spent the past four days together. I'd like there to be more days if I'm honest. I feel like Connor understands me. He doesn't tease me about my incessant need to talk or ask me hundreds of questions about Juilliard or my few years as a professional. And he feeds me. He's always feeding me. I know I've lost a few pounds with the stress over the decision to quit my job, but I still don't look as dangerously thin as I did in my Philharmonic days.

I follow the aroma of coffee and what I think are muffins baking and go down the stairs and into a huge gourmet kitchen. There's a massive island of white marble and dark blue cabinetry. The walls of the kitchen are clad in white cabinetry accented with beadboard inserts. A honed stone countertop snakes around the whole of the kitchen. It's an unusual stone with some sort of swirl of blue and grays. Connor must hire a decorator.

"Feel better?"

I nod. "You cook, too?"

"I dabble. I do own six restaurants, after all."

"Only six?"

Conner grins. "Well, Ox and I own them together. He's mostly the silent partner who puts up a lot of money and complains. I manage and run them and all of that."

"Sounds exhausting."

"It is, actually. Which is what I want to talk to you about." Connor fills a mug with steaming hot coffee and drops two huge blueberry muffins onto a plate. Both are carried to me by the lion. At least, he has that predatory look about him just now that makes me think of the lion tattoo on his back.

I stare down at the muffins. They look amazing. The berries are huge, plump and look as though they're about to erupt with sweet juice the minute I bite into them. They're smeared with melted butter and I find my mouth watering for what is honestly the second time this morning. The first — being pinned under Connor's body in bed. *Down girl,* Inner Foodie scolds the Goddess. *Eat first. Flirt later.*

"What do you want to talk about?" I ask as I pinch off a piece of my muffin. Curls of steam drift upward out of the fluffy pastry.

"I was thinking I'd take some time off — a vacation. It's

summer, after all. Everyone needs some downtime. I want to head up to one of my favorite places by the beach and just veg out, you know?"

"Sounds like a plan." I hope my tone doesn't reflect my disappointment. We just met, and he wants to go out of town for what sounds like an indeterminate about of time. Inner Sex Goddess starts pouting, and I'm right there with her.

"I'd like you to come with me," he proposes. His tone is so nonchalant you'd think he'd just asked me if I wanted more coffee, not if I'd go on a trip with him. Vacation? With Connor? Foodie and Sex Goddess already have their suitcases down and are starting to pack, but Miss Insecurity is not so sure. I stare mutely considering my options.

Connor gives me that amused little smile again and almost laughs.

For someone who talks non-stop, I literally have nothing to say. I totally did not see this coming. But I have to say something. He's expecting an answer of some kind.

"Really?" And that's what I come up with. Oh yeah, I'm a regular wordsmith. I stuff a huge bite of muffin into my mouth to stall. It's rude to speak with a mouth full of food, after all. Maybe that's why he's always feeding me.

"Yeah, I know we're just getting to know one another, but I'd like you to come along. I think it would be fun. We could get to know one another better. And, well, you were unhappy the other night about the fact you haven't been on a vacation in a while. I think you could use some time away, too."

"Connor, I'm unemployed. I can't just drop everything and go on a trip."

"What's your situation? Financially, I mean."

I blanch. That's a very personal question! I mean, yes, I was just upstairs in his bed, where I slept all night in his T-shirt and we kissed this morning and I felt his arousal pressed against me. And why is it that that feels exciting and this feels like an invasion into my privacy? Shouldn't it be the other way around?

"I know it's none of my business. But you don't strike me as the irresponsible type. You drive a hybrid for crying out loud. You've got to have a little put back, right? If you can float your expenses for the next few weeks, I'll pick up the trip. Everything. It'll be my treat. Transportation, hotels, tickets, food, everything."

"Connor, I can't do that. I mean, I could, but I shouldn't. That's too much."

"So, you could swing your bills for a while?" He swallows half of a muffin in one bite.

"Sure, six months or so," I confess.

"Whoa! Really?"

I sigh and give him a half-hearted shrug before pushing the second half of my first muffin into my mouth. I use the time it takes me to chew and swallow to think of what to say. My mother has drilled financial independence into me since I was five years old and started my first savings account. Well, it was a piggy bank, but I was required to save. Every birthday and Christmas, a portion of any money I'd been gifted was put back for "a rainy day." Funny, but when the rain finally came, it wasn't money I needed to clear away the gray clouds.

"I pay cash for everything. Even my car is paid for. All I have is my rent, utilities and living expenses. I canceled all non-essentials the day I quit my job. Besides, people with boring lives have nothing to spend their money on anyway, remember?"

"Lainey Bird, you are far from boring. So, it's all settled. We leave tomorrow. Meet me at the bar at six. You need someone to come by and feed a cat or water plants or something? I can get the kid who housesits for me to do it."

"Connor, I can't go on vacation with you. I have to find a job." Seriously? Problems of the spoiled little rich man.

"You have to clear your head. You have to put some space between whatever it is you're moving away from before you can move on to the next thing."

I'm shaken at how close to mark that comment is. I've known for a while I was running. Running from my parents, running from Juilliard, then from *the one who shall not be named*, then from the grab-ass at Pittman & Wright. Running is exhausting. It is completely irresponsible, but a break from my life sounds like heaven.

"You may be right." He gives me a hard stare at my comment. "OK, you are right. How much did I tell you that night I got so drunk, anyway?"

"You said enough. Please, Raven, I want to do this with you. I want to do it *for* you. For reasons I hope one day I'll be able to fully explain."

He calls me Raven. I haven't had anyone other than my parents and sister call me by that name in such a long time. And the tone of it on his lips sounds like a song, not a curse. Not the way I was so used to hearing before I became Elaine. Oh my goodness, I think I just fell a little in love with Connor Rose.

# CHAPTER SIX

**Monday, June 7**

My suitcases are packed. I even put them in the car. But it's 6:15 and I still haven't decided if I'm doing the right thing. I pick up my cell phone and start to dial Connor's number to tell him I'm not coming. I chicken out before I enter the last number.

I check my email once more, praying there will be a hoard of messages with invitations for interviews, but there's nothing. Well, Eddie Bauer sent me an email to tell me about a sale on swimwear, but that's about the only person who's filling my inbox today, it seems.

I dial my sister. Willow was still a baby herself when I was born — only eighteen months old when I made my grand entrance onto planet earth. And it never occurred to either one of us for even a single second that we were not born to be one another's best friend, playmate, confidant, secret keeper and loyal partner in crime. She's my everything and always will be. I tell her absolutely every detail of my life and trust her to give me the right advice. She answers on the second ring.

"Hey Ray," she says in her husky voice. I love that my sister has this incredibly cool voice. Most people have to smoke like three packs a day for twenty years before they can sound as cool and edgy as Willow. She's never smoked a single cigarette. Hers is all-natural. And it's beautiful. When we sing, our voices melt together so perfectly. But we never sang much growing up. Music can't be a career, after all. So why waste time on it — or so our mother was so fond of reminding us.

"Hey," I say. I'm trying very hard to keep the anxiety out of my voice, but I know she'll hear it.

"What's wrong?" Of course, she detects it immediately. I don't even know why I bother to try to hide it from her.

"I might be leaving to go on vacation for a few weeks," I say evasively.

"Stephen," she calls to her husband. "I'm going to Atlanta. Ray has fallen and hit her head. She's gone crazy or something. Ray, I'm coming. Just stay where you are." I know she's totally teasing. That's what big sisters do, after all.

"Stop it. I didn't hit my head. I'm serious. I'm all packed and everything."

"OK. Where are you going?" The tone in her voice suggests she's playing along on some joke with me.

"I don't know. He hasn't told me yet." My tone makes it clear, this isn't a joke.

"He? There's a he? Since when is there a he?" I can hear her haul in a deep breath. "OK, Ray, I'm going to need you to go back to the beginning of all of this, and start at the top."

And I do. I leave nothing out. Not one detail. I tell her everything about the interview at Pinnacle and meeting Connor at the bar, passing out, then waking up in his bed. I tell her about Ox and Tori, the pizza, the ride on the motorcycle and end with the party last night. I even tell her about the sleepover and Connor's obvious desire to one day get rid of the "no sex" promise he made me last night.

"Wow, Ray. That's a lot. And you're supposed to meet him when?"

"Like forty-five minutes ago," I say, glancing at my watch.

"Shit, girl. Why are you talking to me? Hang up and call me from the road!"

"You think I should go?"

I hear my sister sigh on the other end of the phone and there's a long pause before she finally speaks. She's using her big-sister-loves-me voice, so I know she's being serious now.

"Raven, honey, you've got to let go. Of all of it. Mom and Jemmy and those evil people at Juilliard. They all tried to make you who they wanted you to be. You've never had the chance to just find out who you are. This could be that chance."

"You think?" Tears mist my eyes. Not because it sounds pathetic or because it's true. But because she knows me. And she knows. She knows I'm running, too, and I can't run away from my situation anymore. It's time I find something to run toward.

"I do. And more than that, I think you do, too. This Connor, he's safe? You'll be safe with him?"

"Yes, I will be." I know that's the truth.

"Then you have to do this, Ray. I know it's scary, and you're afraid. But you need to do this."

Tears start to slip down my cheeks. Willow knows me better than anyone, even our own mother. She knows that vacations scare me. I've had the time off, and the money to go on them over the years, but I just never have. I was too anxious. Too much unknown. Too much loneliness.

"I sound pathetic when you put it like that."

"You're not pathetic, sweetie. You're just a little ... lost. It's time to go out and find yourself."

"Thanks. I love you."

"I love you, too. Send me proof of life every day, or I'm calling the FBI on this guy," she says only half teasing me this time.

"I will. I promise."

Fifteen minutes later, I wheel my two large suitcases along the sidewalk and stand in front of the door of the bar. It feels ironic to be in a place called the *Journey's End*, since this is where my journey is actually beginning.

I scan the bar and see Tori sitting with Connor. He looks upset. His head is bowed and he's playing with a pen, twirling it between his fingers. Deep creases crisscross his forehead. Tori has her arm around him and whispers something in his ear and rubs his back in a soothing way. I instantly feel the need to go to him, to comfort him for the obvious frustration he's feeling. What's the matter? What happened? Then, it suddenly occurs to me that his disappointment is probably because of me. He thinks I'm not coming, and it's hurt him. I hurt him.

Tori looks up and notices me, then pats Connor on the back, nodding in my direction. His head lifts and his face instantly brightens. When he glances down at the two rolling bags I'm towing behind me, a hundred-watt smile erupts. He pops up from his barstool and both he and Tori walk toward me by the door.

"It's good to see you, Lainey," Tori says, but I detect a skepticism in her voice. There's no doubt in my mind, she doesn't mean that one little bit. "It's good you actually showed up. I may have been wrong about you." She gives me this little smirk and I can't decide whether she's being sincere or a totally sarcastic pain in the butt.

"You came!" The delight in his voice speaking those two simple words is all I need to hear. I'm doing the right thing. I'm scared out of my mind about what may happen, but I'm doing this. I want to do this. I want to be with Connor.

"You two have a good time. We'll see you soon, Con," Tori says and gives him a quick hug and kiss before floating out the door.

"I'm sorry I'm late. It just took me some time to ... um ..."

"It doesn't matter. You're here. You are coming, aren't you? I assume you didn't get a better offer, and the suitcases are for some other joker."

I laugh lightly before replying. "I am going with you. Eddie Bauer did make me an offer to shop an online sale today. It was a tough choice."

He laughs back at me and then falls quiet. His stare is intent. With slowness, he touches my face, leans forward and kisses me. Just once. And softly. But it's enough for me to feel the happiness in his kiss that I'm here.

"I have a bit of paperwork I've got to finish for Ox before we leave. Have you eaten?"

I shake my head. "You always want to feed me. Why is that?"

"You need to eat, Lainey. You're too thin."

"I thought women could never be too rich or too thin," I retort back.

Connor presses a soft kiss to my ear. I can feel his fingers loosening my grip on the suitcase handles as he assumes their conveyance from me. His breath is hot over my neck. The rush of heat ignites goose bumps over my body.

"One of these days, I'm not going to be able to keep my

promise of no sex during a sleepover. And when that day comes, I want something I can sink my fingers into, Raven."

I gulp silently. His voice is so seductive and erotic, I think my Inner Sex Goddess may have vaporized in a flash of spontaneous combustion.

"Lucas, get a glass of Pino for my girl and a number two special, medium."

*My girl?* I'm Connor's girl? And he said *when* the day comes, not *if.* My palms start to get clammy. This is all happening so fast, my head feels a bit dizzy. Strangely, however, my heart feels just right.

Tugging my suitcases into a corner booth, we snuggle in together — him with his paperwork and me with a perfectly cooked, perfectly seasoned steak and a twice-baked potato. Every morsel is divine.

"I thought you weren't coming," he says, finally stacking his paperwork into a neat pile.

"I almost didn't," I admit. On any other mortal man, my confession would force a look of what could be deemed panic, but on Connor, it merely mimics a mild annoyance.

"I know you're scared. I am, too. It's going to be great though." He takes my hand in his and it's like the entire universe tumbles into place. I can't explain it, but when we hold hands, it's like fitting the cogs of a giant clock in sync so that time moves forward without glitches. And up until now, my whole life feels like it's been one gigantic glitch.

"You know I'm scared?"

"Jesus, Lainey. I'd be worried if you weren't."

"Thanks for that. It helps."

"All right, so you've got everything? Your blanket, jammies and favorite stuffed animal? Night-light? Prescription meds?"

I know what he's asking. I've been on the patch for years, although not for actual birth control. And I did actually think to bring an extra refill for our trip so I could avoid the hassle of having the doctor's office call in a prescription to a local pharmacy in wherever it is we're going — which he hasn't told me yet. But I play back and keep him guessing. Regardless of how much I may be interested, I'm not emotionally ready for sex with Connor.

"Absolutely. There's the patch for my hysteria and my anti-psychotic meds, my pills for mood, twitching and night terrors, oh and the cream I have to use twice a day for this weird rash thing all over my ..."

"Ha, ha, ha." He uses that little smile he saves for when he's amused by me, and I pray I see it every day on this trip. I cannot believe I'm actually doing this. It is by far and away the most insane thing I've ever done. And, oddly, I couldn't be more excited.

Connor and I agreed five weeks was going to be our limit. I've missed a vacation for the past five years, which equates to ten weeks of time off I haven't taken. But there is no way I can be gone that long. So, after much debate yesterday, we compromised on one week per year for a total of five weeks. Although I have absolutely no idea where we're spending these five weeks. He promised me we aren't leaving the United States, and I'm glad to know that. But packing for a trip that could be anywhere from Alaska to Key West is tough. I only hope wherever we go, I can buy what I didn't pack — which is practically every piece of non-business attire I own.

When my steak is finished and his paperwork is complete, we pile into his Mercedes sedan and head out. He informs me he's rented a vehicle for our trip, and I am immediately intrigued. Connor has like four cars. He has the gorgeous little vintage sporty number he drove me home in, a nice big Audi SUV, the Mercedes sedan we're in now and a pickup truck. And that doesn't include his collection of motorcycles. What other type of vehicle could we possibly need?

My answer is found at the Cumming RV Sales and Rental Center off of Highway 19 on the far north side of town. It's called a Korak — a tiny camper we can sleep in and drive. Painted a sharp gray with dark black accents, it fits Connor to a tee. I want to laugh at the name — more irony, or perhaps it's the universe's way of letting me know that I'm doing the right thing. I have never been in one before. Are we driving cross-country and roughing it in this thing for the next five weeks?

"What the heck is this?" I ask, scrunching my nose. I walk around and give the tires a cursory little kick with the toe of my tennis shoe.

"What, you don't like it?" Connor signs a form on a clipboard.

"This is our mode of transportation for our trip?"

"Just wait, Raven, it's like a spaceship inside." His face lights up like the kid who got the Red Ryder BB gun for Christmas with no clue he's almost gonna shoot his eye out. I can tell he's excited to show me everything.

"A spaceship? You mean like the *Enterprise*? Or like a Star Destroyer?"

"Oh, Lainey Bird, I think I just fell in love with you and your cute nerd references."

"It looks more like the S.S. Minnow to me," I tease. It's actually quite nice, and I know he can see that on my face. But I am enjoying this playful banter we have going on, and I'm not quite ready for it to end yet.

"The S.S. Minnow? You mean like from *Gilligan's Island*?" His brows knit together and he tips his head, appearing more thoughtful than stunned.

"Well, actually now that I think about it, it's more like the minnow bucket."

At this, he lets out a long, loud laugh I've never heard before. I can't help but think about what Ox told me last night about Connor never laughing. I smile. I make him laugh. That means I make him happy. I don't make anyone in my life happy, not even myself. But he is happy because of me. My heart soars.

"Perfect. The Minnow Bucket she is."

"Well, let's check out the inside." I pop open the door and climb into to what is quite possibly the sweetest-looking little hotel room on wheels I've ever laid eyes on. Two huge comfortable-looking captain's chairs up front swivel to face the center of the RV. The cockpit behind them does look like a spaceship with glass-paneled controls and hardly a knob or button to be seen.

To my left is a small kitchenette with a dishwasher, microwave, lots of storage and a large refrigerator and freezer. It's not as big as the full-sized one I have at home, but considering the size of the space we're in, it's huge. In front of me is a cozy little banquet table with a bench seat that looks like a place to eat or play cards. A large screen TV hangs opposite it.

"There's a bunk above the cab," Connor points to a small loft space above where we'd be driving. "But I am really hoping we can keep our no-sex sleepover arrangement."

"And *if* I do?" I tease, placing plenty of emphasis on the word "if."

"There's a queen-sized bed in the back along with a toilet, sink and shower. Of course, we won't be spending every night in here. But I think it will be comfortable when we do."

I spend a few minutes looking around while Connor signs the rental paperwork and gets the keys. He's thought of everything. The fridge is fully stocked. There are clean sheets and towels, dishes, silverware and plastic cups. There are even board games and cards if we get bored. It's utterly adorable how much thought he's put into this trip. If only he'd tell me where we are going!

"OK, all set?" he calls to me. I watch him stretch the seat-belt over his thick chest and wonder if it has the tensile strength to keep Tarzan in his chair if we were to actually become involved in an accident. I nod and we back up and head out.

It's nearly midnight before we pull into our first destination, which I'm pleased to discover is a spa in North Georgia. We are ushered to a beautiful hotel suite that overlooks lush vineyards attached to a small winery a couple of miles away. It's too dark to see them now, but the bell captain who brings in our luggage assures us they're gorgeous.

Connor hands him a generous tip and we're left alone in the room ... with each other ... and one bed.

Connor rifles through his one bag and pulls out a pair of cotton sleeping shorts and a white T-shirt and disappears into the bathroom. It's his only bag. Yeah, that's right. One. Single. Bag. I roll my eyes. Well, he does have the benefit of knowing where we're going.

When he comes out, I move in to brush my teeth and pull on my pajamas. When I come out, he's stretched on the bed, a pile of pillows behind him and one of my favorite home decorating shows glows from the TV.

"I love this show," I say, crawling between the covers beside him in my pink cotton shorts and pajama top.

"Me, too. Have you seen this one?" He pats the bed beside him, beckoning me closer. I float up to him like a moth to a flame.

"Yeah, they end up ..." I begin.

He cuts me off with a loud bark. "Ah! Spoiler alert. I haven't. Don't tell me!"

I giggle at him. "Sorry. Hey, you have all the pillows," I pout.

"I'll be your pillow, Lainey Bird." He gives me that happy little smile and pats his shoulder in invitation.

The lost little girl inside me squeals with joy and finds herself a place curled up beside her lion. And that's how we fall asleep on the first night of our vacation. Snuggled in one another's embrace, blissfully unaware of whether or not the dream house makeover was a hit or a flop.

# CHAPTER SEVEN

**Tuesday, June 8**

WE TAKE a tour of the nearby winery after breakfast, and I'm overwhelmed with Connor's vast knowledge of wine. He does own more than one bar, I suppose. I probably shouldn't be surprised, but I am. He asks great questions about the wood they use for the barrels, the aging process and the type of grapes they grow, whether they import pressed juice, and on and on and on. I just know that every wine we sample is delicious. And that tasting wine is like drinking drams of whiskey. A little goes a long way. #wineoclock

I learn more from following him around and listening to him to ask questions than from our guide. We dine on a delicious lunch outside near the vineyard and head back to our hotel.

It's a gorgeous estate converted into a boutique hotel, but it has the customer service and ambiance of an upscale bed and breakfast.

"Aren't we heading out?" I ask.

"Nope. We're here one more night. I have a surprise for us this afternoon."

He evades the questions I ask to get even a clue as to what that surprise might be. Around three o'clock, we check in at the spa. Connor has organized a manicure and pedicure for us followed by a couples' massage. The pampering is a first for me, and I'm undone by the way my mind and body begins to relax after simply having my fingernails and toenails painted. Connor seems pretty comfortable having his nails done, and I'm shocked at the juxtaposition of seeing this huge, tattooed man sitting in the spa chair having his nails buffed to a gleaming shine.

We move into the couples' massage room and I see two tables set up in the middle of the room.

"Go ahead and remove your clothing and get on the tables face down," a nice-looking woman with bright pink hair instructs us. "Your masseurs will be with you in a few moments. Relax while you wait."

Connor starts removing his clothing and placing it on a chair. His boots and socks are first. Then his T-shirt and finally his shorts. I stand and watch in utter amazement as inch by delicious inch of his gorgeous body is revealed to me in full. He's totally unashamed of it, and he shouldn't be. It's glorious. It's like the rock itself birthed this man's physique. It's so toned and strong. The ripples of his tanned abdomen look like soft waves of caramel. I willingly admit that my Inner Sex Goddess wants to lick them up and down to be sure he's actually a man and not a confection.

"Lainey?" he looks at me. I know I'm staring. Who am I kidding? I'm full-on gawking.

"You're naked." I barely utter.

"The massage is better when they can touch your skin, babe." He glides over to me and slowly lifts the hem of my T-shirt up over my head. He kisses me on the lips, letting his mouth trail down my jaw to my neck and collarbone. His hands unclasp my bra and I remain motionless — held prisoner by his kiss along my arm and chest. I can't move. Teasingly, his broad fingers rake gently over my back until he catches the waistband of my cotton skirt. He unties the drawstring and lets it skim over my body to the floor in a puddle. I toe out of my sandals and feel his fingers hook into my panties and then slide them down to my ankles.

"Step out, Lainey." His voice is velvet over stone. For a heartbeat, I close my eyes and shiver.

He's always commanding me. One of these days I'm going to make him beg me. But, as my Inner Sex Goddess reminds me, that day is not today. I do as he instructs and am standing naked before him. My hands instinctively move to cover my body. Connor, thankfully, fixes his eyes on mine and doesn't allow them to wander over me.

"Get on your table and I'll cover you with the sheet."

Wasting no time, I practically dive onto the table and yank the sheet over my bare behind.

I feel his kiss on my shoulder. "Relax, Lainey Bird. We're going to be together for the next five weeks. You don't think we'll see each other in all states of undress? It's fine. You're beautiful. You have no reason to be embarrassed."

I let out a long breath. That is exactly what I was worried about.

"Besides, I undressed you the night we met. Remember? I've seen it all before."

And there's that. My body flushes with the heat of shame. I twist my head and watch him lie down on his own table and cover with the sheet. I'm going to ignore my embarrassment and just try to enjoy this. I play this statement on repeat in my head for the next five minutes while we wait for the masseurs.

"This is a really nice surprise," I confess.

He props his cheek on a forearm and looks intently at me.

"You haven't had a vacation in years. It's been a while for me, too, I admit. I think we could both do better to start this whole adventure off with a little relaxation. You know, put us in the right frame of mind."

I let out a sigh and try my best to relax.

"Don't be nervous, Lainey Bird. I'm right here to watch out for you. That's why I booked it this way."

My shoulders finally begin to unknot at the idea that a total stranger is about to have his hands all over my body. Another man, who is practically a stranger too, just had his eyes all over my body. I roll my eyes at myself and try to push these anxious thoughts from my mind. I flinch at the quick knock at the door.

For the next hour, we are rubbed and kneaded into a Zen-like state of relaxation that can't be described in words. Hot stones are laid on my skin. Oils and perfumes fill the air with lavender and almond and other spicy scents I can't readily identify. It's so overwhelming, I don't even want to fill the silence with words. I doubt I could. If I open my mouth, the only sounds that would come out would be moans of delicious delight. I could definitely get used to this. When I get a job, I'm going to budget for a little spa treatment once in a while.

Connor doesn't speak, and neither do the two masseurs. I can hear the sounds of a tiny fountain in the distance and soft sitar music. I close my eyes, letting the notes and the scents and the touch lift me away to discover the loud amid the quiet.

A warm palm is placed on my forehead and a soft voice whispers, "Relax a few moments. The quiet room has been prepared for you."

A quiet room. The absolute opposite of everything I am. I

hear Connor chuckle a bit when my masseur says that. I deserve that. I know it.

The masseurs leave us and Connor turns his head to look at me.

"How do you feel?"

"Like I'm totally boneless," I murmur. "You?"

"Oh, I've got the bone over here, trust me." He gives me a playful grin.

I look over and see him perched on the edge of the table, a large tent now being erected in the area of his groin.

"Massages always make me hard. It doesn't help that you're naked right here next to me, Lainey Bird."

I slowly pull my torso into a vertical position and for several long moments, we just sit, covered in our thin sheets on our respective tables, peering at one another. Connor is beautiful. And like last night, I can't believe I'm actually sitting here with him. His body twitches and strains under the sheet. He's got to be uncomfortable. Inner Sex Goddess seems to suspend my ability to make rational decisions. Because I'm not sure what possesses me to do it, why I decide it's a good idea, or whether I've thought it through at all, but I let the sheet fall off of me, walk over to Connor and extend my hand to him.

"Let's go," I whisper.

We move into a large room with a huge shower — clearly meant for two people. Connor twists the water faucet in a clockwise direction and we step into the warm stream together.

"You'll want to wash that oil off of you," he says grabbing a loofa and squirting some soap on it. He moves to hand it to me, but instead, I just curl his fingers around it and press it back toward his own body again.

"You do it for me," I command. Inner Sex Goddess takes the helm of my brain and body for a while. She claps her hands and jumps up and down at me. I hope I haven't made a mistake in letting her drive this train wreck for a bit. The truth is, I feel safe with Connor. And I feel sexy. Not ready for actual sex, but a part of me thinks if I'm ever going to allow a man to sleep with me again, it could be him.

His hands find my shoulders and neck, and he immediately begins to move his soapy fingers across my wet skin. Hmm, now I understand why he commands me. It's nice. It's heady. It's sexy. A man who wordlessly does your bidding. Not only because it pleases you, but because it pleases him to have the chance to do it for you. To obey and bring pleasure. Yep, letting Inner Sex Goddess drive is a great idea.

His hands rove over my body from my ears to my toes, not missing a single inch. He caresses my breasts for a long time and spends an equally long few minutes massaging between my legs, although he never tries to touch me inside. He just tickles the hair there and rubs softly against my outer lips.

When Conner is finished, I put out my hand. "Your turn," I insist. My voice is barely a whisper. I've never in my life been this forward with a man. I'm shaking so hard I'm afraid I'll drop the tube of body wash. I mimic his movements, starting at his neck and rubbing my hands across his slick, wet body. I leave the lion for last.

I feel the tiny thin hairs on his chest, the tight peaks of his nipples that harden under my caress, the way his abs clench at my slightest touch.

Working my way down his body, I inspect and admire every hard, rounded curve of every muscle. He is perfection in flesh. And he's here. With me. I fight the urge to ask him why.

When my hand moves to his hardness, he hisses. I lather the small nest of hair around it and gently cup his heavy sack into my palm. His eyes close and his head falls back. He bites his lower lip.

"Please." His voice is barely a whisper. "Please, don't stop. Don't stop."

I literally bite my lip to keep from speaking. I know words would ruin whatever magic my Inner Sex Goddess is conjuring for me right now. I'm not about to break the spell.

My fingers grip the long hard length of him, exploring the veins and cords of muscles in my hands. He's as thick as he is long. I can't even reach around the width of him with my fingers. I slowly begin to stroke up and down in long, soft pulses.

His hands reach out and clutch my shoulders, dragging me closer to him so that he can rest his cheek on the top of my head. His arms wrap around me, pressing our bare chests together. His breathing becomes ragged. Water splashes between us and pools where we are pressed so closely to one another that not even the droplets can find space to seep through.

I hear a groan and then a long, hard guttural breath rise from his throat as I continue to stroke a bit faster.

I stand there, in total silence. For the first time in my life, the silence holds everything together. I need to hear his sighs, his groans, the sound of his racing heart against my ear. I need to listen to his quivering breath and respond to his growing urgency. I need to know what I'm doing to him. He's breaking me, stone by stone, tearing down the tall wall of anxieties and insecurities that have safely managed to keep me at a comfortable distance from any kind of intimacy. I don't know why or how, but I believe I'm doing the same for him.

My fist begins to pump faster and his fingers clench tighter at my shoulder while his breath comes faster and in heavier pants. I continue to slide up and down his length. My stomach touches his. My thighs squeeze against his thighs. My chest presses into his chest and feels like it's too much and not enough at the same time. His arms wrap around me completely and I move faster, sensing his pleasure from the movement.

He hums loud and long and breathes faster. Leaning so hard against him, I feel the muscles in his body tense. His arms wrap around me so tightly I can barely breathe. I feel his entire body shudder, he twitches in my grip and then the hot liquid of his release pours over my knuckles. He doesn't make a sound, doesn't call out my name. He just lets out a long, hard gulp of air and pants quietly, working to get his breath and heart rate back under control. His forehead drops to rest against mine. We stand there entwined in the warm stream of water for a long time. He merely holds me. Remarkably, I can't utter a word.

I nibble at my dinner. As usual, I fill the empty spaces between us with idle chitchat that skates around what happened in the shower between us. I want him to bring it up, to say something. Anything. What if he was put off at how forward I acted. What if I didn't do it well enough. What if he can't respect me now? I worry he regrets bringing me along on this trip and that he thinks badly of me now because I acted so impulsively. The never-ending what-if demons rumble through my mind all evening. The rumbling turns into slight tremors I can see vibrating in my fingertips when I pull back the sheet later that night.

Just as he did the night before, he's propped his torso up on the pillows. I notice, however, that he's asked housekeeping to bring extras for me to lie on. Is that because he doesn't want me sleeping on his shoulder? Doesn't want me close enough to touch him? Worry lines crease my brow.

He pats the bed next to him and draws me to his side again. A tiny portion of me relaxes slightly. Maybe I didn't ruin everything. Maybe he just wants me to know that what happened today was not what he intended. Or what if he wants it all the time now? I don't know if I could muster the courage to be that brave all the time.

He clicks off the decorating show he is watching and kisses my forehead. The room is plunged into utter darkness. His fingers rub tenderly along my upper arm and shoulder. I can't stop the tremors ripping through my body.

"You're shaking, Little Bird. What's the matter?" he whispers.

"I'm fine," I lie.

"Lainey, what's happened to you?" His ragged breath whispers into the darkness.

"What do you mean? Do you mean today in the shower? Because if that upset you, I'm sorry. I'm not a tease, and I never would have done it except that you were so turned on after the massage. I don't really know what possessed me to do it. I've been worried all day that ... that you're ... I don't know, disappointed in me somehow for being so ... so brazen."

He silences my inane ramblings with a hot kiss. "No, Raven. Today was amazing. I loved it. God, you're incredible. Your touch totally undoes me. It's so gentle. I think the fact that what you did was so unexpected is what made it almost ... I don't know. Magical? It was definitely special to me."

My body physically sags onto him now that the weight of my worry is relieved.

"That's what's been worrying you? The hand job in the shower?"

I nod against him. "I don't know. Sometimes, oftentimes, I second-guess the things I do."

"Someone hurt you, didn't he, Lainey? Someone made you feel like you're not enough. Or what you are, who you are, is wrong. What you do is wrong. Didn't he?"

I nod and find a tear emerging from my eye. I wipe it away and threaten the sad little girl inside me to stay her tears or else!

"What happened to you? Who did this to you?" Connor holds me close, and I feel safe here in his arms. Protected and treasured. It's a feeling I've never before experienced in a man's arms. All I want to do is enjoy it and keep all of my dark memories locked away.

"I don't want to talk about it now," I say quietly, praying he doesn't detect the sadness in my voice.

"OK, Lainey Bird. But I want you to tell me when you're ready. I want to know."

"Thank you."

"You're wonderful, you know," he says after a long silence.

"What?"

"You're wonderful. You're crazy talented, so smart, and you make me laugh. You challenge me, and I love that about you. You're always surprising me. And I need you to know that I'll never, ever regret asking you to go on this trip with me. No matter what. I have no doubt that I'll drive you crazy enough to chew nails. And you'll drive me nuts with all that talking. But that's normal. It doesn't mean anything is wrong. I'm not a big talker. But if you ever want to know what I'm thinking or feeling, just ask me. I want you to feel safe with me."

I snuggle next to him helpless to stop the hot tears that drip against his T-shirt. "Thank you for saying that."

I do feel safe. Safe feels like falling asleep in the lion's arms again that night. And safe feels so good.

# CHAPTER EIGHT

**Wednesday, June 9**

A HAND BRUSHES softly against my shoulder. It's warm. The touch is so delicate. I hum at the lovely feeling of it against my skin.

"Good morning, Lainey Bird," I hear a deep voice whisper. The hand repeats the gentle stroking, and I allow one eye to crack open. If this is a dream, I want to keep sleeping. But it's not a dream. It's Connor. He's smiling at me, his hair damp from a shower and falling over his shoulders as he leans down to kiss my temple.

"Hi," I croak. My voice is thick with sleep.

"How did you sleep?"

"Good. You?"

"Better than I have in a long time. It's time to get up. We're headed to Greenville today. I want to be there in time for dinner. I've made a reservation at a friend's place."

"You're always feeding me," I tease, playfully sitting up.

"You're too thin. How about breakfast?"

"See what I mean." I slide my legs around his body and

scoot to the edge of the bed where he sits beside me. I stand up and stretch and in one quick movement, he has his hands clasped around my waist. He lifts me up and moves me to his lap. His lips and nose nuzzle into my neck.

"I can damn near put my hands around your waist, Little Bird. You weigh nothing. I need you to eat."

"I will. I admit I've been stressed about my job, and I guess eating wasn't always a priority. But I swear I've already gained five pounds since I met you."

"Good. You're not going to be stressed. And you're going to eat."

He rises from the bed and stuffs something into his one bag.

"You fit everything you need into that one bag?" I nod in the direction of his duffel on the bed while I dig some clothes from one of my two cases I shoved to bursting.

"Guys are easy. Shirts, shorts, shoes, a couple of pairs of jeans."

I momentarily allow my mind to drift back to our time in the shower after the massage yesterday. And a niggling thought flies through my mind. It's brief, but it gets me thinking and wondering. That's never good on an empty stomach without coffee. "Connor?"

"Yeah?" He tugs the zipper closed with a sharp rip and snatches it off the bed.

"Are there condoms in that bag?" My index finger points to it accusingly.

He drops it to the ground and then stares at his feet. His fingers stab through his still-damp hair. "There are."

I let out a sigh.

"That's not why I asked you to come with me. It's just wishful thinking. The boy scout in me wanting to be prepared — in case." He pulls open the bag and jerks out a box of condoms. He walks them over to where I'm standing and hands them to me.

"You keep them. If we need them, it will be because you have decided we do, OK?"

I take the box from him and drop them into my suitcase. "No expectations?"

"No expectations. But I'm gonna wish on every damn falling star, dandelion weed and wishing well we come to. Just so you know."

I smile and give him a little grin.

"I'm going to load this stuff up in the RV and order us some breakfast. Meet me outside when you're ready. No rush."

He kisses me on the cheek and departs with one of my two bags as I finish packing the other. I vow to repack so I can just bring one case into the hotel on nights when we won't be sleeping in the camper.

I look into the bag again and see that he's gotten a large box of condoms. "That's a lot of wishes, Connor."

"So we're obviously going northeast," I confirm, looking at a foldout map shoved in the RV's glove compartment. "Are you ever going to tell me our final destination?"

"As soon as you ask me," Connor nibbles on a bag of kettle corn. He has the RV stocked with all manner of snacks: crackers, granola bars, cookies, bags of chips, popcorn, juices, waters, soda and candy. This man has a giant sweet tooth, apparently. I help myself to one of the lollipops I find in a cabinet. It's some sort of butterscotch flavor and it's delicious. I can't remember the last time I ate a piece of candy.

"Where are we going, Connor?" My tone is sarcastic.

"Tonight, Greenville. The final destination is my favorite place in the world."

"And where might that be?" I ask. I pop the stick back into my mouth and roll the candy orb around on my tongue.

"Do you have any idea how erotic it is to watch you lick and suck that thing?" I watch as he adjusts his crotch in the driver's seat. I roll my eyes at him and make a show of enjoying the candy just to tease him a little.

"It's 2:22!" He says suddenly.

"So?" I reply.

"So? Whenever all the numbers on the clock are the same, you get to make a wish."

Dandelion seeds. Numbers on clocks. Seriously, what's with this man and his wishes? He closes his eyes to wish and I shriek in horror.

"Eyes open and on the road, pal!"

His voice rumbles in a low laugh that sounds like the purr of a happy kitten. "All right. All right. Don't freak out. I've made my wish."

"What did you wish for?"

"For you to pull that little box I gave you out of your suitcase. After you treat me like that lollipop you've got there." He readjusts himself again and gives me another one of those smiles of amusement. It appears I amuse him a lot. "What did you wish for?"

"I didn't."

"Well, hurry up. You only have a few seconds before the clock changes."

I'm not sure why I feel compelled to make a wish this time, but I do. My wish — my heart's desire — courses through my being. It's the one thing I've always wished for. The one thing I probably will always wish for.

"Got it?"

"Got it."

"What did you wish for, little Lainey Bird?"

"I can't tell you. Then it won't come true."

"Well, if you don't tell me, then I can't make it come true."

I give him a smile. "You haven't answered my question. Where are we going?"

"I already told you."

"Fine, what is your favorite place in the world?"

Connor laughs again and turns up the music. He's made a great playlist of some amazing rock music on his streaming service. One of *Climax*'s songs comes up and the thumping beat fills the camper. I reach over and turn it down.

"Tell me!" I whine like a spoiled child.

"Fine. I'm taking you to Martha's Vineyard."

"What? That's in, like, Massachusetts, right? That'll take forever."

"I have it planned to take three weeks. We'll spend two weeks at my family's little seaside cottage, and then fly home."

"Connor! That's unbelievable. We're really driving all the way up the East Coast and spending two weeks at Martha's Vineyard?" I clap my hands like a child. I feel like a child. A kid on Christmas morning to be exact.

"I hope you're happy. I've got a lot of cool stops planned for us along the way. But we'll mostly be driving in this camper. That's why I wanted something a bit more comfortable than my car. You can stretch out on the bed in the back and we can have snacks and stop and rest ... or whatever ... whenever we want to."

His reference to "whatever" is obvious. I'm flattered that Connor finds me desirable. But I'm worried he'll be disappointed when he learns we won't be having sex. Last night, he made me promise I'd trust him with my anxious thoughts.

And I'm about to test him in his commitment to listen without judgment.

"Connor, we're not going to have sex."

"How can you be so sure?"

"Because, I ... that is, it's um ..." I falter in my resolve. I reach over to turn the music up, and he stills my hand by gently touching my wrist and holding it in his fingers.

"Lainey, tell me. Please." His voice is serious and softer. All playfulness gone. I'm not sure what it is about the way he commands me to do things, but I am powerless to do anything but obey. It's so frustrating.

I let out a long breath. "Look, I don't mean to be a tease. That's what you think of me, don't you? Because of what happened at the spa. I don't even know what on earth possessed me to do that. I have absolutely no clue. Because I'm not usually like that." I'm rambling now, but he just looks at me like he doesn't have the heart to interrupt. I haul in a deep breath, hoping the explanation I'm willing to give will be enough. "I don't really like sex. I'm sorry, but I'm just not that girl. Are you disappointed?"

"No, I mean, yeah. But I respect your feelings, of course. It's just ... what do you mean, you don't like sex?" His expression is not one of disappointment, but rather one of complete and utter disbelief. I know. I know. #freak.

"It's ... um, unpleasant. That is, uncomfortable for me, that's all. I don't really want to get into it. It's embarrassing." I hope that he'll leave it at that, but no. He keeps on.

"Physically, you mean?"

"Do we really have to discuss this?" I plead silently with him to stop. I don't know if I have the courage to say more. To tell him my darkest secret. The one that has derailed me into this life I'm in.

"Yes. I think we kinda do, Little Bird." His voice is adamant. "After the way you made me feel in that shower?

Raven, you can't tell me you don't like sex because it's uncomfortable, and then just expect me to let that go. Why is it uncomfortable?"

"I don't have a lot of experience, I guess. It was just that Jemmy, my ex, well, he was ... well ...it was always painful when we had sex." My face is seventeen shades of crimson.

"Wait a minute!" Connor commands. He swiftly pulls the RV onto the shoulder, bouncing us violently as he careens to a stop from highway speed. He turns and looks at me with an expression of genuine concern edged with anger.

"Do you mean to tell me that some jackass hurt you? Forced you?" Connor's eyes fill with what looks to be bordering on rage. His jaw muscles flex and I can tell he's grinding his teeth.

"No. Of course, he never forced me. It's just that ... well, he didn't mean to ... he never intended to, of course. It's just that I don't have a lot of experience so ..."

"Babe, stop." Connor shakes his head in disbelief. "Raven, I'm sorry, but that's utter bullshit. You know that, right? Being inexperienced has nothing to do with how it feels. Jesus, Lainey, he hurt you, baby." His knuckles trail down my cheek in a feathersoft caress. "And that's not OK." Tears fill my eyes, but I swallow hard, willing them not to fall. For the moment, they obey. But I know it won't be for long. "He's the one, isn't he? He told you that you weren't good enough, didn't he?"

"No." I can feel my stone wall of insecurity being reconstructed again, mortared together by fear, doubt and anxiety. "Just drop it. This is a stupid conversation. All that is personal. We're not having sex. The reason doesn't matter, does it? I'll keep my hands to myself from now on. Let's go. We'll be late for the dinner." I sniffle, but the tears remain unshed. Thank God!

Connor unbuckles his seatbelt and comes to kneel

between our chairs. I have no idea how he fits himself in that snug space, but the fact that he kneels in front of me weakens me in ways I can't begin to explain.

"Nevermind about dinner. Lainey, I'm so sorry he hurt you." His fingers come up and softly touch my neck. "This trip isn't about sex. No expectations, right? All I want you to know is that I'm sorry you were hurt. You deserve so much better, Raven. I won't always get things right, but I promise I won't hurt you. Nothing happens unless you're comfortable. One hundred percent comfortable. OK?" I nod slowly as he speaks. "You are wonderful, remember? You deserve for everything to be wonderful in and out of the bedroom."

The tears pooling in my eyes reach nearly to overflowing, and my heart wants to break. The newly erected stones of the wall around me come crumbling down again. He actually stopped on the side of the road to apologize for what happened with Jemmy? Well, at least as much as he knows about it. And to remind me that he thinks I'm wonderful. I need to be reminded of that. And he somehow just gets it. I don't know whether I'm more touched because of all of that or because he makes me feel brave. He doesn't judge me. Doesn't pry or force me to reveal everything. There's no way I feel brave enough for that. I don't know if I ever will.

"Thank you. It's OK. I'm OK." I whisper, holding back the tears somehow.

"No, Lainey Bird, you're not. Not yet. But you will be. I promise."

Connor's hand reaches and touches my cheek again. He caresses my skin and gives me a compassionate smile.

"Connor, if you're disappointed. I want you to know, I have no intention of teasing you."

"That's not what yesterday was to me, Raven. Shush now. No more talking. I understand. Don't worry. And I still think you're wonderful. Whatever happens or doesn't happen, I'm still glad you're here with me."

He slides back into his seat and fastens his seatbelt again. Wordlessly, he maneuvers the camper back onto the highway. He turns the radio up and *Climax*'s *Youngest Lover* comes over the speakers. I sigh, remembering my wish and wondering if it could ever come true.

Around 4 p.m., we check into a cute little bed-and-breakfast Connor found for us. We have just enough time to shower and change for dinner. I hope my LBD is going to be all right for this place. It's a simple design, V-neck, sleeveless, comes just above my knees. It fits looser than the last time I wore it, thanks to my birdseed habit these past few months. I wasn't necessarily trying to lose weight, but I had no appetite. That has certainly changed.

Connor's "friend" turns out to be a famous chef, Anton Arnaud. I watched him on the Food Network in a mystery ingredient battle last Christmas. The mystery ingredient was cranberries. I was impressed by what he could do with them — even the jellied canned version. Anticipating our meal, I'm actually pretty thankful my dress is a little roomy.

"You know Anton Arnaud?" I hug Connor's arm as we stride into the restaurant. The blast of air-conditioning feels marvelous. The day reached triple digits and I swear the humidity level must have topped the 90th percentile.

"He helped me get one of our more upscale restaurants in Buckhead up and running a couple of years ago. He's actually a friend of Ox and Tori, but we all worked together a lot during the start-up."

"This is so cool." I can't help but gaze around and take it all in like a kid in a candy store. Inner Foodie is floating on cloud nine right now.

The restaurant, like Anton, is French. Connor and I are seated at a long counter that overlooks the kitchen and the chefs and cooks work directly behind it. These coveted seats allow the lucky diners who secure them to not only watch their food being prepared, but to speak to Chef Anton as well. And of course, Connor Rose is one of the lucky ones.

Watching the staff in the kitchen is like watching a well-choreographed ballet. Sparks of fire set the stage. Clinks of metal on metal and sparse conversations of "couper," "émincer," "trancher" and "oui, Chef" provide the symphonic arrangement to the dance. Decked out in their crisp white chef's jackets, the cooks, alongside the penguin-clad servers, twirl and dance across the kitchen and dining room in perfectly practiced movements. It's beautiful poetry. And the aromas that waft through the air are fragrant enough to make me salivate like Pavlov's dog. My Inner Foodie is officially falling in love.

Anton comes over and greets Connor warmly and offers me a customary French greeting with a kiss on each cheek. He's a stout man with a cherry red face and long curved mouth that smiles widely, when it's not scowling at his staff demanding "la perfectionnement". I know a little French, and Anton continues to refer to me as Connor's "la petite amie." It's not just "little friend" as would be directly translated, but "girlfriend" for those who are more familiar with the language. Connor doesn't correct him. I know he doesn't think of me as a girlfriend. It's probably easier than explaining that I'm an acquaintance of less than a week whom he's invited to journey in a camper van with him for five weeks from Atlanta to Martha's Vineyard because she couldn't get hired for a job due to her lack of a personal life.

Yeah, girlfriend is a lot easier. And I don't mind, actually. He did call me his girl once.

For more than four hours, we dine on the most delicious food on the planet. Anton brings us one amazingly beautiful dish after another. Each is more savory and well-crafted than the last, and paired with wines and cocktails carefully selected to amplify the flavors.

During my brief tenure with the New York Philharmonic, I performed in Paris and ate some delicious French cuisine while I was there. Nothing I ate then could rival what Anton and his crew create in this kitchen. He manages to somehow meld traditional French cuisine with more modern influences and adds in slight hints of American and Italian flavors.

By the time we finish the seven courses, drink two entire bottles of French wine with Anton and laugh until our sides ache, it is nearly 2 a.m. We are the last to leave the restaurant.

"I wish you'd give me the recipe for that chicken dish you served to Ox and me that night our restaurant opened. Our chefs have never been able to reproduce it the same way you made it," Connor says, clapping him on the back as we slowly make our way toward the door. Wait staff work busily around us to close up for the night.

"Ah, zat iz becauz I remove ze secret ingredient from ze rezipe," Anton confesses, tapping his finger alongside his nose.

"What do I have to do to get it from you?" Connor begs. The persuasiveness edging the periphery of his voice makes me think he already has something to offer in exchange. The sly look in his eyes tells me he's not ready to reveal it — not yet. I love the way he looks playful.

Anton pulls up some information on his phone, and I hear Connor's device beep with an incoming message. He glances down and lets out a bark of laughter.

"Really? A scavenger hunt?" Connor muses.

"Oui. You and la petite amie can spend ze day finding it. And when you do, you will leave for me ze thing I ask of ze Ox when I help with ze restaurant. Oui?" The long curve of a smile pulls across Anton's face and pushes up the knobs of his full scarlet cheeks.

Connor laughs again and claps him on the back. "All right. You win. What do you say, Lainey Bird? You up for a little scavenger hunt tomorrow?"

I nod eagerly, fueled by the wine and high spirits of the evening. The pleasantness of the friendship between these two men spills over and fills me.

"Oui! C'est très bon!" I make a mock salute. I'm rewarded with a hearty laugh from Anton and Connor and immediately start laughing along with them.

La vie est belle.

# CHAPTER NINE

**Thursday, June 10 (but only barely)**

THE WARM BUZZ of the wine, lingering richness of the food and lateness of the evening wash over me while I change out of my little black shift dress and heels and into my nightgown. I grin at myself and murmur Connor's words over for my own hearing, *You are wonderful!*

When I come out of the bathroom, I find Connor once again propped up on a pile of pillows, tapping the bed beside him in invitation. I smile. I hope this becomes our nightly routine to snuggle together this way. I love the way it makes me feel — treasured, respected, safe.

"Did you enjoy dinner?" Connor asks, after turning out the lights.

"Are you kidding? I ate a seven-course meal prepared by Anton Arnaud. *The* Anton Arnaud The meal was as much of a floor show as it was a dinner, watching his staff prepare everything. The plates looked like paintings. And the food was amazing. It was a perfect dinner, Connor. Thank you so much."

"It was my pleasure, Lainey Bird. I'm glad you enjoyed it." Connor's voice is a rumble of chocolate-covered steel. It gives me goose bumps as I curl a millimeter closer into his hold.

"You seemed to be having a good time, too. Are we really going on a scavenger hunt tomorrow?"

"So it would seem." He kisses the top of my head.

"What is all that about? The scavenger hunt for a chicken recipe?"

"Anton is big into the geocaching thing. He's hidden the recipe somewhere in Greenville. He sent me the GPS coordinates and we get to go searching the area tomorrow."

"And he wants us to leave what exactly for him in return? Something tells me you already knew about this."

"Yeah. I actually brought it. I figured he'd ask me for it. He's always wanted this special guitar pick Ox has. The two of them argued over whether Ox would ever give it to him or not."

"A guitar pick?" My brow scrunches up in confusion.

"Anton is the biggest *Climax* fan you'll ever meet. He went full-on Superfan when Ox called about helping us set up the restaurant in Buckhead. He asked for nothing except the first guitar pick Ox ever used in a live concert. Ox damn near keeps the thing under glass. But he knew we were coming here and asked me to bring it to him."

"So where is he hiding ze rezipe?" I ask in a mock French accent.

Connor chuckles. "Near as I can tell it's somewhere along ze Swamp Rabbit Trail." Connor's voice is playful, but his tone is heavy and sluggish. He's tired. I don't blame him, I am, too. But curiosity wins out over exhaustion.

"Swamp Rabbit Trail?" I ask with a heavy yawn.

"Yep. More than twenty miles of food, parks and beautiful scenery. I thought we could rent some bikes and head out after breakfast — before it gets too hot. Sound good?"

I let out another long, loud yawn. I feel Connor kiss the top of my head.

"Sleep now, my wonderful little Lainey Bird."

"Come on!" Connor's voice is loud. He's shouting. "Move!"

I open my eyes and hear him yelling. He keeps screaming for someone to "move" or "c'mon." I reach to touch his shoulder and lay a hand on his chest. His body is hot, almost feverish. He twists and his fingers grip my wrist, hard. I shriek. The sound emerging from my lungs is equal parts pain and fear. My heart starts pounding.

"Why won't you move?" Connor's voice is urgent, agitated, and he's screaming. His eyes are open, but he doesn't see me. They're glazed, unblinking and ... terrifying. I try to wrench my wrist from his grip, but his fingers tighten and I whimper.

"Connor!" I call out to him, working to keep my voice from sounding panicked. "Connor, let me go. Stop it! You're dreaming."

Connor's eyes blink furiously. He stares into mine for several long moments as if he can't see me right in front of him. My lip starts trembling. I can't help it. His grip on me loosens slightly, and I take advantage and pull away. I slide out of the bed and quickly flip on the light.

Connor's face is pale, his eyes wide. A glossy sheen of sweat is slicked over his skin. He's shaking. "What happened?" he stammers.

I start rubbing my wrist. "You were having a bad dream."

"Did I touch you?" Connor's expression is loaded with alarm. It's a look I barely recognize on him.

"It's all right," I offer softly, still rubbing at my sore wrist.

"No, I'm sorry. Please come here. I'm so sorry."

I make my way back to the bed and Connor instantly envelops my body against his. I can hear his heartbeat hammering against his ribs and the fast pant of his breath. Every muscle in his body quivers nervously.

"Connor, what's wrong?"

"I have nightmares sometimes. I'm sorry. I should have told you. It's just that I haven't had one whenever you're with me. I thought ... I thought maybe, with you, they might be gone. Where did I touch you?" Connor's hands immediately begin searching my arms and hands for marks. I hide the place where he touched me, not wanting to upset him further.

"You grabbed my wrist, it's nothing." He bares the tender skin and then kisses it softly, his lips trembling slightly.

"Did I hurt you?" His voice quavers.

"Not much, you mostly scared me," I reply. "Connor, what do you have nightmares about?" I try to ignore the bruise forming on my wrist. He certainly didn't do that on purpose.

"It's nothing for you to worry about, Lainey Bird. Just lie here with me for a while. I'll be OK in a minute." I click the light off again and slide into the bed beside him. His body is sticky with a sheen of perspiration.

"Connor, please tell me."

He lets out an apprehensive sigh. For several long heart-beats, he says nothing. I notice his breathing and heart rate slow considerably as we lie spooned together in the dark.

"Years ago, I was in the Army. A Ranger. We were on a mission overseas ... Afghanistan. Some of the other special forces guys we were with ... there was an explosion. I managed to get a couple of them out. But ... there was so much blood and three of them ... they didn't survive."

"Oh, God. Connor. I'm so sorry." My heart clenches for him in a way I can hardly describe. It feels like it's breaking.

"It was pretty bad," he says. I can tell that's a tremendous understatement, but I allow him to tell his story in his own words, in his own way.

"And you have nightmares about it?"

"Sometimes." Connor offers simply.

"What can I do for you when that happens?" I ask. I want to offer him the same support he offered to me in the RV when I was forced to disclose my dislike of sex.

"I don't know. But I can get separate rooms for us from now on if you want. I want you to feel safe. I don't want to hurt you."

"You didn't hurt me, Connor." It's only half a lie. The mark on my wrist doesn't hurt nearly as bad as my heart that's breaking for the man who still carries the ghosts from war with him.

He rolls away from me, and I'm face-to-face with the lion inked onto his back. The room is dark, and I'm unable to see the tattoo clearly. I can only make out a faint trace of the haunting blue eyes visible in the ambient light. But I know the lion is there. Just like in the shower at the spa, my fingers reach for him again and I feel the pads of them skate along his bare skin over the lines where I suppose the lion lies sleeping.

Connor's muscles twitch under my touch, his skin rippling as I pet the lion and attempt to soothe him back to sleep. A long, soft sigh escapes his lips.

"That feels so good, Raven. Thank you." His voice is heavy with need. This is what he needs. He doesn't need to be abandoned in a separate room in his brokenness. He needs someone whose heart can glue the cracked and shattered pieces of him back together again. I don't know if that's me, but I want to try.

"Why the lion?" I ask quietly. I force myself to remain quiet for his reply despite the awkward silence that seems to engulf us for so long. I'm just about to give up hope that he'll respond at all when a single quiet word lifts through the darkness.

"Aslan." He offers simply.

"From the Narnia books?" I think back to that sleepover the night of his birthday and the stack of books he keeps beside his bed.

"Yeah. One of the spec ops guys in the bombing had a copy of it on him. I read it. It's an allegory of the Bible, you know."

"I didn't." I continue to quietly and softly stroke the lion's mane. I can feel Connor's heartbeat slowing and the tension in his shoulders relax a tiny fraction.

"It's the story of the Bible. Of Jesus. How he forgave Edmund his betrayal, equipped the Pevensie kids with weapons to defeat evil and then offered up his own life to save everyone. Aslan is Jesus."

"I never made that connection before. But I admit it's been a long time since I've read it."

"I've read it dozens of times," Connor said. "Aslan has my back."

"Interesting thought. But this beautiful tattoo ... you can't even see it."

"I don't need to see God to know He's there — that He protects me and takes care of me. I want others to see it, though."

I lean forward and place a soft kiss on the space I think would be the lion's nose. Connor's body flexes and he turns to lie flat on his back. I readjust myself and curl up beside him, nestling my head into his shoulder — my perfect pillow.

My fingers continue to slide over his skin. I softly skim his neck and then twirl them into the hollow of his throat.

Drifting down over his chest, I rub softly in large figure eights for several long minutes. My short nails finally scrape lightly over the ripples in his abdomen and he lets out a light moan. I snatch my hand away, but he captures my wrist in his fingertips. I can feel the place he squeezed so hard before. It feels bruised and sore. I pray there's no mark there. Connor would never forgive himself.

"No. Please, don't stop. Keep going. Your touch is ... it's comforting."

"How?" I lay my palm flat on his stomach and rest it there, lightly curling my fingers and then stretching them again. I can feel his muscles harden and then relax.

"Your touch is so ... I can't describe it. It's so soft, so easy."

"Women are usually rough with you?"

"Sometimes. They take one look at the long-haired, tattooed guy and just assume I'm a total monster in the sack. They claw and squeeze. It's always so hard."

It hurts somewhere deep down to hear him talk about other women he's been with. I try to listen to him now with the same patience and understanding that he showed when I tried to explain about my brief relationship with Jemmy.

My hand skates lower and I half sit up in the bed and look down at him. His hand finds my face in the dark and brushes a curtain of my hair behind my ear. I lean forward and kiss his chest softly. His skin is so warm, and pulled so tight over rounded sinew. He gives me an encouraging little groan and I wiggle lower against his body until my mouth is over his navel. I swirl my tongue over it, tasting the light scent of the body wash he uses. It's a spicy mix of leather and some sort of herb that smells like rosemary or mint.

I can feel the thickness of him lower, his eager staff twitching and waiting for his turn for kisses. I tug off Connor's shorts and let my lips fall on him softly, slowly, and pull as much of his hard length into my mouth as I can. Connor lets out a loud sigh and I'm undone with the need to comfort and adore this man.

I continue to minister to him with my lips, my tongue, my fingers. I massage and kiss and suckle and stroke. Connor's hands grasp for me, eager to touch me to find some piece of me he can hold onto while his body strains to keep control. I can feel the tension working through his blood under my tongue. His fingers finally encircle my head.

"You don't have to do this, Raven," Connor's torso flexes and he lifts up to his elbows. I know he wants to catch a glimpse of me here, my lips encircling his groin and lapping at his generous length. I'm thankful it's too dark to see much. He hisses through his teeth. I spend time just loving him. His body is incredible. Long, hard, thick and ... perfect.

The moans and growls I'm pulling from him make me feel sexier than I've ever felt in my life. The notion that a girl like me could make a man like Connor so hot is almost too much to believe. No man has ever made me feel like this. Powerful. Desired. Alluring. I am lost in the act.

"Raven, I'm so close. God, I wanna come so bad right now," Connor groans.

I stop before he does. I'm not sure my courage extends far enough to do what I am certain he wants. I kiss my way back up his body and our lips find one another. They clash in a mad tangle of tongue and teeth. My blood simmers under the surface. I'll admit that having him in my mouth turns me on. Big time. It never did with Jemmy. It was an obligation — sort of a requisite a couple of times a month, but with Connor, it's completely different. I give to him. He doesn't take.

"I need to touch you," he gasps. His hands clumsily fumble over my collarbone and shoulders.

"Yes," I breathe quietly as he tugs off my nightshirt and cups my breasts in his hands.

"Christ, I want to bury myself inside you so bad, woman. You have no idea." His lips move to descend to my breasts and I lurch back. I push gently against his shoulders, pulling his lips away from my body.

"Connor, stop. Please." I murmur.

His hands instantly freeze and shoot up as if he has been caught by the police. He's practically panting, but he stops. The minute I ask. The first time. I half expected to have to plead with him, like I did with Jemmy, but he just stops. My heart floods with an emotion I can't describe. Respect? Gratitude? Appreciation? Perhaps a combination of too many expressions to single anyone out as stronger than the next, but they're all there swirling together, willing me to tell him to stop and at the same time urging me to continue.

"Connor, I won't be a tease," I say. My hands tap around on the bed in search of my shirt.

"You aren't teasing me," he says quickly. "Well, you are, but I love it. I know where the line is. I won't cross it. I'm sorry I said what I did. I just got caught up in it all. Do you really want to stop?"

"You mean, you're all right if we just fool around and don't actually have sex?" The idea is as foreign to me as a sleepover with no sex. Jemmy convinced me foreplay was for high school. Sex was for adults. I don't want Connor thinking I'm just some juvenile cock tease set on driving him crazy and then denying him the big finish I know he craves. Despite the fact I crave it, too, I don't think I'm ready to face my fears.

"Are you kidding? This is the most turned-on I've ever been in my life, and I think it's because I know I get to do everything *but* have sex with you. I don't want to stop, but I will."

My hand lands on his thigh. His fingers move to cover

mine and then I lift our hands back onto my breast again. The pad of his thumb brushes over my nipple and I can feel it twist into a hard pebble under his touch. I do want him, but the fear of the pain of his intrusion stops me from saying anything else.

"Lainey, let me kiss you." His other hand slides between the junction of my thighs. I know what he's asking with that commanding tone in his voice. I nod, unable to speak. I want it. I do. I want it so badly.

"Please," I rasp.

He orders me to lie back. I surrender to him. His body covers mine and I feel the weight of his massive bulk bearing down on top of me, pushing me deep into the soft mattress.

"I will only kiss you, I promise. Just my mouth, OK?"

I nod, giving my consent.

His lips stroke my neck softly, his tongue enters my mouth with a long, deep lick before it drifts to my ear. He nibbles the lobe while I feel his fingers slowly pry my thighs apart. They're clamped together with nervous anxiety. Unease over the discomfort that usually follows looms too close to allow me to fully engage with him. I'm so afraid. Afraid of the pain.

"You're wonderful," he whispers against my breast. He teases the nipple with his lips before swallowing it down into his warm, wet mouth. My body arches up to offer him more. The feeling is exquisite. So soft, and gentle. His words caress me just as much as his touch. I can feel my body slipping into submission. Connor doesn't hurt. Everything he does feels so incredibly good.

For long, lingering minutes, he licks one breast and then the other, spiraling me into a frenzy of need so intense I feel as if I may shatter from his touch there. Is that possible? Can a person orgasm from being kissed and licked at her breasts alone? My Inner Sex Goddess begs me to find out.

His hands rove over my hips and belly, keeping well away from my velvety entrance below. Knowing where they are, feeling them work deliberately against my body, calms my anxiety a bit. He's going to keep his promises.

He drops several light, soft kisses at my stomach and then leans up to look at me. I can't see his expression in the utter darkness of the room, but I sense his gaze on me.

"This is where I need you to talk, Little Bird. Tell me everything. Tell me what feels good, what doesn't. Tell me what you need, what you desire. This is for you."

I gulp, and then softly whisper, "I'll try." Because the truth is I'm on the edge of absolute combustion. Words and thoughts are being drowned out of my mind as sensation and ecstasy take over.

I can feel the warmth of his sweet amused little grin as his voice rumbles into my inner thigh.

He peels away my panties and hums in whispered kisses back up my leg.

"You mean, all I had to do to get you to be quiet is to bury my face between your legs? Why didn't you say that from the beginning?"

We both laugh and I open my trembling legs a bit wider for him. The comedy is just the dose I need to relax enough to let him past my defenses.

Connor's pace is both deliberate and patient. The touch of his tongue is hot even against my fevered flesh. I let out a hard gasp at the first contact of his mouth against my intimate folds. The feeling is so soft, so gentle. But it forces intense shockwaves of sensation to ripple through my body, spreading in larger and larger waves as it fans out from my core, down into my limbs and rings through my ears.

"Are you OK?" he asks. I can tell by his tone he's genuinely concerned.

"Yes," I manage to gasp out. "I'm good."

"You're supposed to be talking to me, Raven." His tongue licks through my folds once more.

"I can't. It's too wonderful," I whisper. "Please, don't stop yet."

"I wasn't planning to." His words buzz through my body in hot vibrations that only heighten the sensations. I'm desperate to move, and my hips begin to roll softly as his tongue works against me, finally finding that tiny pearl of flesh begging for his attention.

"Don't chase it," he adds softly. "Just enjoy it."

"God, Connor. I can't help it. It's so close," I breathe. I can count on one hand the number of times I had an actual orgasm with Jemmy. That number would be two. Two times. Jemmy was too rough and too quick. He never really paid any attention to me or what I was feeling. On the rare occasions it happened, it was almost an accident. It wasn't as if Jemmy worked to get me there. He only worked to get himself there.

Connor is his polar opposite. I have no doubt, his own unanswered desire to find release borders on painful at this point, and yet he doesn't complain. He enjoys what he is doing. He keeps checking to see whether I like what he's doing and how he's doing it. I answer "yes" every time, of course. The man's mouth is like pure heaven. "Yes" is the only word my Inner Sex Goddess can remember. The rest of my brain has turned into total mush.

I can feel my body cresting quickly. I'm desperate for release when Connor's mouth stops. He licks up my body, giving my breasts a final kiss, before pressing his body alongside mine. My chest heaves up and down as I pant fervently. My heart thunders in my chest as I work to focus on what is happening. Why is he stopping?

"Touch me," His command this time is pure begging. "I want to come with you. Make me come."

I feel his fingers softly resume a slow gently swirl between my legs, massaging the swollen knot. My inner muscles clench in anticipation of my coming orgasm.

My hand moves to his shaft. It's thick, fevered and slick from his desire. I slide easily over him in an easy rhythm that matches the tempo of his fingers against my flesh. His thumb and forefinger begin to massage and I feel myself ready to explode at any moment.

"Faster, Lainey." He commands me again, and I couldn't care less. I comply with eagerness, feeling his fingers increase their pace against my body as mine do against his.

In a rush of groans from him and my own soft screams, we climax together, our bodies convulsing and shuddering as violent spasms grip us both. Connor's hand cups my belly, his fingers squeezing my flesh, holding onto me while he explodes into my fist, still gripping him fiercely.

Connor's arms enfold me as our breaths race to find balance and our hearts work to regain a steady rhythm again.

We lie cradled together, chest to chest, a cooling little pool of spent desire on our bodies. Neither of us even cares. His breath restored, Connor kisses my forehead and whispers.

"Whoa, Raven. That was incredible." He kisses my head and works to slow his breathing. "Did you like it?" This question is timid. He's afraid I'll say I didn't. I want to put his mind at ease.

"Very much," I purr. My entire body is awash with a sated feeling that has my joints loose, my muscles leaden and my skin replete with a glorious afterglow. It is the most intense orgasm I've ever had. Inner Sex Goddess just lit up a cigarette.

"Everything tonight seemed great. What is it about sex that bothers you, Lainey Bird?" he whispers through kisses into the hair at the top of my head.

"Having someone inside me, I guess. It hurts. Every time,

not just my first — which was bad, by the way. I just lie there, and pray it's over soon."

"Was your former lover ... was he a big guy?" Connor's fingers work through my hair playing with the strands.

I chuckle at his question. Jemmy wasn't large at all. His prick was thin and short. Nothing like the stallion-sized member Connor has rearing up on hind legs. "Um ... not at all."

"And foreplay didn't help?"

"There wasn't usually any foreplay," I say absently. "He just went for it."

"Baby, that's a problem. No wonder you didn't like it. If he didn't take the time to properly prepare your body, sex would be rather uncomfortable for you."

"That's just not how he did it. Wasn't his style I guess." My Inner Sex Goddess has smoke rising up out of her head at the notion I'd even try to make excuses for that douche nozzle.

"Was he your only lover, then?" Connor's voice is soft and quiet.

"Yes, why?"

"Because it's not a matter of preference or style, Lainey. There are rules to sex."

"Rules? For sex?" I nearly want to laugh.

"Yes. Rule number one. You should always feel safe. Safe sharing your body and safe letting your heart go with it. You should never feel like it's an obligation or something you're required to do."

I think on that for a second. Did I feel safe with Jemmy? Maybe at first. No. Not even then. I felt pressured and rushed. Toward the end of our relationship, I felt used. "What's rule number two?"

"Rule number two is that sex is about giving, not taking. My job is to pleasure you to insanity, and your job is to pleasure me. We give to one another, we don't take from one another. Does that make sense?"

"I guess so. It wasn't that way with Jemmy." Jemmy took from me. He took too much.

"Jemmy is a bastard. And if I ever get the chance, I'm going to shove my fist into his throat for what he did to you. No man should treat a woman the way he treated you. Were you two dating or were you just sleeping together?"

"I thought we were dating, but it turns out we were just sleeping together. I wasn't his only one."

I feel Connor's fists clench as I utter these words and instantly regret saying them, although I'm telling the truth. Almost the whole truth.

"Don't," I say, rubbing the lion on his back with my fingertips again. "It's over now. Are there any more rules?"

Connor lets out another breath before he continues. "The joining is the destination, not an orgasm. You can have great sex and not come. It's about being satisfied. Even for men. It is possible to have sex and really enjoy it and not reach climax, and that's OK. It can't be all about that. Then, it's just working a job. Sex is about connection, not orgasm."

I grin against him at hearing that. "Something tells me you rarely have to employ that rule," I tease.

"That's true." We both laugh lightly at that.

"Is that all?" I stroke the lion on his back imagining what it would feel like to run my fingers through the mane — if it were real.

"No. The last one is almost as important as the first one. I doubt you'll have any trouble with it, Little Bird."

"What's that?" I ask, still stroking the lion's mane.

"You have to talk to each other," Conner says. I hear the irony in his tone.

"What do you mean?"

"I need to know what you like, how you like it. If you

need to adjust a position, or ask me to do something. I especially want to know if you don't like something. We have to discuss issues and ideas — games we want to play and fantasies we have. Becoming lovers doesn't give you clairvoyant abilities, you know. Besides, conversation is some of the best foreplay."

"I like your rules."

"I like you," he whispers. "I'm glad you're here with me tonight, Lainey Bird."

Long minutes of silence stretch between us as we cuddle together. Connor wraps us in a soft sheet and a light blanket. I feel his body relax against mine as we drift off to sleep. I'm curious to learn more about this man, however. I work up my courage to ask one final question before I close my eyes and allow myself to completely drift away.

"What were their names? The men you saved in Afghanistan?" I ask tentatively.

"John Galloway and Ian McGuire," he replies in a sleepy voice.

I softly stroke the lion and feel his body relax and finally surrender to sleep again. The darkness shrouds us and, for just these few moments, we are alone in the universe. Trapped somewhere between sleeping and waking, between yesterday and tomorrow, adrift in pillow talk and kisses and touches and ecstasy, and I never want to leave. I want to stay right here, languishing in the in-between with Connor until all the stars in the sky have turned to dust.

# CHAPTER TEN

**Thursday, June 10 (still)**

MY ASS IS SORE. Like screaming. As in it's painful. A little numb voice yells at me to get off this damn bicycle.

"Connor," I whine more than say. "I need a break."

We started out at the bike rental shop just after breakfast this morning. We've ridden what feels like about six thousand miles, but I'll admit, it's been a beautiful ride. Swamp Rabbit Trail is exactly what Connor described. Parks, streams, bridges, even a little waterfall. Summer sun and large white clouds make the whole scene around us look like a postcard. I've taken dozens of pictures. I plan to post them on my newly created Instagram account #naturephotography, and send a few to Willow. She would love this place. Well, I will if I survive this two-wheeled trek Connor has us on.

"We're nearly there, are you sure?" He tries to be encouraging. Like he has for the past two miles, but I can't anymore.

"Hell, yes. I need to walk at least." At this point, I'm begging him, and I honestly don't care.

"Ah, your lady bits angry with you?" He smirks at me again.

"No, but my lady ass is. You're not sore?"

"Are you kidding? I haven't been able to feel my balls for like the last five miles." Connor dismounts and walks his bike. It could be my imagination, but I swear he's limping slightly.

We both break out in laughter and maneuver our bikes into a nearby park. It's a lovely summer day. Huge white puffy clouds drift slowly in and out of shapes that are reminiscent of everything from dragons to pirate ships. I'm thankful for the quiet din of sound that follows us from markets to food stalls and parks where children play. I can't talk to Connor on bikes, really. I need the noise.

We walk our bikes to a huge old sycamore tree. Connor peels off his backpack and lifts out two bottles of water. I drink greedily from mine. It's a sweltering hot day. The southern humidity the area is known for is really showing off, even at ten in the morning.

Connor flops down in a lush green patch of clover and stretches out on his back in the dark shade. He props his head in his hands and lets out an audible yowl of relief. "God, it feels good to straighten my spine for a while. Whose dumbass idea is this, anyway?"

"Yours," I intone, lying beside him. The clover feels so cool on my scorched back. The tank top and shorts I've chosen for today stick to me everywhere. Nearby a bee buzzes. He is probably upset we've just crushed his lunch.

"I'm officially firing myself as social events coordinator on this adventure of ours, Lainey. Any nominations from the floor as to my replacement?"

"I vote for Aslan," I offer, toying with his emotions.

"I second that," he laughs.

"Hey, you hungry?" I ask, taking a whiff of a delicious aroma permeating the thick humid air.

"I could eat," he replies, sitting up. His knees are bent, and he's scanning the various food trucks that have come to the park to attract the lunch hour crowd. The scent of grilled meat and veggies being prepared have my stomach growling. "Oh man, I see what we need," Connor finally says.

He stands up and pulls me to my feet. We wander to a bright red food truck. Just behind it toward a side entrance near the bumper, an older woman rolls a lump of ivory-colored dough with a rolling pin that looks like a broomstick. Sitting on an overturned plastic bucket, she works happily, her hair pinned back in a kerchief. A dusty black apron covers her plain dark dress.

"Gözeleme," Connor says with a purr of happiness in his tone.

"What's gözeleme?" My Inner Foodie desperately hopes it doesn't contain the entrails of any sort of animal whatsoever.

"I had it when I was in Turkey once. She's making a type of phyllo dough, then she'll stuff it with meats or cheeses and cook it on that flat top there." He gestures to a large disk-shaped flat top griddle. It's heated by a propane flame under it. Another older woman wearing a black and white striped bandanna over her hair uses a flat wooden paddle to move around what appears to be an envelope of the thin sheets of dough. I can see meat and cheese and some sort of green inside. Dark brown patches of crisp dough start to color as she flips and moves it around the griddle adding generous brushes of olive oil over it as it moves.

"This looks great. Where were you in Turkey?" I ask Connor, filming the woman as she makes our snack.

"Incirlik Air Base, near the Syrian boarder. I was on mission with the Army." Connor says, leaving out too many details.

"Oh," I mutter softly and let the subject drop. I don't

want Connor thinking about anything that may make him have another nightmare tonight.

A young girl with long jet-black hair plaited down her back asks us for our order. Connor orders me a gözeleme with spinach and feta and he gets his with ground meat and cheese.

I watch dumbstruck as the older woman creates a sheet of dough so thin you could read a newspaper through it. She then sets to folding it in almost a robotic motion. It's obvious she has repeated these steps a million or more times in her life. She makes a large rectangle and then scoops generous portions of cheese and fresh spinach into mine and sets to folding the dough over and over until it creates the envelope shape I saw on the griddle earlier.

In only a few minutes, we're back under our tree with our piping hot snacks, cooling from inside their white butcher paper wrapping. With my first bite, my Inner Foodie falls instantly in love. The exterior dough layers are crisp while the softer interior ones pillow around the freshness of the spinach and tart tang of the feta. I hum in appreciation. I wash it down with the sweet sodas Connor ordered with them and the combination of hot/cold, sweet/savory and crispy/creamy is perfection on my palette.

"Amazing," Connor says, stuffing a huge bite into his mouth. "I want to hire that woman to come make these at the *Day Old Bagel*."

"That's a cute place, by the way. The food was good, too," I offer.

"Yeah, it's coming along. We made big changes to the menu and overall ambiance of the place when we bought it, which met with a lot of pushback from the old management. It's been a pain. The place has more than doubled its average sales, but the former owner insists the way he did it was better."

"More comfortable, maybe?" I add. "Not everyone likes change."

"I suppose. You mind if we just hang here for a while? The thought of getting on that bike is too much right now."

"You don't have to try to sell me. I'm going to pass out from a carb coma right here under this tree. Then I may go shopping in those little boutiques there. I want to get something for my sister on this trip."

"That's right. You mentioned her before. What's she like?"

"Willow. She's two years older than me. She lives in San Diego with her husband, Stephen. She's going to have my first niece or nephew in a few months."

"That's exciting." Connor reaches into his backpack and pulls out his worn copy of *The Lion, the Witch, and the Wardrobe*.

"Are you going to read for a while?" I ask, offering him the last bits of my gözeleme. He shakes his head at my offer, and I crumple the paper around it and set it aside for now.

"Do you mind? We're not in a hurry today."

I shake my head. "Would you read me the part about Christmas? That's my favorite part,"

"It's my favorite, too," he says and quickly turns to the passage. He starts to read, and I'm quickly hypnotized by his low, smooth voice. He's so familiar with the story, he's almost acting out the scene he's reading. As he does, his voice becomes faster and louder during moments of action or suspense and softer and slower during the meaningful conversations between the Pevensie children and Santa Claus. I let my eyes fall closed and allow the sounds of his voice and the birds and the murmur of the crowds at the park to carry me away.

I wake later with my cheek planted on Connor's thick thigh. It's damp from sweat. I've obviously been lying here a while. I let the sunlight in through tiny cracks as I flutter my eyelids open and see two boys kicking a soccer ball back and forth about a hundred yards from our tree. A warm summer breeze drifts lazily over me. It feels too hot and tired to do much more than just breathe down on the earth. It's moving just enough to keep us from melting under the rising heat of a South Carolina summer day.

Beyond the soccer players, high up in the sky, the puffy clouds gather into greying columns that work their way to block out the sun. It's a welcome respite from the blaring heat. In minutes, I feel the cool shade of them wash over my skin.

There is a light scratching sound above my head and I move to rise, but my ear strikes the corner of something hard and a bit sharp.

"Lie down," Connor commands. "Be still."

"Why? Is there a bee on me?" I grin. I begin to stroke at his leg with my fingertips letting the damp hair curl around my fingernails.

"No, I'm sketching and you'll mess up my model."

"Oh, who's your model?"

"Stop moving," he says forcefully, but not meaning it. Not really.

"I'm not moving. I'm talking."

"Well, that's what I'm sketching, so stop moving your mouth."

"You're drawing my mouth?" Teasing Connor may be my new favorite pastime. I smile wide.

"I'm sketching lots of things. Right now, I'm sketching the corner of your mouth. Stop smiling."

Hearing his mock anger at my grin only makes me smile wider. A soft giggle starts to escape my throat and I feel the stifled laugh vibrate through my body against his lap, where my head is resting.

"Well, now you've done it." He lays the sketchbook aside and helps me sit up. "You've ruined the whole thing. You're totally hideous now."

"Let me see," I beg, adjusting my tank top and shorts.

"Nope." Connor slides the small sketchbook back into his backpack and zips it up. He leans forward and kisses me softly. "Time to go. I'm ready to get back to some air conditioning and I've got like six emails I've got to reply to before Ox has a seizure."

"Back on the bikes?" I look around, but they're gone.

"Nope. I called and had the rental company come pick them up when you were asleep. According to the GPS, we need to walk down the path for a while. It's the Ankle Express for us, Lainey Bird."

Our walk along the paved path turns into a nature hike as we follow the flashing blue dot on Connor's GPS device. We finally reach the coordinates and begin looking around. Our search is short when Connor discovers a vintage-looking ceramic chicken, one eye painted closed as if he's winking and taunting us. We break him open back at the camper and Connor uncurls a handwritten recipe.

"Well, I'll be damned. Distilled white vinegar. Who the hell would have guessed that?" He makes that grin when he's amused by something, but it looks different to me this time. Something about his eyes doesn't quite look the same as when he makes that face at me.

We drop the guitar pick off to an elated Anton, and make our way back to the highway and toward the next leg in our adventure. I can't believe I'm hungry after eating the gözeleme earlier, but that's what fresh air and exercise does to me, I suppose. Connor insists he doesn't want a sandwich when I make one for myself, but he does manage to eat three candy bars, four lollipops and half of a bag of red licorice whips and then chew three pieces of bubblegum over the next two hours.

"You're going to be sick," I chide as the sun begins to slip down toward the horizon. The camper gives a little lurch.

"OK, fine, make me a sandwich then," he says, and moves into the right lane to pass a blue minivan.

"Are you sure? It's starting to get late now. Aren't we going to stop for dinner soon?"

"Check the maps app on my phone and see what's nearby," he says, sounding disinterested.

"The cell signal out here is kinda sketchy." I feel the camper make another little hiccup. "Um, should I be worried?"

"Not until a red or yellow light comes on the dash." Connor says, pointing to a space between the spokes of the steering wheel. No sooner do the words leave his mouth than the entire dashboard lights up like a Christmas tree.

"OK, you can be worried now," he says. "Look for a place to park this thing, will ya?"

I quickly scan the map and see a couple of small towns, each about ten miles off the interstate. "Nothing close. We'll have to leave the highway. I'm not sure about that, Connor. It looks pretty desolate around here. And I swear I heard banjos two miles back."

"It's not densely populated, that doesn't make it a crime scene. What are our options?"

"Mayo to the left or Cowpens to the right."

"You're serious?" Connor says, casting me a skeptical look. "Mayo and Cowpens? Those are real places?"

"Yep. Looks like there's some sort of campground near Cowpens, I think. Maybe we could head there?"

"Good idea. Type in the address, we'll let the nav guide us," Connor says.

We make a right at the next exit and amble onto a

country road. I watch the sun begin to shed her bright yellow hue of the day and slip into her amber evening dress. A hint of gold washes over the landscape making it look gilded and glowing.

There is a noticeable lack of any sort of structure that even remotely looks like a human dwelling and no street-lights. The area looks abandoned. Inner Miss Insecurity is visualizing all of those zombie apocalypse movies where the handsome warrior survives and his mousy sidekick gets eaten in the first five minutes of the film.

I glance out the window over Connor's shoulder and watch the sun sinking lower into the sky. When the sun finally slips away, it's going to be very dark. Are road bandits still a thing? Miss Insecurity begins to curl up in her corner. She's not rocking back and forth yet, but it can't be far off. She'll morph into Miss Angry Anxiety. Oh, please, not her.

"Isn't it beautiful out here?" Connor says, nodding to some hills in the distance. "Can you imagine if you built a house here, the sunset views you'd have every night?"

"Yep, right before the darkness creeps in and you're murdered in your sleep or eaten by wild animals." Or zombies.

"Lainey, stop. You're letting your imagination get the better of you. We're going to be fine. Look, there's the camp-ground. It looks nice. And the camper hasn't stopped yet. It's probably just a blown fuse or something."

"You think?" His voice sounds so confident, I find myself believing him even if everything he says sounds like a total lie. Miss Anxiety perishes, and I let out a long breath.

"Absolutely. Don't worry. We're together. I'll take care of everything," Connor reaches across the wide expanse of console space and gives my hand a quick reassuring squeeze. And just like that, I believe him. I do feel safe with Connor, and Miss Insecurity slinks back into her little room and soundly closes the door behind her.

We maneuver the camper into an area with a large sign declaring: the Cowpens RV Park, City Pool, Recreation Hall and Community Center, and follow the directional arrows to the tiny house serving as the rental office.

"I don't want to turn the camper off in case we can't get it to start again. So, you sit tight here, and I'll be right back."

I nod, but the look on my face must reveal I have serious reservations about being alone. I offer a smile, but it feels forced. Perhaps I should install a little lock on Miss Insecurity's door.

"You're good?" He asks, offering me that bemused little grin of his. My smile widens into something more genuine.

I nod again, a bit more convincing this time, apparently, because Connor slips from the camper and into the little house. I watch the numbers on the digital clock on the dash tick by, slowly counting out the seventeen minutes he's gone. I let out the breath I didn't even realize I've been holding when he emerges with a folded piece of paper in his hand.

"Good news, we got a space. It's near the lake, too. Otis, the owner, is going to drive out to help me get everything connected. I also called the RV rental company back in Atlanta and they're going to have a local mechanic come out and check everything over in the morning. But the guy on the phone agrees, it sounds like a fuse."

Connor expertly maneuvers the camper into our designated space. With only a few minutes of daylight left, and he and Otis move quickly to get the water and electricity connected before it gets too dark to see.

"There's a bathhouse about half a mile that way," Otis says, pointing down a dimly lit gravel footpath that meanders through a small cluster of pines. "And there's a little general store about a quarter of a mile in that direction. Just follow the signs. We're pretty full up tonight so you probably won't even need a flashlight. There'll be plenty of light from the other campers."

Otis thrusts out his swollen, weather-worn hand to Connor who shakes it gratefully.

"Thanks for all your help," he says as Otis climbs back into his electric golf cart and heads back to the rental office.

"So, how about we walk to the store and pick up something for dinner?" he asks. "I think you're right. I need more than Hershey bars and Red Hots."

"All right." I'm not sure if it's the temporary fear and anxiety I was feeling before or the increasingly cooler breeze that's blowing, but I need a sweater before we start toward the store. As we walk, Connor takes my hand and tucks it in his. He asks me question after question, forcing an endless stream of conversation between us about nothing important. By the time we reach the little camp store, I feel better. It doesn't escape me he's been keeping the conversation flowing to keep me out of my head and keep the door to Miss Anxiety shut tight. I give his hand a tight squeeze in appreciation.

The Cowpens RV Park General Store looks like something straight out of an 1870s western. There are huge barrels filled with candy, shelves lined with thick black rubber rain boots and walls of hooks looped with shovels, ropes and garden hoses. A separate section has a campsite setup complete with tent, camp chairs, tables and lanterns. While Connor shops there, I move into the grocery section. I grab some onions, peppers and apples. I can't resist a few fresh tomatoes piled in a high pyramid under a handwritten sign proclaiming they're from the world-famous Browns Farm of Cowpens. In the refrigerated section, I snag a package of spicy sausage from a local pork farmer and head toward the register. Connor meets me with a couple of flashlights and two bottles of wine.

"This place is so cute, isn't it?" I gush. "Could you imagine a restaurant like this? A grocery area filled with locally sourced produce, cheeses and baked goods. And a cafe right behind it using all those same things to make some yummy farm-to-table dishes." I yammer on and on with ideas for my imaginary restaurant.

Connor smiles and adds in a few ideas and questions that keep me talking while he consumes an apple from my bag on the walk back. By the time we reach our campsite, there are no traces that Miss Anxiety or Miss Insecurity even made an appearance tonight. A shadow of something braver starts to take shape in my heart. Ironically, it's the shape of a lion.

Our camper comes complete with an outdoor patio, which is where we decide to have dinner tonight. Connor unrolls the awning — not that we needed it in the early evening darkness — unfolds a couple of camp chairs and lights a fire in the little tabletop grill. In minutes, our onions, peppers and sausages are sizzling away, teasing us with the flavored smoke of the delicious meal ahead.

Connor pours wine into two red plastic cups and we sit and toast one another.

"This is my idea of camping," Connor says, first smelling the wine's bouquet after swirling it around in his cup. I don't know what he got, but it must have been expensive because I know my few groceries didn't cost anywhere near the eighty-five dollars he paid when we checked out with the cashier, but it's delicious.

"It's nice," I admit, slicing a tomato to add to our plates. I've also retrieved some brown sugar and cinnamon out of the pantry and cubed the apples, hoping the low coals on the grill will caramelize them enough to be a light dessert.

"Are those for after?" Connor asks, motioning to my apples.

"Yes, is that OK?"

"Perfect. There's some caramel ice cream in the freezer inside. Remind me to get it out when we're ready."

We gorge ourselves on spicy sausages, grilled vegetables, cooked apples and a huge scoop of caramel swirl ice cream. It was no seven-course feast by Anton Arnaud, but it was one of the top five best meals I've ever eaten. All five of which, coincidentally, have been since meeting Connor Rose. Inner Foodie pats her stomach in agreement.

From inside the camper, Connor produces a guitar and starts picking out a few songs that we sing together. It's easy to match a harmony to his voice and the juxtaposition of the harmony being in my higher alto voice gives the chords we create a cool folk song sort of vibe. We sound good together.

Eventually though, our voices tire and Connor turns on some music he has saved to his phone. This man has killer playlists. He drops it into an empty plastic cup and the echo makes it sound like full stereo around us.

"Dance with me," Connor commands. He offers me his hand and I can't refuse. We sway close, our bodies pressing together, his left hand at the small of my back and the right clutching my fingers lightly in his. I curl one arm around his shoulders and hold tight to his fingers with the other. Our bodies weren't this close when we danced at his birthday party just days ago, and I can't help but think it's not just our bodies that have gotten a bit more comfortable being closer.

Connor endears himself to me at a pace I can barely keep up with. In so many ways, we are strangers to one another. But in other ways, he knows me better than even Willow. He knows that my annoying habit of incessant talking is a coping mechanism for my anxiety and he doesn't make me feel bad about any of the insecurities that drive it. He's patient with me, understanding. I have to admit, I haven't had as much fun in my life as I've had since meeting him. He's like having my own personal advent calendar. Every time I turn around, he pops open a new door that leads to unexpected and wonderful surprises. Some small, some big, and all magical. In a matter of just a few days, Connor has won my heart.

"I guess everything did turn out all right after all," I confess. Connor gives me that little smile of his that tells me I've amused him somehow. I see the shift in his eyes and watch as the corners of his mouth curl up to meet them.

A low rumble of thunder interrupts the music. I'd noticed dark clouds moving in as we left Greenville, but didn't think they'd had time to follow us out this far. We ignore the interruption and continue to sway and spin and twirl together until the first fat raindrops start to fall.

I break from Connor's grip and see him laughing. "Grab the guitar and my phone. I'll fold up the chairs and get them under the awning."

It only takes a minute or two to complete the tasks, but when we're finished, we're soaked through. The downpour came fast and hard, dropping a curtain of heavy rain. I can hear the slosh of my sneakers and Connor's boots over our laughter when we finally burst into the camper in a mass of soggy clothes and dripping hair.

Connor looks down at me, my hair lying flat against my face, and curtains it aside. The pads of his thumbs rub gently under my eyes. I have no doubt he's removing the smears of black mascara I put on earlier that now runs down my cheeks in coal-colored rivers.

"You look like a drowned cat," he says through fits of laughter.

I look up, slightly affronted, and notice that he is no better. His hair looks darker when it's wet and hangs in long limp waves plastered to his scalp. The three-day stubble catches random stray strands that cling to his cheek and chin.

"You're a wet hen," I tease back and laugh so hard, happy tears start rolling down my cheeks.

"A wet hen? You mean wet cock, don't you?" Renewed fits of laughter begin and we both start toeing out of our shoes and peeling away wet socks. Connor can actually wring water from his. Which, of course, evokes even more laughter from both of us. I look down to see a puddle spreading around us on the linoleum floor of the camper.

"C'mon, let's get changed. We can watch a decorating show together," he says, and reaches for the buttons of my shirt, slipping the first through its tiny slit. Then the next. I feel my breathing go ragged as I look down and watch his large fingers undressing me. I allow him to continue until he peels away the wet shirt from my skin. It falls with a wet smack to the floor. I look up and our eyes lock.

In the time it takes a single streak of lightning from the storm to lick through the sky behind us, our souls hold a private conclave. Requests are made, permissions are granted, boundaries are removed, consent is given and it's done. And I am undone.

His hands cup my face and his body moves closer to kiss me. His lips are light and sweet. His tongue forces my lips apart and he delves inside my mouth, tasting of sweet wine and apples.

My hand strokes the back of his head and my fingers splay out through his wet hair. Gradually, smoothly, he unclasps my bra at my back. Cool air breezes past when he drags it over my shoulders and it, too, joins my top in the puddle on the floor. His fingers move to slip the button of my shorts loose and then tug easily at the short zipper. Thick thumbs hook into my waistband, sliding my shorts and panties down to my ankles in one slippery wet moment. I'm naked, chilled and burning at the same time.

Our mouths come together again as I pull at the hem of his T-shirt. He's too tall for me to undress standing up. He tugs his wet shirt up and over his head while I loosen the button and fly of his tan cargo shorts, watching as his stiff erection springs out toward me in eager anticipation. Christ, he goes commando? My Inner Sex Goddess already has her legs spread for the lion.

"Go to bed," he commands. And like before, I readily comply to the commands that I know are really his pleas for me to let go and let him make love to me. Tonight, I will face down my fears with the strength of a lion and let him. Oh, will I let him!

I stretch out on the bed and watch the silhouette of him enter the small sleeping area at the back of the camper. He's holding something small in one hand that I can't make out. Perhaps its the box of condoms?

"Condoms?" I ask nodding imperceptibly to his hand.

"No. Do you want them?" His voice is ragged and desperate.

"No. I have a patch, but if you ..."

"You're safe with me, Raven." His voice is just above me as his body looms closer. He kneels over me on the bed. "I promise."

"I know," I say as I loop my wrists around his neck and draw him down for a long, wet kiss.

His lips are on mine, his tongue, his hands all roving and touching. Tweaking, twisting, licking, sucking. My mind empties and I'm struggling to keep up with how he's taking me mind, body and soul. I close my eyes and try to feel him on me, but he's everywhere. His hands touch and stroke, bringing more of the wetness from inside me, which he spreads over the cleft between my spread legs. His mouth, hungry and urgent, suckles at my breasts and then devours my breath from my lips. I feel dizzy and dreamy.

"Raven," his voice vibrates next to my ear. His tongue licks the shell and he nibbles a tender place just below it that sends chills racing over my skin quicker than the lightning flashes outside and pounding of my heart within. Heavy sheets of rain drum on the roof and drown out the sound of its hammering.

"Are you all right, Little Bird?" His breath is heavy and scattered and I can hear the tension of his voice. "You have to breathe."

"Yes. Yes!" I try my best to breathe. His lips are on my nipples again, and I'm absolutely sure now that a woman can orgasm from being touched and kissed here because I'm about to. My body explodes and I cry out. Connor's body half lifts from mine and his fingers stroke lightly at my cheek. The sensation is brief, but powerful, and I recover quickly. Looking up, I see his bright shining eyes staring down into mine.

"Raven, did you just come?" His voice is breathy and feels so far away from me now. I can't feel his heat of it on my skin. He's moving away. I've done something wrong. I am helpless to stop it. Embarrassment and panic begin to creep over my skin in a warm rush. I'm grateful it's dark and he can't see the pink stain on my skin. I am too needy, too desperate for him. Is that a turnoff? Oh God, I've let my eagerness ruin everything. I don't want that. I want more. I fumble to find the words that will bring us back to that moment just a few seconds ago when everything was flame and heat and ... so damn good.

"I'm sorry," is all my pitiful brain can come up with. I close my eyes and hope it will be enough.

"Sorry? Shit, don't be sorry." I feel his fingers and thumb pinch my chin and hold my face to meet his eyes. "Look at me, Little Bird." When I do, he continues, "That's the most erotic thing I've ever experienced. You have no idea how wonderful you are, do you? Damn, Raven, you're amazing, absolutely incredible."

"I didn't think ... it's just you were touching me, and kissing me and I just ... I just ..."

"Exactly, Raven. It was perfect, baby. I loved it. I want you to feel safe letting go with me. I want this to feel good for you."

"Connor, I ..." I stop talking. I want him and I fear him. But the desire is far outweighing the fear. For one night of him with me, I'll suffer through the pain of it. I crave his touch, the feel of him inside me so powerfully no other thought can even inhabit my brain. This cannot stop. Not yet.

"You *are* safe with me, Raven. Just tell me what you want." His voice is slow, soft and feels like a warm breeze against my heart.

"You. I want you. So much." My lip trembles, working to control the tide of lust and need coursing through my veins. That one taste of pleasure wasn't enough. I want more. I need more. I'm an addict to the drug that is his mouth, his hands and his words.

I feel his fingers play lightly at my entrance again. A finger traces the tiny opening that is the door into my body, into my heart. It slips in and I brace for the pain of the invasion, but it doesn't come.

"Is this all right?" His movements are delicate but sure. All I feel is pleasure.

I nod. "Um-hmm."

A second finger joins the first and they probe further inside, spreading me slightly. The pressure is bliss. I let my legs fall apart a bit more. I want him to know I want more. I want it all.

"You're so tiny inside, Little Bird. I'm scared I'm going to hurt you."

"Just go slow, OK?" I breathe and force my breath to try to sound steady and even. I fail miserably. My body craves him with a hunger I can't identify or describe except to keep repeating that I want him. Want. No. It's so much more than that. So. Much. More.

People suffocating want air. Starving men want food. But the desire, the need for the thing that will keep them alive is so much more than want. It's an ache that if not relieved will mean the end of their own life. It's the ache I feel over my entire body right now. I ache for Connor.

He leans over and takes the tiny object he came into the room with off of the small table beside the bed.

"I haven't had time to warm this up. It's going to feel cold. But I think it will help us out. I'll still go slow and if you want to stop, you just have to tell me, OK?"

I feel his fingers touch me again and they're coated in some sort of slick liquid that is indeed quite cold. He rubs it against me and it heats with the warmth of our bodies in seconds. My body's awareness of his touch is heightened. My skin feels so much more sensitive to even tiny, imperceptible movements. His fingers slide into me again, and this time, the feeling is softer and makes me feel even hungrier for him.

"I like that," I murmur, trying desperately to remember the rules and tell him what I'm thinking and feeling. It's so hard when my body is screaming for me to just beg for him. "It feels good. Soft."

"Good. God, you're so hot inside. You feel amazing, Raven." His fingers pump in and out of me slowly, each time sinking further into my body.

I respond to his touch again, my body racing toward another climax. "Connor." I clutch at his shoulders and bring him to my mouth. "I want to ..." I can't finish, my hips buck and start a slow, rhythmic rolling as his fingers continue to slide in and out of me. He withdraws them for a moment and I whimper. When they return, they're slick with more of the lubricant he's brought to the bed with him.

"Don't chase it, baby. We'll get there. Relax and let go." His words. Oh, how this man woos me with his words. The tender gentle meaning behind them, the rough breathy way they sound, the heat of his breath on my skin. I feel the muscles inside my body contract again, releasing a flood of violent spasms that shake my body and force my back to bow, arching into his hand as a second, powerful orgasm claims me.

Connor lies on his side stretched out alongside me. His fingers fondle my breasts, the slickness of the lube and my own release coats my nipples as he rasps and strokes them. He's letting me recover again. Patient. Perfect.

"Come down a bit, Little Bird," he says.

I pant and feel my body begin to relax, the lube turning warm between my legs and at my breasts now. My body is satisfied, but the ache still pulses between my legs. I need more. Connor just grins at me, adoration making his blue eyes fairly glow in the dim light around us.

"You're not going to make love to me? Did I do something wrong? I'm sorry, I ..." His lips silence mine with hungry licks. His teeth capture my lower lip and he sucks it into his mouth, giving it a tiny nip.

"Shh, Raven, you're unbelievable. I've never been with anyone who is so sensual and so sensitive. I absolutely love it. I love it too much. You've got me ready to blow, Little Bird. Give me a minute to breathe or I'm going to ruin this for us. Understand?"

I swallow and lick my lips nodding, although my Inner Sex Goddess is ready to have a full-on tantrum.

"Is the lube helping?" He asks, kissing me softly along my

mouth, neck and shoulders. My body shivers yet I'm still burning at every touch.

"Yes. It's so good." His fingers begin their slow dance at my soaked entrance again.

"Good." His mouth presses the word into the flesh of my neck over and over again as he slides his body over mine. He coaxes my legs wide apart to accommodate his bulk. I feel the tip of his staff nudge at my opening. I lift my hips eager to feel him, wanting to have him inside me. Unafraid of it now.

"Slow. Don't rush. I don't want to hurt you," he whispers and nudges himself inside me a fraction. He moans even at this first contact that is barely more than a touch. "God, Raven."

He pulls back, then presses again, this time inching just a fraction further inside me. My mind clouds with sensation. My body stretches, my skin pulls. But instead of the pain, I feel only fullness. It's as if there's been something missing inside of me all my life, and I'm only now feeling the space fully filled with the one thing that was created to belong there.

Connor groans. "OK?" he asks for the tenth time. I know he's trying to be careful with me, but I can't wait anymore.

I lift my hips up and swallow him down inside me in a long, easy slide. When he's fully sheathed inside me, his body falls atop mine as if I have pulled his strength into me and not just his erection.

"Holy ... Raven ... Jesus." It's all he says in a loop over and over as he slides by fractions in and out of me.

"It feels so good," I whisper. "You feel good," I start my own loop of repeated words. My mind is incapable of anything else. We begin to rock back and forth with one another in a slow, steady rhythm. We're joined, coupled and locked together in a grip I never want to let go. I hold him inside me, pressing my knees around his hips and locking my ankles at the small of his back. He scoops my hips higher allowing me to take him deeper. He growls and then moans. The sounds have the same effect on me as his words.

"I'm not going to last much longer, baby. Damn." He groans into my neck.

"Don't then," I beg. I'm so close and I want us to come together.

We continue to rock, our hips rolling against each other in a seesaw that has me catapulting off of a cliff face and then hanging suspended in the air like a glider. I grip the lion and hold onto his mane as we find release together. The last sound I hear that rings through my ears is my own name — Connor's benediction, *Raven*.

# CHAPTER ELEVEN

**Friday, June 11**
**(but so early, it hardly counts really)**

A FLASH of lightning and a clap of thunder collide in the wee hours of the morning, jolting me from sleep. Outside the storm escalates and the wind rocks the camper back and forth a tiny inch as it blows. I slide out of bed and fumble through a drawer to snag a T-shirt and slip it over my head. The way it falls down nearly to my knees, I know I've found one of Connor's. It smells like him, and I can't help but smile. After cleaning up the pile of sodden clothes on the floor, I dig out my cell phone and check for weather advisories. Surely, some sort of evacuation notice would be issued if any serious storms are predicted. Outside the window near the small banquette, I can see lights on in a few other camps nearby. So, apparently, we're safe. For now.

I push open the fridge and take out a bottle of juice. The soft yellow appliance light illuminates Connor's sketch pad left in a dark corner of the bench seat by the table. I pick it up and flick on the flashlight of my phone. Turning on the overhead light would wake Connor and, after his fitful night last night, I want him to rest.

I flip to the last page and what I see astonishes me. The sketch is undoubtedly me. Pencil lines mesh together in what looks more like a painting than a sketch. The artwork is exquisite. I study my face the way Connor sees it. My eyes are closed in sleep, my hands tucked under my face. I'm smiling slightly, but there's a worried little crease at my brow that leads me to believe that even when I sleep, I'm never really at ease.

Flipping the page, I see myself nude standing in a waterfall, or is it a shower? God, but he's been kind to the shape of my body. My breasts are fuller than I would have drawn them, my hips curvier. My ass is perfect. Is this how he sees me? It's quite a departure from the way I view myself, and I'm slightly embarrassed. I never realized how much he admired and desired me. My Inner Sex Goddess has awakened and is dumping buckets of dampness between my legs. Connor Rose, the most beautiful man on this planet, thinks *I'm* beautiful.

I flip a few more pages and see sketches of lions. Faces of them from every angle. Incomplete designs, partial faces, only lion eyes. I examine pages of them, realizing they are his tattoo. He drew it. It's totally amazing.

I flip a few more pages and see the face of another woman. She is most assuredly *not* me. Her eyes captivate me the most. They're set slightly further apart than on most faces and are narrowed, giving her an almost menacing gaze. She looks at something far in the distance. A lock of hair is drawn as if it were flying across her face in the wind.

I flip back to the picture of me in the shower. I'm looking straight into my own eyes. So are the lions. But she's not.

There are more sketches of her. Dozens of them. She's lying on a bed, wrapped in a tangle of sheets. She's reading.

She's outside with a flower of some sort. Most of them are of her nude. She's gorgeous. The sketches are all just pencil, blacks and whites and grays. But I get the sense she was blond, with light eyes. She's got high cheekbones, perfectly shaped brows and full lips. Her breasts are huge.

But I keep coming back to the last sketch of her. Her full face, nothing more. Her hand lifted and resting on top of her head. Elegant and thin. Dark, mean eyes that look convicting somehow. I cock my head to the side and wonder how a woman so beautiful could look so angry. And who is this person to Connor?

"Shana," I hear Connor's voice say from the entrance into the little bedroom area. I snap the sketchbook closed and fumble to turn off my phone's light.

"I didn't mean to wake you," I stumble over my own voice. "I'm sorry."

Connor walks slowly to the table, picks up the sketch-book. He glances down before he hands it back to me. "Go ahead. Look."

I shake my head, feeling as though I'm being punished for my invasion of his privacy. "I didn't mean to upset you or to pry, I just wanted to see the sketch of me in the park and ..."

Connor tosses the sketchbook back onto the table. It slides off and back into its place in the shadows of the banquette. "Did you see it?"

I nod slowly, hoping the flashes of lightning will illuminate his face enough for me to discern what he's thinking, what he's feeling, but it doesn't. I have seriously overstepped here. I panic searching for a way to make it right again. Nothing comes to mind. Nothing except fear. A terrible fear that I've ruined everything. Again.

"What did you think?" he asks, his voice still giving nothing away.

"You're an incredible artist. The tattoo, you drew that, didn't you? The lion?"

He nods slowly and sits in the passenger seat in the front of the RV. It's turned to face the living space now instead of out ahead through the dash. He's still naked. Still stunning. His fingers rake back his long hair from his face. I can't see his expression through the veil of darkness, but I know he's looking intently at me. He expects me to say something, to ask the questions that burn in my throat, but I can't. Even I know what I did was a violation, and I have no right to know.

"You can ask," he says softly. "But there are things I can't tell you. Not yet."

"Are you still seeing her?" Anxiety and insecurity invade my lungs and force the words out in a rush. I pray his answer is no. I want to be the only woman in his life. I'm not equipped to compete with anyone else. I'd lose.

"No." His answer is quick and I let out a relieved rush of air from my lungs.

"She's beautiful," I tread delicately. My knees tremble. I feel like I'm confessing to every sin in my life and I've been found guilty wanting for excuse. "I'm so sorry if I upset you. Please forgive me, Connor."

"You didn't upset me, Lainey Bird." His voice is barely above a whisper, but something about hearing his little nickname for me puts my heart a bit more at ease. "If there's something you want to know, ask now. I don't know when I'll be able to make you this offer again."

I stand there for several long minutes, trying to think of what I really want to know. "What is she to you, Connor? A lover? A girlfriend?"

"Shana was my wife."

Every bit of air is instantly sucked from the room. A vacuum has been created in its wake, and is immediately filled with doubts and fears and questions too numerous to be identified. My heart begins to pound. No matter how intimate we've been with one another, I am forced to face the reality that I really know almost nothing about this man, and he knows almost nothing about me. We are nothing more than friendly strangers keeping our secrets hidden — letting each other only fall for the parts of us we want to be seen.

I let his words roll through my mind, trying to put them together. *Shana was my wife.* Was? She's not anymore.

"Do you have children?" I stammer.

"No." His tone sounds sad and detached.

I swallow and press with one more question. "Do you two still talk to one another?"

"There was a time when I visited and talked to her often, but she stopped listening. So, I quit going."

"This is painful for you, isn't it?" I pry.

"Was it painful for you to tell me about Jemmy?" he snaps back.

Touché, Connor.

"Yes, very. That was a difficult part of my past I want to just forget. Is that what Shana is for you?"

He nods. "Yes."

Connor lifts his hand, beckoning me to come closer to him. I slowly close the distance on trepidatious feet. "Those sketches are from years ago, Raven. She's not a part of my life anymore." His fingers begin to stroke in soft circles over my back.

"You don't want to talk about her, do you?" I already know the answer to this question.

Connor shakes his head and his fingers glide up my waist, over my breast to the neckline of my T-shirt. "Never."

"I stole this," I say, unable to let the silence get a foothold. I nod down to the shirt I've got on.

"A thief and a spy," Connor *'tisks'* with a click of his tongue. "I'll have to keep my eye on you, Little Bird."

He lifts me slightly and readjusts me on his lap so that I'm straddling him. He leans up and kisses me hard and deep. He's hungry and needy. Heat radiates from his skin. I feel need welling inside me, too. I need to experience the closeness we shared again. I need to know I haven't ruined whatever this is that's growing between us. Because I like it. No, I love it.

I wrap my arms around his neck and shift my hips closer, nudging my damp opening over the tip of a hardening rod that rises up between us. I want him to know I understand.

"I need to be inside you," he growls in command. "Can I? Please."

I sit up slightly on my knees and grip him in my fist. Slowly, I lower my body onto his. The inside of me is slick from desire, the lube and the seed he spilled earlier that night. He's thick and my skin is slightly sore, but the feeling of him entering me is wonderful beyond words. I groan as I take all of him inside me.

"I need you, Raven," Connor says, almost breathless. I know what he's telling me. He wants to forget all of the painful memories I've dragged up. He wants to get lost in pleasure and passion until his body empties all its sadness and anger inside of me. He needs me to take his pain. I need him, too. I need him to need me like this. I need to love him like this. Sex is about giving, not taking. All I want to do is give myself to him.

My head nods and I feel him tilt his hips upward, shifting himself higher into me. He's long, thick and his thrusts are powerful, coming in hard, quick movements. His large hands grip my backside, spreading me open and lifting and lowering me down on top of him. His pace multiples.

I am forced to grip the chair behind him for balance as he works faster inside me. I start to climb with him. His body slaps against mine in hard claps now. His fingers dig tightly into my flesh and I feel him get closer and closer by the second. Finally, with a primal cry, he comes inside me, hot wet spurts of himself find their means of escape — even if just for a moment.

His mouth returns to mine and he kisses me gently, deeply. My hands drop to his chest as I slowly pull myself off of him, but he grabs my hands and presses them to his chest. He angles his forehead against my cotton-covered breast and I feel his shoulders shudder slightly.

Warm wetness dots over my breast. I close my arms around him, drawing him close while his tears come softly and quietly for several long silent minutes. Outside, the storm begins to subside, and I can't help but wonder if the ones that rage inside of him ever will.

His cheeks are still damp when his mouth returns to mine and he carefully lifts us off the chair, my legs still clinging around his waist. We walk a few steps and he drops me to my feet. His body never stops touching mine even though we walk separately into the bedroom area. He holds my hand, taking me back to bed.

We make love again. Slowly this time. Over and over, with kisses and tender touches, until our strength is gone and the night is spent.

# CHAPTER TWELVE

**Friday, June 11<br>
(however, with actual daylight)**

I CAN'T GO BACK to sleep. I lie for long hours, listening to the sound of Connor's hard breathing and cadenced snoring before I finally get up and head out to the general store. Maybe someone there is up early and I can grab some stuff to make breakfast.

I read a book once, in the days when my heart was raw from pain and hurt about the way I show love and the way I like for love to be shown to me. Turns out, I'm a person who shows love with acts of kindness. Apparently, it's also how I offer my contrition, too. Making breakfast is the perfect way to show how sorry I am for violating Connor's privacy last night. Although he seemed OK after we'd had sex, I worry he was angry. Shana wasn't a subject he'd voluntarily brought up. I cannot possibly imagine what sort of a breakup they'd had to create such hard feelings. Connor, with all his as yet unknown parts, doesn't seem to be the kind of person who'd overreact to a breakup.

I am happy to see the store opens at seven, and go in to gather some ingredients to make breakfast back at the Minnow Bucket. I hope that the old adage about "the way to a man's heart" includes scrambled eggs and bacon.

"What's all this?" Connor asks. He tugs on a T-shirt as he steps out of the bedroom. For a split second, Inner Sex Goddess reminds me that the beautiful man standing in front of me made love to me all night last night.

"Breakfast. I thought I'd feed you for a change," I almost get up from my seat at the small table, but he stays me with a hand.

Connor ties his hair back in a messy bun and then uncovers the dishes I've prepared, laid out for him in the small kitchen area. "Scrambled eggs, bacon, tomatoes, fruit." He crunches on a slice of bacon and hums, "Looks great."

"There's coffee, too, but you'll probably want to heat it up."

"You didn't have to do all this, Raven." Suddenly, I don't like my name again. I miss him calling me his Lainey Bird. "But I appreciate all the trouble you went to. Thank you."

He piles the food onto his plate and comes to sit across from me at the small table.

"When will the mechanic be here?" I ask, filling the silence between us. The awkward, painful silence.

"Around nine." He glances at his watch. "Any minute now, I guess."

"I want to shower before we get back on the road."

"Sure thing." Connor swallows a bite of eggs and reaches over to take my hand. My fingers trace the circular rim of my paper coffee cup. I drop my hand into his and feel the warmth of his touch rush through my entire body in an instant.

"Hey," his voice is soft and my eyes lift from where our hands are joined to look into his. "I need to tell you that last night was incredible. I said you're wonderful, but you're way more than that. Are you feeling all right today?"

I nod, but don't speak.

"Did I hurt you, Lainey?" he asks, fear behind his eyes.

"No."

"What is it? Do you regret sleeping with me? The sex, I mean."

I shake my head. "I regret prying. Connor, I'm sorry."

"Do you regret it because you don't want to know what you now know about me, or because you're afraid I'm upset with you." Connor Rose nails me again.

"I'm scared you're angry with me," I confess, adding depth to the emotions.

"I'm not. I've been worried you'll want to turn around and go home now that you know I was married once and it obviously ended in disaster. I am not proud of that part of my life, Lainey Bird. I don't talk about her."

"I don't care that you were married, Connor. Shana obviously hurt you very deeply. I hate that I brought all that pain back up."

"It's been buried too long," Connor says. His fingers close tighter around mine now. "There's a lot I want to tell you. Someday. But it's hard for me. It's still hard for me to talk about what happened."

"It's OK. You're not obligated to tell me anything," I offer.

"That's not what I want with you. Sharing our secrets, our pasts, that's what brings us closer, isn't it? And I want that with you, Lainey Bird. I want 'closer' with you."

We're interrupted by a tap on the camper door. "That's the mechanic." Connor gives me a reassuring smile. "Hit the showers. We'll leave as soon as he's given us a good once-over."

Connor disappears down the steps outside and I can hear

the two men talk, then Connor on the phone with someone. I slip into the tiny shower closet next to the bed and try to wash away all the doubts about myself that seem to loom around me. Connor wants closeness with me. He was worried I'd want to leave. Reliving his past with his ex-wife brought him to tears. I never want that again. But he's right. I want to know more about who he is. I want the closeness knowing everything about him will bring.

But closeness, which I hope means relationship, also means I have to tell him my secrets, too. Relive the humiliation and pain of what happened. Reveal all the ways I'm too broken and damaged to ever be worthy of him. I already feel my heart surrendering to him, but I can't. Not yet. Maybe not ever.

I wash quickly, dress and clean up the food. By the time I'm done, Connor pops back into the camper. "Minor repair. We're good to go."

"What was it?" I ask.

"I'm not even going to pretend I'm the guy who can tell you with any level of understanding what that man just did, Lainey Bird. There were wires and some kind of a screwdriver and bada boom, it was fixed."

I giggle at that. Seems Tarzan has his inadequacies, too.

"So, we're heading out?"

"Yep, it's my turn in the shower and then we're off. I don't suppose you'd want to come in and wash me like you did back at the spa in Georgia, would you?"

"No room. You're barely going to fit in there. Try wedging that monster dick of yours in there all hard and eager, and you might get stuck." I give his behind a loud smack.

Connor grabs me and pulls me tight against his chest. "Monster dick, huh?"

I nod and smile, feeling his sleeping monster already

beginning to morph into the ravenous beast that took me countless times last night. "You've seen it right? You know."

"Hmm. I kind of like that. And he definitely likes you." He kisses me and I know he wants to restore things to the way they were before I went snooping. For that, for this, I'm grateful. So, for now, Miss Insecurity is put back into her room.

"I can see that," I say. I press my pelvis into his hardening rod. It sends a growl up through the lion's chest and into my ear. "Go wash the one-eyed monster and try not to get stuck in there. I'm going to finish cleaning up."

Connor's hands grip my ass and squeeze me. He presses me into him again, forcing that sensitive cleft between my legs to feel that beautiful steel under his shorts. I fight back the urge to moan.

"Where are we going today?" I say, trying to wiggle out of his hold before we end up back in bed again. As much as I would love it, I don't think my underused lady parts could handle more of that monster right now.

"If I get my wish, back to bed." He kisses my neck and nips at the base of it, sending shocks through my body that settle low in my belly.

"Connor, I can't anymore right now," I confess.

He kisses me, deep and hungry. "Later then?"

I nod and he hugs me tightly before undressing right in front of me and then walking down the short hall to the shower, teasing me with a glimpse of the monster and then my lion. My Inner Sex Goddess is officially in love.

It's quite dark by the time we arrive at our next campsite in North Carolina. In practically no time, Connor has the RV set up while I unpack our little patio space. Our campsite has a metal firepit and the campers who used it last left a small pile of cut timber we can burn for a campfire tonight. I have a small blaze going when Connor finishes and joins me.

"The Minnow Bucket is all settled in for the night," he proclaims. "We have a big day tomorrow."

"What are we doing tomorrow?" I ask, stabbing a large marshmallow onto a long stick. I found a bag of them inside along with some peanut butter cups and graham crackers. Connor Rose really did think of everything.

"Surprise." The sly grin on his face says everything.

"I'll need to know what to wear." I taunt him.

"Shorts. We'll be outside. It's going to be hot. And bring a swimsuit. You packed one, right?" Connor lets out a puff of air that extinguishes the marshmallow he's lit on fire before popping it into his mouth.

"Three," I confess. He rolls his eyes at me in the glowing dance of the campfire. I sandwich a perfectly toasted marshmallow between layers of crackers and a peanut butter cup and hand it to him. "Here."

"What? I didn't know where we were going. I wanted to be prepared." I lick a dab of melted chocolate from my thumb and stab another marshmallow onto my stick.

"What the hell is this?" he asks, glaring at my culinary creation.

"It's a s'more. You had all the ingredients, surely you meant to make them?"

"Yeah, but you've got a peanut butter cup on here. What fresh hell is that? You've bastardized a classic."

"I have not! You haven't even tried it. I've elevated a classic. Shut up and eat your s'more."

"Elevated a classic?" he says dubiously.

"Eat it."

He opens his mouth and stuffs the entire thing in, chewing slowly. He tries to hide his reaction, but I can tell he likes it.

"See?" I boast triumphantly, rolling the stick in my fingers to evenly brown another marshmallow.

"Whoa," he exclaims, finally swallowing. "Amazing! The peanut butter gives it just the right amount of salt so it's not too sweet. How did I never think to do that before?"

"You've just got to trust me," I say, lifting my right eyebrow. "I'm no Anton Arnaud, but I can make a mean s'more."

"Trust is a funny thing, Little Bird," he contends, shoving another s'more into his mouth. "It requires a person to feel safe."

"You don't feel safe with me?" I counter. My tone is meant to sound teasing, but honestly, I'm a little hurt. I honestly felt that we did trust one another and feel safe together. How are we having sex and not? Aren't those his rules?

I sandwich another treat and hand it to him. He takes it, but doesn't eat it right away.

"I do," he says, a peculiar smile gracing his lips. It's not the amused grin he typically gives me. Its meaning is deeper. "I need to know you feel safe with me, Raven."

"I thought those were the rules," I echo, the thought already racing through my head.

"Yes, but I'm still nervous," Connor confesses, and offers nothing more. He tosses the uneaten dessert into the fire, then douses it and goes inside to bed. I linger outside for a few minutes longer, replaying our exchange in my head, and then join him.

An odd tension swells between us as we take turns brushing our teeth and changing into pajamas. When I turn off the light and enter the bedroom, Connor is propped up on pillows on our queen-sized bed. It always looks so small with his large body stretched out across it.

As he does each night, Connor invites me to curl up on his shoulder. His fingers slowly stroke the hair at my temples. "I do, you know," he begins out of the blue.

"Do what?" I ask, feeling my eyelids drift closed. My fingers are at his chest, toying with his nipples. I feel them harden, but sex doesn't seem likely. His mood is heavy somehow.

"Trust you. Feel safe with you." He lets out a long breath. "I need you to know that."

I nod my face against the skin of his bare torso, but offer no words. Words here feel wrong somehow. Connor needs peace and quiet and space.

His tone is darker than usual, and I'm nervous about where this conversation is going. I offer a long moment of silence. Then he begins speaking. His voice is low, just above a whisper and it sounds pained somehow.

"I met Shana at a *Climax* concert," he begins. "I was between deployments, home for leave, and playing roadie for Ox so I could earn some extra dough and spend time with my family. She was a typical groupie. Blond, big tits and willing to do whatever a man wanted for a chance to spend a week with a popular rock band. We spent two weeks of the tour together, most of that in bed."

This tale makes me extremely uncomfortable. I don't want to hear about his sexual escapades with his beautiful ex-wife. I wiggle to get away, but Connor keeps me close, pressing my body to his, forcing me to hear it all.

"When I deployed again, she wrote to me. I'd call her sometimes, and we kept our thing, whatever it was, going until I got home. I thought I was in love with her, and she said she loved me. I proposed and we got married six months later. The wedding was this huge ordeal. Her family had money and threw this amazing party. We went on a honey-moon to the Caribbean and never left the hotel room. That's pretty much all the good parts of our whole marriage."

I sense why Connor needs me close now. His fingers stroke my shoulder. The more he talks, the faster he strokes. This conversation is painful for him. But he wants me to know. He wants the closeness that telling me will bring and he trusts me with it.

"I'm sorry," I mutter, not knowing what else to say.

"She bitched constantly," he continues. "She went on tour with Ox and Tori and drove them so nuts, Ox told me to come get her. She got wasted every night. I had to pick her up one night and drag her out of another man's bed. I wanted to kill him, but I knew Shana started it.

"We always fought. Nothing I did was ever good enough. She hated I always had to go away, and I hated it more. Because I knew that when I was gone, she wasn't alone. Our bed wasn't empty when I wasn't in it. We stopped having sex. I couldn't even think about putting my dick into a place where I had no idea who'd been there before me. She disgusted me, and I disappointed her.

"Then, I got orders to go to Afghanistan. It was a bit of an unusual assignment. Usually, my whole unit would go, but this time, it was just a small detachment of us. Shana was pissed at first. Right before I left, though, she came to me crying, and she said she was sorry about all the men. She wanted to make our marriage work and promised she wouldn't stray again. I told her when I got home, I was going to start the divorce process. She was still crying when I left. It was the first time I'd ever made her cry. I felt like shit. My mind wasn't on the mission. I missed so much I should have seen. I should have seen it coming.

"Our mission was to support a spec ops team there for a simple snatch and grab. We were there to snag a professor who was being used to build a nuclear weapon for a particularly nasty terrorist group. He was supposed to meet his mistress at this hotel in a real shithole of a town. My team was there with a group known as the Heathen Brotherhood. Badass group of men. I'd follow those guys to hell if I had to. The whole town was eerily quiet that night. Even for the middle of the night. We all felt it — something wasn't right.

"The Brotherhood formed a column and headed inside the building. One of their guys, Tex they called him, was on overwatch from the building next door. My unit was there strictly for cover and we were scattered in a perimeter a few hundred yards from the hotel. We could hear chatter on the comms as they talked back and forth and they seemed to be clearing their checkpoints easily. Then, without warning, there's this explosion. The blast went straight up. Tex was knocked off the top of the building. How he survived, I have no idea. Fire, smoke and falling chunks of concrete landed everywhere. The other men from my own unit were too far back. It was Tex and me, working to get to the other members of his team.

"Some were blown to nothing more than mist and water. We found random parts of others. We only found two men who were in one piece. And they were both alive. Tex couldn't move their bodies, he was wounded. But even limping with a broken leg, he managed to give me cover while I dragged them out. Bad guys descended on us like vultures on a gut truck. We were taking serious enemy fire. The Delta guys we hauled out were both unconscious. I tried to get them to wake up and move, but they couldn't. I threw one over my shoulder and hauled ass. Then, I went back for the other one. They both survived. But I was seriously fucked up.

"I was burned pretty badly on my back and actually took a round to my leg, but I didn't feel it until the medics arrived. I spent two weeks in a hospital bed down the hall from three guys in the Brotherhood and six men from my detachment. The guys I pulled out were in there a lot longer. The whole time I laid in that hospital, all I could think about was Shana. I blamed myself for her affairs. If I'd only been there, she wouldn't have needed to go anywhere else. I'd failed her as a husband, and I was wrecked. I decided to go home and make things work."

"What happened?" I ask. Tears streak down my face. I can hear the emotion in Connor's voice as he relives the gruesome events he's just entrusted to me.

"When I got back, I called her to come pick me up, but she didn't answer her phone," Connor relays painfully. "A buddy of mine drove me home. Her car was in the driveway, but she didn't answer when I called out her name from the foyer. I searched the whole house. I found her in our bed.

"She was dead." The words echo around us in the quiet darkness, bouncing off the walls and ceiling only to come stabbing us in the heart over and over again like a ricocheting bullet.

"The sheets were soaked with her blood. There were empty pill bottles all over the floor. She'd cut her wrists. And she had my pistol next to her on the pillow in case that hadn't worked. It was my birthday. And my wife killed herself in our bed. On my fucking birthday!"

I audibly gasp. My stomach clenches in a sudden burst of roiling acid. I feel physically sick.

"There was so much fucking blood." Connor's voice breaks. Torrents of tears tumble down his troubled face. I just hold him tighter. His arms cling to me as if it is to the last vestiges of sanity he has. I don't know if there's more to his story, and honestly don't know if I'm strong enough to hear more. But I sit quietly, letting him finish.

"She was pregnant, Lainey. The baby wasn't mine, and she didn't even try to hide it. She put it right there in her suicide note." He's shaking now. "She tried to see if there was anything left between us before I left. And I'd told her I wanted a divorce. The baby's father didn't want anything to do with her. He denied it was even his. She didn't want to have a baby alone and said she couldn't believe I'd want to raise it with her since I didn't even want to be married to her anymore.

"I spent two more weeks in the hospital after trying to wrap my car around a tree doing eighty-five drunk on tequila. Ox and Tori put me there. A rehab place for broken people. I was as broken as they come. It's taken a long time to climb back from that hell, Lainey. Five long years. And I can't even bear to think of her face in that damned sketchbook. I don't want you to see her ugliness. I don't want it to touch you. But now you know. You know what a fucked-up man I really am. I failed her. I failed those men. I failed them all."

Neither of us speaks for a long time. I'm numb. But I can't judge. Not after what I had done. Not after everything that happened at Juilliard and then with Jemmy. I want to tell him I understand that level of pain. I've lived in that hell, too, and sometimes feel like I still am. But I can't. It's all too much. I want to give him my truth, my compassion and whatever comfort he needs. But there's nothing I can give him. Nothing but me, and my own brokenness.

# CHAPTER THIRTEEN

**Saturday, June 12**

HE'S IN A REFLECTIVE, contemplative mood the next morning, trying to push past all he told me last night. I'm at a loss to help him, so I don't try. I pretend to sleep as the sun rises slowly, illuminating our tiny sleeping space in the Minnow Bucket. I keep still and listen to him inhale and exhale. I hear him text on his phone for a while, then lay it aside. He curls his body next to mine and spoons against me tight and close.

"Are you sleeping, or are you playing possum over there?" he whispers so tentatively, I can barely hear him.

"Possum," I reply.

"You're so quiet. It's starting to scare me a little. Look, Raven, if you want to go home, I can get you a plane ticket today."

I roll over quickly and silence him with a long, wet kiss. "Connor, I don't want to leave. What you said last night doesn't change anything except that I feel ... I feel more connected to you." We are connected in a way I can't even describe to him — not yet. We're both bound in our pain, working to try to find normalcy in a life that has given us anything but for a long time. I suddenly don't feel alone anymore. I don't feel scared.

"I'm honored, not upset." I close my eyes, let out a long breath, then open them again. Staring into his dark blue pools, I whisper, "Do you want to end this — our trip, I mean?"

"No. But I need to know you feel safe. That you are here because it's what you want, Lainey Bird. I need to know what you really want."

I swallow. For the first time in my life, I know exactly what it is I want. And it is staring at me with two of the most hopeful navy-blue eyes I've ever seen. The deepest depths of my lovely lion.

"I want you," I whisper, barely audible. His mouth closes over mine and we fall into a thrashing mass of limbs and kisses and strokes and deafening heartbeats. He strips me naked and then tugs down his shorts, freeing himself.

"Roll over," he commands. I twist onto my stomach. He lifts my hips slightly and arranges two fluffy pillows under them. I feel his hand slip between my legs, parting them and spreading warm lube, which we've taken to calling our joy juice, over my already slicked entrance. The sensation is instantly overwhelming and I arch upward into his caress.

"You want this?" he asks, already knowing the answer and nudging the rounded tip of his erection against my entrance.

"Yes." My Inner Sex Goddess is on her knees begging.

"You know the rules, Lainey. I need to give, not take. What do you want me to give you?"

I twist my head around and kiss him as he inches inside me. "Give me all of you, Connor. Everything you are right now. Whatever it is, I want it."

Connor's body presses down over me. His hands cover mine and our fingers fold together curling into lovers' fists. His hips begin a slow tap against me until he's filling me completely. From behind me, he feels even larger than he did before and it's nearly overwhelming. I moan and he stills.

"Talk to me, Little Bird. Am I hurting you like this?" His voice is strained as he works to steady his control.

"No. I want more, Connor. More, please," I gasp.

I can hear the smile in his voice as he promises he'll give me everything I want. His body resumes its thrusting. It escalates quickly, growing harder and faster. I lift and lower my hips in time with his movements and we crest together in mere moments. The feel of him inside me is an explosion of sound and sensation.

Connor growls and then rolls off of me to curl my sweat-slicked body back against him like two spoons again. His softening manhood stays tucked inside me. He swipes the hair off the back of my neck and begins to feast on my flesh there, nibbling and sucking. His stubble has turned into a soft, short beard. I love the feel of it against my skin.

"Raven," he says, and kisses my shoulder. I wait to hear him say more, but he doesn't. He just holds me quietly holding next to him. He doesn't have to say anything else. He doesn't know it yet, but we are born of the same fire.

"I know," I answer. Because I do.

"Are you coming or what?" I squeal like a child. Connor has just handed me two tickets to King's Mountain theme park. How I missed seeing the snaking roller coasters and water-slides on the way to our camp spot last night, I can't imagine.

I guess it really was quite late and rather dark. But they're here before me now, twisting and curling in ribbons of steel. They look like smiles curved in a promise of thrills and adventure.

"And here I was thinking you'd be scared of riding a roller coaster," Conner says. He's got that amused little smirk on his face again. I'm so happy to see it. It spreads into a wider smile that threatens to morph into a full-blown laugh at any minute. I love it.

"Oh, I totally am," I admit, my voice overflows with child-like enthusiasm. "Isn't that the fun? Being scared to death, but knowing you won't actually die from it?"

"I suppose so." Connor hikes his backpack up onto his shoulders. We have our swimsuits, sunscreen and flip-flops inside it along with a few candy bars for Connor. Seriously, this man and his candy addiction!

We enter the park to the sounds of the whoosh of a roller coaster swinging overhead. The smell of cotton candy and deep-fried corn dogs permeates the air even though it's barely past ten. We are among the first to arrive. The sun is already scorching and I'm thankful our passes grant access to the attached water park. We'll be ready for that later.

"Where to first?" I practically bounce on my toes as Connor studies the cartoon-looking map of the park we received at the entrance gate with our colored wristbands.

"Here." Connor points to a place not far from where we're standing. It's marked with a huge glossy-black bird with a single yellow eye and wedge-shaped tail that issues a silent warning. "I saw this ride online and knew we had to come here."

"You got us tickets to ride just this one ride?" We're walking through the park and I stop short when we get to the end of the queue for the coaster. It's called Raven Flight. I can't stop laughing.

We click selfies of us waiting in line. Connor entertains himself by trying to grope my breasts and behind and fool those around us into thinking that he's swatting a bee or flicking a hair from my shirt. It's become an elaborate, playful game by the time it's our turn to be seated in a car.

The seat I climb into is suspended from the top of the ride. Belts are strapped between my legs and over my shoulders and waist before a heavy bar locks down over my head. My heart starts to race and I grip the bar over me. Miss Insecure is in full-on panic mode, but a new smaller character is being born at the same time. She's all fun and laughter and thrill and playfulness.. Miss Adventure, welcome to the world. I put her in charge for the rest of the day. #bringiton

The ride begins its slow ascent and I feel the floor slope away, leaving my feet dangling in midair. The long, loud ticks of the ride bring us up to the crest of the first hill and in a moment, we slip over the edge and slide downward into what appears to be empty space. My chair tilts and I'm in a superman pose, facing the ground, watching it race beneath me in a blur of color and sound. I let out a laugh and look over to see Connor with his arms outstretched and his eyes closed.

I put my arms out and our fingers touch. He takes my hand and we are flying. We arch upwards, twist to the right, and then quickly back to the left again. We repeat this zigzag back and forth a few more times before arching up back toward the sky again. And then we careen down into a loop, coming face to face with first the ground and then the sky. The ride finishes with a corkscrew that leaves me breathless and laughing before we finally lurch to a stop right where we began. We're forced to wait a few seconds while riders ahead of us disembark. The ground slopes back under my feet and I am thankful for the delay. I need my wobbly legs to firm up before I attempt to walk.

"Wow!" I say as we exit, my muscles still twitching and trembling from the adrenaline rush.

"So, you liked it?" Connor says, raking his long hair back into a sloppy twist at the nape of his neck.

"No," I begin tugging at his arm to reenter the queue. "I loved it! Let's go again."

We ride Raven Flight three more times before tackling a log flume, a runaway train ride and finally a slow spin on a giant Ferris wheel.

"OK, so food?" Connor queries as our car tips, suspended nearly at the top of the wheel.

"You and food," I chide.

"I'm hungry. Someone had me working up an appetite early this morning." His hand snakes up the hem of my shorts and tickles at the center of my body with his thumb. I clench when he hits a delicate spot where the tiny knot of sensation is covered by a stretch of blue cotton and lace.

"Hmm," he leans over and kisses my neck. "I know what I want for lunch."

I smile and bend my neck to allow him better access to continue kissing my throat. "You do?"

"Yes. This," he whispers. His thumb caresses softly again and I feel his fingers snake under my panties. I wiggle in my seat and adjust my posture, giving him access to what he wants. He starts to stroke slowly inside me with one finger, then two, working at that needy little nub with this thumb. Our chair swings and we lurch forward, one car away from the apex of the circle.

Connor continues his kneading, the movements slightly faster now. I bite my bottom lip and let my body surrender to his touch. Miss Adventure and Inner Sex Goddess are an unbeatable team.

Connor nips at my neck and kisses me while my body

starts to squirm. When we reach the top of the wheel, I reach my top, too, and curl into a ball as I dissolve into spasms against his fingers. He kisses me long and hard before removing his hand from my panties. I watch as he puts his fingers into his mouth and then sucks on them. And just like that, Miss Adventure has an orgasm. And now she, too, has fallen hopelessly in love with Connor Rose.

"Sweet," he says, before kissing me again. The next time our car moves, we make a complete circle before we stop at the bottom and the door pops open to let us out. I'm exhilarated.

We opt for tacos and then head toward the water park. Connor has reserved a private cabana for us that includes a tiny bathroom — even smaller than the one in our Minnow Bucket — and two plush loungers under a canopy of shade. I slip in to change into my bright pink string bikini, ready for a dip in the pool.

I chose this bikini over the other two for blatantly obvious reasons. It's not the skimpiest one I brought, but the halter top has molded foam padding that makes my B cups look like Cs. And the bikini bottoms hug my cheeks like a couple of baseball mitts. Truthfully, even Miss Insecure likes what she sees in the mirror.

"I hope that water is cold," Connor says, gawking shamelessly at me when I reemerge. "I'm going to need it. And you're not going to sleep much tonight when I'm finally able to get my hands on you."

"It's not only your hands you want on me, is it?" I tease and shrug nonchalantly as I dive into the pool.

"No," he affirms and dives in after me.

In the shower, I discover not only red patches from overexposure to the brutal summer sun, but a couple of tiny little nip marks along my breasts and inner thighs. Connor practically attacked me as soon as the camper door closed behind us. He tore off my swimsuit, and demonstrated his proficiency in his version of the breaststroke before I managed to get into the shower. Despite his urgency and desire, he never forgot lube and asked me several times if I was OK. I was better than OK. Twice.

I take my time in the shower, letting the cool water soothe my sunburn and the tender ache between my legs. When I emerge, our little table is spread with a cloth. Candles are glowing and an unmistakable aroma of garlic, basil and Italian spices waft throughout the Minnow Bucket.

"Connor, what is all this?" My stomach rumbles.

"Dinner. You have got to be starved. You've barely eaten anything all day." He lays pillowing breadsticks onto the table.

"I am," I acknowledge his thoughtfulness. I sit across from him and feel the sting of his invasion as I do. I wince, not realizing I've even done it.

"Raven, are you all right? Is it sunburn?" he asks sharply. When I don't respond right away, he narrows his gaze and adds softly, "Did I hurt you, baby?"

My eyes shoot up to his. "No," I reply instantly. "Well, yes. Just a little sore from so much sex after going so long without it. Pass the salad, please."

"Raven?" His blue gaze fixes on me and feels like cold steel pressing into my heart. "Baby, there are rules. You're not obligated to give anything. You're supposed to tell me ..."

"Connor. You are amazing. I love being with you. Everything feels good. Really, really good. You have my word that if I don't want it, you'll be the first to know. Now, the salad, if you please."

I swear a low growl of disapproval crawls up from his throat as he hands me the salad and then loads my plate with pasta, sauce and a delicious eggplant parmesan.

# CHAPTER FOURTEEN

**Wednesday, June 16**

THE NEXT THREE days fall into a predictable pattern of driving, junk food, sharing stories, driving, more junk food, listening to good music, more driving and more junk food. Each night, Connor and I conclude our bedtime routines by falling asleep cuddled together. The only change is that Connor has switched from his usual decorating shows to cooking shows.

We've also seemed to work ourselves back into our no sex sleepover arrangement. Other than a few passionate kisses, Connor has made no effort to make love to me. I'm shocked to discover that I'm not the least bit concerned that I've done something wrong this time. I know that he's battling his own insecurities that come as a result of what happened with Shana. And, I know part of his hesitation comes out of deference to me as I was a bit sore "down there." He wants to be a good man to me, and I'm letting him.

I make sure to keep his candy stash replenished, and give

him playful pats and touches to remind him he's very much desired and his efforts are appreciated.

On the fourth day, we turn off the highway and onto a dirt road that seems to lead to the middle of nowhere.

"Our campground is pretty far off the beaten path, isn't it?" I comment. It's a passive-aggressive way to ask where the hell we're going, I know. But I know Connor understands I'm curious, but I don't want to second-guess him.

"We're staying with some friends of mine tonight. I hope that's OK."

I sit up in my seat. I've spent the last hundred miles leaning back with my feet propped up on the dashboard. How Connor sits rigid and upright in that driver's seat all day is beyond me. He can't even stand up straight inside the Minnow Bucket. No matter how many times I offer to drive and let him stretch out, he insists he is enjoying himself and politely declines.

"That's great. Who are we meeting?"

"Morris and Georgia Krazanski."

Something in his tone clues me in that these people are more than casual friends. "How do you know them?"

"Dr. Krazanski is one of the therapists who helped me when I was recovering from the death of ..." he stops, not even wanting to utter her name. I get that. He has no idea how much.

"She who shall not be named?" I say, trying to diffuse his pain.

"Yeah. I like that. Thanks. Dr. Krazanski said if I was ever in the area, I should stop by. I texted a few days ago and she and her husband insist on meeting you."

So, Morris Krazanski, as it turns out, isn't the doctor in the relationship. His wife Georgia is.

"I'm honored," I admit. And it's not a lie. I am honored.

"Really? Because we don't have to go if you'd rather not."

"They just want to meet me, and see you. You obviously have a friendship with her; it's not just doctor and patient with this woman, right?" I'm guessing, but the look on Connor's face tells me immediately that I've nailed it.

"Exactly. I thought I'd have a harder time getting you to understand that. But then again, you're not ..."

"She who shall not be named?" I say, this time with a bit more boldness.

"You really are wonderful, Lainey Bird."

Morris and Georgia Krazanski are undoubtedly the cutest couple I've ever met. Their farm is at the crossroads of the Ends of the Earth and the Middle of Nowhere. I swear, there's no cell coverage and they must have to pay to pipe in the sunshine this far off the beaten path. But their house is cozy. Every nook and cranny is filled with some little knick-knack or another. Every piece of furniture has a hand-crocheted doily on it. The wallpaper is floral, the furniture threadbare and the camaraderie amazing. I can see why Connor obviously cares about these people so much.

We're greeted on their front porch with a rolling cart of cocktails. Morris mixes up Cosmopolitans tonight. Apparently, every "cocktail of the day" is different. The drinks are sweet and strong. Miss Adventure throws back a second before I remind her that we can't go overboard in front of Connor's friends.

Morris is a slight man of around eighty with not a single hair on his head. He wears a wrinkled smile that never fully fades and has bright twirling eyes that look like sparking coal dust against his dark tanned skin. Dr. Krazanski, Georgia, as she insists I call her, is a stout woman with fluffs of gray hair that mostly stay in a loose wispy bun on the top of her head. Her full figure is wrapped in a flowing rayon bag of floral material and she laughs so frequently and with such genuine gaiety that it's impossible not to laugh right along with her.

"My goodness, Connor, you look wonderful. How have you been doing?" Georgia asks as we plant ourselves on their front porch and watch Morris mix up his next batch of Cosmos.

I notice Connor sits on the edge of his chair like he's anxious about something. Literally on edge somehow. He reaches over and takes my hand in his and holds it tight. It's hot and clammy. I suddenly realize he's nervous. About me? About what she'll say? Am I here for her approval? Perhaps it has nothing to do with me and everything to do with reliving the horror of Shana's suicide.

"Good. The restaurants are all doing well, and I confronted the manager of the *Day Old Bagel* like you suggested, and I think things will be better going forward."

"Good to hear. And, of course, there's this happy addition to your life." Georgia winks at me.

Connor squeezes my hand. "She's wonderful," he says and I smile at the familiarity of his words.

"How did you two meet?" Morris asks, offering to refill my glass. I shake my head and he moves to sit next to Georgia, which is directly across from Connor.

When I glance over at Connor, he gives me that adorable amused grin of his and he starts talking while still holding my gaze for a few long seconds.

"She got drunk in my bar and passed out. I took her home," he says.

"I see," Georgia replies with a light chuckle.

Morris laughs out loud and adds, "Her home or yours?" he asks, refilling a glass for his wife.

"Mine," Connor says, blushing slightly on his neck.

"I see. And you two have been sharing that little camper, what did you call it, Connor?"

"Lainey named it the Minnow Bucket," Connor grins. Georgia lets out another of her light little laughs.

"Well, I have two rooms made up for you two. You can get some space from each other tonight."

"Lainey and I sleep together. But it's your house, Georgia. You and Morris get to make the rules." I blanch at how candid he is with these people about the details of our relationship. It's probably just second nature to him to share everything, especially with the woman who used to be his therapist. But even for me, the Queen of Oversharing, it's a bit embarrassing. It's probably implied we're intimate, but does it have to be advertised?

"Ah, yes, the rules. I suppose we should review those, shouldn't we?" Georgia says, playfulness in her tone.

Connor's face loses a bit of his cheer with those words. "Nah. No need."

"Good. Well, you two must be hungry. How about I feed you something other than candy bars and gummy bears, huh?"

I laugh at that. Georgia casts a clever little wink my way before adding, "This man has a serious sugar addiction. He really needs therapy, you know."

She, Morris and Connor all laugh at the joke. I'm happy they can infuse some levity into Connor's past recovery. I know he seems well now, but I promise myself to ask Georgia if there is anything I should be watchful for. I want to be able to help Connor in whatever way I can.

Connor carries up our suitcases after dinner. I'm so full I can barely move.

"Morris wants to take us riding tomorrow. Do you want to go?"

"Riding, like on motorcycles or on horses or what?"

Connor grins, amused by me again. "Horses, baby. Want to go?"

"Yes, I'd love it."

"Great. I'll go down and let him know."

Connor is gone for more than an hour and I am already

changed and snuggled under the light hand-sewn quilt on the big brass bed when he comes back upstairs and sneaks into my room. He strips out of his clothes and slides between the covers. I feel his warm body curl around mine. His warm, naked body.

"Lainey?" His voice is a whisper, and he no doubt wants to let me stay asleep, if I am. But I'm not sleeping.

"Hmm?"

Rather than reply with words, I feel his hand snake up from my hip, slide under my top and gently caress my breast.

I hum in appreciation of his touch.

"I'm going crazy wanting you, baby" he whispers softly.

I twist in his arms and lie flat on my back. His fingers skate lower and dip under my panties.

"You haven't acted like you've wanted sex the past few days," I comment. His fingers lightly tickle at the moist area between my legs. "I'm not complaining, it's just an observation."

"I know. I feel really bad about that night after the theme park. I suppose I was a bit too rough. I wanted to give you a few days without me being a greedy bastard."

"You're very good to me," I whisper. His fingers begin to tease at my entrance.

"I want to be a little bad tonight." His finger slides easily into me. "Can I be a little bad, Raven?"

I hum my consent and he strokes me slowly, a second finger now having joined the first. "Christ, you're already so wet. Stay here. Don't move."

Move? I can barely breathe. I ache for Connor's touch inside me like a lioness in heat.

I know where he's gone when I hear a bag zip open and he rummages around inside to find the joy juice he uses on me when we have sex. God, I love that stuff. That tiny little bottle could have saved me so much discomfort with Jemmy.

And I'm reminded of just how little he actually cared for me. That feeling hurts.

Connor smiles and lunges toward me, the lion ready to devour his prey. And I pray I'm the prey. My Inner Sex Goddess is ready for him to completely devour me.

Connor spreads our joy juice over me and then positions himself on top of me. I spread my legs and wrap my knees around his hips, drawing him inside me quickly in one long, smooth motion. He gently eases out and then presses forward again with a rough thrust. The bed gives a mournful creak and the headboard rattles against the wall, tapping it three times.

Connor and I both start laughing hysterically, forcing one another to keep quiet.

"I think Georgia is punishing me for sneaking in your room to share a bed with you," he whispers. "The place is rigged. No sleepovers is a house rule, and I'm breaking that. We need to be quiet."

"I can be quiet, but I think the bed is going to give us away," I manage to say between giggles.

"We'll save naughty for later. I'll be gentle, and it'll be ... good clean fun," he says, kissing my ear. "I do want you so badly."

He eases out of me and then slowly reenters my body while the bed gives another hard tap against the wall and squeaks out a loud protest. This time we laugh slightly louder and Connor rolls off of me with an annoying groan of frustration.

"Looks like it's Madame Thumb and her Four Merry Mistresses singing you to sleep tonight, stud," I laugh. Connor rolls onto his side and tickles me, kissing me until we're both restless and wanting. We don't make love, but the connection we make just enjoying one another like this, honestly, is as intimate as if we did.

# CHAPTER FIFTEEN

### Thursday, June 17

"Her name is Sweet Caroline," Morris says, handing me the reins of a beautiful bay chestnut. I immediately start to hum Neil Diamond's song with the same name. Connor gives me that little amused grin of his. I softly rub the velvet of her the mare's nose and begin to whisper sweet nothings to her. I'm reminded of the times Willow and I spent riding horses at summer camp when I was a kid. Get ready to giddyup, girl!

"You're going to be sweet to me, aren't you beautiful Caroline? We're going to go for a little ride today. It's going to be hot, but so much fun."

"I wish you'd whisper in my ear like that," Connor says playfully. "I'd give you a hell of a ride, baby."

I give his shoulder a tough punch and he pretends to wince, but I know granite can't feel pain. And that's what his shoulder feels like it's made of.

"You two randy lovebirds cut all that out. All that squeaking in that bed last night was enough," Morris groans as if he's exasperated. He winks at me which puts me at ease.

Morris is one of those people who tease as if he's serious and you never quite know if he's truly angered and offended or just genuinely giving you a hard time. This morning, it seems, he is definitely giving Connor a hard time.

"That damn bed is the world's best cock blocker, Morris. What happened to the other bed? The one I slept in when I lived here? It didn't squeak."

My ears prick at these words. Morris helps me up into the saddle. When I find my seat, I chime in. "You lived here?"

"Yep. What, like three or four months, wasn't it, Connor?" Morris says, scratching his head to jog his memory. "Georgia taught him to cook and he was a big help with the animals. The chickens adored him." Another wink. Ah, so this is ribbing Connor again. I smile.

"Chickens?" I ask with a playful chuckle.

"Demon poultry, not chickens. That rooster spurred me every chance he got. I guess he didn't like me touching his ladies." I laugh out loud at that.

Morris and Connor throw their legs easily over their horses and we set out. The sun blazes down with intensity and the humidity is stifling. I'm so hot, but it's too humid to sweat. The stickiness clings to my skin like a wet wool blanket. Connor pulls his hair up into a neat little man bun that sticks out of a ball cap. I am not as smart and pick up my hair feeling long strands of it cling to the back of my neck. I need air. A breeze, something.

"Where are we headed?" I ask Morris, who seems to be allowing his horse, Apple Eater, to amble wherever she wants to go.

"I thought we'd see if the fish are biting down by the stream. You fish?" Morris asks.

"Never have before, but I bet I could figure it out. Which direction?" I call back to him a horse's length behind me.

Morris nods his cowboy hat-clad head in the direction of a

line of trees a good distance away. "All right, I'll see you two slowpokes there." I give Sweet Caroline a little click of my tongue and a tap of my heel and work her into a nice canter. She's got a graceful gait that my spine naturally falls into. I prod her to go a little faster and she's eager to run. The breeze picks up and I'm finally cooling down by the time we reach the water.

Morris calls this a stream, but it's more like a river to me. The water doesn't look like it's moving too fast. I lead Sweet Caroline down and she takes in a long drink. I pull off her saddle and let her sweat-slicked skin cool under a shady tree. "You're making me look good today, girl. Enjoy a little clover snack. I'm going to cool off, too."

I kick off my shoes and socks and wade into the water up to my thighs. It's cold and moving a bit more swiftly than I first noticed. My white T-shirt is splashed a bit by the water dancing off of a cluster of nearby rocks, so I turn to make my way back up to the shore. I see Connor and Morris dismount and lead their horses for a drink. I smile and wave at them. Connor's face morphs into sheer horror and the color drains from it.

"Don't move, Lainey!" He's screaming at me. I freeze. I know without even looking there's something in the water with me. Something dangerous. I have no idea what it is, but Connor's face has paled to a light shade of greenish-yellow that immediately twists my stomach into knots.

"Connor?" I plea.

"Hush. Close your eyes. Don't move," he instructs in a straightforward and authoritative voice.

I can't close my eyes. I'm too scared to move any part of my body. I watch as Connor slowly pulls a pistol from his back and points it just to the left of me, close to the cluster of rocks. My eyes do close then as he takes his aim and squeezes off a single shot. I shriek and scream, curling myself into a ball as a hard splash of water spits over me. My arms and hands cover my head protectively.

I scream again when something strong and stiff comes around my waist and I feel myself being hauled out of the water. My feet are scooped up and loud splashes erupt around me. Blood pounds in my ears. My heart beats like a kettle drum.

"I've got you, Little Bird. You're OK. Just a snake. You're OK," I hear Connor's voice soothe as he carries me up to the tree where Morris comforts the three horses. They're less startled by the gunshot than I am. I guess on a farm they hear it more.

I'm crying, more out of sheer terror than of being hurt. Connor's hands drift over my body and he smooths the hair from my wet face, brushing it back out of my eyes.

"Hey, baby. Look at me. You're OK. Did I hurt you?" His eyes scan me from top to bottom over and over again.

I shake my head no, but honestly, the feeling hasn't come back into my skin yet. It's still tingling with numbness from the sudden onslaught of adrenaline. My hands shake as I reach out and cling to Connor's forearms. He presses his forehead to mine.

"Jesus, that scared the shit out of me." He kisses me hard, and with more emotion than I've ever felt from him before. His lips tremble slightly. He kisses me like I nearly died. I didn't. Did I?

"Wh ... What was it?" My teeth chatter, but I'm not cold.

"Cottonmouth," Morris says, striding from the water with a dead snake clutched in one gloved hand. His head was severed by the shot, but the length of him still curls and twitches as the last bit of life leaves his body. Morris holds the venomous creature up over his head and his tail drags, disappearing below into the water. A bite from that beast would have killed me before we could have gotten back to the house. I shudder and bury my face in Connor's shoulder. I did nearly die.

He squats down beside me as I try to regain my equilibrium. I see the gun on the ground by his foot. "That bothers me, put it away, please," I say, nodding to the gun.

"It can't hurt you, Lainey," Connor says, moving to pick it up.

"Just put it away," I demand, feeling silly for my sudden fright of guns. I've never been scared of a gun before. Not that I've ever even been around one before.

"You're just spooked. I'll take you back to the house," he offers.

I shake my head. "No. I know my way. You two stay here and fish. I saw a bunch of rods and things up river a bit. I'll be fine."

"I don't want to leave you."

"Just help me get Sweet Caroline's saddle back on her. My hands are shaking."

"I'll do it. You just get her settled so she can ride, Connor," Morris says. He's tossed the snake back into the water and I watch its now lifeless body floating away in the fast-moving current.

In a half hour, I'm back at the house. Donovan, a farmhand, takes Sweet Caroline and promises to turn her out for me. I head back inside and guzzle down two huge glasses of water and try to breathe normally. Georgia finds me in the kitchen.

"You're back so soon? Fishing's not your thing, is it?"

"Fishing is fine. Snakes aren't my thing," I manage.

"Jesus, did you get bitten?" She lays a hand on my back and does the same eye scan Connor did, checking for signs of a bite.

"No, thank goodness. Connor shot it. I guess it was good that Morris gave him a pistol to carry."

"Morris doesn't own a pistol, honey. Shotguns, a revolver, yes. But no pistol," she says, shaking her head. "But Connor is never without his."

"You mean he's had a gun with us in that camper this whole time?"

"Probably. That seems to bother you?"

"Well, it's just, well ..." I let my voice trail away. Connor isn't dangerous, but guns are.

"You worried he'll go crazy and try to hurt himself or something? You don't need to be. Connor isn't a danger to himself or anyone around him."

"No, no, of course not," I stutter.

Georgia pulls out a chair at the tiny kitchen table. The worn yellow Formica tabletop feels cool on my arms as I plop down into a matching lemon-colored vinyl chair.

"How long have you and Connor known one another?" she asks. "I know it's none of my business, and you're not required to answer. I'm just curious."

"Not long. We met and started this crazy journey five days later. We've been traveling for just over two weeks."

"Oh, that's a long time," Georgia says, nodding knowingly.

I cock my head to one side and stare at her. Three weeks is hardly any length of time to really know someone.

"You think I'm nuts to say that, but I promise you it is a long time. You two have been together for three weeks, basically 12-hour days, not to mention nights? Well, that's like 42 dates. If you think of a six-hour date, usually twice a week, that's like you and Connor dating for ..." she pauses to count on her fingers, "four or five months. Most couples know whether they're going to be together for just a while or forever for a lifetime after about that long. Especially at your age, dear."

"I guess I've never thought about it like that," I admit.

"And living with someone in such a tight space. I'm sure

he's driving you crazy by now." Georgia offers one of her light-hearted laughs.

"The candy thing is ridiculous," I confess. "I mean, it's nonstop. And there are wrappers everywhere."

Georgia laughs her sweet, light laugh again. "I used to find little stashes all over the house. It's a comfort food for him, I guess."

"He told me what happened to him ... with Shana, I mean," I confess. I want her to know what he's revealed to me. I hope she can help me understand him more fully.

The smile fades from Georgia's face. She lifts an eyebrow. "Did he?"

I nod. "He said he was really messed up for a long time. Morris said he lived here with you for a while?"

"He stayed with us a while," Georgia confirms. "Connor wasn't really as messed up as he was lost. Trust me I know. Really, he just needed time to process everything that had happened to him. He needed to come to grips with the fact that Shana had her own problems. He could never have helped her — no matter how good of a husband he was to her. And, if you ask me, he was a good husband to her. Much better than many I see come through my practice. Well, used to see. I'm retired now."

"He didn't want to go home?" I ask.

"Connor was battling more than just the loss of his wife, Lainey." Georgia hesitates.

"He told me about Afghanistan, too," I divulge, feeling a heavy sadness dump into my heart.

"You two have shared a lot," Georgia reaches out and taps my fingers with hers. "Connor's sister and Ox are good people, but they only want to baby him. Connor doesn't need to be babied."

"I can understand that," I admit. "He needs to feel useful,

strong. I think he needs to feel like he can be there for someone else. Is that right?"

"Exactly right, dear," Georgia says. "You seem to understand him quite well. His struggles with PTSD will linger with him for the rest of his life. It's something he has to take day by day. That's what he learned here with us. At least, it's what I hoped he learned."

"It was nice of you to let him stay here," I acknowledge.

"Nonsense. That man worked himself to death, practically running this farm on his own once he got the hang of it. Managed the seasonal help we hire during harvest time. He was useful and felt needed, which he was. I taught him a few of my favorite recipes, too. Lord, that man can eat!" We both laugh at that, knowing it's no exaggeration. "He bragged on my cooking, told me I should open a restaurant. I told him to take his inheritance and open his own restaurant. He was welcome to my recipes."

"The tomato pie is yours, isn't it?" I inquire.

"You've had the tomato pie? Yes, only he uses basil instead of thyme. Was it good?"

"Very. They're serving it at the *Day Old Bagel*."

Georgia nods. "I'm glad. Does he still work himself to death?"

"Yes. He plays hard, too, though. Most nights I feel like I'm passing out, not falling asleep. I'm so tired. I can't keep up with his energy." I blush slightly, imagining what she must think when I say that.

"There are rules, Lainey. I hope Connor has explained that to you by now. You should always feel comfortable saying what you're feeling and asking for what you need. If you want a break, ask for it."

"Oh, he did. I didn't mean about sex," I divulge. I can't believe I'm talking about this. "Sex with Connor is incredible. He's very passionate and he cares for me. He always takes time to be sure I enjoy everything. He's considerate, but not so gentlemanly that he doesn't get to enjoy himself, too, if you understand."

Georgia laughs and stands up to pour the last of the coffee from the carafe into a nearby mug. She dumps a puddle of cream into it and then sits down again, still chuckling to herself.

"I didn't mean in bed, dear, although it's good to know you two are enjoying a healthy sexual relationship. I mean with you two being in love with one another. The rules are for life and love, not just for sex."

"Oh," I flush, a bright crimson spreads over my face. "Sorry. Overshare. I'm working on that. But we're not in love."

"Nonsense. I know love when I see it and you two are most definitely in love with one another. Connor is for certain. Hasn't he told you already?"

"What? No. I mean ... we don't really discuss our ... that is, we don't really talk about how we're feeling." I say those words and then quickly realize it's not true. We're constantly sharing our emotions through the stories of our past, the music we play, small touches of affection and all the little quirky nuances that have come to make up the routine of our travels.

"Connor has invited you on this journey. He cares for you. You two enjoy one another sexually. I see the way he looks at you. He can't look at you and not smile. He's very much in love with you, Lainey."

I grin when Georgia mentions his smile. "All of this time, I thought that little smile just meant he was amused by me."

"So, you've noticed it, too. You have your own little tell-tale signs, you know. The way you look at him, and always light up when he touches you. It's more than being new lovers. You're in love with him too, aren't you?"

In love? With Connor? Georgia's words seem obvious and yet at the same time, I'm stunned to hear them. I care for Connor, and I love being with him. I feel safe with him and I've told him more of my past life than I've shared with anyone except Willow. We understand one another. He totally puts up with my need to talk incessantly, and even uses it to help me cope with situations that make me feel nervous or uncomfortable. And the sex is amazing! But when we're together, it's more than just a physical thing. I feel like he's really and truly loving me and I'm loving him.

Holy crap! I'm totally in love with Connor Rose. My eyes widen and my head suddenly feels dizzy. How could I have been so oblivious?

Georgia smiles warmly and gives that little light giggle that makes her so endearing. "You're good for one another," she says. "Something tells me that all the broken pieces of your heart fit exactly into the shattered places left behind by his own tragedy. And that's really what we're looking for in love, isn't it? It isn't about fixing someone's broken heart. It's about filling in the cracks with your own love. The love that's left over from pain and loss."

"How did you know?"

"That you've experienced pain and loss?" She laughs at me now. "Everyone has, dear."

"How do I do that? Fill in the broken spaces? When he needs me or has a nightmare, I don't know what I should do."

"He's still having the nightmares?" She tisked at that. "Oh, poor Connor. He seems angry when he's triggered, I know. But really, he's just scared. And big, burly Army rangers with tattoos and that tough biker look don't get scared. And that scares him, too. It's a vicious cycle. Just hold him, dear. Tight and close. That's all he needs. To know he's got no reason to be scared."

"Thank you, Georgia," I say quietly. She picks up her coffee cup and half walks, half waddles to the door.

I head upstairs to take a long hot bath. I want to think about what Georgia has said to me. By the time I'm dried off, dressed and back downstairs, reading a copy of interior design magazine I found in the living room, Morris and Connor have come back from riding and fishing. A long string of fish is clutched in Connor's fist. His face cracks into a wide smile. It's the same amused little grin I used to just enjoy — but I see it now. He does love me. And I love him.

Dinner with Georgia and Morris is at 4:30 in the afternoon. By 5:30 p.m., they've dozed off in their recliners in front of a baseball game they're watching with the sound turned off. I have no idea where Connor has disappeared to. I spend an hour cleaning candy wrappers out of the Minnow Bucket and wash a couple of loads of laundry.

"Hey, Lainey Bird," I hear Connor's voice call from just outside the camper. I poke my head out and give him a big smile. "What are you doing?"

"Searching for candy wrappers. It's a fun game, wanna play?" I taunt.

"I know, it's a terrible habit. I can help you clean up." He pops up the two camper steps and pulls me to him. He kisses me. His skin is so warm and he smells like sweat and sunshine.

"I've got it. What have you been doing?" I ask. Knowing Connor, he is probably working on something special for Morris and Georgia before we leave tomorrow.

"Setting up something for us to do. You wanna go, or do we need to finish here first?"

"I'm done here. I just want to get the clean linens back on the bed, but I can do that later. What did you set up?" Miss Adventure is intrigued.

Connor just gives me his sweet smile and a wink. "You'll see."

We walk hand in hand through a wide meadow that Connor explains will be cut for hay for the horses for winter. We stop by a piece of broken wooden fence where a line of empty cans has been set out about three or four feet apart.

"What's this?" I ask, pointing to the cans.

"You're going to learn to shoot."

I spin on my heel with a hearty "hell, no." Connor grabs my arm and spins me back around.

"Hell, yes. Lainey, I didn't like that look on your face today. I know the snake really freaked you out, but if I had to guess, I'd say my pistol did more. It's not some sort of a trigger of a bad memory or something, is it? No one you know has been hurt by a gun?"

"No, but they're dangerous. They kill people." I think about the fact that Connor has probably killed people in battle. I instantly regret what I've just said. I bite my lip and feel the heat of an embarrassed blush wash over my neck.

"This gun has never killed a single person. People kill people Lainey, and they don't need guns to do it. Trust me."

"You've killed people." It's not a question, but he answers anyway.

"Yes, I have." His gaze is stern and almost warns me not to take this conversation further.

"Guns scare me," I confess.

"I know. And this pistol is in our RV all the time. If you ever need to use it, I want you to know how. So, I want you to feel comfortable."

Before he hands me the gun, he releases the magazine inside containing the bullets. He slides back the top half of it and a final bullet falls into his hand. "It's not loaded." His index finger slides to the trigger and he pulls several times, demonstrating the weapon won't fire.

"Just hold it," he says, offering it to me.

I take it in my hand. The metal is warm where Connor has been gripping it and it's a good deal heavier than I imagined it would be.

Connor takes his time to show me all of its features, the magazine release — never call it a clip, he warns. Clips are what girls wear in their hair. The slide release, the double safeties, the sights. The thing is much more complex than I originally thought and I'm now very impressed at people who can master it.

Connor hands me two tiny earplugs and tells me to keep my sunglasses on. I stuff the foam pieces into my ears and can now only hear the sound of my own breathing. It's hollow and echoes and suddenly, bam! The shot comes much too hard and much too fast. Connor loads the pistol again, takes aim and pulls off a single round, flicking one of the cans from the fence rail.

Then, to my horror, he hands me the gun. It's much heavier now and I need two hands to hold it up, where Connor just uses one.

"Hold it here," he says, adjusting my hands around it. I am shaking. "That hand position where you look like you're holding a teacup in a saucer looks cool in the movies, but if you hold a gun like that in real life, the slide is going to come back when you shoot and bite you." He pinches the tender skin between my thumb and index finger, showing me where I could potentially get hurt.

"I don't want to do this, Connor," I beg and I know I

sound like a girl. Even Miss Adventure hides out with Anxious and Insecure right now.

Connor's eyes bore into mine. "I'm right here. Nothing is going to happen. Take a deep breath. All I want you to do is squeeze the trigger. Don't try to aim for anything."

I hold the pistol the way he's shown me and squeeze my eyes shut as I pull hard against the trigger. The weapon explodes in my hand, sending shock waves rippling through my arm. The recoil has kicked my arm nearly straight up and I've lost my balance. The entire experience is much more violent than I imagined.

Connor stands, hands on his hips, grinning and then laughing at me, not with me, the same way he did when I shot back the sipping whiskey. Miss Adventure has just been issued a challenge. She comes out of the corner, dusts herself off and is determined to show this man no fear. I like this chick. #gunslinger

Make no mistake, there's fear. Lots and lots of fear. I'm just determined not to show it.

"OK, quick draw, you've done it. We can end the lesson here today." Connor holds his palm out to take the weapon back. But I shake my head.

"Again," I demand. "Tell me what to do."

Connor quirks a brow and the teasing fades. A more serious expression materializes across his face. "That's my girl."

For the next fifteen rounds, I shoot. Connor stands slightly behind me with his hand on my back, issuing directions into my ear. By the time I'm done, I've learned how to load and unload the weapon, and I've even hit two of the cans on the fence rail.

"You're a hell of a shot, Lainey," he says, pulling the foam from his ears. "If I ever nearly get bitten by a water moccasin, I'm going to let you kill it for me. I'm really proud of you."

"Thank you," I say a bit shyly, realizing I never thanked him for killing the cottonmouth before it bit me. Morris had told the story to Georgia over dinner and said the snake was just inches from me and had its mouth open to strike. Apparently, it had been sunbathing on the rocks and didn't appreciate my interrupting his afternoon repose. Hearing those details made me shiver, and I was thankful Connor changed the subject as soon as the tale was done.

"I just hope you're not afraid of guns anymore. This was really more about you facing something you're afraid of than really learning to shoot. You know that, right?"

"I do. It's not that. I mean, yes, I'm thankful for you teaching me, but I was referring to the snake today. I never said thank you."

"Lainey, I've never been so scared in my life. I can't think about not having you in my life. If anything had happened to you ..."

"But it didn't. You made sure of that."

"I'll always make sure of that, Lainey." He kisses the top of my head and stands holding me while the cicadas chirp and mosquitoes buzz in our ears.

We clean up our mess, close up the RV and head back inside and upstairs before nine. Connor joins me in the shower that night, bringing us both to orgasm so quickly that my head spins. He says he is desperate for me. I guess he is. He also promises me that he doesn't care if the camper rocks or squeaks, he is going to take me again tomorrow, and the next day, too. My Inner Sex Goddess marks her day planner with bright red hearts.

# CHAPTER SIXTEEN

**Friday, June 18**

TURNS OUT, the red ink doesn't even have time to dry. We are less than fifty miles from Morris and Georgia's house the following morning when Connor stops the camper at a rest area. Without a word, he leads me to the back bedroom area and spends more than two hours licking, kissing and petting me so seductively that I climax three times before he finally lets himself go inside me.

Boneless and pleased beyond anything I'd ever felt in my life, I sleep for the next three hours until we stop at our next destination in Richmond, Virginia.

"I'm glad you got a good nap earlier," Connor says, as I finish dressing in our hotel room in Richmond. "We're going to be out pretty late. I'm used to the hours, but I know you're not. You nearly turn into a pumpkin at the stroke of nine."

I laugh at that, but he's right. The few nights we've stayed out late, it's been a struggle for me to keep my eyes open and I always have a horrible sleep hangover the next day.

Although he refuses to tell me what tonight's surprise is, Connor insists I wear something sexy, yet casual. I try on the last of three outfits. This one earns me a lascivious look — my clue that I've finally achieved the right balance between a vixen and an angel. Turns out, that look is a pair of tight jeans, heeled ankle boots and a red silk tank. Connor has me wearing it backwards so the deep V is now in the front and shows more of my décolletage than I have ever dared to bare. I pull my hair up into a loosely braided twist and add some black leather earrings with this cool hippy fringe. I have to admit, I like the way I look.

I give myself a long once-over in the full-length bathroom mirror. I look the same. Same brown hair, same eyes, same thin figure. But I know that the girl staring back at me is not the same as the one who left on this trip with Connor. I've eaten at five-star restaurants, been on geocaching adventures, ridden wild roller coasters, danced, camped and lived more in the past week than I have in the last ten years of my life. And the reason is standing just outside our hotel room in the hall, waiting to whisk me out for another amazing night. The man I love. The man who has helped me to become a woman I love, too.

I take one look at him by the elevators and my mouth goes instantly dry. Connor is stunning. His long hair is tied back, which I love, and he has on a pair of dark jeans and a black T-shirt that clings to him like a second skin. I can count the six-pack he has under it. He forces me to take a selfie of how awesome we look and we head out of the hotel and into a waiting limo.

"A limo? This is a special surprise, then?" I quirk a brow. "You're not going to give me even a tiny little hint?" I bat my eyelashes at him in mock pleading. The truth is, I don't need to know where we're going to already be certain it's going to be an amazing evening. Because Connor is amazing.

"I really want it to be a surprise, but I guess you could say we're going stargazing."

"Stargazing?" My curiosity is piqued.

"Yep. This is actually Ox's surprise for you. I just get to be the one who enjoys watching you love every minute of it." Connor's oversized paw cups my hand and holds it tight as we weave through the lights of downtown Richmond in our sleek, black limo.

It pulls in at the rear entrance of some sort of a large building. There's no signage, but there seems to be an awful lot of activity, and a few police officers mill around on the sidewalk. What the heck is this?

An enormous black man with a clipboard and an earpiece asks for our names. He's intimidating as hell, but Connor seems nonplussed.

"Connor Rose and Raven Flynn," Connor says and takes my hand again, letting our fingers twine together. I have no idea what's on the other side of the black metal door behind the giant with the clipboard, but whatever it is, Miss Adventure and my Inner Sex Goddess are one hundred percent on board.

"Oh, yep. Got you right here. Go right in. Straight back to the right. Ask for Sam. He's expecting you."

"Thanks." Behind the door, we are enclosed in such darkness, it creates instant blindness. A faint blue light shines from somewhere in the distance, and turns out to be some sort of indicator light behind a thick black curtain hanging in front of a door. We walk around and are met face-to-face by a stunning blond with the biggest tits I've ever seen. No way those are real. Her hair color isn't real either. Upon closer inspection, her lashes, her fingernails, not even her blue eyes or suntan are real. This woman is ninety percent plastic. She gives us a huge bright white smile — OK, plastic and veneers, apparently — and Connor asks for Sam.

"Oh, you must be Ox Carr's friend. Follow me." She gives Connor a look from head to foot that lasts just a little too long for my liking.

We follow her through a maze of narrow corridors to an area that looks like it's the back of an elaborately built stage.

Out of the shadows comes a thin, dark-haired man who wears ripped dark jeans with a heavy silver chain looping over one hip. He's not wearing a shirt and has a chest covered in swirls of tattoos on prominent display.

I audibly gasp. I would know this man anywhere. Inner Fangirl has just fallen into a swoon and is out cold. Holy. Shit.

"Hey, Connor. And it's Raven, right?" He just said my name and I grip Connor's hand so tightly he can't let it go to shake the one outstretched toward him. He finally shakes my hand loose and gives the man a wide smile.

"Jesus, man, it's been years. How's your sister?" His voice rasps out. My mouth falls open at the sound of that all too familiar voice.

"She's good. Good to see you too, Sam. Thanks for setting this all up for us. Tori sends her love," Connor replies. It takes my brain an entire second and two heartbeats to realize Connor knows him. Connor knows Sam Slade!

"It's my pleasure. Who's your hottie?" Sam nods to me and smiles. Inner Fangirl is now surrounded by a full-on medical team shouting "clear" as they attempt to restart her heart. Sam Slade just called me a hottie!

"Raven Flynn, I want you to meet Sam Slade."

Sam Slade. The name rings through my ears. I choke. I can't speak. Sam is none other than the lead singer of *Limitless*

—only one of the best rock bands in the entire world! Lead singer, guitar player and one-time love of my life — OK, when I was seventeen, but still. Whether it's a killer plastic surgeon or the ten pounds of makeup he looks like he's wearing, he looks exactly the same as the poster on my old bedroom wall.

"Oh, my God! I can't believe I'm meeting you," I manage to croak out as Connor and Sam have a laugh at my Inner Fangirl, who is now about to pass out. I shake his hand and realize I'm holding it for an awkwardly long period of time.

"I heard that you're a musician yourself," Sam Slade says to me. Sam Slade says to *me!* My pulse flutters and flips as Inner Fangirl, now somehow revived, is floating around with beating hearts in her eyes. My Inner Sex Goddess may or may not be giving those abs and ink a closer look, too.

"Raven played for the New York Philharmonic. Cello," Connor brags. My Inner Sex Goddess makes a note to give this man whatever sexual favor he asks for tonight because his tone is one of utter pride.

"Damn. You're like the real deal. We just ram our dicks out to the girls and scream in harmony." Sam Slade laughs and juts his groin in my direction.

"Hey man, careful where you point that thing," Connor jokes. Another man I also recognize comes up behind Connor and slaps him on the back.

"The baby Ox," he says laughing.

"Jesus," I mutter in awe of the musician standing before me. Evan Jax, drummer extraordinaire. He's a recent substitution to the band after their previous drummer was sent to rehab. Evan has way more talent than the other guy, and is super hot. He's also very young. No way he's more than twenty-one. He only wears jeans and ink — no shirt. It's an ab-fest around here and Inner Fangirl and Sex Goddess are both salivating.

"Hey, Evan. This is Raven," Sam introduces me. Sam, that's right. I am now on a first-name basis with famous rock stars. Me! #coolgirl

"Kick-ass name, babe. When you're ready to fly with a real lover, let me know. These hands are good for a lot more than beating a drum." He gives me a salacious wink. I see Connor roll his eyes a little, but Fangirl is unconscious again.

"It's nice to meet you." My mouth is totally dry. I can't speak. I'm actually standing here and conversing with *Limitless*. Well, they're doing most of the talking. Which is starting to freak me out, because I don't think I've ever been struck this dumb before.

"We gotta be on our game tonight, man. Raven, here, is a real musician. Played cello for the New York Philharmonic," Sam says, jutting a thumb in my direction.

"No shit?" Evan says, raking his hands through long wavy blond hair. His eyes are hypnotic. A light cinnamon color with flames of honey and copper that make them look almost haunted. I wonder if they're contacts.

"No shit." I hear myself say. "I played with them for three seasons, actually."

"Too bad we don't have a cello, you could play with us tonight," Sam says, and he doesn't even sound as if he's being polite.

"Too bad," I repeat. I honestly think if I had a cello right now, he'd have me playing right alongside the band. My heart amps up another ten beats per minute.

"She'd class up your act," Connor adds. "Now where's everyone else? I want to introduce Raven around."

Sam and Evan, who goes by Jax on stage, lead us to a large greenroom where I meet Ziggy Morris, the bassist, and Ban Braxton, guitarist and sometimes singer. After the cursory polite small talk and nice-to-meet-yous, the band escorts us to a small area backstage where we can wait while the opening act prepares to start.

As soon as they are out of sight, I grip Connor's arm and squeal into his ear. "Oh, my God! We're backstage at *Limitless*! Connor, I can't believe I'm here. Please tell me we're going listen to them play from backstage."

Connor gives me that grin that's just for me and breaks into a light laugh. "Baby, we're not only here for the whole concert, but we've been invited to the after-party with the band. We're all staying in the same hotel."

I literally jump up and down on my toes, silently shrieking with a girlish enthusiasm I haven't felt since the day I got my letter from Juilliard.

"So, you like tonight's little outing?" Connor gives me a quick kiss on the mouth and his eyes sparkle into mine.

"Connor," I breathe. "Every time I think you can't top whatever it is we've done before, you go and do ..." I gesture around me, "This! I could kiss Ox for this. How does he know them?"

"Ox and Sam have known each other for years. *Climax* used to open for them and vice versa. These guys used to come over to my house for cookouts and stuff. They're practically my uncles. Well, except for the new guy, Evan. He's a kid."

"Miss Flynn?" Plastic Boobs calls to us. I nod and she hands me a sheaf of papers. I flip through and see it's the sheet music to *Limitless'* opening song. And it's signed by every member of the band, "To Raven, may music forever bless your soul."

And Fangirl dies on the spot and goes straight to heaven.

# CHAPTER SEVENTEEN

**Saturday, June 19
(but only by 12 minutes)**

THE CONCERT IS one of the best I've ever attended. These guys should call themselves *Relentless* or *Tireless*. The non-stop energy, pyrotechnics and haunting rock harmonies are spot on. My heart beats in time with the music and my blood burns with the fireworks. It is all over too soon for me. But then we jump back into our limo and head for the after-party at our hotel.

The band has rented the entire downstairs ballroom. Small local bands take turns providing music while alcohol flows freely. I've danced with Sam, Evan and Connor and my cheeks are hot from exertion and copious amounts of vodka. I am not a drinker. I'm going to pay for this tomorrow, but I don't care. I just slow danced with Sam Slade! Inner Fangirl, finally revived, is practically panting. She's all fluttery and tongue-tied, but Sam is a total sweetheart about it and just keeps smiling at me.

I glance over his shoulder and see Connor talking to

Plastic Boobs. Her hand is on his arm and is traveling up to his shoulder. She gives him that look. Every woman knows that look. The "fuck me" look. The look that has my Inner Sex Goddess and Miss Insecurity conspiring to incinerate this woman. She leans up and whispers something in his ear and then turns his cheek and ... no! I can't watch. She kisses him. Well, she either kisses him or she's trying to taste test his tonsils.

A sickening feeling washes over me, and I feel myself sway slightly on my feet. I look up and Sam's face peers into mine with something akin to enjoyment and amusement. My gaze instantly flicks back to where Connor and Plastic Boobs are sitting. Sam cranes his neck to follow my eyes.

"That's Becca," Sam says. His tone would imply he just tasted something sour. My stomach roils again.

"An employee?" I ask. The vodka is seriously beginning to disagree with my anxiety.

"Groupie. She follows us around like a little lost puppy dog. We throw her a bone once in a while, if you know what I mean. Well, a couple of the guys do. A couple of us are too old and too married for that shit. Looks like she's got her sights set on Con. Hope he's had all his shots."

The music fades, and I make an excuse to Sam that I'm not feeling well and slip up to our hotel room. It wasn't a total lie. The vodka has decided to leave my body violently under a torrent of tears.

When I've wretched all the sin I can from my stomach, I stand up and stare at myself in the bathroom mirror. My silk blouse is wrinkled from sweat and dancing. My hair has fallen out of its cute braid and dark pools of running mascara make my eyes look like a mask on a raccoon. Crying has made my nose red and puffy. I'm horrified at how I look. It's not just the aftereffects of too much loud music and vodka, I look desperate and pathetic. I thought he loved me.

I twist the knob of the shower and jump in with all my clothes on. Sliding back against the cold tile wall, I feel the warm water soak into me as heartbreak leaches out.

I wake up alone in the king-sized bed of our hotel room. The numbers on the clock beside me scream that it's just after 3:30 a.m. The hotel room is dark. Connor isn't here. Fresh hot tears pour from my eyes again. I don't want to think about it, but I know where he is. He's drowning in a sea of plastic tits and needing a shot of penicillin.

Miss Insecure gives me all of her best doubts. I'm not good enough to be anything more than a fun summer fling to a man like Connor Rose. I mean, look at him for goodness' sake. He's Tarzan and the God of Sex and Orgasms for crying out loud. I'm just for fun. I'm not the kind of woman men like that keep. I never have been, and I never will be. Tears rock me to sleep again as the quiet demons weave their dark magic over my dreams. He can't love me.

I wake up and glance at the clock again. It reads 7:48 a.m. My eyes are so swollen and sore from crying I can barely open them. When I can finally focus, I see a long, hairy hard arm draped over my hip. I breathe a slight sigh of relief. At the same time, I feel rage burn against my eyes again, but no tears come this time. They aren't any left.

He's still wearing his clothes from last night, even his boots. He smells of stale booze and marijuana smoke. I don't want to be here when he wakes up. I slip from the bed and into a swimsuit and head down to the pool.

I stare at the pages of a book I'm pretending to read, words swimming past my eyes as I mindlessly turn pages. I order a sandwich and eat an early lunch. I swim a few laps and then slink back to my chaise in the shade. My thoughts tumble around and around in my head. I love Connor, I know I do. I thought he loved me. But there's no way he can. How can a man who is in love with me go off and screw some blond bimbo from a rock concert?

I'm a fool. My mother used to tell me when I was a child, "Fool me once, shame on you. Fool me twice, shame on me." Well, shame on me. I let myself get sucked into a man's lies. Again. Into a man's bed. Again. I let him use my body for nothing more than his ticket to pleasure and my ticket to pain. Again. I lift my sunglasses and wipe the tears from my eyes. I breathe deeply and try to stay the tide of emotions threatening to overwhelm me in a tsunami of brokenness.

"You're punishing me, aren't you?" I hear Connor's voice growl beside me. He's standing over me, rubbing his fingers through his long damp hair.

"I'm reading," I say, not looking up to meet his eyes.

He sits on the empty lounger next to me. His hand splays over my bare knee. "You would make me chase you out here at the brightest spot in the entire hotel. It's to torment me while I try to survive this damn hangover, isn't it?"

"Maybe you shouldn't have stayed out so late and had so much to drink then," I snap.

"You're angry?" Connor says. His hand stills, but it doesn't lift from my skin.

"No ... I ... you. Where were you last night? I woke up after three o'clock ... alone."

"Um, hmm. I was ..." he starts. I wave my hand dismissively.

I don't want to hear about him and that awful woman. I cut him off with a contemptuous tone. "I don't want to hear about you buried in that woman's plastic pussy all night, Connor. Spare me the details."

Connor begins to laugh and flags down a waiter. "Can I get some water, please? Like a gallon of it?"

The waiter smiles and nods, then disappears, while Connor works to bring his irritating laughter under control. I cannot believe he's laughing at me.

"Plastic pussy? You surprise me, Lainey Bird."

"Don't call me that. If that's the kind of woman you're after, then by all means, go after it. I'm sure you can find her in her thong somewhere around the hotel playing nice with all the Hugh Hefner look-alikes."

Connor is nearly doubled over with laughter now. The waiter returns with his water and hands him a napkin to wipe the tears of laughter from his eyes. Honestly, I want to punch this man right now. Anger has replaced my jealousy and hurt feelings. How can he just sit there and laugh at my pain? Bastard!

"I'm not going to sit here and be the brunt of your joke. I'm going to pack. I'm going home, Connor. Blow Job Barbie can take my place."

I swing my legs over the side of the lounger and make for the lobby of the hotel. I've got to somehow navigate the lobby to get to the bank of elevators that will take me to the sixth floor and our room. And I have to do it with tears clouding my eyes, and my chest heaving, working to keep sobs quiet so the midday crowds won't notice. Before I am halfway through, I feel Connor's arms around me, dragging me into an oversized chair.

"Let me go," I fume.

"Lainey, stop." His voice is firm, but gentle.

The tears begin to well again, held back only by my earlier outrage. Captured by his arms, held close to his body, smelling the scent of his body wash — I'm helpless. I am weak and I know it.

"Baby, stop. Listen to me." Connor's arms wrap around me

and he kisses the top of my head. Oh, please, don't do this. I can't manage to make myself leave this, and I need to. I need to go!

I shake my head from side to side. I don't want to hear it. I don't want the excuses and the reasoning. I don't want to believe another string of lies only to be made a fool of again and again while I watch my heart be torn to shreds by the jaws of the lion.

Connor's hands hold me tighter and begin to stroke me softly. "Sweetheart, you've got to talk to me. What's going on? You disappeared last night. I spent hours looking for you. Then today you're mad as hell at me and I have no idea what I've done wrong."

"You can sell that crop of lies to someone else, Tarzan. I told Sam where I was going. I didn't feel good. The vodka made me sick. I came upstairs." I push back from his chest and swipe violently at my cheeks.

"Baby, you got sick? I didn't know. Sam left the party early. Are you OK? You shouldn't have been alone. You should have told me you needed to leave."

"Well, I would have loved to have you come with me, but Silicone Sally had her tongue down your throat. So ..."

"Lainey, it wasn't like that. What is all this really about? You're this upset because some groupie came on to me? Talk to me. Those are the rules, Lainey. This doesn't work if you don't talk to me."

"This?" My tone is louder than I want it to be. I pause a moment and glance around to discover that no one in the lobby is paying the slightest bit of attention to me. Of course, they're not. I'm not worth anyone's concern. I lower my voice. "What exactly is this? What am I to you, Connor? Am I just some summer fling? Is that all you want from me?"

"Lainey," his voice has taken a sharp edge I'm not accustomed to. It's unnerving and causes Miss Insecurity to call a halt to my verbal assault. "Listen to me. What do you feel, right now? At this moment. Don't worry about how I'll react. Just say it. Tell me."

His voice is urgent and demanding. I can't force myself to ignore his orders.

"I'm jealous," I blurt out. New tears fall hotly and quickly down my cheeks. "And I'm angry because I feel foolish and ... used, and I don't know ... cheated somehow. Betrayed. I thought we were ... you know ... a thing, and then I saw you kiss her, and I just ... I can't compete with that, Connor."

I let my head fall against his shoulder and let out a long breath, trying to reign in the sobs that threaten to pour out of me. His lips press against my forehead and his voice shushes me softly.

"I'm sorry, Lainey. Please, don't cry. I'm taking you upstairs. C'mon." I let him lead me onto an elevator that I'm thankful is empty, and then to our room on the sixth floor. He sits on the bed, leaning against the headboard, and pulls me close to him. Just like he does every night.

"Nothing happened with her, Raven." Connor's fingers stroke my arm softly. "Girls like her and Shana, they're all the same. They don't give a shit about anyone but themselves. She knew I was with you — hell, everyone did. I promise you, baby, I've made it very clear I am not traveling down that road again. Not ever. Evan ended up taking her upstairs around 2 a.m."

My tears slow and dry. "You ... you didn't sleep with her?"

"No, Lainey Bird. No. The only woman I wanted last night disappeared on me. One minute you're dancing with Sam and laughing and the next ... you're gone. I got frantic when I couldn't find you. I went looking for Sam, but Ziggy told me he'd gone upstairs with his wife an hour before. I was ready to go door-to-door in this fucking hotel when I came up here a little before 4 a.m. and saw you sleeping. God, baby.

I was so damned relieved. You can't know how worried I was. Sam and his guys are OK, but some of the folks that come to these things ... they get fucked up ideas about what women want when they're stoned."

"I'm sorry, I didn't mean to worry you, I ..."

"You had too much to drink? You got sick?" He interrupts, obviously more concerned over me than an apology.

I hold up four fingers, and Connor lets out a low-pitched whistle between his teeth. "Damn, baby. You can't handle that much. What were you thinking? You should have come to get me."

"I would have except ..."

"Except Becca?"

"Yes."

"You and I are together, Lainey. I'm sleeping with you and only you. I want only you. That gives you the right to come up to anyone and assert yourself."

"Connor, I have no claim on you, I'm just here because ..." I hesitate, letting my words fall away. Connor lets out a sigh of frustration and stabs his fingers through his hair.

"What? You're what? Damn it, talk to me, Lainey. I need to know you feel safe with me. Rule number one!"

"It's just I ..." I can't bring myself to say the words. They feel juvenile, awkward, and unwanted, like soured milk on my tongue. Miss Insecurity seals my mouth shut until I hear Connor say...

"Tell me." His blue eyes glower into me. The eyes of my lion. He's the King of Beasts and I am nothing more than a subject under his command.

"I don't know what I am to you, Connor. If you say I'm just your lover, you should know that's not how I feel about you, about us. I want to be more to you, Connor. You've come to mean so much to me." I finally manage to say. The words come in a wild tumble piling over one another and crowding in a cluster of syllables.

"I guess ... I want to be your girlfriend," I blurt out.

"My girlfriend?" Connor says, all amusement gone from the grin he gives me.

I nod my head. "Is that dumb?"

"Yes. Maybe. No," he stammers. "I'll admit though, I haven't had a girlfriend in a very long time, Lainey Bird. I'm kinda rusty with all this. I mean, the last girl who I called my girlfriend got my class ring. So, I'm not sure what I'm supposed to do to let you know that you're mine and I'm yours."

"I'm yours?" I repeat, liking the sound of the words and hoping he'll say them to me again.

"Yes, you're mine, and I'm yours."

We sit and he holds me for an impossibly long minute, until our souls have the time they need to reconnect and put all of the anxiety behind us. Finally, Connor leans forward and kisses me long and deep.

"I have an idea. Go take a shower. Get all that sunscreen off your skin. Wear something loose."

"Connor," I start, but he just leans forward and kisses me again more delicately this time. I rise to my feet and then turn back to give him a quizzical stare.

"Trust me," he says with a quick slap to my bikini-clad bottom. "Go."

I take the fastest shower of my life and come out to slip on my favorite pair of yoga pants and a lightweight tank.

"All right, let's go. There's a car waiting downstairs," he says grabbing his wallet and phone.

"A car?"

"Yep."

"Where are we going?" I can hear the nervousness in my

voice and the playfulness in his when he replies to my question.

"You need ink." He says simply.

"You want me to get a tattoo?" My eyebrows shoot to my hairline and all hell erupts inside me. Inner Sex Goddess thumbs through tattoo design books, Miss Insecurity paces and Miss Adventure gives herself a pep talk.

"Yep. This whole thing we have between us, Lainey Bird, it's new and special. And I want to commemorate it with something special."

My entire body convulses in a shiver that pricks goose-flesh over every inch of my being.

"Is this some sort of a test? Connor, no. I can't. Tattoos are permanent. I can't ..."

"I know they are, Lainey. I have some. Are you worried I'm going to ask you do a whole leg or a sleeve or something?" I nod as he continues to talk, although I have no idea what to think. "Don't worry. We'll put it someplace discreet. And it will be small. Something the artist can finish in one sitting."

I swallow. Anxiety and fear battle for seniority as I think of every hidden part of my body and then quickly toss away ideas. "My lower back, maybe? A tiny butterfly or some-thing?" I suggest, hoping I can make this as painless as possible.

"A tramp stamp? No way. And no butterflies. You're getting something classy and cool. You're my girlfriend, after all." He gives me a little wink, and my stomach does a flip-flop while Miss Adventure tosses back something for courage.

"What did you have in mind?" I wait for an answer as our driver snakes us through town to River City Ink.

"You'll see."

# CHAPTER EIGHTEEN

**Saturday, June 19**
**(the longest afternoon of my entire life)**

I SHAKE VIOLENTLY on the narrow table. A thousand bees, no, a million of them, sting me over and over. The pain doesn't stop. I bite my lip and try to breathe. Connor holds my hands and reassures me I'm doing well. But the truth is, I feel like I'm about to pass out. Damn, this hurts!

"Connor, how much longer?" Tears prick against my eyes. The skin along my rib cage is nearly numb from the pain, but not quite.

"Not much longer, baby. You wanna take a break? You've been going for like," he glances at his watch, "an hour."

"No. I wanna finish this. But I can't take much more."

"You're doing great, baby. Let me get you a soda. Just hang in there. Damn, I'm impressed with you, Raven."

I sip the soda and it does help soothe me a bit. I clench my hands around his. The bees keep stinging and stinging. Just a few more minutes, I tell myself. Just a few more.

Miss Adventure may have ventured into her first misadventure. #stingink

# CHAPTER NINETEEN

**Sunday, June 20
(it's all a blur)**

A STERILE WHITE cotton gauze patch is taped over my lower back and side. The artist who inked me gives me instructions I don't even register. My head feels fuzzy, and I'm pretty sure I passed out right before he finished. I'm sure Connor knows what to do. My job is just to keep breathing. Thank God, the bees have stopped at least. The relief of not being tattooed eases me a bit. I can finally unclench my teeth and relax, so I do. So much so, I dose off while Connor goes next. He won't tell me what he's had stamped on me or what he's having put on his own body.

We get back to the hotel and he carries me back to our room. I am so tired. Emotionally worn out. Spent. I still feel the bite of the tattoo needle. It hurts. But now, I'm just too exhausted to care.

I drift off to sleep with visions of yellow jackets chasing me through a hayfield. I run as fast as I can toward a creek. The water swirls and coils up from the riverbed following the trail of a bird in flight and then rises up into the air. It darkens and morphs into the giant mouth of a snake, fangs bared. Behind me the bees swarm. In front of me, the water snake is set to strike. I scream until my lungs explode. Then, from out of the rays of the sun, a lion descends to scoop me into his jaws. My legs collapse, and the world goes blank.

I wake up sweating and find someone touching me. Connor is touching me. It stings where his fingers lightly brush against my back. It burns, and I want him to stop. I open my eyes and see I've collapsed onto a chair in the Minnow Bucket. I have no idea how I got here and I don't care. My head swims and my stomach hurts. I close my eyes and pray the spinning and weariness subside.

When I wake again, we are moving. Connor is driving and I'm asleep on the bed in the back of our RV. How long have I been lying here? My eyes strain to focus, but I finally see a sign that says we are just seventy-eight miles from Washington, D.C. Whoa! What happened to me?

"Hey, Little Bird," Connor calls to me from the driver's seat. "You need to get up. Come sit up here with me."

I move slowly. The patch of skin over my back feels numb. I want to pull the patch off and see what Connor has had inked on me.

"Don't," Connor says, spying on me through the fancy camera system he uses to see the back of the RV. "It'll gross you out to look at it now. It's bloody and scabbed and you won't appreciate the design. Give it another few hours or so."

"What did you put on me?" I ask. My arms and legs feel as if my bones are filled with lead. They're so heavy. I move slowly up to the front and flop down into the captain's chair next to Connor.

"Drink," he says, pointing to a large soda in the cupholder. I twist the cap and do what he says. I pause before putting it to my lips and give him a long, hard stare.

"Don't worry," he says. "You're OK. You passed out at the shop for a while. I feel really bad you were in so much pain. You've been sleeping all day. I guess last night really did you in."

"How long did I sleep?" I ask, realizing I do actually feel rested for the first time since we set out on our cross-country road trip in the Minnow Bucket.

Connor looks at the clock. "About sixteen hours."

"Sixteen hours? Are you kidding?"

Connor shakes his head. "How do you feel?"

I pause and consider his question. I take stock of myself. The place on my hip and a little up toward my rib cage is sore, but not hurting. My body feels a bit sluggish, but otherwise, I actually feel pretty good. I feel totally rested for the first time in days. My head is clear and I don't feel anxious about anything. I do feel something, however.

"Hungry," I reply.

"We can stop in fifteen minutes, or you can grab a candy bar from the back. I'm sure you're starved."

I grab one of his favorite candy bars, unwrap it and break it in two. I give him the larger of the two pieces and he smiles at me with his little grin.

"Connor," I say, letting the chocolate, caramel and nuts roll around on my palate. Inner Foodie is singing. "Did I pass your girlfriend test?"

"It wasn't a test, Lainey Bird. But if it were, you'd have passed with flying colors. I'm sorry it was a bit more than you could handle. I didn't think the design would be that involved. But you're going to love it. Will you forgive me for that, Raven?"

"I forgive you," I say. I take another swallow of my soda before handing him the bottle. He takes a long drink and hands it back.

"But Connor, you should know," I add emphatically, "I don't think I'll want to do that ever again."

"No, probably not," Connor smiles.

My skin itches around my new tattoo, and I'm honestly shocked I actually went through with getting it. I can't believe I let him talk me into something so ... so permanent. And yet, he didn't talk me into anything, really. When he suggested it, it was unexpected, but the more I considered it while we drove to the tattoo parlor, the more I realized I wanted this. Not for him. For me.

I look over and watch him while he drives. I thumb through my Instagram account at all the new likes and followers I've gained after posting pictures of us at the concert, backstage with the band and then later at the after-party. #limitlessrocks Ugh, that party. I can't be mad at Becca, though. If it wasn't for her, I doubt I'd be looking over at my *boyfriend* right now. My boyfriend.

I shoot a text over to Willow.

**Me: Did you see my IG?**
**Willow: Hell yes! You're an official rock star, Sis. You look amazing btw. Everything but ink.**
**Me: Got that, too!**
**Willow: *wide-eyed surprised emoji* WTF?**
**Me: Connor had a tattoo artist put a design on me in Richmond after the concert.**
**Willow: A design, of what? Did it hurt?**
**Me: IDK. I'll see it when we stop tonight. He wanted to give me something so everyone knows I'm his. And yeah, hurt like hell.**
**Willow: Know you're his what? If ropes and floggers are involved, I need DETAILS ASAP!**
**Me: LOL. No! I'm his girlfriend.**
**Willow: *heart-eye emoji* Aww.**

**Me: IKR**
**Willow: Happy?**
**Me: So. Happy.**

I smile at the message. I am happy. I like this feeling of knowing someone, and having someone know me. That thought brings a dark cloud to my mind. Miss Insecure shakes out her umbrella. Connor really doesn't know me, though. He doesn't know what happened. How pathetic I am. I can only hope when he finds out, he'll still want me, flaws and all.

My Inner Sex Goddess scolds me, and Miss Adventure wags her finger at me. I know I need to tell him, but I'm so scared. Afraid of what he'll think. Terrified that all the happiness I'm feeling now will dissolve in the light of the truth of who I really am — a failure.

When we stop for burgers and shakes at a takeout diner a few minutes later, I swallow my pride and share a bit more of myself with him. Connor trusts me with his whole story. I can tell him one thing, right? Just one. That will be enough. He doesn't have to know it all. Just this. This will be enough. I'll say it, and it will be done. Rip the Band-Aid off.

"After I left New York, I had a really hard time with things. It took me a long time to get through it. There were lots of pills — anti-depressants and anti-anxiety pills and so many doctors. Each of them had me on something different. I hated the feeling they gave me, so I quit cold turkey. I shouldn't have done that. I was sick for so long. Every day, too nauseated to eat, too weary to sleep, too sad to even cry anymore."

Connor puts down his half-eaten burger and reaches across our small table to take my hand. He says nothing. His eyes are soft and pleading with me to tell him more. "I know that feeling," he says softly. I nod. I know he does.

"I got a job for an advertising agency based out of Chicago, where my parents live. The agency transferred me to Atlanta after a couple of years, and I really loved it. For the first time in a long time, I felt like I was moving past everything that — well, everything that had me feeling down for so long. I was working to become an account manager and eventually have my own team. But then, my boss, Morgan Wright, propositioned me in his office one night. Said that if I wanted to move up in the company, I needed to be 'a good girl' and prove myself to him. When he started to unbuckle his belt, I ran. I reported it to HR the next morning. The manager just shook her head at me. He'd beat me to it. He'd already been in a few days before and told her his version of offering me an 'advancement opportunity'. He said I'd cornered him and threatened to report him for sexual harassment if he didn't give me a promotion. I couldn't believe it! I quit that day."

Connor's grip on my fingers tightens while I tell him the story of Morgan Wright, the shitbag. Connor's jaw clenches, I know he's angry.

"I didn't encourage him ..." I supply that critical bit of information, quickly hoping to diffuse his anger.

"Of course, you didn't, Raven." Connor pulls his fingers from my hand and rakes them through his hair. It's long and loose today. "What an asshole. You did the right thing. It wasn't safe for you to be there around that fucker."

"Thanks. It's been a few weeks, and apparently, he's put the word out that I'm a risky hire. I've had interviews, but no offers."

"No wonder you didn't take vacations for so long," he says with total empathy. "Come here to me, baby." Connor pushes himself into the passenger seat up front and I curl into his lap, our fast-food dinner all but forgotten.

"Fuck, Lainey. I'm so sorry that happened to you." His tone is not one of pity, but of understanding. "You're wonderful, though." He kisses me softly. "Really, you're the most amazing person I've ever met, Raven. I promise, I'm going to help you get past this. We're going to relax and have fun, right?"

I nod slowly.

"I promise you, you're going to be all right," he says before kissing me again.

I give him a smile. How many times did I hear those words from my mother? Or the students and teachers at Juilliard? Or Jemmy? Jemmy used, "I swear," and "I promise" as much as he did "hello" and "goodbye." Deep down, I never believed any of them. I always knew they'd all turn around and hurt me again in exactly the same way. Their words were hollow and empty, and I could hear the echo of my pain ringing through them.

Connor's voice is different. There's something behind it the other voices never had. Not even my mother's voice. It's love. Connor Rose loves me. And he's not going to break this promise. His words are solid and sure. My heart knows it.

Our RV is valet parked at the Watergate Hotel in D.C. It's a gorgeous hotel. Our modern room is decorated in cool caramels, grays and whites. It has a small balcony overlooking the interior of the hotel. It's sparsely furnished and feels open and clean. Only the essentials are included. It's perfect.

We unpack and Connor orders room service and arranges for laundry service to clean our clothes tomorrow. I'm impressed at how he thinks of everything. No detail is left to chance. The entire trip is organized and orchestrated to be sure I have the time of my life. And I am. I've missed so much over the past five years. I was hiding. Hiding from the world and hiding from myself.

I wanted to protect myself from hurt. Instead, I sheltered myself away from the joy the world has to offer. Life is a two-sided coin. There is pain and devastation and loss, but there is beauty and laughter and love, too. Connor has shown me that. He's opened himself up to me, and has made me feel safe in doing so with him. It's hard for me to speak my truth — to reveal the many ways I'm broken inside. It scares me that I'll be too much for him. But each time I brave my fears and tell him a little more, I feel less heavy, not more anxious. It's the opposite of how I thought I'd feel.

I undress and pile the clothes I've been sleeping in for the past two days into the laundry bag the hotel has provided. The white gauze patch is still there covering the tattoo Connor has put on my body, claiming me as his own.

"Don't take that off yet," Connor warns. "Just shower with it on. I'll be there in a minute."

I nod, grinning at the idea that he plans to join me in the oversized shower. Showers with Connor always seem to involve some sort of sexual activity. I suppose I started that a few weeks ago in Georgia at the spa. Wow! A few weeks? That's all it's been? But Georgia — Dr. Krazanski — was right. All of this time with Connor is like dating in dog years. One day is equal to a week. A week is equal to a month. And by the time we're done and on our way back home, it will feel like years with this man.

Steam fills the bathroom as Connor steps in and clicks the glass shower door closed behind him. He washes me slowly, starting with my hair and then down until every inch of me is clean. Then, it's my turn to return the favor and I can feel his arousal begin to flex, as the one-eyed monster wakes up between his legs. My Inner Sex Goddess is now soaking wet at the prospects ahead of us tonight.

When we step out of the shower, Connor goes to one knee and kisses all around my new tattoo. The tape used to keep the gauze on peels away easily. He kisses the spot and I feel it burn slightly as if my skin has been scratched, but it's not painful anymore.

"It turned out so great, Lainey Bird. Are you ready to see it?" His eyes are alight with excitement and I can tell he's pleased.

I nod, eager to see how this man has marked me. I'm nervous, too, but mostly excited. I know whatever it is, it's going to be stunning. When he stands and moves aside from the mirror, I am not disappointed. It's quite honestly the most beautiful thing I've ever seen.

A thumb-sized dandelion has been painted in black on my skin. Tufts of seeds being blown in a wish float up and over my back and rib cage, up to my shoulder blade. As the seeds float away, their shape morphs into tiny birds. Ravens. I feel myself in this tattoo. Wishes cast into fate's breeze where I am set free — where I fly.

I inhale sharply. The skin still looks angry and red, but the tattoo is gorgeous and I'm thrilled beyond words at how carefully Connor chose the exact right thing. He's freed me. He's marked me. He loves me, and no matter what happens between us, I will forever be free. No longer trapped in the seeds of my wishes. There's a word beside the stem of the dandelion written in a curling script. It's hard to read in the mirror.

"What does it say?" I ask, trying not to touch it.

"Evermore." Connor says. He's moved behind me and has his arms wrapped around my breasts, touching and caressing them slowly and tenderly.

"What does that mean?"

"I got the idea from this poem Edgar Allen Poe wrote about a visit from a raven. He was mourning his lost love, a woman named Lenore. He was in despair, truly broken-hearted. But then this raven comes to him simply saying 'Nevermore' over and over. Poe wants to be uplifted, but he can't move beyond the sadness. The raven doesn't care. She just sits, listening, speaking her one word. In the end, he feels his loss, but I think he also feels the company and friendship of the raven. She understands his pain. And instead of removing it, she shares it with him. That's you, Lainey Bird. You're my raven, come to be mine. To share and banish my pain. You have already. I will have you as a part of me, not 'Nevermore,' as the raven replied, but forever, 'evermore'."

Connor's words are beautiful and I see the emotion of them on his face, watching us in the mirror. Our bodies naked, wrapped around one another, and for this one moment, perfect.

"It's beautiful, Connor," I whisper. The words stutter on their way out, trapped in the knot of emotion in my throat.

He kisses me. A hot, wet kiss of dancing tongues and unspoken desire so intense my skin tingles with it.

"Take me to bed," my Inner Sex Goddess speaks aloud.

Connor makes love to me slowly, but we rise quickly, feeling our bond with every long, easy stroke of our joining. In moments, we are panting, climbing and then flying together.

Our limbs collapse against one another, limp and fully sated. When my breath stills and I can finally speak, I ask him what I had wanted to ask earlier in the bathroom before he'd wooed with his beautiful words and my mark. His mark.

"What did you have done? At the ink shop?" I ask. Connor rolls over to reveal the lion. In his mane, twisted among the wiry hairs and whips is a raven. Its wings are a glossy black, reflecting greens and purples as the light dances off of it. Like the lion, it looks as if it could take flight and swoop around the room in a moment. It's stunning. It's me.

"It's gorgeous," I say, wanting to finger its delicate plumage, but keeping my distance. His skin is tender still, too, no doubt.

He rolls back over and holds me close in his arms. His lips are on my ear and I can feel his breath against my skin. "You're mine, Lainey Bird. My girl. My Raven."

"Yes," I breathe. "Evermore."

# CHAPTER TWENTY

**Tuesday, June 22**

I'VE BEEN to Washington D.C. several times in my life. I've seen the national monuments, I've toured the Smithsonian museums. But there is something wonderful and new about seeing them with Connor. Instead of walking for miles around the city, he books a twilight tour of the war memorials and we are driven through D.C. just as the lights begin to twinkle and the stars peek out from behind a purpling summer sky. We sit atop an open-air bus, sipping ice-cold lemonade.

The statues are haunting in the glow of the lights that illuminate the faces of the fallen. Our last stop is at Arlington. It is nearly dark, but Connor seems as if he would know the way to his destination even if he was blindfolded. Three small white crosses mark the names of the men who died in the bombing in Afghanistan. Connor doesn't speak. He just stands with his hands in his pockets, quietly whispering to the ghosts of the fallen who had been brothers in arms to him.

The experience is sobering and so much more emotional than I dreamed it would be. Looking up from the three headstones engraved with the names and ranks of U.S. Army Special Operators Mark Freedoms, William Greer and Nathan Fairsmore, my eyes gloss over thousands upon thousands of small white markers. The straight lines of them crisscrossing seem to disappear over the horizon. I feel hot tears well up in my eyes. There are so many of them. So many soldiers who have been willing to go into battle for our nation and the ideals it stands for. The idea is staggering.

"You OK, Lainey Bird?" Connor's voice is tinged with sacrifice and loss.

I can only nod. Words are too much — even for me.

"Don't cry for them. They're together with their brothers here. These are the people they were fighting for." His arms wrap around me and his fingers drift softly over my skin.

"People think we fight for oil or for sand or for freedom. But we don't. We fight for the man standing next to us. And all of those who stood before and all those who will stand after."

Connor's words comfort me a little. The idea that these men and women aren't alone, that their spirits are at rest with those people they fought for, eases me some. Connor sends the tour bus on ahead without us. We'll call a cab when we're ready, he tells the driver who also wipes tears from his eyes. Even though he's probably seen this scene a hundred times, it never gets easier.

Hand in hand we walk through the cemetery back to the entrance. The park closes in a few minutes. I should be completely freaked out, walking among the dead in near darkness like this, but I'm not. Miss Insecurity is at peace. She has been for a while now, only coming out of her quiet closet when truly fearful things occur.

"Why did you join the Army?" I ask quietly. "Was your

dad in the service or something?" I knew that both of Connor and Tori's parents were killed when Connor was younger, but he never told me how it had happened.

"No. My parents were in New York City on September 11, 2001. They were visiting an old friend and meeting with some financial people about investments and stuff." Connor's voice grows quiet again. "They died in the World Trade Center bombing."

"Oh God, Connor, I'm so sorry."

"It was a long time ago. I was kinda lost for a while. I spent a lot of time with Ox and the band and found more trouble than I did direction. Tori is the one who put it into my head to join the Army. She said I needed discipline. When I did join, my commanders found out I was pretty good at being a hard-ass, and I got my ranger tab shortly thereafter. The rest is history ... until Afghanistan."

"Tori must feel a bit responsible for what happened to you there, and with Shana and everything," I say, compassionately.

"I never thought about that, but yeah, I guess she might. She babies me about everything, and I used to think it was just some kind of mother-hen act. But there's truth to what you're saying, Lainey. She shouldn't feel that way though. Soldiers fight wars. They get hurt. They die. It's what I signed up for. I was old enough to know."

After we make love that night at the hotel, I curl quietly next to the lion beside me. Equal parts protector and defender. I brave my fear and finally touch the raven on his back and understand why he had the artist place it there. Then, I run my fingers along the deep scars in his skin. He'd said he'd been injured, but I had no idea. Most of his tattoo covers them, but I can feel the ridges and dips in his muscles under the wings of the raven. Scars hidden and protected by a bird, both omen of luck and of death. A raven, like me.

# CHAPTER TWENTY-ONE

### Friday, June 25

"I CAN'T BELIEVE this is the end of our time in the Minnow Bucket," I say, heaving a suitcase off the bed. It's taken me an entire day to repack both of my suitcases which are now stuffed to bursting with trinkets I've indulged in at each of our stops.

"Yeah, we can do the train from here to New York City. And then to New Bedford where we'll take the ferry to Martha's Vineyard. You're going to love the house. I can't wait to get there."

"Yeah?"

"Yeah. It's small, but it's right on the water. Last season, I had some sand brought in and it's really nice to just stretch out sand sunbathe."

"You had sand brought in?" I laugh a little at that.

"Yeah, the beach is kind of rocky and I've gotten spoiled by my trips to the Gulf."

I can hear the excitement in his voice when he describes

this special place. He says that it's his favorite place in all the world, and I'm thrilled he wants to share it with me.

"All right, last selfie with the Minnow Bucket," he says, just before we hand the keys over to the rental agency in northern Virginia. #camperlife

It's funny, but I'm going to miss that tiny little space. Connor and I connected there and it will forever be special to me. Because, I suppose, this new beginning of my life is so closely connected to a new beginning with him. And Connor will forever be special to me, too.

"Sad, Lainey Bird?" Connor asks, giving my nose a quick kiss as we board the commuter train to Manhattan.

"A little," I admit softly.

"Me, too." He laces his large fingers between my slimmer ones, and we sit quietly just holding hands as the train carries us one leg closer to Connor's favorite place.

It doesn't escape me that I'm quiet, letting the sounds come to me — the chugging engine and screeching steel of the train, the hypnotic vibrating whir of the air conditioner and faint thumping of Connor's pulse beating under the thin skin of my own wrist. I look over and his head is turned. He's looking at me, giving me the smile Georgia noticed just days ago as his smile of love.

"What?" I ask, flashing my "love smile" back.

"You're quiet," he says softly.

"Don't tell me you wish I'd talk incessantly, because that can be arranged," I tease.

"No." He laughs playfully at me. "But I miss it a little. I know that being quiet either means you're too freaked out to speak, or your Little Bird heart is peaceful. I think it's peaceful right now and that makes me happy."

"It is. And it makes me happy, too."

New York City was home to me for seven years. And being back here — hearing the noise, smelling the foul air and staring out at the smog brings back a rush of bad memories. There were too few good ones during that time to connect to this place. My heart instantly tenses the minute we get off the train.

"You know, I can take you to the best bagel shop in all of New York. It's just this tiny little hole-in-the-wall place. But, you know, those are the best places. Oh, and doesn't Anton Arnaud have a place here? I think it's got like two Michelin stars or something. We'd probably have to bribe him with more *Climax* mementos to even get a reservation. Speaking of *Climax,* have you talked to Tori or Ox? I wonder how they're doing with the restaurants while you're away."

Connor tugs me into a corner of the train station, pushes my back against the wall and stands squarely in front of me. He leans down and kisses me once, hard and quick. He's so huge, and standing so near, I can't see around him. My heart hammers my palms sweat and my breath falls so shallow it nearly stops altogether.

"Breathe, baby. You're OK," he says in my ear.

"I know I'm OK," I say. My voice holds more confidence than I feel. "It's New York. I used to live here, remember?"

He shakes his head and leans down and speaks softly into my ear. "Something about this place upsets you. I want you to know that whatever it is, it's not going to come between us. I'm here. You're wonderful, you're mine and you're going to be fine."

I let out a deep breath and nod, pressing my forehead against the hard muscles of his chest. "I'm good," I lie, but try to sound convincing. I manage to hold back the tide of my tears until we check into our hotel and I can escape into the seclusion of the shower and drown them under the stream of hot water.

Connor orders grilled chicken, sautéed vegetables and a bottle of white wine from the hotel's room service menu and we eat mostly in silence in our suite.

"We're going shopping tomorrow," he says, setting our cart of dishes in the hall to be collected later.

"Shopping? For what?" I never had enough money to really shop in New York, but if he's looking for souvenirs, I remember a few places where we can stop.

"For you. I scored us great seats to see the New York Philharmonic tomorrow night, and I want you to have a new dress. Something red or dark blue maybe. I think you'd look good in dark blue."

I feel all of the blood drain from my face as Connor talks. He wants to take me to see the Philharmonic? "No!" I squawk without preamble. "I mean, shopping is fine. But no dress. No concert. I'm sorry. I can't."

"Lainey, what is it? I thought you'd be glad to see people you know," Connor sounds nervous. I feel sick.

I shake my head, feeling the hurt and shame and fear churning up inside my stomach. I'm going to throw up. I dash off to the bathroom, letting the door lock behind me, and I waste every morsel of my delicious dinner and flush it away.

Connor is practically pounding on the door as I dry heave into the toilet. "Lainey, damn it. Let me in. Right now."

I stand up while he keeps knocking, and run some cold water over my face and hands. In the mirror, I'm a ghost staring at my own pallid skin with haunted eyes. My hands shake. I click the handle and slide down the wall to the floor as he steps inside.

Connor's arms catch me and I let myself fall into them.

There is nothing else I can do. The tears come. One for every tiny broken piece of my soul destroyed and shattered over the years. Shoulders shaking, I weep until my body is wrung dry of every drop it can spare. I'm nauseous, dizzy and humiliated. I cover my face with my hands.

Connor lifts me and carries me in his arms to the bed. Producing a cool washcloth from the bathroom, he wipes my forehead, but says nothing. I can't speak. I can only look into his eyes, begging for the pain to stop. But I know that even my lion can't make it stop. Nothing can. I bury my face into his shoulder and feel him hold me tight against him while sobs shake my body against his.

"I've got you. It's going to be OK, Lainey Bird. I promise."

"I can't go, Connor. I can't. Please, don't ask me to do that."

"Lainey, why not? What happened?" Connor slides wet strands of hair off my damp cheeks. His eyes look troubled.

"What if he's there? What if ..." the thought of seeing Jemmy again brings up a new wave of nausea, and I debate whether I should head to the toilet again. But Connor continues to bathe my face and neck with the cloth. And the queasiness subsides, for now.

"Who, baby? Who is scaring you like this?" Connor's expression is desperate for answers, but I can't bring myself to push the words out. It hurts all over again. It hurts too much. I'm so ashamed.

"I just can't go, Connor. That's all. Please, please don't make me go." I continue to cry, gripping the front of his shirt into my fists, clinging to him, to my lion.

"I don't care about the concert, Lainey. Jesus, look at you, sweetheart. You're shaking all over. You physically got sick at the idea of accidentally bumping into someone. Is it Jemmy?

Is that who's hurt you so badly you can't even confront the notion of seeing him again?"

I nod. But I say nothing because there's too much to say, and not enough words.

Connor holds me closer and pats my back. "Lainey, just say the name, that's all I want. Tell me the name of the person who has you so upset." Connor strokes my hair and kisses the top of my head.

For less than a minute, he leaves me on the bed. He turns off the light and closes the blinds, making the softening light outside disappear. We are bathed in a light glow from the night-lights that glimmer from the outlets around the room.

"Jeremy Forester, Junior. Jemmy." Vocalizing the name aloud leaves me further drained and exhausted.

"Who was he to you?" Connor asks.

"Once upon a time, he was everything. But I was nothing, and so that's what he became to me, too. Eventually." I struggle to find a way to explain.

"Is he involved with the orchestra in some way?" Connor asks.

"He's the concertmaster," I say in a numb monotone. "Maybe he is. He was when I was here five years ago."

"How did you two meet?" He takes me back to the beginning. Like a time machine of torment, back to a place I never want to go again.

"He was at my audition. — a fellow Juilliard alumnus. He said I played well and he hoped I got picked up. Then, he asked me to dinner. He invited me to his place and tried to have sex with me, but I wasn't really interested. I was eighteen and still a virgin. I didn't want my first time to be a one-night stand."

"Good for you," Connor agrees.

"He said it was a pity, because he could put in a good word for me with the selection committee."

Connor says nothing when I relay this, but I hear the sharp intake of his breath and feel his muscles clench.

"I didn't sleep with him. Not that night. But he asked me out again anyway and said he'd still put in a good word for me. I got picked up, and, then he said I owed him for getting me there. The next time we went out, he asked me to have sex with him again." I feel the pain welling inside me. My core clenches as if he were hurting me again. "He was so damn persistent, Connor."

I hear the start of a string of curses forming under Connor's breath, but he inhales and exhales slowly before asking quietly, "He forced you, Raven? He raped you?"

I shake my head. "Not really. I mean, I agreed to it. I let him. But I didn't want to. He went too fast. It hurt *so* much." I clench every muscle in my body and curl tighter into Connor's body. "I hated it. I didn't want to see him again, but he said he loved me. He said he was the one who got me in, and he could take me out if I didn't agree to continue to see him — sleep with him. He has a real ego, that man. No one has ever said no to him in his entire life, and he wasn't about to let me be the first."

"What happened, Raven?"

"We dated off and on for the next couple of years. Almost every date ended with required sex, but eventually I fell into this sort of comfort zone with him. In some ways, he was nice to me. Took me places, got me gifts, spoiled me on my birthday and at Christmas. He convinced me this was love. And I was beginning to convince myself that it was love, too. What did I know?"

Connor sits and continues to rub my back, holding me close while I work up the courage to share the rest of the story with him.

"The whole cello section got a night off and all of us girls — there were three of us — went out for a night on the town

— dinner and drinks and people-watching in Times Square. We were having so much fun. And then I saw him. He was kissing another woman. His hand was up her shirt. There was no confusion about what was happening. I confronted him right there. He laughed at me and said that I was fun, but I wasn't someone he could ever be serious about. By the time I could even gather the courage to leave, they were all laughing at me. All of them."

I hear another sharp intake of breath. I know this hurts him to hear the same way it hurt me to hear about Shana.

"When my third season started, the conductor asked to see me after rehearsal. He said Jemmy had expressed concerns over my dedication to the Philharmonic. Two performances later, I was put on suspension. I was going to have to audition for my spot again. Jemmy told me that I shouldn't bother. I wouldn't be picked this time. He was going to make damn sure the name Raven Flynn was on every national orchestra's black list. My professional days were over.

"I auditioned for the Boston Pops and the Florida Orchestra, but was told they couldn't use an inexperienced cello player, no matter how well I played. I was 'too young — too naive in the ways of the world' to be participating at this level," I snort with disappointment.

"What did you do?" Connor asks. I sink down and rest my head in his lap, feeling the hard muscles of his thighs against my cheek. His fingers continue to stroke through my hair, soothing me as I slowly release every drop of pain from my heart into his veins.

"I went home with my tail tucked between my legs. My mother never approved of my playing professionally. She said music was a nice hobby, but nobody ever made a living at it. She was adamant Willow and I have lucrative careers. She said we should never be dependent on a man to support us. I heard 'I told you so' for two straight years."

"But you told me your father supported you all, didn't he?" Connor asks. His finger curls a lock of my hair and then releases it over and over.

I nod. "He did. But, according to my sister, Daddy had lots of women outside of his marriage. It's why we moved to Chicago. Mom said she didn't want him seeing his women anymore and insisted we move. So, Daddy got the firm he worked for to transfer us to the Chicago office. He cared about Mom, he wouldn't divorce her. But he couldn't be faithful. Free love and all that. She felt trapped. She had no education, no job experience and two little girls to raise. She stayed with him for the money. They have always had a loveless marriage, a marriage of convenience.

"She hated my cello playing. I suppose that's one of the reasons Mrs. Dean took such a shine to helping me. She knew I wasn't getting support at home. She invited a friend of hers who taught at Juilliard to come to one of our concerts. I had a solo piece, and when Mr. Emerson heard me play, words like 'prodigy' and 'scholarship' were thrown around. When they offered it to me, I took it. I loved nothing more than music. It was the only thing I had.

"When I got to Juilliard, I really thought I'd find like-hearted musicians. I'd finally find my people and have friends and mentors to teach me. What I found instead was a group of bloodthirsty cutthroats who would do anything to be the best. They were ruthlessly competitive and cruel. I finished school a year early just to get away. I got an audition with the New York Philharmonic, and that's when I met ... Jemmy." My voice trembles as the words tumble out.

Connor pulls me close and hugs me tight. His muscles strain under my hold.

"God, Raven. Your poor heart's been beaten up for so long. I'm so sorry, baby. What happened isn't right or fair. You're an amazing musician. I wish you could have kept going."

"Me, too. But I went to college online, got a degree in business and that is that. I became Elaine Flynn of Pittman and Wright and ..."

"... and stopped going on vacation?" Connor finishes my sentence.

"Yes. For so long, Connor. All I heard were the voices of these people telling me to stop being who I was. To be quiet and be afraid. For so long, I wondered if I'd ever hear my own voice again. A couple of times, on this trip, I feel like I have. That day in the shower at the spa, the first time we made love, and sitting there in that chair getting this tattoo, I heard it then. But sometimes, I'm just not sure if I'm still in here anymore, Connor."

There it is. I gulp for air. My soul feels as though it's bleeding to death. I've stripped all the scars away, and the wounds underneath now run red with all of the shame and sorrow over my life I've carried for so long. I know what he's going to say. I should have stood up for myself. I should have fought back. I should have fought for myself. But I was too battle weary to try. Too beaten down to muster the strength for another fight. I simply gave up. I'm weak. I'm pathetic and unworthy.

"I'm so proud of you, Raven," Connor says, kissing my face. His cheeks are damp with his own tears. He kisses my forehead and my temple and my closed, swollen eyes.

"What? You're not serious. You can't be." I lean back and look into his face twisted with understanding and compassion. "Not after everything I just told you. I'm humiliated at who I am. The way I let myself be used and walked on. They crushed me. They crushed me because I'm weak, and I'm a coward."

"Are you kidding me? Raven, you've got to be the strongest, most courageous person I've ever met." His hands cup my cheeks and he holds my face, forcing my eyes to meet his gaze. "Look at everything you've been through, Lainey Bird. Your mom clipped your wings, and you flew to Juilliard. Fucking Juilliard, Lainey! Do you know what a fucking big deal that is? And they put you in a cage of solitude and fear, but you flew on to be a professional with the New York Philharmonic. I don't care what that asshole told you — you did that all on your own. And then after that sorry son of a bitch hurt you, you had the courage to go back into the lion's den to regroup. You had the courage to start your whole life over again."

I let his words, his voice — steeped in emotion and filled with love — wash over me. I let them soak in between the broken places of my heart and repair the tattered strings of my soul's tapestry. I wasn't brave. I was flying, I was running away — the leg-shackled bird with the clipped wings.

"Really? That's how you see me?"

"Yes, baby, really. I'm so proud of you, Raven. Baby, we have to go tomorrow. I know you're scared, but you have to. You have to show those assholes that they can't cage a raven."

"I'm a bird, not a lion, Connor." He kisses me full and deep.

"You are wonderful, Raven. I'll be your lion."

# CHAPTER TWENTY-TWO

**Saturday, June 26**

I STAND in a dress shop on New York's Fifth Avenue. My gorgeous long-haired lion gawks at me while sales ladies offer us espressos and champagne. I try on my fourth dress, but they're all magnificent.

"You're gorgeous, Lainey Bird," Connor says, and I swear, he's drooling. The dress I have on is navy blue with spaghetti straps and a low draped neckline that falls damn near to my ass in the back. There's a slit up one leg that stops three inches above my knee. It hugs my body so close I can barely breathe.

"I like it. How much is it?" I twist to see if I can decipher the numbers on the tag that's been tucked in under my arm.

"Who cares?" Connor says, waggling an eyebrow. "You've got to have it." He leans forward in the chair he's been holding down for the last half hour and licks his lips. I swear, my Inner Sex Goddess just purred. No, she roared!

"Oh, my God! Raven Flynn, is that you?" A high-pitched female voice calls from the door of the dressing room. When

I turn around, Presley Templeton, one of the viola players from the orchestra — and one of the only women I could have truly considered a friend — waves to me.

"It *is* you! Oh, my God, it's so good to see you. You just fell off the face of the earth, what like five, six years ago." She hugs me tight and then holds me at arm's length to get a good look.

"Jesus, you look amazing. What have you been doing?"

I smile and motion to Connor standing behind her. "Traveling. I'm just in town for a couple of days. We're passing through on our way to Martha's Vineyard."

"Well, hello, sexy and stunning." She takes a moment to lick her lips and look Connor up and down. "And just what might you be called?" Presley was always a hopeless flirt. I shake my head amused that some things never change.

Connor stands and extends a hand. "Connor, I'd like you to meet a friend of mine from my Philharmonic days. This is Presley Templeton. Viola. Pres, this is Connor Rose, my boyfriend."

Connor casts a quick glance and an easy smile at me, seemingly approving of the title.

"Connor, is it?" She shakes his hand and offers him an overtly flirtatious smile before turning back to me and winking. She mouths the words, "h-o-l-y s-h-i-t!" And then fans her neck with her hand. *Yeah, hot and mine*, I think to myself, grinning.

"You're a far cry from that bastard, Jemmy, I must say," she says, looking back over her shoulder at Connor. He instantly tenses at the mention of the man's name. It's like he wants to beat the idea and memory of him with his fists if he can't get them around the actual man.

"Is ... is he still playing with you all?" I ask reluctantly. My voice shakes. I let Connor talk me into attending the concert, but I'm still terrified he'll be there. I'm unsure what I'll do if I actually see him there.

"Hell no! You know he slept around, right. Well, he used to tell his conquests he would blackball them from professional orchestras if they didn't sleep with him. Prick. Well, he picked the wrong girl — the conductor's granddaughter. Practically raped her on their first date. Big mistake. Jemmy got tossed out on his ear. He played for the Russian ballet for a season, but tried his little stunt with one of the girls there, and they deported him. I'd be surprised if he could get a gig playing for a bar mitzvah. Last I heard, he teaches junior high school band back home somewhere in Iowa or something. Loser." Presley makes an "L" with her thumb and forefinger and taps her forehead.

"Really?" I shouldn't ever be glad about anyone's misfortune, but I'll be honest, knowing he is reaping what he's sown is freaking great. For a split second, I regret it couldn't have been me who started him on his path to ruin, but I let that go in exchange for an inner celebration of his utter humiliation. No one deserves it more. Miss Insecure and Miss Adventure officially hang streamers. I wink at Connor and smile widely. We are going to a concert.

Of course, I buy the dress. Connor insists on shoes, a wrap, a matching sparkly clutch and some gorgeous earrings. After lunch, at my favorite hot dog cart, we hit the computer store to check out some new wireless headphones he's been hoping to find for Ginger's birthday. While I wait for him to look around, I watch a demonstration of on one of the latest tablets. I'm drawn to the salesperson's electronic magic show, and before I know what I'm doing, I'm slapping my credit card on the counter for hundreds of dollars' worth of the first gift I'm ever going to give my boyfriend.

"I got you something while we were out shopping today," I say. I hold the flat box close to my back trying to hide it. I'm so nervous to give this gift to Connor, and I can't explain why.

"You bought me a present?" Connor seems a bit surprised by this.

"I did. I ... I'm not sure if you have one, you probably already do, and this was probably just a stupid idea, but I saw it today, and it just make me think of you and ..."

I'm rambling. Connor's warm grin stops me dead in my tracks. He pushes back his long, gorgeous hair. "Do I get to see it, baby?"

I slowly hand Connor the box. He pulls the bright silver paper and white satin ribbon off and lifts the lid. My heart pounds. I am so worried he won't like it. Miss Insecure is back, chiding me for spending so much money on something he probably already has. He'll think it's dumb.

He peers down at the slick black rectangle and smiles. Hitting the lone button on the bottom, he brings the tablet to life, broadly admiring the sleek thin lines of the device.

"You got me an iPad?" His eyes dance with excitement. I let out a breath.

"Yes, well, there's this app on here," I say, touching the small icon that opens up a drawing program on the touch-screen. "And you can create artwork and sketch with it. There's more in the box. There's this special pencil thing that you use to sketch on it."

Connor presses the stylus against the slick glass of the tablet and watches as a broken graphite line streaks across the page.

"Whoa, that's so cool." He mimics the action again, criss-crossing line after line.

"The man at the store said there are haptics or something in the stylus that make it actually feel like you're drawing with a real charcoal pencil or a marker or whatever you want. It sounds like it, too. You can choose what you want to draw with and all the colors are right here."

I demonstrate techniques from the brief tutorial the salesman at the store showed me. Connor watches with wide eyes.

"You can print it, or send it via email or even take a picture of it."

"Lainey," Connor says, and then just stares up at me with an expression I can't quite identify. "I'm speechless, baby."

"You like it?" I twist my fingers together, fidgeting.

"I love it! It's one of the coolest things I've ever owned. It's like a sketch pad with endless pages, and I can share them all with you."

"With anyone," I smile a bit, pleased and relieved that he likes my gift.

"I'm going to make my first sketch. You sit right there." Connor flops onto the edge of the bed while I settle myself on the edge of a chair, posing like a glamorous movie star.

I watch as he sketches. He glances up at me a few times, his brows narrowing in concentration. I am eager to see what he is able to create with this technology. He has such amazing talent.

After a few short minutes, he turns the screen around to me, but he makes me close my eyes first.

"OK, you can open your eyes now," he says. I crack my eyes open and tears prick at the corners the moment I realize what he's drawn.

It's my tattoo. I always suspected he'd been the one who'd drawn it, but could never confirm that with the artist who did it for me. A dandelion with tiny wishing seeds that morph into a flight of tiny ravens. And under the picture are three tiny words, "I love you."

My hands fly to my mouth and I try to contain my emotion, but it's impossible. I'm sob and I'm overjoyed and I'm overwhelmed all at the same time. He loves me. I've hoped and assumed, but knowing makes it so real. So certain. They are words I have waited to say to him. I wanted to hear them first. I wanted to be sure my feelings would be reciprocated before I offered up my heart, and here they are in front of me in his own handwriting, written under the symbol of my soul he created just for me.

Connor gives me his little smile that I know now is mine, and joyful tears drip down my face.

"Does that make you sad, baby?" Connor asks, knowing it doesn't.

I shake my head violently. "No. Connor, oh, I love you back."

In a heartbeat, Connor lays the tablet aside and wraps me in his arms. "I love you so much, Lainey. This is such a beautiful, thoughtful gift. *You* are the most wonderful gift. I should have said it long before now. I should have said it the minute I realized it, the minute I knew you loved me back."

"When? How ... how did you know I love you?" I say and kiss his warm lips.

"I knew when you got on the back of that bike — the way you held on to me. I knew when I had a nightmare. I knew every time you'd watch those decorating shows with me, knowing you'd seen them all already. I knew when you picked up all my stupid candy wrappers I leave everywhere and never once complained. I knew when you held a gun, when you let me make love to you. And I know it every time you look at me, Raven. I can see it in your eyes. You've never said those words to me, but it's the things you do that tell me day after day how you feel about me. I've been such a coward not to say it until now."

"I suppose we have both been a bit nervous, then," I confess.

"Maybe so, Lainey Bird, but now you know. You can be sure. I am absolutely, and completely, in love with you."

His lips fall over mine and we are lost in the kiss, the touch, the taste, the lust and the love that exists between us. We celebrate it over and over again as our bodies come together in nothing but love. #headoverheels

The concert is magnificent. The Philharmonic plays a collection of music from Mozart, and the performance is flawless. I am captivated equally by the genius of the music and by the generous man who brought me to hear it. My love for him, his love for me, and our love for the music inter-mingle with the night and the city lights and everything beau-tiful the world has given us. Moonbeams radiate through every pore of my being, giving my skin a mesmerizing aura. I'm absolutely glowing, and I can't stop smiling.

"How about drinks at the Russian Tea Room?" He asks, kissing my bare shoulder.

I hum my approval.

"OK, I'll get the car. You just wait right here, and try not to get lost in this crowd, Lainey Bird."

I stretch up, which thankfully for the three-inch heels I have on, isn't as far as I normally need to, and kiss his mouth. "Or, we can skip drinks and I can just have you." I hum again and feel my inner lion start to purr.

A few minutes later, I feel a tap on my shoulder. I turn,

grinning widely, ready to see the face of my lovely lion staring back. But it's not him. The face in front of me is cold, pale, and thin. and The steel in his eyes instantly sends ice into my veins. Jemmy.

"Hello, Raven," he says. I never realized how nasal his voice sounded before. I didn't realize what a small man he really is. Not just in character, but in stature as well. Next to Connor, Jemmy could hardly be called a man. He isn't a man. He's a troll with a penis.

I recoil, putting as much additional space between us as possible, but we're unfortunately crammed close together with the crowds all lining the hall. "Jemmy," I choke out. I swallow, hoping to moisten my throat, but I can't. It feels tight — hard to breathe all of a sudden, and hot.

"I didn't know you'd be attending this evening," he says with a snake oil smugness. "I'm in town at the request of the conductor, of course. He asked me to come and do some work with the librarian to prepare a few pieces for their next concert."

"How lovely for you," I murmur. I work my feet back a few inches, but it's not enough. I'd heard lines like this from him so many times before, believing every single one, but I know now this is a lie. They were all lies. He's nothing but an insecure worm. I turn away from him and scan the crowd for Connor. I need my lion.

He runs a finger down the back of my bare arm. I cringe. "Well, look who's gotten all sexed up with a little peek-a-boo tattoo," he says. His eyes scan my body like an x-rated x-ray machine. My skin erupts in goose bumps, feeling dirty. "You know, we can head back to your hotel," Jemmy leans forward, his acrid breath touching my skin. Shivers of disgust travel down my spine. "For old times' sake. Are you here with anyone?"

Before I can turn back around, I feel his fingers lift

quickly from my body. When I spin to look at what's happening, I see Jemmy's hand being squeezed tightly in Connor's oversized paw. My lion. I let out a long, hard breath.

"No, as a matter of fact, she's not here alone, asshole," I hear Connor growl. Jemmy swallows and turns five shades of white. "My question is why you think you can touch her."

"My apologies. I didn't realize..." Jemmy begins, his voice leveling up an octave.

Connor leans forward, his penetrating gaze casting daggers into Jemmy's eyes. "I know who you are you sorry son of a bitch. I know what you did to her. And, so everything's clear, I want you to know who I am and exactly what I can do to you." Connor's knuckles begin to whiten with the pressure he's putting on Jemmy's hand. It's his bow hand.

Connor's voice turns to a menacing growl. "I am the man who knows a treasure when he sees one. The man who is going to take this beautiful woman home tonight and give her everything you never could. I can do great and terrible things to you, Jemmy. So, if you ever even so much as have a wet dream about Raven, I'll personally ensure you never play the violin again." He leans in and whispers something I can't hear, then gives his wrist a tweak before letting it go with a snap.

Jemmy rubs aggressively at his hand, now free of Connor's grip, and backs up knocking into several people in the crowd. Connor's arm is around me, his glare at Jemmy sending death warnings like arrows.

"I'm sorry, Raven," Jemmy mumbles through the crowd. "I'm very, very sorry."

Even after we've been in the town car a few minutes, Connor is breathing hard and keeps clenching and unclenching his fist. I'm too shaken to enjoy a nightcap now, so we head back to our hotel.

"Are you all right?" Connor asks for the fifth time as we pull up to the hotel.

"I told you, I'm fine. I'm not the one who was nearly eaten by a lion," I quip.

Connor guides us into our room and flicks on the light. He pulls hard to loosen his tie. God, he's gorgeous tonight. He fills out a black suit perfectly. The King of Beasts, properly attired in glorious splendor.

"Thank you for what you did for me tonight. I told you I was a coward," I say apologetically. My eyes dip to my feet. "I don't have the strength. I didn't know what to say."

His thumb and forefinger angle my chin upward so I'm looking directly at him. "You are wonderful, Raven. I'll always be there for you, just like you're there for me."

He leans down and kisses me, softly and gently. Flutters of need begin low in my belly.

"Are you sure you're OK?" He asks for the umpteenth time.

I nod and hum, snuggling into the heat of his body, my cheek burrowing into the dress shirt buttoned over his chest. His hardness, his scent, the feel of skin has me tingling all over. The familiar burn he ignites lighting up inside me. I look up and smile.

"What?" He quirks a brow.

"You are the man who is going to take me home and love me like he never could, remember?" I offer playfully. I slip out of my heels. Connor's fingers trace along the hidden zipper along my side. One hand slips into the back of my dress and caresses his mark.

Connor's stony expression finally eases and he gives me an amused grin. When I see it, I know everything is good again. "I am."

"Then you should get to loving me," I say, lifting up onto my toes and kissing him.

# CHAPTER TWENTY-THREE

**Sunday, June 27**

CONNOR MAKES love to me all night long. When the sun begins to peek over the skyscrapers outside our window, I can barely move. I'm blissfully exhausted. I can't imagine how he's not. He's ordered me to say in bed, order room service and rest while he tends to a matter of business with his lawyer in Manhattan. It's an order I'm only too eager to comply with. Even my Inner Sex Goddess is sore from Connor's amorous attentions. At times, he was gentle and sweet, coaxing pleasure from my body with the experienced hand of a man who knows every trick of the trade to bring a woman to climax. Then, his thrusts would turn primal as he claimed me over and over, growling out his own pleasure. The man is a beast between the sheets. My beast. #luckyme

At five o'clock in the afternoon, I emerge from a nice hot bath to a knock at the hotel room door. Connor probably just forgot his key, so I wrench it open, surprised to see a delivery man carrying a long white box.

"Miss Raven Flynn?" he inquires politely.

"Yes," I finger a piece of wet hair and clutch my robe tight around my neck.

"Mr. Rose asked me to deliver this to you with instructions to be downstairs at 6:30 p.m. sharp."

"I see." I accept the box and hold up a finger. He smiles as I take it. "Wait, let me get you something," I pause, backing a little bit into the room to fetch my purse.

"No need, ma'am. Mr. Rose took care of it." He gives me a two-fingered salute and turns to disappear down the corridor.

I practically run to the bed to see what's in the box. I untie a thick black satin ribbon and lift the white lid to reveal a cloud of white tissue paper. I fold it back and find a black strapless evening outfit. The bustier is adorned with black sequins. Layers of light sheer black fabric flow down to a full-length skirt — that isn't a skirt at all, but wide-legged pants that flow out like a full ball gown. The hem is trimmed in the same black sequins. It's gorgeous.

Inside is a handwritten note with a tiny sketch of a bird in one corner. It looks as if he's used his tablet to write the note and make the sketch and then printed it out for me. I bite my lip, loving this special touch.

*Raven, please wear this and be downstairs at 6:30. The doorman will have a car waiting. I'll meet you when you arrive. And stop worrying, it's a good surprise. — C*

I smile because I was worrying. And now, I'm just excited. Connor's surprises are the best, and I have no doubt this one will be, too. I hurry to dry my hair, apply some makeup and slide into the beautiful outfit he's given me.

The doors of the elevator slide open at exactly 6:29 p.m. An older doorman at the hotel hands me a single white rose. "Miss Flynn?" he says nodding and tipping his hat to me.

"Yes, thank you." I take the rose and lift it to smell its sweet scent.

"Your car is waiting. One moment." He waves down a

shiny black car parked across the street and opens the door to hand me inside. Then, I'm whisked away like Cinderella in her carriage.

"Where are we headed?" I ask the driver.

"57th Street and Seventh Avenue," he says in a proper British accent that oozes charm. His answer tells me precisely where we are going, and at the same time tells me absolutely nothing. I sit back and try to enjoy the ride. I shove Miss Insecure back into her closet and lock the door. I give the key to Miss Adventure who grins like a Cheshire cat. My Inner Sex Goddess is still recovering from last night.

We pull up to a building I know all too well. Connor stands in a black tux waiting for me. He looks amazing — hair long, flowing over his shoulders, and a freshly shaved jaw that only draws my attention to his very kissable, warm mouth. A mouth that draws my mind back to all of the sinfully delicious things he did with it last night.

He kisses me softly and I melt.

"What are we doing here?" I ask, looking at the darkened building. When there is a performance, Carnegie Hall is aglow with lights and sound and people milling around everywhere. Tonight, the venue is eerily dark and quiet.

"You look incredible," he says. He kisses my cheek and offers me his arm.

"You didn't answer my question," I counter, allowing him to walk me through a side entrance into the building. Once inside, I'm met by a thin Asian woman with long straight black hair and charcoal eyes behind gold wire-rimmed glasses. She's grinning from ear to ear.

"Good evening, Mr. Rose, Miss Flynn. If you'll follow me. I have everything ready."

"Everything ready for what?" I ask both her and Connor, though neither answers me.

"Go with Mrs. Kim," he says. "I'll see you in a minute."

Connor takes my rose, twists off the stem and tucks it into the lapel of his tux jacket. Taking my hand, he pulls it to his lips and plants a soft kiss against my knuckles. "See you soon."

"What?" I ask, as I'm practically pulled away. Mrs. Kim navigates me through a maze of corridors and halls before we step out onto what I'm sure is the backstage wing. On the stage, I see a single chair, a microphone on a stand and a cello. My heart stops. Miss Adventure has thoughts on letting Miss Insecurity out of her locked closet, but I mute her for a moment. It's a dress rehearsal probably. A famous cellist, perhaps?

"Are you ready?" Mrs. Kim inquires.

"Ready for what?" I ask, glancing around to see who the performer could be.

She smiles broadly and graciously gestures toward the stage. "To play Carnegie Hall, of course." She extends her hand palm up in invitation toward the chair. My eyes grow huge.

"What? Me?" I press my hand to my chest and gulp. I actually gulp.

"Mr. Rose set this up for you. Your audience is waiting. When you're ready," Mrs. Kim says, still smiling warmly.

Without my consent, my feet start to walk to the center of the stage, although I have no idea what I'm doing.

As I approach the chair, I hear an announcer's voice welcoming the ladies and gentlemen who have gathered for the evening. It sounds pre-recorded. Everyone is reminded to silence their cell phones and refrain from flash photography. But then, I am introduced by name, and I know it's a live announcer's voice. I swallow down hard and try to stay my hammering heart. The disembodied announcer's voice returns and informs the audience that I'm playing a selection of personal favorites. A drumroll beckons and the footlights blaze to life, temporarily blinding me. The curtains sway and then slide slowly back revealing a sea of red empty audience chairs. Well, almost empty. Seated in the center of the first row in the orchestra section are four people. I can barely make them out in the glow of the spotlight now shining on me. But I can hear their applause and see Connor's smiling face.

My hand flies to cover my mouth and I want to break into tears. But I don't. My Inner Maestro instructs me to warm up. I take a seat, curling the instrument to my body. I wrap my legs around my wooden lover and pull the bow across the strings to start a long slow scale.

When it's done, I clear my throat, bow my head and glance over the copper light that dances across the strings of the cello. I lift the bow and press it down, curling my fingers to form the first chord. The bow flashes quickly back and forth, flying over the strings. My hand and fingers dance, pulling notes and chords from its body like strings of sweet taffy. They snap and twirl and twist and are pulled again as the melody transitions from a spritely dance to a slow ballad. My heart and fingers know the music and the notes as if I am recalling my own name.

A dandelion wish morphs into a raven in flight. Of course, I've flown on a wish before. At the spa in Georgia when our trip began, but even before that on the back of Connor's Indian and tucked in his bed for a sleepover. As I pluck each note, I celebrate every flight — the amusement park, the Minnow Bucket, shooting the pistol, shopping, sketches, bike rides, candy, campfire food, dancing, music, concerts and ... my life.

Connor is right. I'm not running away, I'm flying toward myself. And here I am. Willow told me to take this trip with Connor to discover who I am, and now I know. I am Raven.

My spirit soars over the seats, the music hall, the skyscrapers and the city, out into the world of possibilities.

I continue playing through one piece and into the next, pausing for only a moment before letting my mind trace the musical scores I once practiced for hours a day. A concerto, an overture, a prelude, a folk dance. One after the other until my fingers are cramped and sore.

When the music is finished, tears stream down my cheeks. I lean the cello back on its stand and bow. I give thanks to the four people who are on their feet clapping for me. I can see them more clearly now. Tori, Ox, Connor and a young woman, who I can only guess is Ginger.

Mrs. Kim waits patiently in the wings for me and I walk with her to the sound of their cheers and Connor's catcalls. My feet barely touch the wooden planks.

"That was beautiful," she says. "And may I just say, if that wonderful man ever asks you to marry him, say yes."

I laugh, wondering if that particular wish could ever come true. And hug her. "Thank you for your help. I know it took a monumental effort to get this all set up."

"It no work at all, trust me. I mean, any friend of Tori's is a friend of mine."

"You know Tori Carmichael?" I ask, doubting the woman who doubts my affections for her brother would ever help set this up.

"Of course. She's launching a fashion line here in a few weeks. I'm one of her business partners."

I look down and see she's wearing a pair of Tori's jeans. And they are spectacular. She twists so I can see the pockets on the back and I give her a big thumbs up.

"C'mon. You're signing autographs and taking pictures with your fans."

# CHAPTER TWENTY-FOUR

**Monday, June 28 (the wee hours)**

"You're quiet," Connor says in the cab on the way home. Wine and laughter flow together in a heady mix that has me reeling from the surreal events of the evening.

We spent four hours and more money than I care to think about at a posh Big Apple eatery after my concert. Both Ox and Tori toasted me at least twice. Ginger, a clone of her beautiful mother but with her father's emerald green eyes, told me over and over how impressed she was with the concert. Connor couldn't stop complimenting my "extraordinary talents and skills." My Inner Maestro likes having groupies. #fanclub

"Hmm?" I turn my gaze from where I'm staring out of the cab's dirty window, distracted by the flurry of activity all around us. The sidewalks bustle with people. Bright flashing lights show every shop and restaurant are open. It truly is the city that never sleeps. Even at 2 a.m.

"You're very quiet," he repeats. "Was it too much tonight?"

"It was. It was so much, Connor. But it was perfect." I snuggle next to him. "I hardly know how to thank you."

"Hmm," he muses playfully. "I can think of a couple of ways."

"Name it. Whatever it is, you deserve it. Nothing you could do could surprise me more than that, Connor. I want to give something to you."

"I can have anything?" He cocks a brow and his eyes turn into dark pools of lust.

"Anything." I gaze up at him, knowing exactly what he wants. I want it, too.

He slips his hand into his jacket pocket and pulls out a butterscotch lollipop. "Go ahead and get warmed up then, Lainey Bird. You're going to be busy again tonight."

It turns out, I enjoy the "anything" Connor has in mind. I tell him just that as I slowly peel away my clothes and get down on my knees in front of him in our hotel room. I relish the delight I can give to him. I slip open his belt, then unbutton his pants. Cupping him, he hisses his pleasure and I know he's staring down, watching me. Sliding his zipper down, I brush my lips over him, nipping softly and then lapping hungrily. He groans and his fingers fist into my hair. This isn't an obligation. It isn't a payment or an earned reward. I'm giving to him, and in doing so, I'm giving to myself, too. Giving love.

# CHAPTER TWENTY-FIVE

**Tuesday, June 29**

THE FIVE-HOUR TRAIN ride and two-hour ferry ride to Martha's Vineyard is my least favorite part of the trip. I miss the Minnow Bucket and the private closeness Connor and I had while we traveled in it. But the reward of finally reaching Connor's house along the quiet New England village is worth it all. It is small, exactly as he described — only two bedrooms. But a castle compared to the Minnow Bucket.

It's a powder blue-shingled building with white trim and a bright yellow door. It reminds me of the sun is rising into a blue summer sky. Inside, a palette of cream, beige and light blue flow from one room to the other. A small kitchen gleams in all white, but it doesn't appear sterile at all. Personal and eclectic accessories that look like they have been collected over many years fill the counters and cabinets in every room.

It's a family home. His family's home. The one bit of his parents that remains for him and Tori.

Well-loved books with familiar titles fill the bookcases in

the small living room just off of a quiet eating area in the kitchen. The bookcases are flanked by two blue and white checked chairs and two long white slipcovered sofas. A light blue and beige rug covers whitewashed wood floors, and a well-used white brick fireplace anchors the entire room. A wall of French doors leads out to a deep porch decorated like an extension of the living room complete with lamps and thick, comfy blankets. Beyond that is the cape, shining and sparkling, as the sun dances off of the quick little waves that lap the shore like an eager puppy.

Connor shows me around, stopping to introduce his parents and his childhood through photographs scattered around the house. Family snapshots show smiling faces and a trouble-making little boy who looked like he was a real handful. Connor was a lion cub.

The bedroom we share has a big king-sized bed with a linen-covered headboard. The bedding is solid white, simple and elegant. A light yellow chair sits propped against the window, well-worn and faded from the sun streaming in. The only other piece of furniture is a small double dresser painted in a cornflower blue.

"What do you think?" Connor asks, stowing our luggage in the closet.

"It's gorgeous," I say, taking it all in again and again. Each time I scan the room, my eyes find another small treasure — a clock, a glass jar filled with broken colorful sea glass, a piece of driftwood acting as a bookend — that makes the space feel like a home.

"I can see why it's your favorite place on earth. It would be mine, too. I can't believe you brought me here, Connor. It's lovely."

"You're lovely." His hands move to my jaw, capturing my face in his hands, and he bends down to kiss me. His lips are warm and inviting and press against me in a tender display of emotion. "I love you," he says. I will never grow tired of hearing the words. Nor will I ever grow tired of saying them.

"I love you back," I repeat.

# CHAPTER TWENTY-SIX

**Monday, July 5**

CONNOR and I managed to pull ourselves from our lazy habits of life at the beach in time to enjoy the Fourth of July weekend celebration. The island comes alive for two whole days. We watched the boats come into the harbor, decorated from bow to stern in red, white and blue. We ate grilled hot dogs and ate way too much ice cream. Fighting our way through flocks of tourists in town for the holiday, we made it to nearby Edgartown where the whole community turned out for a parade. We skipped the fireworks display that night since Connor isn't comfortable with the sounds of explosives, but it didn't matter. He gave me my own private fireworks display in our bed. The man definitely knows how to light up my night and send sparks flying. My Inner Sex Goddess couldn't be more delighted ... or exhausted. #rocketman

I stretch out on the sand, testing the sore muscles of my inner thighs that were pulled over Connor's rigid body for most of last night — and most of the morning, too. He can make me come so quickly when he lets me be on top, which he's taken to doing every time we have sex now as a sort of contest to mark a personal best time. It's a fun little lover's game that has my sinew screaming.

"Keep arching your back like that, and I'm going to see if I can break the three-minute mark." Connor teases.

"You've got to give me a break tonight, babe," I beg. "Maybe we can just have a sleepover?"

He grins with that sweet love smile and blows me a kiss. "You got it. I hereby institute the 'no sex rule' for the next twenty-four hours. Though it won't be easy. You could try looking a little less sexy in that swimsuit."

We laugh at our escapades as I open up my coverup, giving him an eyeful, and then quickly close it again. That crazy man, I muse to myself. I adjust my sun hat and stare down at the water. A woman and her son throw stones, trying to see who can skip them the farthest, with the boy always winning. His short legs carry him back and forth, dodging the waves as they crash onto the beach. Blond hair flows down his back.

"That kid looks like he could be yours, Con,"I tip my chin to the boy.

"No way," Connor grins. "He's too well-behaved."

"I bet you'll have a litter of beautiful babies someday." I reach down to tug a bottle of water and my newest Sophie Riley book from the bag I brought down from the house.

Connor leans back in his chaise and tucks his head under his hands, elbows outstretched. "Not me. I'm not having any kids." His tone is casual. A bit too casual to be joking. I sit up a bit straighter. Why wouldn't he want a family?

"What? What do you mean? You don't want kids? Why?"

"I don't want that, Lainey." He pulls his sunglasses down from his nose. "Sorry."

"What do you want then?" I'm totally taken off guard. I know Connor loves me. I know we're happy together. His family is amazing and I know, based our discussion of all of his childhood antics of summer spent here, that he had a happy childhood. I shudder thinking this is more of the damage "she who shall not be named" has done to him.

"You," he smiles, but it's not his usual amused grin. This one is forced. "You want a beer?" And now he's deflecting.

I shake my head "no" and not just to his offer of a beer. No to this — this reticence. If I have to follow the rules, so does he. Rule four: we talk.

"Seriously, Connor, what are we going to do when we get back to Atlanta? I mean, I'm eventually going to get a job. I'll work nine to five, probably more like eight to six, and you'll work when?" I struggle to sort through the images flashing through my brain. This is a fairy tale, and one I fear isn't destined to have a happily ever after ending.

"I usually go in around four and stay till close. Two or three in the morning at least," Connor says. He adjusts his shoulders against the back of the chair uncomfortably.

"See. And I'll work Monday to Friday and you'll work ..."

"Weekends are my busiest times, Lainey." He offers me his hand. "Don't worry. We will make it work. I'm yours and you're mine, remember?"

"OK, but then what?" My heart starts to beat a bit faster. Maybe that beer would have been a good idea. Connor is the most amazing man I've ever known. I love him. I want a future with him, it's my dream. My most fervent wish. The one I make every time the clock shows all the numbers the same, every time I blow the fluff from a dandelion. But I also want a family of my own.

"And then what, what? Does there have to be something more? Isn't this enough?" His voice is calm, reasonable and utterly annoying.

"It's unbelievable. But you don't just want to date me forever, do you? What do you want from love, Connor?" I'm pushing his buttons now, I know I am. And he resists. I can see it in the way his jaw tightens and his lips press together. The more truth he shares, the more my heart breaks.

"Lainey. What do you want?" He asks quietly, cautiously.

"I asked you first." I force him to say it. Say what I know is just behind those perfect lips, inside that delicious mouth. He doesn't want me for anything more than this. I'm wonderful, sure. But it's not enough for me, not for Evermore.

"Answer me," he says in a no-nonsense firmness. His voice takes an edge. I square my shoulders and haul in a breath. I'm going to ruin everything. Again.

"I want to get married one day, I suppose." My own voice sounds weak, scared. I am weak. I'm a coward, no matter what he tells me. "I want a family of my own. I'm not too old ... yet, if I don't dillydally around."

"Babies?" He actually laughs out loud. "I'm sorry, but we want really different things. I don't want to get married again. And I definitely can't do babies, Raven. I have my reasons. Working late nights at bars and restaurants, is chief among them. That doesn't exactly mix well with parenthood."

I'm crushed. I lick my lips and stare back out at the water again. The waves rise up to a hopeful peak and then crash down forcefully on the rocks below before receding back into the ocean.

"Let's just be us, like this? Aren't you happy with us?" Connor sits up and leans forward, his demeanor growing more earnest and deliberate.

"Of course, I'm happy. I've never been happier." I feel myself about to surrender. Cash in all of my dreams for him. He'd be worth it, I know he would. But in the past month, I've tasted the air on my wings. I know what life could be — what I truly envision it to be for me — for us. It's too soon to give up on it now. I choke on the words as they come out in starts and stops that sound anything but convincing.

"But I want this relationship to be going somewhere serious, don't you?"

"It is serious. It is to me. Why do you need a piece of paper and some ceremony to prove that?"

"What?" My eyes narrow and my brow furrows. How is this my life?

"Lainey, look, being married taught me that I'm a pretty shit-tastic husband. I love you, but I can't get married again. Marriage was a one-time deal for me. I had my one time, it was a disaster and now I just want to be happy."

"So, you never want to get married?" Tears gather. I don't want them. I don't want to hear this. His words are equal parts shocking and distressing. Miss Insecure threatens to break down her closet door, but Inner Sex Goddess blocks the way. He's joking. He has to be.

"No, baby, I'm sorry. I don't." His voice is kind and almost remorseful. "Look, I'm doing my best with the whole boyfriend thing, OK. Let me get used to that for a while. Then maybe we could talk about moving in together or something like that." His tone is one of love and tenderness, but his words feel like a dagger, slicing at my heart.

"Boyfriend thing? You're uncomfortable with a committed relationship? And what do you mean 'maybe' move in together? We've been living together for the past five weeks." Anger rips through my voice and suddenly rule four sucks.

"Don't turn this into a therapy session, OK. If you want me, this is how you get me. I've made enough concessions to have you as it is." Disappointment and annoyance drip from his words. Good, now he knows exactly how I feel.

"Concessions? What exactly is that supposed to mean?" I fold my arms over my chest. I need a barrier between him and my heart. I need fortified, reinforced steel, but my indignation and arm-crossing will have to do for now.

"The boyfriend thing. I actually hate that, Lainey," he says dismissively. "Not because I want to date anyone else, I don't. But because I don't want our thing to be about labels. Why can't we just be together? We're good together. I like who I am with you. You're easy and, until just now, pretty simple." What is he even saying?

"I'm a complicated label now?" And just like that my Inner Analyst polishes up her black glasses and pulls out her notebook.

"Lainey, Jesus! How did we even get onto this subject? Why can't we just enjoy the beach? We can discuss all of this when we get home." Inner Analyst scribbles so furiously that she has to turn a page in her notebook.

Connor disappears inside the house, murmuring something about needing a beer. I am numb. Inner Analyst tries to console me. *He's experienced a great deal of trauma. As have you. It's clear that while the two of you can offer one another a friendship with lots of benefits, you want different things. We should start regular sessions to help ease your transition after this breakup. I will conduct them during the middle of the night when you should be sleeping. We'll meet later.*

Break up? Connor and I are going to break up? *Yes,* my Inner Analyst nods. *You don't want to date for the rest of your life, do you? You want to get married, and that's not going to happen.* I shake my head. Stuffing my feet into my flip-flops, I wrap myself in my coverup and start walking toward the road in front of the house.

"Lainey, where are you going?"

"For a walk," I say bluntly. "I need to think."

"Lainey, look, I promise we will talk about all of this. Later. OK?"

He actually sounds like he means that when he says it. But I know it's just his way of telling me that when we talk later what he's really going to do is turn up the charm and try to convince me to keep things as they are. And why wouldn't I want that? Connor is wonderful. He loves me. He's amazing. But I want more. I want evermore, just like he had put on my tattoo.

I walk around the tiny island, stopping for lemonade and a cookie. I finally wander back to the house around sunset, but Connor isn't there. There was a time when I'd totally freak out about that. I'd worry and wonder about what he was thinking of me, how he was judging me and being angry that I can't do something he wants — which isn't even a bad thing. But that girl is gone. She's flown away and she can never come back.

# CHAPTER TWENTY-SEVEN

### Tuesday, July 6

I PACK the next morning while Connor sleeps on the sofa. I heard him come in around 10 p.m., but he grabbed a blanket and stayed on the couch. I'm actually glad. I'm not strong enough to be curled up into my lion again.

I'm dressed by 7 a.m. and hear the wheels of my cab crunching outside. I wake Connor as the driver packs my suitcases into the trunk.

"You're dressed very early," he says, rubbing the sleep from his eyes. He looks like he hardly slept at all. I know because they're the same eyes that I looked at in the mirror this morning that didn't sleep at all.

My fingers tremble and my heart aches. I can barely get out the words. "I want to say goodbye, Connor."

"Goodbye? What do you mean? You're leaving?" My heart crumbles when I see the hurt and sadness in his eyes.

"I think it's for the best," I offer, tears clogging my throat and almost paralyzing my vocal cords.

"What the fuck, Lainey?" Connor is fully awake now. Sadness twists into full-on fury. "The best for who?"

"For both of us, Connor." I shake my head and look down. Then I muster every ounce of courage I have left and look up into his dark blue eyes. "If I stay here another three or four days, I'm just going to let you convince me that you're right. That I should just leave well-enough alone. But I don't want to do that." The tears begin their slow steady trickle and his fingers reach up to brush them away, but my fingers do it first.

"I love you," he says softly, reaching for me. "I didn't say I wanted this to end, ever. I just said I didn't want to get married. We've only been together a few weeks, Lainey. Why can't we give this some time and see where we are a few months from now?" His voice pleads with me. It would be so easy to cave to him.

I shake my head slowly and free a few more tears. "No, Connor. By then, you'll be too much a part of me, and I won't be able to let you go. And I need to let you go. You'll devour me. I don't want to say no to my wishes anymore, Connor. You showed me that. You think we don't know one another, but I know you. I know you're scared because of what happened with Shana. I know you still blame yourself, but you can't. She had her own problems."

"Yes, she did," he fires back. "And if I was any kind of a decent husband to her, I'd have seen that and gotten her help. I'd have been there for her. I will not do that to you, Lainey. I love you too much." The look of helplessness in his eyes feels like a razor to my heart. I have to look away.

"I love you back," I say tenderly. "You know that. I am so grateful to you for everything." I pause to regain my resolve. "But I want evermore with you, Connor. A future of 'us', not 'you' and 'me'. Not just dating. Not just filling time until you figure things out. I'm going home."

"What? Right now?"

I nod silently and pick up my purse.

"So, this is it? We're done?" He rakes his hands through his long hair, lightened with bright streaks of blond from the summer sun.

"What is the point of going on when we want to reach two very different destinations, Connor? This is our journey's end. I'm sorry, but staying would be too painful. I love you so much. You'll swallow me up, like a lion. I'll watch myself disappear again into someone else's version of what and who I should be, and I can't do that. If I disappear again, I'll never find my way back." I lift to my toes and kiss his cheek softly. "I love you."

His arms pull me in tight to his chest. The muscles twitch with his own emotion. "Don't go, Raven. Please, don't go, baby."

I push lightly out of his arms, walk out to my cab and tuck myself inside. In the window's reflection, I watch as the little blue house and my sad lion fade into the distance.

# CHAPTER TWENTY-EIGHT

Saturday, July 17

THERE'S a coffee shop around the corner from my apartment that just happens to be directly across from the *Journey's End*. I park myself on one of the high-top stools behind a narrow table in front of a large picture window that overlooks the bar. It's become my new form of self-torture. Every morning, I wander in for my usual latte and a daily dose of Connor. He's yet to notice me there, and I'm glad. Today, I check emails and apply for jobs online and watch Connor across the street in his bar.

And even though I know I shouldn't, I find myself coming here every day just so I can get a glimpse of him. See him, without being seen by him. Because no matter how much it hurts, I still love him. I think it will always hurt. Because I will always love him. I watch him smile at customers. He rakes his hands through his hair. He knots his hair in a little sloppy man bun in the back. It's been two weeks and he hasn't called. Hasn't texted. Inner Analyst keeps telling me he won't, and I know she's right. I still find myself checking messages a million times a day ... hoping. Willow said we need time apart — time to think. All I do is think of him.

I'm reminded of him practically every moment of my life. Every time I see the ink on my back, I think back to the weeks we shared together, falling in love and learning about ourselves and each other in ways so much more intimate than sex. And, heaven help me, I think of sex. I miss him holding me. I miss falling asleep watching decorator shows, resting against his chest.

I still watch the shows he likes, even though I've seen them all more than once now. Like I said, my own version of self-torture. He's the man of my dreams, but not the man who wants to make my dreams come true. The irony is almost more than I can bear.

My daydreams of Connor are interrupted by a text from Willow.

**Willow: How are you?**
**Me: Good**
**Willow: Liar. Has he called?**
**Me: No**
**Willow: Hon, you can't work this out if you don't talk to him. Call him.**
**Me: I can't.**
**Willow: Yes, you can! CALL HIM!**
**Willow: Don't make me put my pregnant ass on a plane, Ray!**

I smile slightly at her empty threat.

**Me: It hurts. I miss him.**
**Willow: I know. It will all work out, Ray. I promise.**
**Me: Thanks. Kiss the baby for me.**
**Willow: Done. Love you, Sis.**

**Me: Love you!**

"You've got a good perch here, Lainey Bird," I hear a low voice say behind me.

My lips curl into a smile when I turn to see Ox Carr standing behind me. Once a rock star hero, now a man I can consider a friend. I reach up and hug him warmly. I look around for Tori or Ginger, but he is alone today.

"How are you?" I ask. "How is ... everyone?"

"I'm good. Going through some stuff, but it's all good. Tori's launching her new clothing line next week. And Ginger has a new boyfriend." At this last statement, Ox rolls his eyes. "I hate him, of course. Mostly because I think they're sleeping together, and I want to murder him for it. He has till Christmas to put a ring on it before I call some of the guys Connor knows from his ranger days to encourage the guy."

"Dad life is hard," I mutter. He nods.

Ox tips his chin in the direction of the *Journey's End* across the street. "He looks all right, but he's not. He's fucking miserable without you, you know?"

"No. I don't." I glance down at my phone. "We haven't talked since Martha's Vineyard."

"For the record, I think he's making the biggest mistake of his life in letting you go. You saved him from himself. He needed to be there for someone else for a while. He needed to be needed and loved. I think, more than anything, he needed to see he could be the man he always thought he should have been with Shana. You did that for him."

"He did it for me, too," I add, praying my river of tears stays behind the dam of pretense and my "I'm doing fine" façade.

"You should call him," he says simply. I wish it were that simple. I wish I could just call and, with a few words, we could heal and bring our hearts back to our last night in New York City when the world was perfect.

"He doesn't want to hear from me, Ox."

"Hmm." He half grunts, half speaks. "Connor said the exact same thing when I told him to call you. Both of you are lying, you know."

"Ox ..."

"I know. I know. It's none of my business."

"No, but thank you for caring. Tell Tori good luck with the launch. I'll be the first to order some jeans from her."

"I'll tell her." Ox hugs me tightly and then turns to leave the little coffee shop and let me drift back through my memories and wishes of Connor, alone again. Just before he walks out the door, he stops and turns to look at me. He wags a finger at me and looks a bit more upbeat.

"Can I come to see you next week sometime? Thursday maybe? There's something else I want to discuss with you." His eyes light up, but he doesn't give any hints.

I open my mouth to reply, but he stops me with a hand and interjects, "And don't worry. It's not about Connor. Thursday?"

"OK, Thursday."

# CHAPTER TWENTY-NINE

**Wednesday, July 21 — Thursday, July 22**

I'VE COMPLETELY FORGOTTEN my promise to Ox about meeting up on Thursday when my phone rings at a little past 7 p.m. on Wednesday evening.

"Elaine Flynn?" A male voice speaks on the other end of the phone.

"This is Lainey," Inner Analyst has just made furious notes on her pad again as I relapse and refer to myself by Connor's nickname for me. I sigh inwardly. We'll be having a long discussion about the reasons I slipped and called myself that tonight. Probably at 2 a.m. That's our standard appointment time. I toss and turn until she cracks open the notepad and we start to hash things out. On nights when she's too tired, Inner Sex Goddess berates me for losing the best lover I'll ever know. And I know she's right. The lion has ruined me for any other man.

"My name is Houston George, I'm one of the owners of the Three Bulls Winery. We're based in California."

"Yes, Mr. George, what can I do for you?" His name

299

doesn't ring any bells. I quickly scan my application list, searching for a point of contact I may have sent a resume to, but there's no Three Bulls Winery on my list anywhere.

"I hope you don't mind. A friend of mine, Cyrus Goldstein, interviewed you a couple of months back for a position in marketing with Pinnacle."

Mr. Pencil Tapper, how could I forget. It was his ridiculous comments that had driven me to drink — literally — at the *Journey's End*. It was that ... what was his name? ... that man that started the whole thing that had led me on a journey of a lifetime only to end up with the heartache of a lost life.

"Yes?"

"Well, he shared your resume with me, and I think you'd be a perfect fit for us out here. Cyrus tells me you're a workaholic and we could use one. We're currently looking to revamp our entire marketing and public relations message and we need someone with experience and dedication who can put in an extra mile."

"That's me," I say lightly. At least, it was.

"Great. I'd love to have you fly out here. I know it's short notice, but we need to move quickly on this project. Our team can make all the arrangements. Could you come tomorrow afternoon? We could spend the day Friday talking and you can see our operations here over the weekend."

"Yes, I can come tomorrow."

"Great. My secretary will email over the itinerary. I look forward to meeting you tomorrow."

"As am I. Thank you, Mr. George," I manage to eke out before he signs off the call. I let out a sigh of relief. A job. Thank God! #workinggirl

On Thursday, I overthink and overpack and opt for an Uber rather than pay for parking at the Atlanta Airport. I've made plans to stay over for a few days and visit Willow and

Stephen and catch up on all the baby news. I check my app and see my driver is still a good half hour out, when my doorbell rings.

"Hey, Lainey," Ox says cheerfully. He looks down at the suitcase by the door. "We did say Thursday, right?"

He's holding a bright yellow box with a silk sunflower attached to the top with a piece of raffia twine.

"Ox, hey. I'm so sorry. I completely forgot. I'm going to have to reschedule. I got a last-minute interview out in California. I'm leaving in a little while. But I'll be back next week. We can get together then if you want."

"An interview? California is a long way away, Lainey."

"I know. But maybe it's for the best, Ox."

"Who's the interview with?"

"Three Bulls Winery. A smaller winery, but they've got some gold under their belt. They're looking for a new Director of Marketing for a total revamp of their brand."

"Sounds like a lot of work," his brows knit together.

"It will be. But I can do it." I hope I sound more eager and hopeful than I feel.

"I have no doubt. Here, these are for you." He hands me the box and steps inside to close the door behind him. I tug off the lid and see a pair of jeans tucked into folds of yellow polka dotted paper.

"Tori launched her new line of women's clothing, and made those for you. She said they're a little longer than Ginger's since you're taller."

I hold them up and examine the pockets. They have tiny cellos embroidered in the corner.

"Oh, Ox. Tell her they're amazing. I love them. I'm going to throw them in my suitcase right now."

"You driving yourself to the airport?"

"I've got an Uber coming. The driver should be here in twenty minutes or so."

"Cancel it. I'll drive you. We can talk on the way."

"Really, Ox? There's no rush. I can see you next week."

"No. What I have to say can't wait. The wine people will liquor you up, and I want to make my offer first." Ox picks up my suitcase and we head for his Mercedes parked outside.

"Offer? What kind of an offer, Ox?"

"Job offer." He tucks me into the supple black leather in the front seat of his coupe, and we curl into the slow-crawling traffic. "I'm getting a band together," he begins.

"Really?" I am all ears. Inner Fangirl is using Inner Analyst's notepad.

"Well, not *Climax*. Their day is done. But I got an idea on Connor's birthday. It was nice just doing the acoustic thing. We were making some wicked harmonies. You've got a good ear."

"Thanks." I am waiting for him to get the part where he makes me an offer. My mind is reeling at what it could possibly be.

"I want you to be our manager," he says, turning onto the interstate.

"What? Me?" Inner Fangirl has just spiraled into orbit while Inner Analyst takes notes. This has something to do with Connor, she can just feel it.

"Yes. You're perfect. I want you to arrange gigs, run the marketing, do all the PR for the band. I want to keep it local to start — just stuff in the Southeast for now. See how we do. I can offer you a decent starting salary, nothing extravagant, but it'll keep you in lattes. Oh, and twenty percent of the band's take. Industry standard is thirty, but I honestly don't know how well we'll do right out of the chute. And we want your input on music, too."

"Ox, I ... I don't know what to say."

"Say you'll think about it while you're in California." I watch him negotiate Atlanta traffic and I know he's serious about this. "I mean really think about it. This is a totally legit offer. I've already talked it over with a couple of the other guys in the band."

"Who's in the band?" I ask dubiously. Inner Analyst sits back in her chair, her glasses hanging on the tip of her nose in anticipation.

"Well, Sam Slade for starters. And another buddy of mine, Memphis, who will be good on guitar. I want you to sit in on some sessions with us, too. I found this killer instrument called an electric cello. Can you imagine? Your stroking that thing would be bad as fuck!"

"Sam Slade and Ox Carr start a band. That's like the perfect rocker love child, Ox. You're going to take the music scene by storm. You'll educate a whole new generation of music lovers on what real rock and roll sounds like."

"See, you're already writing ad copy," Ox says. His round Santa laugh fills the car.

"And what about Connor?" I ask quietly.

"What about him?"

"What is he going to say about all of this?"

"Does that really matter? Besides, he has enough on his plate right now selling all the restaurants."

"What? He's selling all his restaurants?"

"Yep. He's going to hold on to the *Journey's End* — just going to be a silent partner. His buddy, Lincoln, is going to run it. He'll do a good job."

"Why?"

"Well, with me starting up the band and Tori's time invested in her new fashion venture, he'd be managing them all on his own, and that's just too much. He's got something new he's looking to get going."

"You have to let him know. I won't let it affect my decision, but I want to know what he thinks about my working for you. I don't want to cause any problems with your family."

"Working *with* us, Lainey. You'll be working with us."

I give him a hard stare in reply.

"OK, I'll talk to him. But this is your choice."

I hug him goodbye at the airport, and board my plane. I sit back in my seat and my mind starts immediately daydreaming about managing a band. Not just any band, a band headlining Ox Carr and Sam Slade. Inner Fan Girl is starstruck. Inner Sex Goddess is drooling. Miss Insecurity paces — again. My Inner Analyst takes copious notes while The Maestro tries to imagine what an electric cello and acoustic guitar duet would sound like. Miss Adventure is raising a glass to toast them all. Me? I'm smiling. For the first time in weeks, I'm smiling.

# CHAPTER THIRTY

**Sunday, July 25**

"Oh, my word, look at your sweet pregnant belly!" I gush over Willow's rounded shape. I roll my hands around it and lean down to kiss against the skin holding my future niece or nephew.

"Oh, I'm so happy to see you! I've missed you so much," Willow hugs me and tears of affection spring to her eyes.

"What is it? What's wrong?" My brow crinkles together and I search her eyes for the answer.

"Ignore me, I cry at everything," Willow says, swiping at her full cheeks. She looks so adorable all pillowy and round. Her face is filled out, flush and glowing.

"Believe her," Stephen says, carrying my suitcase down the hall to their guest room. "Yesterday she cried at a beer commercial."

"Well, those horses were so sweet," Willow says, wiping her eyes. Stephen rolls his eyes and disappears down the hall.

"I love you, hon." He calls to her waving a hand.

Willow and I flop onto the sofa and clutch our hands

305

together. "How did the interview go?"

"It was great. Willow, these people are so dynamic, and the company has huge opportunities for growth. They've offered me nearly an incredible salary plus bonuses. It's going to be a ton of work. They want me to completely revamp everything — labels, branding, websites, advertising. I'd have my own office, two assistants and a creative team. And the winery is so pretty. Every view looks like a postcard."

"It sounds too good to be true, Ray." Willow says beaming. "I'll be so happy to have you back in Cali, I can't stand it. Mother will be glad, too, although she'd never tell you. She's moving back here to be closer when I have the baby."

"And Daddy?" I ask eagerly. Willow just shakes her head sadly.

"No. He's staying in Chicago for now. But let's not talk about that. Tell me more. Tell me everything." She puts her chubby ankles up on an upholstered ottoman and rests her hands on her expanding stomach.

"Well ..." I start and then suddenly stop. I've told Willow everything my whole life, and yet I wonder if I should tell her about Ox's offer. What would she say?

"What? What are you not telling me?" Her eyes narrow as if she's trying to use her big-sister superpowers to divine my secret.

"I kinda got another job offer," I mutter slowly.

"Really? Where, from whom?" Willow looks excited and it makes me feel excited, too.

"Ox Carr is starting up a band. With ... wait for it ... Sam Slade!" We both squeal excitedly. "And they've asked me to be their manager. Willow, I'd get to plan all the gigs, help with the music and even get to perform some. Ox says he's found me an electric cello. I checked it out online and it's unbeliev-able. I'm dying to get my hands on it." I can hardly stop myself from chattering away.

"I'd be doing all of the PR and marketing, negotiating appearances, contracts, tours, everything. We haven't discussed hard numbers yet, but he's promised me twenty percent of the band's take which would be huge. Because, I mean, it's freaking Ox Carr and Sam Slade for crying out loud."

"Oh my God, Ray!" Willow squeals. "Are you kidding me? This is amazing. Manager of a rock band? You'll get to have your music and marketing and Ox Carr and Sam Slade. You've idolized those men for years. I remember your room growing up was practically wallpapered with pictures of them."

"I know. And they're such nice people," I add, thinking back to my night in Richmond with *Limitless* and my dance with Sam. Which, of course, makes me think of Connor and the tattoo and everything that has happened. I push those thoughts aside and focus on my sister.

"Ray," Willow says, her voice edging into that big sister tone again. "You have to do this."

"What?" My eyes narrow.

"The band. This is your dream. Your music and your marketing talents coiled into one job with people you've always wanted to work with and know. How can you turn that down?"

"I know. But there's Connor," I offer. The only negative to the entire thing.

"What about him?" Willow says, dismissing my objection. "He let you go, Ray. He doesn't get a say."

"I know, but he's going to be at functions. Ox is his brother-in-law. I'm going to see him a lot. And I just don't want there to be any awkward tension that would spill over into the work, you know?"

Willow pats my hand and then rubs her stomach. "Ray, what about you? How are you going to feel about all this?"

"Weird. Good. I don't know." I let my head fall to her

shoulder. She smells like gardenias and Earl Gray tea. I inhale and let the soothing scent calm me a bit. "I miss him so much, Willow. Part of me wants to do anything to keep me near him, and part of me wants to get as far from him as possible so it won't hurt so much. Working in California, I'd never have to see him."

"Ray, you love him?" She asks. She knows I do.

"I think I always will, no matter where I live or where I work."

"Well then, you have to decide which you want more — your dream to have a family or the one man you'd ever have it with."

"What am I supposed to do, Willow?" My heart squeezes and I feel her hand take mine and hold it tightly.

"I can't tell you that, Ray. But I don't think I have to, do I? You already know what the right decision is."

I smile and hug her close.

"Oh, here," she places my hand on her stomach. I can feel the flutters of the new life inside her body, kicking against my hand. My face lights up.

"Oh Willow, I wish you'd find out whether you're having a boy or a girl. But either way, I think you're having a soccer player."

My sister shakes her head with a wry smile. "We want to be surprised."

I smile back.

"Just promise me one thing, Ray," she says pressing my hand against her firm belly again. "You'll come and meet him or her when I deliver. Atlanta is so far away."

My brow crinkles and I rest my head on her shoulder again, comforted by her love and support. My sister is a duplicate of my heart who lives and walks around right before my eyes. Willow is my best friend. She understands what it is I must do. That alone is all I need.

# CHAPTER THIRTY-ONE

**Wednesday, July 28**

IT's a Wednesday afternoon and the *Journey's End* is crowded. Some sort of party, I assume. Connor pours drinks, his hair pulled back in a low tail at the nape of his neck. His shirt is misbuttoned, and I wish someone would tell him. He smiles at the customers. The smile is fake. To everyone else, it looks genuine, but I've seen his real smile, and this is a poor facsimile. He's tired. I wonder if he's been having nightmares again, and if anyone new is soothing the lion while he dreams. No, I can't think about that. I can't let my mind wonder if that's why his shirt is misbuttoned today. That he woke up after making love all night and threw on his shirt as she was trying to drag him back into bed. Nope. Can't think about that. My Inner Analyst makes more notes that we'll no doubt ponder in the wee hours of the morning tomorrow.

I sip my overpriced latte and look out of the large plate glass window of the coffee shop and watch Connor some more. Before I dial Ox, I offer a prayer that he's all right with this.

I start talking as soon as he answers. "Hey, Ox. It's Lainey. Listen, I've thought about your offer and I have an answer for you. Can you meet me later?"

"I can meet you now. You want sugar in that latte or what?"

I put down my phone and scan the customers inside the coffee shop. His head stands out above the crowd and I smile and wave. I must have been too distracted by the lion next door to notice Ox when he walked in.

He wraps me in a hug and flops down on the stool beside me. Now we're both staring out of the plate glass window into the *Journey's End* at Connor Rose.

"Did the winery offer you a job, too?" he asks.

I nod.

"And you've decided which it's to be?"

"Almost. You have to agree to twenty-five percent. But not starting until the first quarter that the new band makes more than two million in sales. Until then, just my salary and expenses. And I get final approval of all creative. Including the band's name. I don't want you guys calling yourselves the *Electric Ponytails* or anything stupid like that. I get it in writing that Connor has nothing to do with our agreement."

"That's it?" Ox confirms, giving me a happy Santa laugh.

"Nope. You buy the electric cello. That thing looks so cool."

Ox smiles broadly. "You'll take the job?"

"Of course. It's a dream come true for me, Ox. You know that. And I'll work very hard for you, I promise."

"I know you will. And don't worry about Connor. He's neck-deep in his own new thing. I told him about the offer, and he's cool with it. He agrees you're be the best person for us. I think he's actually rooting for you, if you want to know the truth."

"I'm glad. What's his new venture?" I ask cautiously.

"He's going to do this neat Farmer's Market grocery store thing with a farm-to-table restaurant in the back. Just a breakfast and lunch place. He says he needs more time off for life balance or some shit like that. It's pretty amazing though."

"He's actually doing it!" I say, my face beaming. My mind drifts back to our conversation that night in the tiny town of Cowpens. The night of the storm when we made love for the first time. My body erupts in gooseflesh that I am helpless to control. Just the thought of the way he touched me. God, I miss him. I miss the sex, but I miss the closeness more. I just miss Connor.

"You knew about this?"

"We talked about it once. Very briefly. What do you know about it?"

Ox cocks his head to the side and stares down at me. "You got time to take a ride with me?"

"Well, you're my boss. What do you say? Can I shirk off this afternoon?"

"C'mon." He pulls me in for a hug.

An hour and a half later, Ox and I stand outside a small white building in what I am sure is the cutest small town in America. The large glass windows on the storefront are papered over so I can't see inside, but construction work signals a renovation is underway. Ox has a key and we enter through the back door. The place is open and spacious. Flooring and cabinetry have already been installed. The fixtures and design all remind me of Connor's family's place in Martha's Vineyard. Except for the dining room of the restaurant.

Boxes are spread out on the floor, filled with decor for the merchandise shelves that are temporarily leaning up against one wall. Peeking through one box, I see a model Ferris wheel, a bicycle basket filled with silk wildflowers and a glass jar of colorful seashells. And there are framed sketches and pictures of us from our trip in the Minnow Bucket.

The dining room looks like the Watergate Hotel with its caramels and grays. Tears prick at the back of my eyes. All the decorating shows we watched are coming to life in front of me. All the nights cuddled next to Connor as he slowly built his dream in his head one piece at a time. We designed it. And now he's building it. My heart is ready to burst.

"It's so beautiful," I say, trying to suppress the emotion in my voice. It's impossible, but I try anyway.

"Yeah. I like it." Ox moves over and pulls a long, paint-smattered drop cloth from over a plank of wood leaning against a wall. Underneath, the sign for the front is revealed. A tiny raven is painted in black against a light blue backdrop. In her beak, she holds a dandelion seed. Written in a loose calligraphy hand are the words "Little Bird Cafe and Grocery."

My whole body responds to the vision of it. I try to hide my face in my hands. But I'm helpless to stem the tide now. I fight back against the emotion as Ox moves to hold me, but it's not his touch, not his comfort I want. He's not the man I need.

"Oh God, Ox." I clap my hand over my mouth, but it does nothing to stop my sobs.

"He's poured every ounce of himself into this place," Ox says, cupping a large arm around my thin shoulders. "And none of it has anything to do with the Army, or what happened in Afghanistan or with Shana. It's just you. That's all that's in him now, Lainey Bird. And if you leave, I'm afraid there won't be anything left of that man."

I bury my face into his thick chest. "I love him so much, Ox. I don't know what to do."

"Lainey," Ox croons softly as he pats my back. "He's suffering just like you, girl. He'd kill me for telling you, but he is. You two have got to talk to each other. I can't stand to see either of you miserable. Fly back to him, Little Bird. He needs his raven."

# CHAPTER THIRTY-TWO

**Wednesday, August 18**

WHO KNEW SO MUCH legal paperwork is required to start a band? I've been going blind staring at contracts. I promised Ox and Sam I'd do a good job for the new band, *Dante's Muse,* and I have pushed what should have taken months into three weeks.

Connor, too, it seems has been drowning himself in work. Ox let it leak that The *Little Bird Cafe and Grocery* is set to open next weekend. Anton Arnaud is even coming down to do a special guest chef pop-up night for the grand opening. Connor thinks Anton just called him out of the blue, but the truth is, I now owe the Ox Carr Superfan the first guitar pick from *Dante's Muse's* first gig for the favor.

I've relived every moment of the day I spent at the *Little Bird Cafe and Grocery* and gone over and over in my mind what Ox told me. More than a few times, I have held my finger over Connor's contact number to call. I have composed dozens of texts, but could never get the courage to send one.

Then two days ago, I saw it. A missed call while I'd been

in the shower. From him. My heart beat like it did the first time he kissed me just seeing his name cross my phone screen. He didn't leave a message. He didn't have to. That one tiny step was all I needed to finally find the nerve. Inner Sex Goddess, Analyst, Insecure, Anxious and Adventurer all conferenced. An important decision had to be made. In all honesty, it had already been made a weeks ago. It was being willing to admit it out loud to myself first, and finally to Connor.

He is the only man I could ever imagine myself being with. Ever imagine I could marry. Or have a family with. But he doesn't want those things. He just wants me.

So, I could have a life with marriage and family to some as-yet-unknown man who would never be the love of my life, or I could have a lifetime of love with my soul mate who will never give me his last name or his children.

So, on this Wednesday afternoon, two days after his name flashed on my phone, I find myself sliding my body into the perfect fitting jeans Tori made for me and a white T-shirt. OK, I bought it a size smaller than I normally wear, so sue me. Inner Sex Goddess thinks he'll like it. Inner Analyst agrees and Inner Fangirl knows that Ox and Slade would approve — if they actually saw me in it. Funny, but Miss Insecurity hasn't made an appearance in weeks, and I'm glad.

At 2:30 p.m., I work up my courage, swallow my pride, march into the *Journey's End* and take a seat at the bar. I glance at the sign and then see the bartender saunter toward me. There's an odd smile on his face like he's amused with me about something. I'm staring. It doesn't matter to me anymore if he knows.

"The view's included, but you have to buy a drink," he says, exactly as he did all those weeks ago. The first time.

"OK, I'll have a beer then," I reply, considering my options at the tap.

"Nah, you look more like a whiskey girl to me," he says and reaches around to pour me a glass of the *Breckenridge* he keeps on the bottom shelf — a bottle hidden from the eyes of the average customer.

"And just so you know, you don't shoot it, you sip it."

"Thanks for the warning." I sit and sip my drink while he rubs a wine glass with a towel and then slides it into the rack above his head. Still broad, still muscled, still turning me on.

"Will you want another one?" He asks, giving me that grin again.

"No thanks. The last time I had whiskey in this place it landed me in some strange man's bed."

"Yeah?"

I nod at him. "Yep. It was actually the best mistake I ever made in my whole life. I fell in love with him."

Connor walks around the end of the bar and comes toward me. I spin my stool around to face him. He spreads his legs on either side of me pinning me in place. There's no warning to what he's about to do, he just does it. He just leans down and kisses me. The electricity I had come to love so much returns like a boomerang and supercharges every atom of my body, shooting through it with painful pleasure. God, I've missed this man so much.

"Lainey Bird," he murmurs, not letting his mouth leave mine for more than a second. His kiss devours me. Like a lion.

My arms wrap around this powerful lion's broad back and I cling to him like static on silk. He grins at me and flexes the muscles from under the thin cotton of his black tee. Connor's fingers press into my skull, urging me forward. Closer. Deeper. "Damn it, I've missed you so much." He murmurs into my ear. His voice is laden with raw emotion he's narrowly keeping in check.

"I've missed you back," I manage to croak out. My mouth is not my own, it's his now. Evermore, his.

"I love you," he whispers as a tear slips down his cheek and disappears into a newly-grown beard.

"I love you back," I reply as he kisses me again, more deeply this time. I have no doubt every customer in the place is staring at us making out in the middle of the bar like two randy teenagers, and I couldn't care less. My body, my very soul, has been starved of this man for far too long. Finally, he breaks away, but keeps my face held firmly in his large hands.

"Connor, I'm so sorry. I never should have left that day. I need you. I need you more than I need anyone or anything else. And if you want to date me forever, then OK. If you're the only family I ever have, that's OK, too. It just has to be you. It can't be anyone else. We'll be who we are — no labels, no pressure."

The words barely escape my mouth, and Connor shakes his head. "No, my little Lainey Bird, I was wrong. I don't know what I was thinking. I could never be who I was before with Shana because you've changed me. You've made me a different man. A better man. Better in every way. I'm so sorry I hurt you, baby. God, you have to know I want you. I want the entire world to know you're mine. All mine. I want you to wear my mark, my name, my ring. I can't live without you, Raven. I need you, too. I need you with me every day— in my bed, in my life, even in a tiny-ass RV."

I'm shaken to my core. I never expected to hear these words nor the intense emotions with which they're spoken to me. "Connor, you don't have to ..." he silences me with a kiss so hot, it makes every other kiss we have shared seem cold by comparison.

"I don't have to. I want to." He wraps his arms around me again and whispers into my ear. "I love you, Raven. And I want you to know that I *am* going to propose to you. And you're going to marry me. Soon. Not today. Maybe not even in the next few weeks. But I swear to you, Lainey Bird, you're going to be mine, physically, emotionally, legally and in every way."

"I'm already yours, Connor." I say, pulling back to see a single tear shining in the corner of one navy blue eye. The eye of a lion. My lion. #evermore

# CHAPTER THIRTY-THREE

### Wednesday November 15

"OH MY GOD, Connor, it's a boy! A boy!" I find Connor in his office at the *Little Bird Café*. His new assistant, Glory, takes Connor's iPad from him. That iPad, the same one I gave to him in New York, stays almost permanently attached to his hands these days. He and Glory are probably managing next week's order with it. That woman works magic with Connor. She keeps him organized, sends him home at a decent time and only allows him two candy bars a day with nary a wrapper in sight. I adore her.

"A boy? When?" Connor asks.

"This morning. Oh, Connor. I have a nephew. Isn't he beautiful?" I slide my finger across the screen of my phone to show him the half dozen photos that Willow and Stephen have sent, but he's distracted by something. Glory just nods and slips back to her laptop at her desk.

"Glory, make him pay attention to me," I pout. "Look at those eyes. And that sweet chin. Oh, Connor his toes. Couldn't you just eat them up? Look!"

Connor laughs out loud at me. Even Glory fails to keep her amusement under wraps. "That's kinda weird isn't it? To want to eat a baby's toes?"

"It's not. Connor, just look at them. Are you looking?"

"I'm looking, Lainey Bird. I'm looking. But I don't want to eat them. Sorry."

Connor rests his chin on my head while I continue scrolling through pictures. Things between us have been incredible. But today I feel his attention being pulled away again as Glory shows him something on the iPad, then goes back to her computer.

"Do you want me to come back? You seem really busy." I start to feel like my intrusion is merely being tolerated while other important work is being neglected.

"I'm sorry. Forgive me. I'm all ears now. Tell me everything."

"Well, he has a beautiful head of dark curly hair and Willow's eyes. He was nine pounds, six ounces and twenty inches long."

"Damn, poor Willow," Connor says.

He glances at something Glory has handed him to look at on his tablet. He nods and swipes with his finger as if he's signing something. I'm starting to grow a little frustrated with him.

"What's his name?"

"Willow didn't send that to me. But he's gorgeous."

"He's a tank. That's what I'm going to call him. My nephew, Tank."

"Connor, that's so sweet. He's not technically your nephew, but you can be his UC, just like you are for Ginger." I smile widely. I haven't brought up the matter of his proposal since the day he mentioned it. But every once in a while, he reminds me it's coming. And I believe him. But a gentle reminder that I'm still waiting can't hurt, right?

Connor gives me a smile. Oh, that smile. The one that's only for me. It's my favorite curve on his entire body. It means he loves me. And he knows when he smiles at me like that, all I hear is "I love you."

"I love you back," I answer to his unspoken declaration.

"We'll find out his name from Willow and Stephen when we get there tonight." He looks over at Glory who is giving him the thumbs-up sign.

"Flight leaves in three hours, Mr. Rose," she says in her light Southern drawl. "I'll arrange everything else while you're en route." My mind spins, looking down at Connor and watching Glory disappear, closing the office door behind her.

"I have this idea," Connor says. "A little surprise for you. I thought we'd fly to San Diego and meet *our* new nephew. We can stay a few days, so you can be with Willow and the baby and your parents on Thanksgiving. I need to talk to your father, too. Then we can rent ourselves a little RV and head to Vegas. We can get married there and honeymoon all the way back home. There are lots of rest areas along the way." He arches a brow suggestively.

My mouth falls open. One hand claps over it in shock as Connor drops to one knee and pulls a small black box from his pocket. He lifts the lid to reveal a stunning engagement ring blinking back at me.

"Marry me, Lainey Bird," he commands. And my heart can do nothing but obey.

"I want you to be my wife," he says, peering up into my misty eyes.

He slides the ring onto my finger. Then, he kisses me softly. "Please, say you'll be my wife, Raven. Be my evermore?" he asks.

"Yes," I reply, happy tears splashing down my cheeks. "Yes. Always. Evermore."

# CHRISTINE ROBERTS

# THE END

**THANK YOU** for reading *Evermore: Heart of the Raven*. I hope you enjoyed the story of Connor Rose and Raven Flynn. If you would like to know more of their story, keep scrolling to read a sneak peek of its **COMPANION NOVEL scheduled to be released in the summer of 2022**, *Evermore: Soul of the Lion*. This is Connor's version of the story and includes tidbits of their journey Raven didn't include, plus an additional epilogue that reveals how Connor and Raven spend their lives as a married couple. You won't believe what happens!

Discover more about the lives of the two soldiers Connor saves in the bombing in Afghanistan in original Heathen Brotherhood series available on Amazon and on Kindle Unlimited. This four book series includes: *Conflict of Devotion*, the story of John Galloway; *Second to None*, the story of Ian McGuire; *Sacred Trust*, the story of Oliver and Maisie; and *On Her Behalf*, the story of Tex Morgan.

Subscribe to the Christine Roberts Author Page on Amazon or follow her on Instagram and Facebook to get the first peeks at the story of Nathan Fairsmore's widow in the *Heathen Brotherhood: Legacy* coming fall 2022.

## WELCOME TO THE HEATHEN BROTHERHOOD

# EVERMORE

*soul* of the *lion*

# CHAPTER ONE

## Wednesday, June 2

"HEAD LICE? SERIOUSLY?" I glare down at Marie. I don't want to give her a hard time about having to leave work early, but damn. Head lice? How is it that we can cure nearly every childhood disease known to man, but this parasite we can't do anything about?

"I'm sorry Mr. Rose. But Dan is on deployment, so it's just me. I can get my mom to watch the kids and work a double on Saturday if that helps?" She looks scared I might fire her. Damn it.

"Marie, it's just plain ol' Connor, OK? Your kid comes first. Don't worry about it. I can cover for you for a couple of hours today. Just let me know if you need anything, OK?"

"Thanks, I really appreciate it."

I wave her off. She played the deployment card. She knows that's my weakness. I remember what it is to be a solider overseas. You have to keep your head in the game, but it's hard when all you can think about — worry about — is whether your family back home is all right without you. If they're sad, lonely, needing you, and you're not there. It's a hard thing to deal with. Dan doesn't need that stress. He's a good guy, and his wife mixes a hell of a margarita.

I hear the door open and Marie waves as she walks out. A few seconds later, the door chimes again and a customer walks in. Holy hell, she's pretty. A bit thin for my taste, but damn, she's got legs for days. Legs are definitely my taste. They're curvy and long and telescope out of a black suit skirt that skims above her knees. No stockings, and three-inch black heels that are sexy as hell.

She's got beautiful dark brown hair and when the lights catch it just right, I can see shimmers of gold in it. She sits down at the end of the bar and takes a few seconds to look around. It's her first time here, obviously. But I would have remembered if she'd been in here before. I would have definitely remembered those legs.

I approach her and clear my throat. She's gawking at the taxidermy animals above the bar. There are four of them: a zebra, a cheetah, a rhino and a lion. They're the inspiration for the whole place. They reminded me of an old photograph I'd seen in school of Ernest Hemingway in Africa. Then, in my research, I found a cool quote that gave me the name for this place. *"It's good to have an end to journey toward, but it is the journey that matters in the end."* It felt fitting for the place. I was ending one journey with the army and starting this — running my own bar. So, I call it the *Journey's End*.

Most people think the animals are fakes, but for the money I paid for them, they better not be. Her gaze finally leaves the lion and she's looking at me, but not saying anything.

This is awkward. She's staring at me. With these eyes that are so dark they're black. Who the hell has black eyes? If I start staring this could go on for a while. I could seriously get lost in those eyes of hers. They're Audrey Hepburn eyes, large and almond-shaped with thick dark lashes that float all the way up to her perfectly arched eye brows.

I tip my head slightly, but she's still staring. It's like she can see me. Really see me. Scars, tormentors, lies, the diseased heart that beats in my chest. And then, deeper to the last speck of hope that still glimmers somewhere so deep down, I can't feel it most days. A tiny shiver runs down my spine. I can't take any more of this.

"The view's included, but you have to order something," I finally say. I almost don't want to break the spell she's got me under, but I don't make payroll by letting women ogle me.

"Can I get you something?" I ask.

"Um, yeah. A beer, I guess?"

Great. First Marie's kid gets lice, and I get stuck behind the bar. And now I'm waiting on what I'm sure is a non-drinker. "Sure, what kind?" I ask ready for the blank stare I know is coming. This chick has no idea what she wants. She's probably a white wine kinda girl, if I had to bet. Not sure why she'd ask for a beer.

"Excuse me?" She murmurs. And there it is. I pull my long hair into a knot on the back of my head and watch as the glazed over look spreads over her face.

"What kind of beer do you want? We have lots on tap, and if you don't like any of those, we have bottles." Does she seriously think beer only comes in one variety? What fun would that be? She glances over the taps and looks totally overwhelmed.

Her shoulders wrap up a little higher around her ears and her posture curls inwardly just a bit. If I didn't know better, I'd say she looks like one of those little bugs I used to play with as a kid. The kind when you tap with a stick, and it curls up into a ball leaving the exoskeleton around the outside its body to protect it from being eaten. And right now this little thing looks like she's about to be eaten by the world. She looks up at the lion again. Yeah, the world has is ready to devour this one today.

"Tough day, huh?" I guess.

She only nods, but her expression is clear. She doesn't need a beer or a white wine she needs a whiskey. She needs a whiskey and a good, long, hard kiss. I'd volunteer to get a taste of that sweet mouth. She isn't wearing much make-up, but her lips have this amazing light natural plum color. Full, plump and sweet. I'd love to find out if they're as soft as they look. I force my gaze back up to her eyes. Those glassy black eyes that are staring into me again. Damn, but this woman is beautiful.

"Yeah, you could say that. I was really hoping to land this great job, and I honestly thought I had, but they turned me down."

"That sucks. Maybe a beer isn't what you need. Maybe you need something else. You like whiskey?"

A whiskey? Did I seriously just ask the woman who can't even order a beer if she wants a whiskey? She needs it though. Maybe something with training wheels. The really good stuff. My favorite brand. She'd like that.

"Maybe," she answers a bit timidly.

Maybe hell. This woman looks like the world has eaten her up and then spit her back out again. I offer her a glass from my personal bottle. It's a small batch brand, a bit pricey for a daily drinker, but so good. I could never keep it on the shelf at the bar for customers. The clientele at the *Journey's End* wouldn't pay the twenty bucks I'd have to charge for a shot. But I keep a bottle for myself for after hours while I balance the till and finish late night paperwork. She only asks me how much.

That's right. She mentioned she was interviewing for a job.

"It's on me," I offer. I look down at her and realize I'm

smiling at her. Now, why in the hell would I do that? She's just a chick. Like every other chick who comes into my bar and sits down with a sob story to tell. The faces change, but the tale is the same — the lost job, missed promotion, break up, make up. Whatever. I pour a shot into an old-fashioned glass and slide it over to her. As she puts it up to her nose to give it a cursory sniff, I pour her a glass of water. Bartender's habit I suppose.

I watch her flip the end of the glass up and toss the entire contents of the glass to the back of her throat. Holy hell! I can't stop my laugh at her coughing and sputtering. I bet that burns like hell right about now. She guzzles the water and her eyes tear up.

"You're not supposed to shoot it, honey. It's a sipping whiskey. That's why I didn't pour it into a shot glass." I can't stop snickering at her. Poor thing. She didn't even get to taste it. She murmurs something and then scoops up her purse to leave. And I don't know why, but I don't want her to go. I grab her glass, drop a sphere of craft ice into it and pour her another dram, a bit less than the last one.

"Oh, no you don't. You need a do-over there tender-foot" Her eye glances to the glass and then down to her purse. "And don't worry. It's still on me."

This time she takes a sip and, I can tell by the look on her face, she likes it. What's not to like? Aged in rum barrels for no less than fourteen years, it's smooth and has strong overtones of caramel and vanilla. It's meant to be savored and enjoyed. And this woman looks like she could use some enjoyment right about now. She also looks like she needs a meal. Damn, she's skinny. Not so skinny that she looks sick, just like she needs feeding. She's just a tiny little thing. Small-boned with delicate features like a little bird.

"You eaten today?" Yeah, that doesn't sound stalker crazy at all. "I mean, you want a menu?"

"Oh yes, I've eaten. I had a granola bar and two bottles of water today." She actually says that as if it's real food. Granola and water? No wonder she's so damn thin.

"Birdseed and water isn't food, honey. Let me get you a menu." This woman needs feeding. Especially after two whiskeys. Her eyes already look like they're a bit glazed.

"What sorts of salads do you have?" She asks flipping through the menu.

We offer several really good ones, actually. But a salad? No doll, no salad for you. You need real food, meat, potatoes and possibly dessert. I'm not sure where this need to care for and comfort her is coming from, but it feels right somehow. Tonight this woman is finally going to get the break she needs in her life. Perhaps a hot meal and a couple of whiskeys are the part I can play in it.

"We don't do salad, honey. How about a cheeseburger? If you're a vegan or something, we can do mushroom or black bean."

Those inky eyes dance a little at the mention of a cheeseburger. Good.

"OK, cheeseburger, I guess. But can I get it with cheddar instead of American? And I'd like steak sauce instead of mustard. And no lettuce, unless it's not iceberg. If it's iceberg, then none. Oh and no mayo."

Sure thing, Sally Albright. I want to roll my eyes, but really, I've heard worse. Like the lady who asked me to cut the crust off of her son's hamburger bun. Seriously? I cut the crust off of white bread and put a burger on it. Kid was happy, Mom was happy. Tip sucked. Just goes to show, no good deed goes unpunished. I could be the poster child for that slogan.

As I type her order in, it actually does sound pretty good. At least she's got a palate that knows how to mingle good flavors together. I charge it as a comp. Tonight the little bird eats for free.

When it comes, it's picture perfect. I love it when the staff gets it right. It's not often, but when they do, it's great. Emilio is running the kitchen today. I make a note to praise him later.

It takes her like an hour and a half, but she finally finishes every bite and I feel better. Especially since while I had to go to the office to take a phone call, she ordered another whiskey. Ted, who's working the bar tonight, wouldn't dare serve her from my personal bottle. He poured her a Larceny. Just as good. And if it's her third, she probably wouldn't taste the difference too much. I notice he also adds a splash of water to it. Good thing, she's a bit tipsy.

Tipsy and chirping up a storm. Lord, this woman's mouth runs non stop. I clean a few glasses and listen as she pours her heart out.

"I mean, I have two Clio awards, you know. They don't just give those out to anyone. But that doesn't matter, I guess when you don't have the Twitter or FaceGram, or whatever the heck it's called," she cheeps on while a regular couple comes in for their daily after work cocktail.

They're a nice couple. He's an office guy, wears a suit and tie everyday and I have no idea what she does, but she dresses well — not a suit, though — and always has her hair and makeup done. They've been married for like forever. And like clockwork, every day at five sharp, they walk in. He's a Jack and Coke, she's a cabernet. Every damn day. They sit and chat about their day and sometimes order an appetizer or dinner. But mostly it's just the one drink, long glances and a nice tip. Lucky bastard. The kind of affection and devotion I see between the two of them when they just look at each other and talk is the personification of romance and real chemistry. It's what I always wanted. What I thought I had once. But know now, I never will.

The little bird at the bar is still chirring away to Ralph

another regular who comes in half hammered a couple of times a week. He's a Miller Lite. He only gets three here before we cut him off, and he knows it, so he makes them last as long as he can. Even he looks glazed over from all her yammering.

"I mean, what's the big deal if a person doesn't take a cavation. It's not like I don't have a life. I have a life. I work. I'm good at my work, I guess. I think I am. Maybe I'm not. But who would I go on vacation with anyway? Cavations ... I mean, vacations, are supposed to be fun, but they just make me feel more pathetic and lonely. I'd rather just save the cash and feel lonely at home with the travel channel."

"I know what you mean. More money for beer." Ralph answers.

"And whiskey," The little bird chirps back. And she's quiet. For like two-point-eight seconds.

"This place is cool. Do you think those animals are real? I mean, I know they're real, they're clearly not imaginary, but do you think they were once alive? I wonder what it must have been like to shoot one. Not that I shoot. I hate guns. And I'm not a proponent of animal abuse or anything, I just can't imagine what it would have been like to have been in Africa and actually seen a real lion in the wild. I'd probably just be scared. Everything scares me. Well, it does now, but it didn't use to. I was brave once. I used to do things. I just don't do things anymore. I guess."

I find myself listening to her more than I'm not. Well, all right, in my defense, she's has this kick ass voice. It's not high and whiney like a mouse's voice. It's kinda lower, more sultry. And the accent is unusual. Not southern, even though I've heard a "y'all" in there once or twice. A transplant to Atlanta, obviously, but I can't tell from where.

She mentions the places she'd like to go, the things she wishes she could do, but then stops herself from believing she ever could. Why couldn't she? She's on her fourth whiskey now, and I've already told the night shift staff that she's not driving herself home. Her words are starting to slur and she's not really making much sense anymore, but that doesn't stop her. She just keeps chirping away. It's endearing, a little, actually. I can't help but be drawn in by her.

I shake my head trying to ignore it — this feeling she gives me. But I can't. Little bird needs a friend, someone to believe in her. Just one, and I bet she'd fly.

She teeters on her heels to the ladies room and I'm given a chance to admire those great legs again. I always did love a great set of legs. And hers are spectacular.

Just after ten, Collette pulls me aside. She probably has another table pissed that she screwed up their order. I swear, if I could get this woman to have just one night where I didn't have to comp an entire table, it'd be a freaking miracle. She's a shitty waitress, but for some reason the guys all request her section. Well, for two reasons. Pretty big reasons that tend to play peek-a-boo from the low cut tops she wears. And the guys who sit in her section tend to stay and run up big tabs, so I guess that's worth a comped meal here and there.

"There's a woman passed out in the ladies' room," she whispers. "Should I call 911?"

I shake my head. Hell no! That's the last thing I want. All I need is for lights and sirens to pull a drunk woman out of my place and load her up into an ambulance. I glance over my shoulder and see the Little Chirping Bird isn't on her perch. Shit.

She's totally passed out on the tile floor. Apparently, she did her business, washed her hands and then fell like a sack of potatoes onto the floor. Thank goodness it doesn't look like she hit her head. She comes to for a few seconds and says she's fine and needs to settle her tab. Right. Fine.

I pick her up. Man, she weighs nothing. I take her

through to my office. The door is just off the short hall where the restrooms are located so I don't have to carry her through the main dining room in front of our guests. I lay her out on the sofa and tell Collette to bring me her purse from the bar.

I retrieve her wallet when she brings it back. R. Elaine Flynn, 2564 Westview Road, Apt. 6, Chicago, IL. Great. My plan was to sneak her into my car out the back and take her home, but no way I'm driving from Atlanta to Chicago. And as nervous and high-strung as she is, if she wakes up in the emergency room, she'll have a total freaking panic attack and probably go insane. Nope.

"What are you going to do, Connor?" Ted asks looking down into her pale face.

"Not to worry, Ted. She's a friend of mine. I'll take her back to my place. She'll be fine once she's had a few hours to sleep this off."

"Want some help getting her to the car?" He asks.

"Nah, I've got it. Just tell Lincoln I'm heading home early tonight. He's the manager on duty to close, anyway. I was just filling in for Marie." The afternoon conversation with Marie comes back to me in a flash. Her shift would have ended at five when she had to leave to get her son from his baseball practice. I glance down at my watch. It's almost 10 p.m.

I shake my head and want to cuss myself a blue streak. I should have been gone hours ago, but I stayed just so I could hear the little bird on her barstool chirping at me. No, not a little bird.

R. Elaine Flynn. Elaine. She doesn't look like an Elaine. Lainey, that suits her better. A little Lainey bird. I smile and look down into her face. It's a beautiful face. Soft rounded cheekbones that sit up high. A long chin and thin nose and huge eyes. And those damn plum colored lips.

I have no idea why I do it, but after I get her into my car and buckled in, I lean down and drop a single small kiss on her mouth. It was so wrong. But, damn, I just couldn't stop myself. Her mouth is completely irresistible. She smells of the sweet caramel of the whiskey. I brush my thumb over her cheek feeling the softness of her skin — like a peach, smooth and sweet. Lord have mercy, I could totally fall for this woman if I let myself.

We almost make it all the way inside my house before she throws up all over my front entry. Her body would eventually purge the poisons on its own. I've seen drunk people in my bar too many times not to know when it's coming. I'm just glad I am able to point her to the bushes and save myself from being bathed in it. She, on the other hand is not so fortunate. What a mess. Bless. Her. Heart.

I get her upstairs, and undressed and clean her up the best I can. She comes to for a few seconds here and there, but doesn't seem to mind that my hands are all over her bare breasts trying to clean her up. And they are fabulous breasts. Not large, but then again, that's never really been my thing. The centers are the same sweet lilac color of her lips. Her body instinctively reacts when I brush over them with a warm soapy cloth and I watch with increasing hardness at the little plum-colored centers twist into points.

She's in no condition for sex, however, so I drape her in one of my *Climax* tees and put her in Ginger's bed and close the door.

I'm not sure why I think of that bed and that room as my niece's. She doesn't stay here with me as often as she did when I got this place. And even then, it was probably more to keep me company than anything else. Ginger knew I was hurting after everything that happened in my life, and it was better for me to have someone here. It will be nice not to sleep alone in this house again tonight.

My cell phone buzzes in my pocket. It's my brother-in-law,

Ox. I have no doubt, Lincoln blabbed about what happened if he called or came by the bar tonight.

"Hey man," I prepare to give my excuses.

"So ... I pop in for a beer tonight, hang out with my favorite brother-in-law, and I hear you've gone full-on caveman carrying out a comatose hottie. I didn't realize you were into necrophilia, man."

"Fuck you, Ox. She passed out in the bathroom. You want me to call the cops and have blue lights advertising the fact our bartenders over served a beautiful woman until she passed out?"

"So she's a beautiful woman, is she?"

"She is the most beautiful woman I've ever met, man. Great legs. Black eyes. I mean, really. Totally black. But can't hold her whiskey worth a damn."

"Where is she now?" You know, I swear I can hear his eye brow arch up when he asks that.

"In Ginger's room. And before you ask, I'm in my room."

"OK, OK. I hear you. How are you? I didn't even know you were heading up to *Journey's End* tonight."

"I needed to pick up some files for the accountant. I was there like ten minutes and Marie's kid's school called. He has lice. She had to leave, and I offered to cover the bar for her."

"Damn. What about *Day Old Bagel*? Any thoughts on how we're going to deal with the management?"

"I was planning to make a surprise visit tomorrow. If Smitty doesn't get on board, I'm going to have to let him go. He can't deny we're doing great. I know you promised him he could stay on, but damn it Ox, I'm not about to loose money because he's a stubborn ass."

"Don't stress about it, bro. When he gets that first bonus check, he'll see things our way. We still on for lunch Friday?"

"Yeah. There's something I wanted to talk about with you, though. Can you cook the pizzas at the *Journey's End*?"

"Sure. This about work?" This time I can hear the smirk.

"Isn't it always?" I answer.

"You work too much, Connor," he says. He uses the voice that speaks more of a loving father than of a brother-in-law and friend. To me, he's really been all three. "I know your birthday is coming up. You doing OK with all that? 'Cause you know you can talk to me if you need to. Talking is one of your rules, isn't it?"

"Yeah it is. I'm OK. Just beat. I'll call you tomorrow."

We hang up and I let out a long breath. My birthday is only days away. It's an anniversary of both life and death for me. The memories haunt me. I'm not sure why, but when I lay down in my own bed a few doors away from her, I'm convinced the Lainey bird is going to keep the ghosts away. And when the sun comes up a few hours later, I realize she has.

# CHAPTER TWO

**Thursday, June 3**

A HALF HOUR into my regular workout, my cell phone rings. Even as early as it is, most people know I'm up. I never miss a workout. This home gym is like a second church to me.

Every Sunday I sit in a pew, sing hymns, hear sermons and bathe in forgiveness. But every other morning at six sharp, I'm here. The pew is replaced with a workout bench. I grunt out my pleas for strength and mercy rather than sing. My muscles shake from fatigue. I bathe in sweat. It's my penance — a way to punish myself for everything I should have done, my sins of omission. It keeps my head clear, and helps me keep my shit together. But it's also given me a pretty ripped body. Maybe that's what the little Lainey bird was gawking at last night. Maybe it wasn't my broken soul she was seeing after all.

I set my weights down and glance at the phone. It's Ox. Again. If he's calling me this early, it can't be good news.

"Now what?" I answer, breathing heavy. There's no need

for me to pretend I don't know it's him. Or that he is the bearer of bad news.

"Good morning to you, too," he says cackling at me. Ox has this laugh that he just can't control. And when it really gets going, it has an infectious quality that makes everyone around him want to laugh even if they have no idea what's so damn funny. This morning, however, was not one of those times.

"Sorry. Good morning. What now?" I bite back.

"I just got a call from the Day Old Bagel. Smitty is at it again. He's using the old menus. The waitstaff doesn't know what to do. Micah is the one who called. Can you swing by there and see if you can throw some of that restaurant-owner muscle around?"

"Yeah, I'll take the little drunken bird over there when she finally wakes up. Smitty thinks we're not paying attention. I'll call him. I'm over his bullshit."

"Thanks."

"Why can't you go?"

"Um ... well, I'm ... uh, busy right now." Ox stammers. I can hear Tori's voice on the other end of the line telling him to hurry up. Geez, those two don't stop. Since they got married at seventeen, they've been at it like rabbits. You'd think after all these years of marriage, they'd move out of the honeymoon phase, but they just love each other so much. I am equal parts revolted and envious.

"You're not busy. You've just got your face between my sister's legs. You guys are disgusting. Grow up, Ox. You're part owner in these restaurants too. You have to deal with the confrontations head on. Silent partners aren't exactly silent when our bottom line is on the line."

"Screw you, man. I'll go by when we're done. I mean, this afternoon after they close. OK? Are you happy now?"

"Fine."

I hang up on him before the heavy breathing starts and finish my workout. I take my time to shower and check my e-mail before heading upstairs to see if the Lainey bird, is awake yet. I tap lightly on the door and see her sitting up in the bed. She's squeezing her temples. I can't help but grin. I bet she's seriously regretting her visit to the *Journey's End* last night.

"Good morning, little bird," I whisper. She looks sleepy and tousled and so incredibly sexy. Her in my T-shirt is such a turn on. "Well, you don't look as bad as I expected. How do you feel?"

"I'm dying." Her voice is raspy.

"You're not dying, honey. You're just hung over. I guess whiskey isn't your thing, huh?" I reply. I almost can't stop myself from laughing at her. I walk closer to the bed. I don't want to scare her, but I want to know she's all right. She's still swaying a bit.

"How many did I have?" She's pressing at her eyes now. Yeah, I know that feeling. And she's right, it does feel like you're dying.

"Last I counted, four, possibly five." I hold up five fingers and her eyes take a second to focus, but she sees me. She's OK.

"Oh God. Aren't you supposed to cut me off at some point when I've been over-served?" Wait, she's chastising me?

"Yep." *Yeah, honey, like this is my fault.* "But you seemed fine. Until you weren't. I wasn't going to let you drive home, but you were chatty and coherent the whole time. Well, until you went to the bathroom and passed out."

"I passed out in the ladies room?" She looks terrified and utterly embarrassed. I can see a faint blush creeping over her face and it's adorable. I didn't know anyone blushed anymore.

"Yeah, one of the waitstaff found you. They wanted to call

the ambulance, but I told them you were a friend of mine, and I brought you here."

"Where is here? And where are my clothes?" She turns her head to glance around the room and that's a big mistake. She turns a little green before taking a steadying breath.

"Relax, little bird. You're at my place in the city." I've never been one to mince words, but telling her about her behavior for the rest of the night isn't going to go down well at all. "And you sorta threw up on your clothes, so I washed them and put you in my T-shirt."

And now, she looks like she's having a full on panic attack. This girl watches too many CSI murder shows on Netflix.

"Calm down, I didn't try to fuck you or anything. You're perfectly safe. I just didn't want you waking up with a charcoal tube down your throat while EMTs tried to pump your stomach. I figured you'd wretch it up on your own, and you did."

"You're washing my clothes? Like in a washing machine?" The bird squawks.

"Um, yes?" Shit. She had on a suit. I didn't even think to check the label. I'm guessing I should have sent it out for dry cleaning. Damn, why do I never think of these things?

"Listen here, Tarzan, that was a $500 suit. It's silk. It's dry clean only. Didn't you read the label?"

It only takes a minute to pull her clothes from the dryer to see they are completely ruined. They've shrunk and the jacket has turned into this wrinkled mass of fabric that can't even be recognized as clothing. I totally screwed this up. I stride into the room to face the music and see her face twist to horror when I hold up her clothes.

"I'm so sorry."

"Great. Now what am I supposed to wear?"

"I'm sure we can find something for you." Lainey looks to be about the same size as Ginger, my niece. A little taller, maybe, but she'll probably have some clothes that will fit. I know she keeps plenty here. There were a few times, while she was in college, she had to call me for a ride from a party where she'd had way more than she needed to drink. She'd crash at my place, and then nurse her hangover without Tori and Ox going nuts. Uncle Connor's, UC she calls me, house is her safe place. I rummage through the closet surprised at how much stuff she keeps here.

"You want me to put on your girlfriend's clothes?" Lainey is practically shrieking. But as soon as she's done, she squeezes her head. Serves her right. Like I said, poster child for no good deed.

"Relax. They're not my girlfriend's."

"You're married?" The statement rocks me to my core. The ghosts have morphed into demons thinking about Shana. I push them away, but not before they get their shadowy hands around my heart and squeeze.

"No, Lainey bird, not married." Not anymore and not ever again. "My niece stays with me sometimes. This is her room. She's got a shopping addition and keeps some stuff here. You guys look be to be about the same size."

"My name is Elaine," she flings back at me.

If she would have asked me to call her Elaine, I might have. But it's much too fun to see the little bird get her feathers all ruffled up over the nickname I've given her. Besides, her name doesn't quite fit her somehow. She doesn't seem to be an Elaine to me at all. Lainey fits her much better.

"I saw on your license," I reply. "It also says you live in Chicago."

"I know. I've been meaning to get it changed, but I keep forgetting." She's lying. Everything about her body language tells me so. Not to mention the fact that anyone who alphabetizes her credit cards, isn't going to forget to renew a driver's license.

I realize, looking at this woman in my house, in my shirt, that she doesn't even know my name. What had she called me earlier? Yeah, right, Tarzan. I grin inwardly at that, a bit more than flattered that she thinks I resemble some sort of Jungle King.

"I'm Connor Rose. But I think I kinda like Tarzan better," I admit freely.

"Thank you for taking care of me, Conner Rose, but I'd really like to just take my doll clothes and go home now." I'm disappointed she's so quickly dropped the Tarzan. It would have been fun if she'd have played back a little. But I suppose I am a stranger and she is hungover. Maybe once she gets to know me, that could change.

I struggle to compose my thoughts. I want her to get to know me. I want to know her. I like her. This chattering little Lainey bird all tousled and defiant in my house. I'm shaken by the realization. It's been five years, and I haven't felt this way about any woman I've met. Why now? Why this one? I want to keep her close a little longer. I need to see what this is ... this interest in her. Maybe it's just lust. But maybe it's something else.

"Look, why don't you get a shower. We can grab some food, and I'll take you back to the bar to get your car. I still think you're a bit messed up, and I don't think you should drive."

She tries to stand up, and wobbles a little on shaking legs. The shirt barely covers her ass and I'm reminded of what I saw under it all last night. I don't process a word she's saying staring at her legs. Damn, this legs!

She's nodding so I am hopeful she's agreed to my offer. I point toward the bathroom and hope I remember to say something about where she can grab towels and shampoo. I turn and leave her to her ablutions. Closing the door behind me, I realize my palms are sweating, my heart is hammering and my inner Tarzan is hard as a rock.

What is this woman doing to me?

I pound downstairs determined to get rid of whatever attraction it is I think I could be feeling for her and call Smitty at the *Day Old Bagel*. Figures, he's on the golf course and not at the restaurant ... again. How he thinks he can be a site manager and never actually be on site is beyond me.

"Ox called and said the wait staff is a bit confused as to why there are two different menus. Did you redesign the menus and not tell us?"

He gives me some cock and bull story about customers asking for old favorites. This man is an absolute idiot. How in the world he managed to make a dime on this place for the last ten years baffles me. When we bought it, the kitchen was way out of code, the menu outdated, suppliers were overcharging him, he was overstaffed and had zero marketing. In just over a year, we're doing double the business and have tripled our profit margins, and he still refuses to embrace the changes.

"Look, Smitty, I appreciate that the regulars need their fix. Just have the kitchen make it for them. But don't start using old menus again. It's confusing. Not just for the wait staff, but for the customers — all the new customers we've brought in." He's ignoring me, and I've gone from slightly annoyed to completely pissed. My tone sharpens. This guy has got to go.

"I'm meeting with Ox tomorrow and we're going to be discussing the direction of current management at all of our stores. This episode isn't going to bode well for your future with our organization. Change is difficult, but inevitable, Smitty. You have to get on board or move on. Do you understand?"

He says he does, and that he'll be sure to tell Micah, the

dining room manager on duty, to be sure all the new menus are being used. But I'm still going to stop by and check. I did offer to feed Lainey bird anyway, right? And she needs feeding. She needs care. And it hits me.

After disconnecting the call with Smitty, I text Dr. Georgia Krazanski, my therapist. She's been retired for more than a year now, and she doesn't charge me, so I wonder if she's still my therapist or just a close friend who knows all my dark shit and lets me call and talk to her whenever I need to.

**Me: I met a girl.**

**Georgia: Hey Connor. Good for you.**

**Me: It's weird.**

**Georgia: What is?**

**Me: I'm attracted to her, but not just physically.**

**Georgia: How would you describe it?**

**Me: Like I want to help her, protect her somehow. Dumb?**

**Georgia: Is she in trouble?**

**Me: No. Unemployed, but smart. She'll get something soon, I know.**

**Georgia: I have water aerobics. Call me tonight. Let's discuss, if you want.**

**Me: OK.**

**Georgia: I'm glad to hear this, Connor. It's been a long time coming. Things might be rough for you. Call me anytime.**

**Me: Thanks**

I take a few deep breaths and thank God for Georgia. I pop back upstairs to check on my Lainey bird, but she's gone. It takes a few minutes to find her. She's poking around my music room.

The space is supposed to be a formal dining room, but Ox insisted it be turned into a music room. Not only is Ox Carmichael my business partner in ownership of six successful Atlanta eateries, but he's my sister's husband, best friend and former lead singer of the number one best selling rock group, *Climax*. He's an honest-to-goodness celebrity. He's obsessed with music. He and my sister have a nice place in Buckhead, but my place is the only one big enough for a music room. It's outfitted with all sorts of instruments Ox and his former bandmates like to experiment with. The baby grand is mine, but everything else is rented until they get bored with it.

This month we have a harp, a cello and a few guitars that will probably be purchased by Ox. He really likes the twelve-string. I find Lainey bird eyeing the cello.

"Do you play?" I ask. My voice startles her out of some sort of trance the instrument seems to have put her under, and she jumps and gives a little squeak.

"I used to, a little," she says shyly. She's nervous.

"Play something for me."

"No, it's been too long." Her words say she's reluctant, but her eyes and her body tell me she's dying to touch it, hold it, make it sing for her. If I had to guess, I think she could probably squeak out a scale, at the very least.

"Please." That's a word I never use. I'm the boss. I'm the owner. I make decisions, I issue directives and the mission gets carried out. I don't ask please. There's no need. And yet, here I am asking her. What would Georgia make of this?

She sidles up into the chair and wraps her legs around it. I'm instantly aroused watching her caress this thing like it's some sort of long-lost lover to her. She gives the bow a cursory inspection.

I watch her take in a deep breath and lay her fingers naturally over the neck, her fingers automatically finding their position for her first note. Her eyes float closed and the bow slides across the strings. In an instant, it see-saws back and forth as notes and chords float up into the air and shroud us in a tender embrace of sound.

I have no idea what's it's called, but I know I've heard this piece before. No matter where or when I've heard it, it's coming alive for me right here in my house with this incredible person calling to life the voice of this instrument that seems to have so much to say. It's Lainey's message translated through pitch and tone. She speaks of longing, of love, of fury, of frenzy and of peace all at once. A snapshot of my soul.

Her fingers fly over the strings, her bow bouncing back and forth. Her body rocks as she plays, her eyes remaining closed. She's baring her own soul to me right here, right now. It's the most sensual, intimate act I've ever witnessed. It has me completely spellbound.

The quick short notes bounce from low to high and then spiral around again and again like a bird's flight through the air. She is the bird and this cello — this music — is what's carrying her through the clouds. It hits me. She needs me. She is a broken little bird. She needs to be loved and protected. I feel it in her music, and I see it in her body as she plays. I need her, too. I need to be needed. I am both undone and reborn as the last note draws out into silence.

The emotion overwhelms in a way I can't describe in words. The little bird clearly knows how to fly. But somewhere along the way, her wings were clipped. She is waiting to be set free again. With absolute certainly, in this moment, I know she is meant to be mine. Lainey is meant for me, and I am meant for her. We are meant to fly together.

She sits staring mutely at me. I stand, in silent awe of her. The gravity of the moment pressing against us equally.

"That was the most beautiful thing I've ever heard. Where on earth did you learn to play like that?" I break the silence and the spell the music has cast over the whole world, or so it seems as if it has.

"Mrs. Dean taught me at PS 163 — middle school," she admits with an expression akin to, what? Embarrassment? No, she's not embarrassed, she's grieving. I can see her eyes filling with tears. There's something very emotional for her about her playing. Music obviously touches her deeply — well, either the music or the memories it conjures.

"Are you OK?" I venture carefully. If she has demons of her own, and I have forced her into waking them somehow, I want to be cautious.

"It's been a really long time since I've played," she says faintly. I understand now. It's the memories. Her own ghosts are alive again, born out of her playing. I wish I could feel badly that I'd brought them back from the grave she'd buried them in, but I can't. She's freed me in a powerful way just now. But I understand the power of ghosts and demons, and say nothing more.

"Let's get you some food, Lainey bird," I say casually.

"My name, is Elaine," she reminds me and not for the first time.

"I know," I smile at her. It comes easier now. "Lainey just fits you better." It's my own nickname for her. Something special I can give her that no one else can. Because she is special. She's already becoming someone special to me, and I want her to feel it for herself too one day. Someday, I am certain, I will see this little bird fly again. On her own.

We walk outside to my waiting car. Today I'm driving my 1960 Ferrari California Spyder. And, OK, I admit, I brought out the roadster to impress her. It's my favorite car, and I can't always drive it. Sexy as hell with an alloy frame that has the curves that remind me of Lainey's body. Slim, but smooth and just begging for you to run your hand over them.

Mine is a beautiful Ferrari Bordeaux red I had custom blended for the project. I sunk every nickel I had at the time into it. It was a way to not only restore the classic automobile, but myself too, I suppose. I did most of the work myself. The evidence of healing lives in the shiny chrome and tan leather upholstery. In it, I can outrun the demons when I need to.

I found a shell of a body of the old Ferrari in a junk yard years ago and had it hauled out and cleaned up. It cost a fortune even with more modern parts to replace the original ones I couldn't afford or couldn't find. Fully restored, it would fetch more than $20 million, but mine is worth a paltry two or three with the more modern elements.

It clings to the road on sixteen-inch custom wheels. When it takes the corners, it feels as tight as a virgin on prom night. A four-speed manual, she's a sport to drive in and of herself with a zero-to-sixty time of less than seven seconds, and a top speed of nearly 150 mph. It's nothing like the super cars they build for the road today, but she gives me a thrill every time I take her out.

Lainey gives me a side eye at first. Obviously, my overt effort to impress her hasn't gone unnoticed. I'm not ashamed about that. What guy wouldn't want to impress a beautiful woman? But she's instantly caught up in the story of how I found her.

"This is seriously the coolest car I've ever seen." She's biting her lower lip and giving the car a salacious little grin that would usually be reserved for lovers. I adore it. And I like that she can appreciate the beauty and artistry of it, even if it is a car.

"Thanks. I don't usually take her out, but it is so nice today, I'd thought I'd let her stretch her legs a little. We've got about twenty or thirty minutes, depending on traffic, to get to the bar."

"After breakfast, right?" She turns that sexy, flirty little grin in my direction. And just like that, she has me. Again.

I don't know if I'm more pleased she's agreed to have

breakfast with me, or that she's impressed with the car. Or maybe, if I'm lucky, impressed with me. I'm not going to push my luck, and I'll assume it's the car. We hop in, and I drive straight to the *Day Old Bagel*. I promised Ox I'd pop in today, and I do want to check on the menus. I can kill two birds with one stone. And feed Lainey in the bargain. Everyone wins. Mostly, I do.

The restaurant is crowded for a Thursday. There's a large party sipping cocktails on the deck. The hostess recognizes me immediately, and we're shown to a table on the patio facing the park. She knows this is my favorite place to sit.

Micah, the potential new store manager, comes to my table with my usual coffee. I like that they take the time to remember what I order and how I like things. I know they're not just doing it because I'm the owner of this little brunch stop. They do it with all of their customers. My niece and her friends come in and mystery shop for me. So I know it's not just me. It's the kind of customer service we need to set ourselves apart from the dozen other charming Southern eateries in this part of town. There are too many places that can serve a decent omelet and cup of coffee. It's these touches that make a place you want to keep going back to. And I'm proud of it.

I'm also pleased to see the new menus are being laid out on our table. Glancing around, I see they're on all of the tables, and I smile a little. My smile only grows when I see Lainey. She glances around and watches a few families enjoying the park. It's a great day for it. Summer in Georgia is usually unbearable, but God has blessed us with a cold front, so temperatures are less humid and only set to reach somewhere in the low 90s today.

We order and my mind is racing — all with thoughts of Lainey, my little Lainey bird. I can't get over the feeling I had in the music room earlier. She's stunning sitting across from me with the sun hanging low behind her. It gives her a halo of gold that makes the color in her hair morph into a rainbow of hues from a rich caramel to dark roasted coffee beans. I love the streaks that show up in her loose pony tail. And those obsidian eyes shining back at me through the soft gray lenses of her sunglasses.

I don't hide my stares. I want her to know. I want to tell her, but I can't. I want her. I want to kiss her sweet plum-colored lips and touch those perfect breasts again. I want to feel her legs wrapped around me like she held the cello today. But I want so much more than that. I want to feel her. I want to know the touch of her hands on my skin. I need to feel the touch of her heart against mine.

For so long I believed myself too broken to even harbor feelings like this. They were dismissed and swept away under a rug of self-doubt and self-loathing. But with Lainey, I can't escape them. I can't escape her.

"What?" She breaks the silence with one simple word.

"You've really never been on vacation?" I'm not sure what prompted me to ask the question, but I'm curious to know more about what she was chatting about at the bar last night.

"What? How would you know that?"

"You're a real chatty Cathy after about your third whiskey."

"What ... what did I say?" A look of chagrin washes over her face.

"You said the man who interviewed you yesterday wouldn't give you the job because you didn't go on vacation."

"I said that after the third whiskey?" She asks blushing again.

I just nod. Fuck, she's adorable.

In her most regal tone, she declares, "Well, then let it be known throughout the land, I am officially a two-whiskey girl." I chuckle a little at her comment. She's funny and has a great wit. I *really* like this girl.

"He said that while my credentials were exemplary, he just couldn't help but think work was my whole life. He was afraid if he hired me, I'd be chairing the local Overachievers Chapter of Work-a-Holics Anonymous."

"Is it true?" I'm slightly amused by her comment and concerned at the same time. I know from first-hand experience that people who work too much do so because they're avoiding something else. Something at home — or, in my case, the nothing at home.

"What?"

"Would you be?" I hope she'll tell me more of what drives her to punish herself from enjoying life.

Micah brings our food and she tucks into the tomato pie she's ordered along with some sausages and fruit. I'm glad she's got a good appetite, but she's stalling to answer me. The pause is answer enough. It's the nothing that keeps her working so hard, not something she's avoiding. She hums slightly with her first bite of pie and I'm pleased. The pie is Georgia's recipe and a favorite of mine. I love that she is enjoying it.

"Maybe," she says flatly.

"Where did you go on your last vacation?" I prod.

"San Diego." She replies quickly. Almost a little too quickly. It's a cool city. I love California — in small doses. I was born and raised in the South, and it's my home. But California captivates me with its vineyards and beaches and perfect weather.

"Oh? When was that?" I reply tucking into my egg white omelet with bacon and cheese. I always order it with whole wheat toast with butter and blueberry preserves. It's not a dish on our menu, but all the waiters know it by heart. It's my order.

Lainey and I volley question after question as I slowly pull the truth from her. She's living a shell of a life at best. Her "vacation" was actually a family funeral. I'm also pleased to learn there's no boyfriend, and equally saddened to know there's no close girlfriends with whom she regularly hangs out. She's alone, but also seems lonely. Me too, sweet Lainey bird, me too.

Lainey is married to her job by default because she doesn't have personal connections in her life. It all hits a little too close to home for me. Is this what Ox and Tori see in me? Is this why they've tried so hard over the years to set me up with women? Being alone, I can do. But, I'll admit, the loneliness stings in the quiet of the night when the sheets in the bed are cold.

It takes the entire ride to the bar for me to work up the courage to ask to see her again. But I fall over my words and just say, "Tomorrow. Noon," when she inquires about returning Ginger's things. Ginger would never miss them. I just want to see Lainey again.

I'm turning into a mono-syllabic fool as Lainey stares at me blankly unsure as to what I've just said. I want to say more. I want to tell her how her music touched me. How similar we are, and how much I want to see her again — so I can learn to know her. I want to kiss her. And then, overwhelmed by the desire of that last thought, I hold back no longer.

I step forward without preamble, without innuendo and simply take her into my arms and press my lips against hers. I'm instantly intoxicated with the feel and the taste of her. In a rush of long-dormant desire, I claim her. My tongue seeks hers with an urgency that both delights and unnerves me. Her mouth is so soft, so warm. Her lips were made to fit mine. They're lush and pliant, and I want more and more of them.

I can feel her palms pressing against my chest and my

breathing ceases. I have to stop now before it's too late. I pull back and stare down into her dark charcoal eyes. And I realize it's already too late. One taste and I'm addicted to her. I know I'll never be able to get enough.

"Noon, tomorrow, Lainey bird. Be here." I growl out desperately trying to hold back the raging lion inside that wants to devour her right here on the sidewalk.